Henry Childs Merwin

**Road, Track and Stable**

Chapters about Horses and their Treatment

Henry Childs Merwin

**Road, Track and Stable**
*Chapters about Horses and their Treatment*

ISBN/EAN: 9783337416454

Printed in Europe, USA, Canada, Australia, Japan

Cover: Foto ©Andreas Hilbeck / pixelio.de

More available books at **www.hansebooks.com**

# ROAD, TRACK, AND STABLE.

## CHAPTERS ABOUT HORSES AND THEIR TREATMENT.

——fortis equus, spatio qui saepe supremo
Vicit Olympia.

BY

# H. C. MERWIN.

BOSTON:
LITTLE, BROWN, AND COMPANY.
1892.

𝕴nibersity 𝕻ress:
JOHN WILSON AND SON, CAMBRIDGE.

TO

# ANNE AMORY MERWIN

This Book is Inscribed

IN GRATEFUL ACKNOWLEDGMENT OF HER ASSISTANCE

AS HORSEWOMAN AND CRITIC.

# NOTE.

OF the chapters in this book, the second, sixth, and last, dealing with "Trotting Families," "Saddle Horses," and "The Care of Horses," are now published for the first time. The remaining chapters originally appeared in the Atlantic Monthly, from which they are reprinted by the kind permission of the publishers of that magazine. The opportunity of republication has been taken to revise and enlarge these chapters.

CONCORD, MASSACHUSETTS,
October, 1892.

# CONTENTS.

# ILLUSTRATIONS.

# ROAD, TRACK, AND STABLE.

# I.

## THE ETHICS OF HORSE-KEEPING.

IF a man could go into open market and for two or three hundred dollars purchase the lifelong devotion of a friend, though a humble friend, it would be accounted a wonderful thing. But that is exactly what happens, or might happen, whenever a horse is bought. You give him food, lodging, and the reasonable services of a valet, in return for which he will not only further your business or your pleasure, as the case may be, to the best of his ability, but he will also repay you with affection, respond to your caresses, greet you with a neigh of pleased recognition, and in a hundred ways of his own exhibit a sense of the relationship.

There are men to whom a horse is only an animate machine: they will ride and drive him, hire grooms and draw cheques for his sustenance and keeping, but all without a single thought of the animal as having a character, a mind, a career of his own; as being susceptible to pain or pleasure; as a creature for whose welfare they have assumed a certain responsibility, of which they cannot get rid, although they may forget it or deny its existence. Even among people who are intelligent, religious, and kind-hearted, as the world goes, there is sometimes found, as we all know, especially when their own convenience is concerned. an astonishing indifference to the sufferings of dumb beasts.

Never shall I forget the shock produced upon my infant mind by a case of this sort in which a deeply venerated bishop was the actor. The good man described in my presence the great difficulty that he had recently experienced. upon arriving in town, in obtaining a conveyance from the railroad station to the house where he was to stay, two or three miles distant. Through some mistake, no carriage had been sent for him; and by the liverymen to whom the bishop applied he was told that all their horses were so wearied and jaded, a huge picnic or funeral having just occurred in the village, that they absolutely could not send one out again. But the successor of the Apostles so wrought upon the stable-keepers by his eloquence — thus he narrated, without suspicion of the awful judgment that was passing upon him by youthful innocence, sitting unnoticed in a corner — that some unlucky, overtired brute was finally dragged from his stall and sent off upon the five-mile jaunt. Now the day was warm, to be sure, and the bishop a stout man; still. being in the prime of life, he could have taken no harm, but rather good, from the walk; and yet neither when he hired the horse nor when he related the transaction did it occur to him that the act was one of inexcusable cruelty. How many people, indeed, know or care what is the condition of the livery horses that they hire from time to time? How many, when they summon a cab, so much as glance at the beast in the shafts? But it is almost always possible to make a selection, rejecting the palpably unfit, choosing the fit horse; and if everybody took even this slight amount of trouble, the employment of broken-down cab horses would cease to be profitable.

There is a good deal of hard-heartedness in our Puritan blood as respects dumb animals. I once spent several weeks on a farm where many beasts of various kinds were kept. The family was of pure New England stock, farmers for many generations back, — stalwart, intelligent, honest people, pillars of the church, leading men in the village, but in their treatment of dumb beasts without feeling or compunction. If the cows did not enter their stalls at the proper moment, they were pounded with whatever weapon came handy; horses were driven when they were lame, and neglected when they were tired. Every animal on the place was in a continual state of hunger, and none ever received a kind word or a pat of the hand. That on all convenient occasions I surreptitiously fed the occupants of the barn, horses, cows, oxen, and bull. is a fact which I may be permitted to state, lest I should include myself in the condemnation of these hard-hearted farmers; and I recall with pleasure the anticipatory neighing, the scraping of hoofs, and the rattling of chains that soon became a regular occurrence whenever I set foot upon the threshold. I have known better educated, village-bred persons of the same stamp, men of a kind that command, when they die, half-column obit-uary notices in the papers, who took a vicious de-light in stoning dogs off their lawns, and who would have been moved to scorn by any show of affection for a horse.

People whose attitude toward dumb animals is of this character not only fail of their duty, but miss a vast amount of happiness. Horses are to be enjoyed in other ways than those of riding and driving. To become familiar with their characters and peculiarities, of which latter horses have many; to see them com-fortable in their stalls, sleek, well fed, well groomed, warmly blanketed; to give them affection, and to re-ceive it back; finally, to take a pride in them, and, frankly speaking, to brag about them without being more unveracious than a fairly good conscience will allow, — this it is to enjoy a horse. In this matter, as in all others where motives are concerned, the good and bad, or at least the good and indifferent, in human nature can be made to co-operate; the sense of duty may be reinforced by a more spontaneous feeling. namely, the pride of ownership. In fact, to lay a foundation for the exercise of this quality should always be a chief object in buying a horse. Let your new purchase have that about him concerning which you can declare, with sufficient plausibility to defy absolute contradiction, that he stands in the very front rank of equine excellence; as that he is the most speedy. or the most enduring, or the handsomest, or the gentlest, or the most intelligent, or the toughest, of animals. If these qualities fail, we come down to minor excellences, such as the fineness of his coat, the beauty of its color, the silkiness of his mane, the length of his tail, or the nobility of his descent. It is quite possible to buy for a small sum horses of unexceptionable pedigree; and though a well-bred weed or screw really travels no better than a "dunghill," yet his breeding will always command admiration, and cast a reflected glory upon his owner. The point of superiority may be this or that; enough that it distinguishes your horse from the ruck of horses, and justifies in some measure, at least to the world at large, the pride and pleasure that you take in him. This reference to the opinion of others as a guide for our affections, even when a human being constitutes the object, is one of those vile traits that lie hid in the murky depths of our nature. Was it not remarked by George Sand, who knew the human heart, and certainly took no pessimistic view of it, that men love women not for what they think of them, but for what they suppose other people to think of them?

And yet there is another aspect of the matter. Just as disinterested affection, or something approaching it, may exist between man and woman, so it is possible to be fond of a horse, and to be happy in his well-being, with no admixture of those baser feelings to which I have alluded. I wish that you, gentle reader of this book, might be induced to try the following experiment. We will suppose that you have a stable with an unoccupied stall in it, and by preference, though it is not essential, that a paddock is

appurtenant to the stable. (Not everybody, indeed,
is so fortunately situated, but still the conditions just
mentioned are by no means uncommon.) Now let us
suppose further that you go into the market or to
some private person and purchase, as you may easily
do for forty or fifty dollars, an old, broken-down
horse, of whom a long hard day's work has been, and
unless you intervene will for some years yet continue to be extracted. Take him home, and watch
the quick transition from misery to happiness. He
comes into your stable with stiff, painful steps; his
legs swollen from hock and knee to ankle; his ribs
clearly visible through a rough, staring coat; and,
above all, with that strained, anxious expression of
the eye which nobody who has once seen and understood it can ever expel from his memory. It is the
expression of despair. You take off his shoes, give
him a run at grass or a deep bed of straw in a comfortable loose box, and forthwith the old horse begins
to improve. Little by little, the expression of his eye
changes, the swelling goes out of his legs, and it will
not be long before he cuts a caper; a stiff and ungainly one, to be sure, but still a caper, indicative of
health and happiness. He will neigh at your approach, and gladly submit his head for a caress,
whereas at first he would have shrunk in terror from
any such advances. (It may be ten years since a
hand was laid upon him in kindness.) If you have
any work for him to do, the old horse will perform
it with alacrity, exerting himself out of gratitude;
he will even flourish off in harness with the airs of
a colt, as who should say, "There is life in me yet;
don't send me to the knacker; behold my strength

and agility." [1] Treat him as you would treat him if he had cost you a great sum, or as if you expected to win a great sum through his exertions. Let him have good blankets, good grooming, and all the little attentions of a well ordered establishment. Is there anything ridiculous in this? Shall not the stable, as well as the house, have its sacred rites of hospitality? Shall not the old cheap horse be made as comfortable as the young and costly one?

And here I anticipate an obvious criticism. "The horse should be killed, and the money that it costs to maintain him be given to the poor." I grant it. Let the old horse be shot, and let the two dollars and fifty cents per week necessary for his support be given in charity. But see to it, ye who might maintain an equine pensioner, and forbear to do so for reasons of conscience, — see to it that the poor be not defrauded of the sum thus saved for them.

Doubtless the ideal manner of keeping a horse is that practised in Arabia, where, we are told, he is treated like one of the family, being the constant companion of the children, and allowed to poke his nose within the tent and in all the household affairs. Unfortunately, our habits of living will not permit such intimacy, although I have seen a yearling colt within the walls of a country dwelling-house, taking a moderate lunch of oats from the kitchen table, and afterward, with ears erect, briefly surveying the outside world through the drawing-room window. Mr. Briggs's introduction of his hunter to the dining-

---

[1] The final illustration is a portrait of an old cab horse, rescued in a moribund condition, and rejuvenated in the manner stated in the text.

room on Christmas night, in the animal's professional capacity, and the consequent results to the china, will occur to the reader as a similar case. But although such instances must necessarily be rare, and are not, perhaps, exactly to be imitated, it is possible for every horse-owner to cultivate the social and affectionate side of the animal's nature by talking to and caressing him, by visiting him in the stable, by making him little gifts, from time to time, of sugar and other dainties. Petting like this undoubtedly tends to render high-spirited horses more tractable and safer on the road than they would be otherwise.

Mustangs that have been allowed to run wild on the prairies until they are brought to the East and sold can rarely be broken so as to be safe in harness; but ponies of the same breed that have been in actual use by the Indians are very trustworthy. Such ponies, like Arab horses, have become domesticated, and cease to regard human beings as their natural enemies.

Few persons, moreover, realize how much a nervous, timid horse dislikes to be left alone, especially amid terrifying or even unusual surroundings. I once brought on a steamer from Portland to Boston a high-strung Morgan mare that I had owned but two weeks. She had never travelled thus before, and during the first hour or two, if I left her alone for a moment, as happened once or twice, she became distressed and alarmed in the highest degree, sweating profusely and struggling to get loose; but when I returned she would immediately become calm again, rubbing her nose against me as much as to say, "For Heaven's sake, don't leave me alone." The same horse (I have her still), when tied in front of a

strange house, always greets me when I come out
with an eager, enthusiastic neigh, as if she had begun
to despair of seeing her master again.

Nevertheless, whether from the want of ancestral
usage or otherwise, horses, it must be granted, are
less sociable with men than are dogs. Nor can I
agree with the remark recorded as having been made
by the famous sportsman, Thomas Assheton Smith,
(but perhaps incorrectly,) that "horses are far more
sensible than dogs." The converse, I should say, is
true. Dogs are more sensible, more intelligent, more
affectionate, and, as a rule, more trustworthy than
horses. So much justice requires that we should
admit, although the contrary is often maintained by
persons well informed upon the subject. Who, indeed,
has not heard the intelligence of the horse eloquently
defended by some hard-headed, hard-drinking old
horseman, who would seem to enjoy a perfect im-
munity from all sentimental considerations? But he
does not. "If we could have come upon Diogenes
suddenly," Thackeray somewhere remarks, "he would
probably have been found whimpering in his tub over
a sentimental romance." And so the old horseman,
being fond of horses, knowing them, but knowing
nothing else, deriving both his livelihood and his
pleasure from them, unconsciously exaggerates their
good qualities. But, on the other hand, the horse is
far more intelligent than most people suppose, and
there are certain qualities in which he excels all
other dumb animals. "The conspicuous merit of the
horse, which has given him the dearly paid honor of
sharing in our wars," says Mr. Hamerton, in a charming essay, "is his capacity for being disciplined; and

a very great capacity it is, a very noble gift indeed, —
nobler than much cleverness. Several animals are
cleverer than the horse in the way of intelligence;
not one is so amenable to discipline." [1]   This is
true, unless an exception should be made in favor
of the elephant.  But Mr. Hamerton omits to state
— except perhaps by implication — the very respect
in which the superiority of the horse to all other
dumb animals is most important and most striking,
namely, the fineness of his nervous system.  All the
great achievements of the horse; all his wonderful
flights of speed and feats of endurance; all his capacity for being guided, restrained, quickly turned,
and stopped, for being urged to the limit, and beyond
the limit, of his strength, — all, in fact, that is glorious in him springs from the sensitiveness of his
nervous organization.  In this respect no other dumb
animal that I know of will bear comparison with the
horse.  Mr. Hamerton well says, in contrasting the
horse and the ass: —

"I have never yet seen the donkey which could be
guided easily and safely through an intricate crowd
of carriages or on a really dangerous road.  The deficiency of the ass may be expressed in a single word,
— it is deficiency of delicacy.  You can guide a good
horse as delicately as a sailing-boat; when the skilful driver has an inch to spare he is perfectly at his

---

[1] Mr. Hamerton adds that the horse is not observant except of
places.  But this is a great mistake.  A strange footfall in a stable
will be noticed in a moment by all the occupants of the stalls.  A
lively horse observes the least movement of his groom or rider, and
his curiosity is extreme.  On strange roads horses always drive
better than on familiar roads.  They are more alert and go faster,
so as to see what is coming next.

ease, and he can twist in and out amongst the throng
of vehicles, when a momentary display of self-will in
the animal would be the cause of an immediate accident. The ass appears to be incapable of any delicate
discipline of this kind."

What makes the horse so delicate an instrument to
play upon is the quick and fine connection between
his nerves and his brain, and the sensitiveness of his
skin. People who have never entered into the art of
driving or riding, though they may both drive and
ride all their lives, think that holding the reins is
something like steering a heavy boat: pull to the
right if you want to go in that direction, pull hard
if you want to stop, and so on.[1] But the real art of
driving and riding is the exercise of a light, firm,
sensitive hand upon the reins, and the continual play
of intelligence, of command on the one hand and
of obedience on the other, between the man and
the horse.

The same nervous development that makes the
horse a sensitive, controllable, pliable animal makes
him also capable of great feats. To run or trot fast, in
heat after heat, requires not only mechanical fitness,
such as well proportioned limbs, good bone and muscle, good lung power, etc., but also an inward energy,
the " do or die " spirit, as horsemen call it. Many a

[1] Opinion as to what constitutes excellence in horse-flesh is very
diverse. I remember once hearing the praises of a certain Dobbin
sung with great enthusiasm by a literary man. This was the most
perfect horse in the world; but, on cross-examination, perfection
was found to reside in one quality, — wherever you left him, there
the animal would stand without being tied. You might be gone a
year, and come back to find him still waiting for you in the middle
of the road.

horse has speed enough to make a racer, but lacks the
requisite courage and determination. "She was tried
a good mare, but never won anything," is a phrase
of frequent occurrence in William Day's reminiscen-
ces. There are cases in which thousands of dollars
have been spent for fast trotters that were afterward
sold for a few hundreds, simply because they were too
sluggish and faint-hearted to keep on after they became tired. On the other hand, almost all the fastest
horses, the "record breakers," whether among racers
or trotters, have been remarkable for their nervous,
"high-strung" constitutions. The trainer of Sunol
(the California filly, who has a three-year-old record
of 2.10, and who at four years of age trotted a mile
upon a kite-shaped track in 2.08¼), after describing
the great difficulty that he experienced in breaking
her, says: "Not that she was actually vicious, but
she had and has a will, a temper, and a determination of her own, and at that time every individual
hair seemed to contain a nerve."

Even among the best breeds of cart horses, such as
the Percherons and Clydesdales, the same quality is
not altogether wanting, and in general it distinguishes,
as I have said, the horse from all other dumb animals.
It follows, of course, that the horse is the most irritable of creatures, the most easily worried and distressed. Little things, such as no other animal, man
included perhaps, would mind, annoy and exasperate
him. If, for example, you notice a row of express-
wagon horses backed up against the curbstone, you
will easily perceive that every horse there has his
temper permanently ruined by the frequent passing
of vehicles before him, thus obliging him to turn

his head. Harsh treatment, though it stop short of inflicting physical pain, keeps a nervous horse in a state of misery. "An hostler's angry tone will send a quiver of fear — I have seen it scores of times — down a whole barnful of stalls."[1] On the other hand, it is perfectly true, as a besotted but intelligent stable-keeper once observed to me, "A kind word for a hoss is as good sometimes as a feed of oats." A single blow may be enough to spoil a racer. Daniel Lambert, founder of the Lambert branch of the Morgan family, was thought as a three-year-old to be the fastest trotting stallion of his day. He was a very handsome, stylish, intelligent horse, and also extremely sensitive. His driver, Dan Mace, though one of the best reinsmen that the track has produced, once made the mistake, either through ill temper or bad judgment, of giving Daniel Lambert a severe cut with the whip, and that single blow put an end to his usefulness as a trotter. He became wild and ungovernable in harness, and remained so for the rest of his life.

One of the best, most docile, most intelligent animals that I have known was a powerful brown horse belonging to a veterinary surgeon. When the doctor was making professional visits in the city where he lived, he would often walk from one stable to another, and beckon or call to the horse to follow him. This the latter would always do, waiting patiently meanwhile. But if any strange man or boy mounted the gig and attempted to drive him off, he could not be made to budge an inch. This animal

---

[1] I quote this just remark from a published sermon upon dumb animals, delivered by the Rev. G. L. Walker of Hartford, Conn.

showed his intelligence and docility in many other
ways; and yet he had begun his career in harness by
killing two or three men, more or less, and the surgeon, who perceived that the horse was naturally
kind, and that his temper had been soured by ill
treatment, purchased him for a song. He served his
master faithfully for more than twenty years.

I do not mean to say that a nervous horse is always
courageous and always intelligent, nor to imply that
courageous intelligent horses are invariably nervous.[1]
But these qualities commonly go together; and as the
horse is distinguished from all other dumb beasts by
a highly developed nervous system, if I may be for-
given for repeating the statement, so the finest specimens of the genus are usually those in which this
development is most conspicuous. Hence, in dealing
with the horse, more than with most animals, one
ought to exercise patience, care, and, above all, the
power of sympathy, so as to know, if possible, the
real motive of his doing or refusing to do this or
that. To acquire such knowledge, and to act upon
it when acquired, is a large part of the ethics of
horse-keeping.

In the matter of shying, for example, great dis-
crimination needs to be exercised. Everybody knows

---

[1] It happens sometimes, though rarely, that a courageous horse
is sluggish and has to be "aroused," even by the whip. Such an animal is the trotting stallion Wedgewood, one of the best "finishers"
ever seen on the track, and famous for winning races of numerous
heats against speedier but less enduring competitors. Another type
is that of the ambitious, but soft and washy horse, who goes off
at a great pace, but soon tires. The ideal roadster starts slowly,
gradually warms to his work, and after ten miles or so (just when
the inferior horse has had enough) begins to be full of play.
Such pre-eminently is the habit of the Morgan family.

that when horses are in good spirits, especially in cold weather, they will often shy at sights or sounds which under other circumstances they pass by without notice. In such a case it is always assumed that the horse, out of roguishness, is simply pretending to be afraid; and commonly this is true. Frequently, indeed, horses work themselves into a condition of panic for the mere fun of the thing, — to enjoy the pleasure of running or shying off from the object of their half-real, half-fictitious terror, just as a school-girl might scurry through a churchyard at dusk.

In one of Mr. Galton's books there is a passage about wild animals which throws light on the conduct of some tame animals. He says: " From my own recollection, I believe that every antelope in South Africa has to run for its life every one or two days upon an average, and that he starts or gallops under the influence of a false alarm many times in a day. Those who have crouched at night by the side of pools in the desert, in order to have a shot at the beasts that frequent them, see strange scenes of animal life : how the creatures gambol at one moment and fight at another; how a herd suddenly halts in strained attention, and then breaks into a maddened rush, as one of them becomes conscious of the stealthy movements or rank scent of a beast of prey. Now this hourly life-and-death excitement is a keen delight to most wild creatures."

But there is more behind. I am convinced that nervous horses, when in high condition, and stimulated by the cold or otherwise, are often actually frightened by objects which do not thus affect them

at other times. Their nerves, being more tense, send
a different message to the brain. I have seen a man
of robust constitution, but just getting out after a
long illness, jump like a colt when a piece of white
paper blew across the sidewalk before him. Now,
what illness had done for his nerves, high condition,
cold air, want of exercise, will do for the nerves of a
horse, especially if he be a young horse; and the
moral is, that for shying thus brought about the whip
is no cure. In fact, even for intentional shying the
use of the whip does more harm than good; it is per-
missible only when the horse refuses to approach or
to pass a particular object. If he cannot be led or
coaxed forward, then it is well to employ punish-
ment, for he must never be allowed to disobey.

The success in equine matters of which Americans
can fairly boast is due chiefly to the fact that we have
consulted the equine nature. Our trainers, perceiving
that the horse is a nervous, timid, and yet docile animal, have endeavored to win his confidence, rather
than to subdue his spirit. Instead of breaking colts,
we "gentle" them; and that single word developed
in the daily usage of the stable eloquently indicates
the difference between the old method and the new,
between American horse-training and foreign horse-
breaking. The superintendent of a large stock farm
states: "At the age of six months we take up the
colts and *gentle* them. After several weeks of this
work they are again turned out. At fourteen months
old they are taken up and driven double with an old
horse, and in a short time they are put in single harness." In smaller establishments even greater pains
are taken to domesticate the colt from infancy up-

ward; and in general the method is to accustom him
gradually to the bit, to the harness, to being driven
and ridden, so that his education is completed by a
succession of small steps, each achieved without a
struggle, without rebellion, without exciting the fear
or hatred of the colt. The result is that our horses
are commonly gentle. I have seen a high-spirited
stallion, on the fourth occasion of his being in harness, driven to a top-wagon, and going so kindly that
the owner did not hesitate to take his child of three
years with him.

In England great improvement in these matters has
been made in recent years, but the British horse-
trainer is still behind the age. Vicious horses, again,
are far more to seek here than is the case abroad.
Abroad there is no difficulty in providing those horse-
breakers who perform in public with specimens on
which to exert their skill, — with "man-eaters," con-
firmed kickers, etc. But in this country, when such
an exhibition is to be given, say in New York or in
Boston, it is found almost, sometimes quite, impossible to procure a beast savage enough to do credit
to his subjugator.

John Bull has accomplished wonders with horses,
and nobody, I presume, has lighter hands or more
"faculty" in the management of them than the gentlemen of England. But the understrappers and
grooms, the breakers and trainers, lack the sympathetic understanding, the gentleness and patience,
that are essential for the proper education of a horse.
To discover what could be done by the exercise of
these qualities was, I make bold to say, reserved for
the American trainer; and anybody who studies the

history of the trotting horse will perceive the truth
of this statement.

I read lately of a former well known M. F. H. who
kept an enormous equine establishment, and yet
among all his men there was but one fit to be in-
trusted with the exercise of his best hunters.

To create the trotter, increasing his speed within
seventy-five years from a mile in 2.40 to a mile in
2.08$\frac{3}{4}$, was perhaps an even greater achievement than
the development of the modern thoroughbred in the
one hundred and fifty years that have elapsed since
the importation to England of the Godolphin Arabian.
The utility of the achievement is another matter; and
I should confess to some sympathy with the critic
who was inclined to estimate it lightly. But whatever we may think of the result, whether or not we
hold that a 2.08 horse is greatly better than a 2.40
horse, the value of the process by which this result
was reached can hardly be exaggerated. The trainers
of the American trotter have taught the world the
best lesson that it has ever received in the ethics of
horse-keeping.

The case of Johnston, the famous pacer, illustrates
what can be accomplished by humoring the sensitive
equine disposition. "He was," writes John Splan,
his trainer and driver, "the most nervous horse that
I ever saw, and I found that in shipping him about
from one track to another he became more nervous
and irritable. If you left him long alone in the stable,
he would tramp around like a wild animal, and get
himself in a sweat. If anybody went into the stall
next to him, and began to hammer or make anything
like a loud noise, he would try to climb out of the

window. Whenever a stranger stepped into his stall
he would give a snort and back into the farthest corner." Splan. with some difficulty, obtained the services of a quiet, faithful "rubber" or groom called
"Dave." Dave procured a dog as additional company for Johnston, and these three remained inseparable through the period of Johnston's training. It
was a matter of course that the groom should sleep
in the stall, but he never left it, day or night, having
all his meals brought there. Under this treatment
Johnston rapidly improved. He became less nervous, ate better, and in the event lowered the pacing
record to 2.06¼, a mark which has not yet been surpassed upon a regulation track.

There remains only one branch of the subject which
I feel bound to consider, namely, the duty of the
owner toward the horse that has grown old and in-
firm in his service. I say little about the man who
employs horses in the course of his business; let him
settle the matter with his own conscience, though I
cannot refrain from the obvious remark, that whereas
it might be a poor man's duty to sell his superannu-
ated beast for what he would bring, lest his family
should suffer, so it would be the rich man's duty to
dispose of his work horses in a different manner. But
as regards horses bought and used for pleasure this
general rule seems to me undeniable, that the owner
is morally bound to protect them from cruelty when
they become old or broken down. He may do it by
killing them, or otherwise, as he sees fit. But how
seldom is this duty performed! It is neglected, possibly, more from thoughtlessness than from intention.
A span of carriage horses, we will say, after some

years of service, lose their style; they become a little
stiff. a little "sore forward," it may be; one of them,
perhaps, is suffering from incipient spavin; and on
the whole it is thought high time to dispose of them,
and get a fresher, younger pair.   Accordingly, John,
the groom, is directed to take them to an auction
stable, and in due course Dives, their old master, receives in return a cheque, — a very small cheque, to be
sure, but still large enough to make a respectable contribution to foreign missions or to purchase a case of
champagne.   That is all he knows about the transaction, and he does not allow his mind to dwell upon
the inevitable results.   But let Dives go to the auction
stable himself; let him observe the wistful, homesick
air (for horses are often homesick) with which the
old favorites look about them when they are backed
out of the unaccustomed stalls; then let him stand
by and see them whipped up and down the stable floor
to show their tardy paces, and finally knocked down
to some hard-faced, thin-lipped dealer.   It needs very
little imagination to foresee their after career.   To
begin with, the old companions are separated. — a
great grief to both, which it requires a long time to
obliterate.   The more active one goes into a country
livery stable, where he is hacked about by people
whose only interest in the beast is to take out of him
the pound of flesh for which they have paid.   He has
no rest on week days, but his Sunday task is the hard-
est.   On that sacred day, the reprobates of the village
who have arrived at the perfect age of cruelty (which
I take to be about nineteen or twenty) lash the old
carriage horse from one public house to another, and
bring him home exhausted and reeking with sweat.

His mate goes into a job wagon perhaps, possibly into a herdic, and is driven by night lest his staring ribs and the painful lameness in his hind leg should attract the notice of meddlesome persons. The last stage of many a downward equine career is found in the shafts of a fruit pedler's or junk dealer's wagon, in which situation there is continual exposure to heat and cold, to rain and snow, recompensed by the least possible amount of food. It may be that one of the old horses whose fate we are considering is finally bought by some poverty-stricken farmer; he works without grain in summer, and passes long winter nights in a cold and draughty barn, with scanty covering, and no bed but the floor. It is hard that in his old age, when, like an old man, he feels the cold most, and is most in need of nourishing food, he should be deprived of all the comforts — the warm stall and soft bed, the good blankets and plentiful oats — which were heaped upon him in youth.

If, as is probably the case, the old carriage horse has been docked, his suffering in warm weather will greatly be increased. That form of mutilation which we call docking is, I believe, inartistic and barbarous, and I do not doubt that before many years it will become obsolete, as is now the cropping of horses' ears, which was practised so late as 1840. But still I should not utterly condemn the owner for docking his horses, or buying them after they had been docked, which comes to the same thing, if his intention and custom were to keep them so long as they lived. But to dock a horse, thus depriving him forever of his tail, to keep him till he is old or broken down, and then to sell him for what he will bring, is the

very refinement of cruelty. The Anglomaniacs. to
whom we owe the revival of docking, should consider
that in our climate of flies and mosquitos the practice
is infinitely more cruel than it is in England.

I have endeavored to show that the horse is an
animal peculiarly capable of suffering, and to suggest
some of the ways in which his suffering can be prevented or alleviated. Of late years, thanks largely
to anti-cruelty societies, the horse has been less abused
than was formerly the case. But let any one, and
especially any one who may have a fancy for the
human race, consider what awful arrears of cruelty
to dumb animals have accrued at its hands. Let him
think of the horses that have been baited to death. as
bulls are baited; let him think of the unspeakable
remedies that have been applied by ignorant farriers
and grooms, such as the forcing of ground glass into
the animal's eye; let him think of the horses that
have been "whipped sound" in coaches and heavy
wagons, — that is, compelled by the lash to travel
chiefly on three legs, one leg or foot being disabled,
until the overwrought muscles gave out entirely; let
him think of the agonies that have been inflicted by
beating and spurring, of the heavy loads that a vast
army of painfully lame, of diseased, and even of dying
horses have been forced to draw. Let him take but a
single glance at the history of the human race in this
respect, and another perhaps at his own heart. and
then declare if it be not true, as was once remarked
to me,[1] "Man deserves a hell, were it only for his
treatment of horses."

[1] By the late John Boyle O'Reilly.

## II.

## TROTTING FAMILIES.

THE American trotting horse is derived from these sources : —

The English thoroughbred.[1]

The Norfolk trotter.

The Arab and Barb.

Certain pacers of mixed breeding.

And just as the best running horses now extant in

[1] A thoroughbred is one all of whose ancestors, back to the eighteenth century, are recorded either in the English or in the American Stud Book for running horses. The American work is a continuation for this country of the English. The first volume of the English Stud Book was issued in 1808, and an annual volume of each book is published.

A thoroughbred is, therefore, a horse of pure running stock. The origin of this stock, which is chiefly Oriental, will be found stated briefly at page 118.

England are descended from three or four animals
foaled in the eighteenth century, and bred chiefly
from Arab importations, so the American trotter of
to-day can usually be referred to one or more of the
following ancestors : Messenger, True Briton, and Diomed, thoroughbreds ; Bellfounder, a Norfolk trotter ;
Grand Bashaw, a Barb ; Pilot, a Canadian pacer ; and
Blue Bull, a pacer from the State of Ohio.

Of these horses Messenger has played the greatest
part.  He was a gray, foaled at Newmarket in England in the year 1780, and imported to this country in
1788.  For a thoroughbred, he was a plain, almost
coarse animal, with a big, bony head, low withers, upright shoulders, and a rather short, straight neck.  But
his shoulders were deep and strong, his loins and quarters very powerful, his legs flat and clean.  He had big
knees, big hocks ; and his windpipe and nostrils were
described by a contemporary writer as being "nearly
twice as large as ordinary."  He stood 15¾ hands high,
and, "whether at rest or in motion, his legs were always
in a perfect position."  The low withers, the upright
shoulders, the plain head, Messenger inherited from
Sampson, his great-grandsire,[1] a black horse ; and these
peculiarities, as well as the black color, were so extraordinary in a horse of Oriental breeding, that suspi-
cions have been entertained as to Sampson's pedigree,
and some writers have asserted that his dam was a Lincolnshire cart mare.  But the best authorities do not
appear to share these painful doubts, and Sampson may
safely be regarded as a true thoroughbred, close to the

---

[1] Messenger was by Mambrino, by Engineer, by Sampson, by
Blaze, by Flying Childers, by the Darley Arabian.  Messenger's dam
was by Turf, by Matchem, by Cade, by the Godolphin Arabian.

Arab foundation. At all events, he was superlatively excellent both as a race horse and as a sire, and Messenger inherited most of his good qualities, but not his extreme speed. Messenger, though running bred, was a natural trotter, — the more so, perhaps, on account of his somewhat straight shoulders and low withers. It is true indeed that certain of our very fastest trotters, notably Axtell and Palo Alto, have sloping shoulders and fairly high withers ; but the Messenger or Sampson conformation is that of the typical trotter. Maud S.,[1] Sunol,[2] and Nancy Hanks[3] are built thus.

Messenger was an animal of great soundness and vigor. One who saw him taken off the ship was accustomed to relate that three other horses, his companions on the long voyage, "had become so reduced and weak that they had to be helped and supported down the gang-plank ; but when it became Messenger's turn to land, he, with a loud neigh, rushed down, with a negro on each side holding him back, and dashed up the street at a stiff trot, carrying the grooms along in spite of all their efforts to bring him to a standstill." "When Messenger charged down the gang-plank," Hiram Woodruff declared. "the value of not less than one hundred million dollars struck our soil."

Messenger died of colic. at Oyster Bay on Long Island. in January, 1808, being then twenty-eight years of age, and having attained such a height of equine reputation that he was buried with military honors, and a charge of musketry was fired over his grave.

---

[1] Her record is 2.08¾.
[2] Her record is 2.08¼ on a kite-shaped track.
[3] See page 87.

Nearly fifty years later, in November, 1854, an old bay horse called Abdallah was turned out on the sands of this same Long Island, and abandoned to die of cold and starvation. He had been sold for thirty-five dollars to a fisherman, who attempted to put him in harness. But Abdallah had never been broken to harness, and being of a vicious temper he kicked the fish-wagon to pieces, and thereupon the fisherman cruelly cast him adrift. Abdallah was a grandson of Messenger,[1] and, so far as we know, the best of his descendants in that generation. He was an ugly, rat-tailed horse, but big, strong, tough, and a fast trotter. Unlike the Messenger stock in general, he had fine sloping shoulders. Abdallah was the sire of Rysdyck's Hambletonian,[2] who founded the noted trotting family called the Hambletonians.[3]

The dam of Rysdyck's Hambletonian, known to fame as the Charles Kent mare, was of a lineage entirely different, for her sire was Bellfounder, a Norfolk trotter. Bellfounder was imported in 1822 by Mr. James Boott, a rich merchant of Boston, Massachusetts, who paid seven hundred pounds sterling for

---

[1] Abdallah was sired by Mambrino. Mambrino was by Messenger, out of a mare by imported Sour-Crout. Abdallah's dam was said to be by another son of Messenger.

[2] The sire of his grandam was called Bishop's "Hamiltonian," after Alexander Hamilton. The name was however corrupted to "Hambletonian," which was also the name of an English race horse bred in Hambleton, a district of Yorkshire.

[3] Of the twenty trotting stallions who stand highest on the list, judging by the records of their sons and daughters, all but two are descended from Rysdyck's Hambletonian, either on the paternal or maternal side: and of those two one is also a descendant of Messenger (in a different line), and the breeding of the other is unknown on the dam's side.

him. He was a handsome round-built bay horse with black points, and he is said to have trotted in England nine miles in twenty-nine minutes and thirty-eight seconds, and two miles in six minutes. Bellfounder was of the same blood from which the modern hackney is derived, and of much the same origin as that famous Marshland Shales whose name is preserved in the works of George Borrow. An old advertising card was discovered some years ago, in which it is stated that Bellfounder's dam was Velocity. In 1806 Velocity was matched to trot sixteen miles within an hour on the Norwich road, and although she broke into a gallop fifteen times, "and as often turned round" (that being the penalty), she won the match.

Bellfounder was described as "plump in form and muscular in all his parts," and as having "a fine, slashing gait." He contributed to the Hambletonian family that mildness of temper for which, unlike the earlier Messengers, they have always been distinguished.

Rysdyck's Hambletonian was an animal of extraordinary appearance, looking very much as a locomotive might look if it were turned into a horse with no more changes than were necessary to effect the transformation. He had a long, round body, like the boiler of an engine, of almost the same girth throughout. His neck was short and straight, and he had a big, ugly head, surmounted by ears which, though large and coarse, were a little too well shaped to be positively ill-bred. His expression was good, phlegmatic but amiable, and full of character. He stood very firm and solid, on feet perfect in shape and texture; and his legs were flat, clean, heavily muscled, and free from gumminess or swelling even in his old age. It is hardly necessary to add that his tail was set low and carried low, for there was nothing ornamental about Rysdyck's Hambletonian. His hind quarters were very powerful, and he had great length from hip to hock. The rump was rather round than sloping. Altogether he presented the appearance of a serviceable, practical beast, fit, when well warmed up, to trot for a man's life, as the phrase is, but neither beautiful nor lively. In color he took after the Bellfounder strain, being a rich, deep bay with black points, and this color was transmitted to his descendants with singular uniformity.[1]

The Hambletonians, indeed, have a marked family resemblance. They are almost always big bay horses, with large ears, drooping tails, a long, wide gait, and a sleepy disposition. Thus it appears that they are ill adapted for roadster purposes, whether in form, in action, or in character; and the predominance of the family is, on the whole, to be regretted. It has increased the speed, but lessened the beauty and dulled the spirit of our average harness horse. Hambletonian himself had no record, but he was undoubtedly fast. His chief points of excellence were his long trotting gait, his muscular development, the fine quality of his bones and sinews. It is estimated that he sired about 1,340 foals, and of these only forty made records of 2.30 or better. Hambletonian's reputation is

---

[1] The following measurements of Hambletonian may interest certain of my readers. He stood 15.1 at the withers, and 15.3 at the rump. His knee was $13\frac{1}{2}$ inches in circumference, his hock $17\frac{1}{4}$ inches. From the centre of the hip-joint to the point of the hock he measured 41 inches; from the point of the stifle to the point of the hock, the length of his thigh was 24 inches.

established by his more remote descendants, in whom the cart-horse qualities inherited from the Bellfounder strain were overcome by an infusion of thoroughbred or Arab blood. His best sons were invariably from high-bred mares. Perhaps the best of all was Alexander's Abdallah.[1] This grand horse came to an end more untimely and no less cruel than that suffered by his grandsire Abdallah. In February, 1865, just before the Civil War closed, Alexander's Abdallah was stolen by a Rebel guerilla from his owner's farm at Woodburn, Kentucky. The next day he was recaptured by a Federal soldier, ridden fifty miles unshod, and then abandoned at the roadside without food or shelter. He died a few days later of pneumonia. Among his few descendants are Belmont,[2] Almont, and Thorndale, all of whom founded subordinate trotting families, and the famous Goldsmith Maid, whose career will be glanced at in a subsequent chapter. Other noted sons of Rysdyck's Hambletonian are George Wilkes and Electioneer, both of whose dams were of the Clay family (presently to be described), Volunteer (whose dam was a high-bred mare called Lady Patriot), Happy Medium, Harold (the sire of Maud S.), Strathmore, Dictator, and Aberdeen. At present, the two most popular trotting families are those founded by George Wilkes and Electioneer, respectively. Both of these horses were bred in New York State, but Wilkes passed the greater part of his life in Kentucky, and Electioneer stood for many

---

[1] His dam was a small, wiry bay mare, who showed signs of high breeding. Her pedigree is untraced, but she is said to have descended from Mambrino, son of Messenger.

[2] Sire of Nutwood and of Wedgewood.

years at the head of Governor Stanford's famous farm in California. He is the sire of Sunol, of Palo Alto, whose dam was a thoroughbred, of Arion, and of many other fast trotters.

Neither the Wilkeses nor the Electioneers pure and simple are possessed of much style or beauty, nor are they suitable for roadster use ; but some of the younger branches in each family where other blood has been introduced excel in these respects, as well as in trotting speed.

There is another strain descended from Messenger scarcely inferior to the Hambletonians in speed, equal to them in soundness, and far superior in point of elegance and spirit. This is the Kentucky family of Mambrino Chief,[1] and more especially of his son, Mambrino Patchen. The dam of Mambrino Patchen was the Rodes mare, by Gano,[2] a thoroughbred. Mambrino Patchen himself was a very beautiful black horse, about sixteen hands high, with sloping shoulders, high withers, a fine arched neck, a tail well put on and well carried. In fact, this whole family is noted for the proud and graceful carriage of its tails, so much so that some detractors have insinuated that artificial means were used to produce this effect. An own sister of Mambrino Patchen was Lady Thorne, perhaps the best trotting mare, all things considered, ever bred. She was a blood bay, 16¼ hands high, with the marks

---

[1] Foaled in 1844 ; by Mambrino Paymaster, he by Mambrino, a thoroughbred son of Messenger. The dam of Mambrino Chief cannot be traced, but she was a fine, strong, courageous animal, and a great roadster.

[2] Gano was a son of American Eclipse. The grandam and great-grandam of Mambrino Patchen were also half-bred horses of much quality, sound and long-lived.

of a thoroughbred. Her record is only 2.18¼, but she
beat all the fastest horses of her day, including Dexter,
Mountain Boy, Goldsmith Maid, American Girl, Lucy,
and George Palmer, and had it not been for an injury
to her hip received while she was being taken from
a car she would doubtless have lowered this record.
The accident compelled her retirement from the
turf. There is a tradition that Dan Mace once drove
Lady Thorne a mile in 2.08 and a fraction, and it is
fairly well established that she trotted a trial mile
in 2.10½.

The best son of Mambrino Patchen is Mambrino
King.[1] now twenty years of age, but still a prize
winner at horse shows. There is a singular unanimity
of opinion about this animal, for, so far as I can as-
certain, all who have seen him pronounce Mambrino
King to be the handsomest horse in the world. Such
is the judgment of Mr. Robert Bonner, for example,
in this country, of Mr. Burdett-Coutts in England, and
of those Continental connoisseurs in horse-flesh who
have visited this country. Among the latter is Baron
Favorot de Kerbeck, a French Colonel of Dragoons,
who, with two other officers, was sent to the United
States by his government, a few years ago, to inspect
our horses. He reported : —

"Mambrino King is the most splendid specimen we
have had an opportunity of admiring. Imagine an
Alfred de Dreux, a burnt chestnut, whole colored,
standing 15.3 hands, with an expressive head, large,
intelligent, and spirited eyes, well opened lower jaws,
well set ears, the neck and shoulders splendidly shaped.

[1] His dam was by Edwin Forrest, a half-bred horse raised in
Kentucky.

long, and gracefully rounded off, the shoulders strong
and thrown back well, the withers well in place and
top muscular, the ribs round and loins superb, the
crupper long and broad, limbs exceedingly fine, the
joints powerful, the tail carried majestically, and all
the movements high and spirited, — imagine all this,
and you will have an idea of this stallion. He is as
fine, if we look at him in front, as he is in his hind
quarters, the whole animal being an embodiment of
purity of lines, elegance, and elasticity. He is in fact
perfection."

Some years ago Mambrino King was stigmatized by
many practical horsemen, whose ideal trotter was a
coarse-bred brute, as the Dude Stallion; but since his
sons and daughters have displayed both speed and
gameness in numerous hard fought races, Mambrino
King's solid qualities are no longer questioned.

Having, then, such horses as Mambrino King. as
Quartermaster,[1] Alcantara,[2] Ivywood,[3] and many others
like them, it seems absurd that we should import for
our driving hackneys from England. which do not surpass the American horses just mentioned in any respect, and are far inferior to them in speed. In this
connection I will quote a remark from the present
Duke of Marlborough's account of his visit to the stock
farms of Kentucky. "The small farmer," he says,
"drives an animal that would leave the English farmer
on his way to market in the last parish, while the
amateur can buy for £150 to £200 a pair of animals
which could not be obtained in England for double the

---

[1] A great-grandson of Mambrino Patchen, sired by Alcyone, a
son of George Wilkes.

[2] A grandson of Mambrino Patchen, own brother to Alcyone.

[3] A son of Wedgewood.

money, and are able to go at a speed far greater than our best Norfolk trotters can manage."

I have now indicated the two most important trotting families descended from Messenger, and there are others but little inferior. Vermont had the Harris Hambletonian, a grandson of Messenger, out of a gray "English mare." He was a gray himself, and so were most of his descendants. This horse was the sire of Sontag, who once beat Flora Temple in a match race, and grandsire of the Morse horse, among whose descendants was Lulu, with a record of 2.14½, and Governor Sprague, a trotting stallion of high reputation.

Maine had Winthrop Messenger and the Bush Messenger. The Bush Messengers were almost invariably chestnuts. Fanny Pullen, dam of Trustee,[1] the first horse to trot twenty miles within an hour, was a Bush Messenger.

Still another Messenger strain, and one of more "quality" than the rest, is that of the Champions. In the first quarter of this century, one Mr. John Tredwell of Long Island had a pair of extraordinarily fast and enduring road mares, called Amazonia and Sophronisba, the former being of Messenger descent, and the latter a granddaughter of imported Baronet.[2] In 1823 both of these mares produced foals by Mambrino, son of Messenger. Amazonia's foal was Abdallah, sire, as we have seen, of the famous Rysdyck's Hambletonian, and Sophronisba's foal was Almack, sire of Grinnell's Champion,[3] first of the name, and

---

[1] His sire was imported Trustee, a thoroughbred.

[2] By Vertumnus out of Penultima. Baronet, a bay horse, was noted for his beauty.

[3] The dam of Grinnell's Champion was by Engineer, and his grandam by the famous American Eclipse.

founder of the family. This horse was thus described by one who had seen him : —

"He was a golden chestnut, about sixteen hands, with a perfect diamond on his nose, and two white socks behind. In his general make-up he partook much of the thoroughbred appearance : the lightness of his head and neck, his wiry leg and elastic movement, his glossy coat and waveless mane and tail, shaded from a darker hue to a bright tint on the edge, — in all a perfect type of the high-bred runner. He was exhibited at the State Fair at Auburn, New York, in 1848. I can never forget, though I was very young at the time, this eventful show, as he assumed a position among his rivals which bade defiance to the artist. He seemed to realize the admiration with which he was regarded by the immense throng about him."

The rich chestnut color, the high spirit, the well-bred look, displayed by Grinnell's Champion, distinguish the family to this day, and it is probably owing more to accident and mismanagement than to any deficiency that the Champions are few in number, and of less reputation than the Hambletonians. The fastest of the family was the Auburn horse, who belonged to Mr. Robert Bonner.[1]

The Auburn horse was the last of those famous trotters which, as one writer remarks with pardonable extravagance, were stabled in Hiram Woodruff's brain.[2] In the autumn of 1864, just before winter

---

[1] He was a son of King's Champion, his dam being by Red Bird, son of Billy Duroc, by Duroc, son of imported Diomed.

[2] Mr. Woodruff, a genius in the art of horsemanship, and a very honest man, was the author of " The Trotting Horse of America," by far the most interesting work upon the subject. ·

closed in and the ground became frozen, the Auburn horse showed a flight of speed that set Mr. Woodruff's household and stable in commotion. On alighting from the sulky, he declared that he had just been carried faster than he ever rode before in his life, and he made the same remark to Mr. Bonner later in the day, when that gentleman paid the stable a visit. "But," said Mr. Bonner, "you rode at the rate of two minutes to the mile behind Peerless for a quarter. Do you mean to say that you rode faster behind the Auburn horse than behind the gray mare?" Woodruff answered, "Faster than behind the gray mare, — faster than I ever rode before behind any horse." This was probably true, for he was a man not given to overstatement; but early in the following spring, before the season opened, Hiram Woodruff died, and the Auburn horse did not long survive him.

So much for the chief strains of trotting blood derived from Messenger. Next in importance among founders of the trotter comes the Barb or Arab, Grand Bashaw, who was imported from Tripoli in 1820. He is described as a very beautiful little black horse, about 14.1 high, with a small star in his forehead. He died in Pennsylvania in the year 1845. Among his sons was Young Bashaw, a larger and much coarser animal, and gray in color like his dam, who was Pearl, by Bond's First Consul; his grandam was a Messenger mare. Young Bashaw sired Andrew Jackson,[1] the fastest trotting stallion of his day, a black horse, strong, compact, and short-legged. When Andrew Jackson was foaled, his dam was the property of one Daniel Jeffreys, a brickmaker, and the

---

[1] His dam was a pacer, and nothing more is known of her.

first act of the little colt was to tumble into a pit
where clay had been mixed for making bricks. He
was rescued from this hole in a very sorry condition,
and either on account of the accident, or from natural
weakness, he was unable to stand upright. His pastern joints bent under his weight, and altogether he
appeared to be so wretched and worthless a creature
that Mr. Jeffreys gave orders to have him killed.
But his wife interceded, begged that the foal's life
might be spared, and undertook to look after him
herself. The colt was accordingly permitted to live,
a little careful nursing soon brought him round, and
thus, through the pity of a woman, did the ancestor of all the Clays escape being murdered in his infancy. It is an odd fact that Vermont Blackhawk,
founder of the trotting branch of the Morgan family, and one of the handsomest horses that ever
lived, was also condemned to death by his owner
because of the weak and ugly appearance that he
first made in the world. In his case it was the
groom who successfully interceded for his life. The
same thing is true of Santa Claus, one of the best
grandsons of Rysdyck's Hambletonian. Andrew Jackson was the sire of Henry Clay, founder of the Clay
family, his dam being a Canadian trotting mare called
Surrey, of unknown breeding.

Some writers assert that Henry Clay's good qualities as a trotter were derived from the Messenger
element in his composition: but it is a striking fact,
that in form, in disposition, and in color he resembled
his great-grandsire Grand Bashaw very closely. He
was a coal-black horse with a beautiful white cres-
cent on his face, "very perfect, the line of it extend-

ing up and down, that is, one horn above the eyes, the other below." He had the curved neck, the fine sloping shoulders, the round swelling barrel, the small ears, the springy pasterns, the tough, round feet of a Barb or Arab horse. In the hind parts, however, he took after his dam. His hips were sharp, the rump was long and drooping. He had great length from hip to hock, the invariable formation of a trotter, and his tail was thick and wavy, with a few white hairs at the dock.

"In disposition and temper," writes Mr. Randolph Huntington, " he was a very lovable horse. The last time I went to see him was in October, 1865. Henry Clay was then twenty-eight years old. Mr. Fellows, who owned him, knew that I loved the old horse, and asked me if I would not like to see him out. However, not wishing to trouble him, and knowing that Henry Clay had long been blind, I answered, 'Never mind,' but the door of his box was swung wide open, and after a cheerful, 'Come, Henry,' from his master, the old horse sailed out into the barnyard with as lofty and as sure a step as though he could see every spot in which it was possible to place a foot."

Henry Clay was a horse of great bottom and of sound constitution, as is sufficiently proved by the fact that he lived to be twenty-nine years old, notwithstanding the hard usage to which he was subjected. There is a tradition that he was once driven ninety miles in a single day, and started the next afternoon in a race which he won. However this may be, it is certain that for many years Henry Clay belonged to an owner who cruelly abused him. It seems to be the natural amusement of a drunken man to ill-treat

a horse, and Henry Clay was one of that innumerable
company of dumb beasts whose fate it has been to
supply this kind of entertainment for the superior
animal. When his "peculiar turns were upon him,"
writes one who knew both horse and man, " W——
always wanted to drive Henry Clay. At such times
the city of Rochester, which is twenty-eight miles
by road from Geneseo, was the objective point.
When ready to return, after an experience that tries
men's nerves, he would get into the wagon, take out
his whip, and, giving it a wide swing, exclaim, 'One
hour and a half into my barn,' — which the horse
had to do. Sometimes his carriage would break down.
The President of the Livingston Agricultural Society,
the late M. L. Cummings, wishing at one time to
see W—— on some important matters, waited for
him in his barn, and W—— finally drove in hanging to the dashboard, the hind axle dragging, both
hind wheels gone. The horse was dripping wet, and
panting so that Mr. Cummings (a first-class horseman) thought that he would never recover his wind.
W—— took out his watch, looked at it, and exclaimed, · He did it, or I would shoot him. One hour
and a half, twenty-eight miles!'"

On another occasion W—— struck Henry Clay
with a club, breaking one of his ribs, and the injury
left its mark on the skeleton of the horse, which
is still preserved in the National Museum at Washington.

The Orloff trotters of Russia were bred in much
the same way as the Clays, and there is a resemblance
between the two families. Some years ago there was
an exhibition of Orloff trotters at a State fair held in

Central New York, neai the former home of Henry Clay, and many farmers who saw the Russian horses there protested at what they considered an imposition. "These are not foreign horses, they are nothing but Clays," was their criticism.

For many years, while the Hambletonian star was rising, the Clay family were undervalued and misrepresented; but finally, when it became apparent that the most successful Hambletonian sires, George Wilkes and Electioneer, were out of Clay mares, and that in many other cases Clay blood had helped to produce extreme speed, this prejudice was dissipated. It seems to be true, however, that there is a slight tendency in the family to sulk at critical moments. "It was undoubtedly," says Mr. H. T. Helm,[1] "a mental quality, which, when they were collared by an antagonist, and likely to be forced to the utmost, caused them to sulk and refuse to do their best." And Mr. Helm adds that Boston, the famous four-mile racer, and Harry Bassett. his grandson, both exhibited the same trait.

I have stated already the maternal lines coming from Clay stock in which chiefly distinction has been won. There is also an important California family descended from the Clays in the paternal line. This is the family founded by The Moor, among whose descendants are Sultan, and the son of Sultan, Stamboul, whose record is 2.11. These California Clays are very beautiful horses, having almost the finish and quality of thoroughbreds.[2]

[1] "American Roadsters and Trotting Horses." A valuable work, of which I shall make frequent use.

[2] The breeding of this family is as follows: Henry Clay sired

It is an interesting fact that the Hambletonians, the Mambrino Chiefs, and the Clays all have a hall-mark, so to say, of their own, not found of course in every individual belonging to their blood, but still extremely common. In the Hambletonian family this is a white hind foot, mottled with black; in the Mambrino Chief family, especially in the Mambrino Patchen branch, it is one hind leg gray from foot to hock; in the Clays, it is a few gray hairs at the root of the tail.

Having now indicated in a general way three of the main sources of trotting speed. — namely, the Messenger strain as exhibited especially in the Hambletonian and Mambrino Chief families, the Bell-founder or Norfolk Trotter strain as represented in the Hambletonian family, and the Grand Bashaw or Barb strain preserved in the Clays. — I come to the fourth main source of trotting speed, namely, the Morgans, a New England breed.

In the troubled year 1788, one Colonel De Lancey, a King's officer, and a patron of horse racing, was in command of a regiment stationed at a point on Long Island connected with the mainland by a long bridge. As his private charger, the Colonel had a very hand-some bay stallion, a thoroughbred, called True Briton,[1] and afterward Beautiful Bay.

Cassius M. Clay out of a well-bred but untraced mare. Cassius M. Clay sired Clay Pilot out of a mare by Pacing Pilot (a Canadian horse of unknown pedigree), second dam by Gray Eagle, an in-bred Diomed. Clay Pilot sired The Moor out of Belle of Wabash, a very blood-like animal, a thoroughbred, or nearly thoroughbred, granddaughter of imported Fylde.

[1] True Briton was by Lloyd's Traveller, by Imported Traveller. Imported (or Moreton's) Traveller was bred by Mr. Crofts. He

Some nameless person, perhaps a patriot ambitious to despoil the enemy, or, as is more likely, a miscreant bent upon plunder, stole this True Briton, and ran him across the bridge to Connecticut, and thereupon he became an American possession, and was kept at East Hartford. This horse was the sire of the bay colt afterward known as Justin Morgan. The dam of Justin Morgan is represented to have been of the Wildair breed. Wildair, a horse of the very first quality, was imported from England, and afterward repurchased at a high price and returned to that country. According to other accounts, Justin Morgan's dam was descended from the Lindsey Arabian, a noted animal kept first in Connecticut and afterward in Maryland.[1] At all events, it is probable

was sired by Partner, grandson of the Byerly Turk, and grandsire of King Herod. The dam of Traveller was by Bloody Buttocks, the Arabian. The dam of Lloyd's Traveller was by a son of Old Fox, out of Miss Belvoir.

[1] The story of this horse is a romantic one. In return for some very important service, he was presented by the Emperor of Morocco to the captain of a British frigate, who took him on board and set sail for home. Being obliged to call at one of the West India islands, the captain put the horse ashore in order that he might exercise himself in a large enclosed yard near the sea. Unfortunately there was a pile of lumber in this yard upon which the horse climbed, and, the lumber slipping, he fell and broke three of his legs. In the harbor at the time there happened to be also an American ship commanded by an acquaintance of the British officer, and, as this vessel was intending to remain there for some weeks, the horse was given to the American captain, who brought him on board, put him in a sling, and succeeded in setting his broken legs. The animal finally arrived in the United States in good condition, and was sent to Connecticut, where he soon made a reputation. He was now called Ranger. During the Revolutionary War some Virginia officers, including General Harry Lee, were struck by the great excellence of certain horses ridden by soldiers from Con-

that she was nearly, if not quite, as well bred as
True Briton, for so remarkable an animal as Justin
Morgan could hardly have been a mongrel.

It must be remembered that at the time when
Justin Morgan was foaled the typical thoroughbred
was very unlike the thoroughbred of the present day.
He was close to the Arab foundation, and conse
quently he was a shorter-legged, rounder built, more
compact animal than the race horse of the nineteenth
century. Such was the famous and beautiful Gimcrack,[1] foaled in 1760. It is not surprising, therefore,
that Justin Morgan, though well-bred, was a chunky
little horse, with short legs and round quarters. He
had a fine mane and tail, a short, powerful back, a
longish body, strong, oblique shoulders, a delicate
ear, a noble head, and the most intelligent, expressive,
and courageous eyes that the spirit of a Houyhnhm
ever looked out of. He stood fourteen hands only,
and weighed about nine hundred pounds. He was
foaled in Springfield, Massachusetts, in 1793, and as
a two-year-old he was taken in part payment of a debt
by a school-teacher named Justin Morgan, who brought
him to Randolph, Vermont. The horse died in 1821,
near Chelsea, Vermont.

necticut. On inquiry, they learned that these horses were sons
of Ranger. There were sixty of them, all grays, in a troop commanded by Captain Tallmadge, who is said to have lamented the
loss of one of them more bitterly than he did the death of a trooper.
The Virginia gentlemen made up a purse, and sent one Captain
Lindsey to inspect Ranger, and, if the horse answered the account
that had been given to them, to purchase him if possible. Captain
Lindsey accordingly bought Ranger and took him to Virginia, where
he was known as Lindsey's Arabian. He was a gray, high-spirited,
of a proud and commanding appearance.

[1] Gimcrack was by Cripple, by the Godolphin Arabian. He
stood only 14.1 hands.

Justin Morgan was no trotter, and not till the third or fourth generation did a trotter arise in his family, but he was distinguished in three ways, as a draught horse, as a short-distance runner, and as a military charger or parade horse. In his day there were no race-courses and no stated races in Vermont; but when the sporting element gathered at a tavern on a spring or summer evening, they were wont to amuse themselves by running their horses on the level road in front of the tavern, the prize being a gallon of rum, and in these races Justin Morgan is said never to have been beaten. On the same occasions a contest would often be had in pulling logs; and when the other horses concerned had done their best, it was the custom of Justin Morgan's owner to hitch him to the heaviest log that had been stirred, then to jump on himself, and the little horse never failed to move the load. When ridden at a muster, his proud carriage made him the cynosure of all eyes; and he was so intelligent and tractable that women could ride him. In fine, Justin Morgan was an animal of extraordinary utility and style. To an extraordinary extent, also, he stamped his image and impressed his qualities upon his descendants.

Unfortunate indeed is the American in whose ears those magic words, "Morgan horse," awake no recollection, or not even a thrill of sympathetic interest. For nearly a century the Morgans have served the farmer, the stable-keeper, the minister, the country doctor, the mounted militiaman, and all other people who desired to travel quickly or to be carried handsomely. Wonderful truly (and perhaps at times a little apocryphal) are the stories of Morgan intelli-

gence. of Morgan speed, and of Morgan endurance,
that are told by the dim light of a lantern in many
a country livery stable in Northern New England.
I remember — But at present we are concerned with
the Morgan merely as a trotter, and so I reserve
my stories of Morgan roadsters for a subsequent
chapter.

Justin Morgan's finest son was Sherman, whose dam
was a small but highly bred chestnut mare. Sherman
himself, a bright chestnut in color, stood no taller than
a pony, for he measured only 13¾ hands. He weighed,
however, 925 pounds. Sherman was the sire of Vermont Black Hawk, and Vermont Black Hawk founded
a trotting family. His dam was a half-bred "English" mare from New Brunswick. She stood sixteen
hands high, and weighed about eleven hundred pounds.
Vermont Black Hawk was foaled in 1833; he was a
little under fifteen hands, and jet-black in color. This
horse, besides being a trotter, had every quality of a
good roadster: he was strong. speedy, enduring; he
had a lively but pleasant disposition, and he was remarkably handsome. His back was short, he carried
his head high, and he possessed that elastic "trappy"
gait which is the true roadster way of going.

His most distinguished son was Ethan Allen, a very
beautiful little bay horse. whose dam was a highly
bred gray[1] mare, said to be of Messenger descent.
Ethan Allen's trotting action was wonderfully smooth
and pure. He has a record of 2.15[2] with running

[1] Both the black color of his sire and the gray color of his dam
are very infrequent in the descendants of Ethan Allen. They are
commonly bays or chestnuts.

[2] H. B. Winship, a descendant of Ethan Allen, has since trotted
a mile in 2 06 with running mate.

mate, and he was, I believe, the first horse to be driven in that somewhat ridiculous fashion. The manner is, to provide strong breeching covered with sheepskin, and to make the traces of the runner shorter than those of his mate. The runner thus pulls the trotter along, very much as a boy is pulled by a wagon when he " cuts behind," and hangs on to the tail-board.

Ethan Allen's record in single harness is 2.25¼. This discrepancy of 10¼ seconds between his record with and his record without a running mate is greater than it should be, and is probably due chiefly to the fact that his hind legs were faulty, his hocks being somewhat weak, and his pastern joints too long and delicate, so that he could not maintain his speed except for a short distance. These defects he inherited from his dam. One who knew the horse well wrote of him : " He works with the least possible waste of motion. His stride is as precise as the stroke of a pendulum, and so true does he carry his body, so graceful his head and neck, and so animated his carriage, that he seems to ·light up' all over. and presents a most perfect, sylph-like form of elegance."

The best son of Ethan Allen was Daniel Lambert. who became the most distinguished progenitor of trotters that has appeared in the Morgan family. His dam was Fanny Cook. a chestnut. and a daughter of Abdallah. son of Messenger and sire of Rysdyck's Hambletonian. Thus in Daniel Lambert the Messenger and Morgan strains were united. and this combination has since produced many fast trotters.[1] In Daniel Lambert disappeared the faulty conformation that Ethan Allen inherited from his dam, and he was not

---

[1] Notably Jack. 2.12¼. and Pamlico, 2.16¾.

inferior in beauty to his sire or grandsire.  He was a
chestnut, with mane and tail some shades lighter, the
mane being very silky, and the tail long, wavy, and
well carried.  This peculiar coloring of two shades of
chestnut is still very common in the Lambert family,
and, seen at its best, nothing could be more striking or
picturesque.  The Lamberts are apt to be a little hot-
headed, but they are intelligent, docile when properly
treated, very spirited, speedy, and courageous.  Perhaps it would be no exaggeration to say that the finest
gentlemen's roadsters bred in this country have been
of Lambert stock.  Daniel Lambert himself was a
horse of commanding style and of magnificent carriage.
For many years he was kept in the vicinity of Boston,
but late in life he was brought back to Middlebury,
Vt., where he had been raised.  On this occasion all
the inhabitants turned out with a brass band to wel-
come him home, and there was a procession through
the village streets.  "The old horse," relates an eye-
witness of the scene, "kept time to the music, and was
the proudest creature that ever walked on earth."

I have mentioned the pacer as one source of trotting
speed.  Why he should be such is a problem much dis-
cussed, and not yet solved, although an important suggestion on this subject has been contributed by Hark
Comstock.[1]  He conjectures that the pacing gait is
apt to result when thoroughbred horses are first crossed
with ordinary mares; and he shows that pacers have
been common in those parts of the country where this
condition obtained.  Moreover, there is, I believe, no
case where a very fast trotter has come from pacing

[1] *Nom de guerre* of Mr. Peter C. Kellogg, an original and instructive writer on the trotting horse.

stock, except when this blood was qualified by that of high-bred horses. The great Smuggler[1] was of pacing-thoroughbred descent. Both Maud S. and Jay-Eye-See are descended on the maternal side from a Canadian pacer. Their grandsire was Pilot, or, as he is now more commonly called, Old Pacing Pilot, — a Canadian horse with all the characteristics of that race. He was coal-black, with a long, thick, "wavy" mane and tail, and hairy fetlocks. He stood a little under fifteen hands. His head was plain, but not coarse, his neck fairly long; he had a sloping rump, and his hocks were well let down. He was a very muscular, compactly built, stout, tough horse, full of "character," and he could pace a mile in 2.26, carrying a weight of one hundred and sixty pounds on his back. Pilot was a typical Canadian, descended probably from Norman horses brought into Canada by the French, and rendered smaller, tougher, and longer-haired by the severe climate and rough fare.

By far the best son of Old Pacing Pilot was Pilot Jr., a handsome gray horse, whose dam was Nancy Pope, a Diomed mare, nearly if not quite thoroughbred; and it was Pilot Jr. who sired the dams of both Maud S. and Jay-Eye-See.

There is another trotting family descended from a pacer, which is far more numerous though somewhat less distinguished than the family of Pilot Jr. Many years ago there was in the mountainous part of Ohio an extraordinary looking horse owned by a man named Merring. This horse was dubbed "Merring's Blue Bull" by the local wag, — "Blue" on account of his color (which was that rare shade commonly known

[1] See page 100.

as mouse-color), " Bull " on account of his thick neck,
— and the name Blue Bull, thus given in scorn, became in the third generation a badge of honor.  Merring's Blue Bull had a son called Pruden's Blue Bull,
no less remarkable in appearance than his sire.  He
was a big horse, at least 16½ hands high, weighing
twelve hundred pounds, — a mouse-colored beast with
a white face, a black stripe down his back, three white
feet, and legs marked like those of a zebra.

A writer in the American Horse Breeder gives the
following description of him : " He was a deep mouse-
color, generally called blue, blazed face, glass eyes,
heavy black mane and tail, black stripe down his back,
legs white to the knees, and from there up had yellow stripes around them.  He was a powerfully built,
heavy-bodied, close-ribbed horse, with an enormous
beefy neck, a natural pacer, and ungainly in action.
Many of this family were natural pacers, and but few
proved to be good riding horses, on account of their
awkward and stumbling gait.  They were, however, a
strong, tough, hardy race of horses, and served admirably for heavy teaming in this hilly country before
the days of turnpikes and railroads."

Merring's Blue Bull and his son Pruden's Blue Bull
were, then, clumsy pacing cart horses, and Wilson's
Blue Bull, son of Pruden's Blue Bull, looked much
like his sire and grandsire ; and yet he is the founder
of a trotting family almost if not quite as numerous
as the Wilkeses or the Electioneers.  Wilson's Blue
Bull, the only Blue Bull up to his day who had attained the slightest distinction, was foaled in 1844.
" His appearance," as related by an experienced horseman, " was the most peculiar I ever saw.  From a

side view one would judge him to be a draught horse,
but a front or rear view would dispel the illusion. His
hind legs were sickle-shaped, front knees sprung back-
wards, legs wide and thin, very short from knees down,
great length of arms, with muscles long and massive,
hips extending so far forward and shoulders so far
backward that there was not length enough of back
for an ordinary riding saddle to be properly adjusted.
He seemed to be made of hips and shoulders, but had
good length of belly. His only gait was a pace. I
have often seen him pace with a running horse beside
him, and for a few hundred yards he would always
come out ahead."

He had a sleek, short coat, and this and his sloping
shoulders were his only indications of good breeding.
As he was the single son of Pruden's Blue Bull, and
the single grandson of Merring's Blue Bull, to attain
reputation as a trotting sire it is fair to assume that
he derived his good qualities in great measure from
his dam. She was a "sorrel chestnut," about 15.1
high, with good trotting action, considerable speed,
and great endurance. On one occasion she was ridden
eighty-seven miles in eleven hours by a man who
weighed one hundred and eighty pounds. Her sire
was Young Selim, of a family called Truxton,[1] and
Young Selim is supposed to have been a half-bred.
Early in life Wilson's Blue Bull lost an eye, and was
deformed by a kick which broke one of his fore legs.
Thus his extraordinary and ugly appearance was

[1] The original Truxton, a son of Diomed, was owned and
raced by President Jackson. General Stonewall Jackson's favorite
charger was a sorrel called Truxton, probably a member of the
same family.

heightened, and, until a few chance colts by him began to show great speed, he was held in the very lowest estimation.[1] Moreover, his descendants are remarkable not only for speed, but for beauty and finish, and the term "Blue Bull" now suggests qualities the very opposite of those for which it was given. The Blue Bulls, however, are thought to lack gameness.

Of the six horses that I mentioned in the beginning of this chapter as being, in a general way, the foundation stock of the American trotter, there remains only one to be described, and that is Diomed, a thorough-bred, and a contemporary of Messenger. Messenger as a sire of running horses was a failure. Of all his foals, only one, a filly called Miller's Damsel,[2] attained distinction on the running track; but Messenger, though running bred, had good trotting action, and the gift of imparting it to his numerous descendants. Thus, as we have seen, he played a leading part in the development of the trotter.

The case of Diomed is very different. He was a successful runner himself, and from him descend the stanchest, speediest runners that have appeared on the American turf. But he was not a trotter nor a sire of trotters, and his foals were few in number, so that upon the general harness horses of the country the influence of his blood was very slight. On what ground, then, can he be regarded as one of the half-dozen foundation horses from which the American trotter is chiefly derived?

[1] He began his career precisely as did the Godolphin Arabian, and his value was discovered in the same accidental manner.

[2] And her dam was by a son of Diomed.

Diomed owes this distinction to the high quality of a few trotters that have descended from him in the maternal line. If the pedigree of all horses that have made 2.30 or better were consulted, Diomed's name would appear so seldom as to make his part in the development of the trotter seem very insignificant. But when the pedigrees of the select few that have trotted in say 2.12 or better are examined, Diomed's name appears so frequently as to suggest something more than a series of coincidences.

Before stating a few of these cases, I will take a brief glance at Diomed's history. The first "Derby" was run at Epsom on May 4, 1780, and it was won by a "compact, well formed chestnut colt, the property of Sir Charles Bunbury." This was Diomed. He was bred by the Hon. Richard Vernon, of Newmarket, and foaled in 1777. Diomed was by Florizel, by King Herod, and his dam was the famous Spectator mare.[1]

James Rice, who wrote a History of the British Turf, says: "It has been the fashion to underrate the Derby victory of Diomed, but the history of his three-year-old career on the turf shows that he was a good performer, and won or received a forfeit in all his engagements, proving himself thereby one of the best three-year-olds of his time."

Diomed was brought to this country in 1799, having been purchased for the small sum of fifty guineas, at the age of twenty-two, and he died in 1808, which was also the year of Messenger's death. He left, as I have

---

[1] To show the Oriental richness of his pedigree, it is sufficient to state that he traces to the Leeds Arabian nine times : to the Darley Arabian seven times; to the Byerly Turk five times; to Curwen's Bay Barb twice; to the Bald Galloway once; to the Godolphin Arabian twice; to Flying Childers four times; etc.

said, only a few foals in this country, — less than a
hundred; but those few appear conspicuously in the
pedigrees of our fastest horses, whether at the running,
the trotting, or the pacing gait.

The best son of Diomed was Sir Archy, foaled on
the banks of the James River, in Virginia, in the year
1805.[1]  Sir Archy was a thoroughbred of the very first
breeding, the speediest, gamest race-horse of his day,
and his descendants have not been unworthy of their
origin.  Sir Archy was of a rich bay color, with one
white hind foot, and he is thus described by Frank
Forester :  " He was a horse of commanding appearance, standing fully sixteen hands in height, possessing great power and substance.  He was eminently
superior in all those points indispensable to the turf
horse and mainly contributory to strength and action.
His shoulder, one of the most material parts of the
horse, was strikingly distinguished, being very deep,
fairly mounting to the top of the withers, and obliquely inclined to the hips.  His girth was full and
deep, back short and strong, thighs and arms long and
muscular, and bone of excellent quality.  His front
appearance was fine and commanding, his head and
neck being beautifully formed, the latter rising well
out of his withers.  Take Sir Archy as a whole, and
he had more size, power, and substance than are often
seen combined in the full-bred horse."

Sir Archy beat all the best horses of his day in this

---

[1] His dam was the imported mare Castianira by Rockingham.
Rockingham was the best son of Highflyer, who in turn was the
best son of King Herod, one of the horses to whom all the fastest
thoroughbreds are said to trace.  The dam of Rockingham was
Purity, by Matchem, another member of the great trio just indicated, out of the famous mare known as Squirt.

country, and his owner challenged the world at four-mile heats. Boston, a grandson of Sir Archy, started in forty-five races and won forty, of which thirty were races of four-mile heats. Lexington, son of Boston, was also a noted long-distance runner. Both Boston and Lexington were inbred to Diomed.

When we turn to the very fastest trotters and pacers, we find, as I have stated, that the blood of Diomed, chiefly through his son Sir Archy, figures not very remotely in their pedigrees. Thus, Miss Russell, dam of Maud S. and of Nutwood,[1] was out of Sally Russell, a daughter of Boston, and the dam of Miss Russell's sire, Pilot Jr., was by Havoc, by Sir Charles, a grandson of Diomed. The grandam of Jay-Eye-See was by Lexington.

The dam of the wonderful Arion, whose two-year-old record is 2.10¾, was by Nutwood, just mentioned. In the pedigree of Direct, the pacer who holds the fastest record, of Allerton, of Nancy Hanks, and of others scarcely inferior, will be found a double, and sometimes a triple and quadruple cross of Diomed blood. If it be asked what essential quality these horses may be supposed to derive from Diomed, the answer would be that it is gameness, endurance, or "nerve force." Speaking generally, Messenger contributed the action, and Diomed contributed the inward spirit, both of which are necessary to bring a trotter to the wire in superlatively fast time.

Other thoroughbreds that figure largely in trotting pedigrees are Trustee, Glencoe, and Margrave; and it is a notable fact that all these names, as well as the

---

[1] His record is 2.18¼, and no less than seventy-five of his sons and daughters, including pacers, are in the 2.30 list.

name of Diomed, appear in the pedigree of Dame Winnie,[1] the thoroughbred dam of Palo Alto, the fastest trotting stallion yet produced.

A controversy has raged bitterly among fanciers of the trotting horse, and still rages, as to the amount of thoroughbred blood that is desirable in a trotter. The anti-thoroughbred party declare that "trotting instinct" is what makes a trotter trot, and that every thoroughbred cross tends to weaken this "trotting instinct." The other party maintain that superlative speed for a mile or more, at any gait, be it run, trot, or pace, can be obtained only through the courage, through the bone and sinew, of the thoroughbred. In their view, the ideal pedigree for a trotting horse is one which contains only just enough cold blood to furnish the requisite action, — that bending of the knee and long stroke of the hind leg which are not natural to the thoroughbred. Electioneer, for example, had excellent trotting action, and transmitted it to his colts from thoroughbred or half-bred mares.

This is not the place to engage in the controversy, but I cannot resist making two remarks that bear upon it. First, then, beauty, style, a high spirit, intelligence, and courage; these surely are desirable qualities in a trotter, — the last named is an indispensable quality, — and their only source is thoroughbred or Arab blood. But secondly, in a degree, there is

[1] Dame Winnie, a chestnut, is by Planet, by Revenue, by Trustee. Planet's dam was Nina by Boston. The dam of Dame Winnie was Liz Mardis by Glencoe. The second dam of Dame Winnie was Fanny G. by Margrave. Her third dam was Lancess by Lance, by American Eclipse. The fourth dam of Dame Winnie was by Aratus, son of Director by Sir Archy.

such a thing as a trotting thoroughbred. That is, when a family of trotters has been subjected for a considerable period to race-horse usage, it tends to acquire race-horse or thoroughbred traits. Courage, a fine nervous organization, muscle, and lung power are developed by the severe contests, the high feeding, the careful training, which fall to the lot of a trotter, and when this process has been continued for some generations its effects are marked.

The breeding of trotters is only beginning to be a science. In the early days, pedigrees were very slightly considered, and the transmission of qualities was not appreciated or understood. Then came a period when the value of pedigree was over-estimated; or, more correctly, when the value of such trotting pedigrees as we had was over-estimated. It must be remembered that the trotter is not a fixed type; he is commonly of mixed descent, and therefore members of the same family, own orothers and sisters, for example, may differ widely in capacity. This is true of course, in some degree, of thoroughbreds, but it is far less true of them than it is of trotters. Almost any thoroughbred in training can run a mile in 1.42 or 1.43, and as the fastest will run it in 1.35½ or thereabout, the difference between them is not very great. But the fastest time for a mile at the trotting gait is 2.08¾, and there are many very well-bred trotters who cannot trot a mile faster than three or even four minutes. This wide difference is accounted for by the fact that the trotter has scarcely emerged from the mongrel state, and consequently the own brother of a very superior animal may " throw back," either in himself or in his descendants, to some an-

cestor of inferior quality. There is an example of
this in the family of Maud S. Harold, her sire, is
also the sire of thirty other trotters, whose record is
2.30 or better. Harold has a brother called Lakeland
Abdallah, far superior to himself in size, in beauty,
and in apparent power, and yet as a sire of trotters
Lakeland Abdallah has been an utter failure. He
has but a single representative in the 2.30 list. Of
course his opportunities have been less than those of
Harold, but still they have been considerable.

However, by a process of selection, these discrepan-
cies are diminishing. One by one, those branches of
a trotting family in which speed has not been shown
are dropped; only successful sons of successful sires
and grandsires are looked to for the transmission
of speed. The lines are drawn in, comparatively
few strains are cultivated, and thus a thoroughbred
trotter tends to be evolved. It is probable that in
the near future the breeder will be able to predict
of a given animal, This horse will trot in 2.20; and
doubtless fifty or one hundred years hence a much
higher rate of speed will be insured by certain lines
of breeding.

It is commonly believed that horses, as a rule, take
their form and gait from their sire, and their disposition and nervous system from the dam; and there
are many facts which appear to support this theory.
Certain horses, conspicuous among whom is Mambrino Patchen, have had their reputation made chiefly
by their daughters, and for this reason they are called
"Great Brood Mare sires." Pilot Jr. is another
noted member of this class. On the other hand,
Rysdyck's Hambletonian, and many other famous

horses, are distinguished more through their sons than
through their daughters. Now Mambrino Patchen
and Pilot Jr. excelled in nervous energy which they
derived from the thoroughbreds in their ancestry;
whereas Hambletonian excelled in gait and structure,
and was deficient in nervous energy. Hence it would
seem to be true that the outward form is derived
chiefly from the sire, and the inward energy from the
dam, inasmuch as Hambletonian's sons, inheriting
his superior structure and gait, surpass his daughters;
and Mambrino Patchen's daughters, inheriting his
superior nervous system, surpass his sons. However,
these general rules are subject to many exceptions.

But there is one principle in relation to trotting
horses which is, I think, admitted on all sides. The
single quality that the "record breakers" have in
common is nervous energy, — that mental or physical
trait, or that relation between the mind and the body,
which enables or compels the muscular system to
accomplish the utmost of which it is capable. A
good shape, good lung power, good action, — these of
course are indispensable, and they are found in many
a trotting-bred horse; but the motive power which
lies back of the mechanism ultimately determines
the animal's speed for a mile, if not for a quarter;
and it is chiefly in this power that the record-breakers
excel their contemporaries.

Now, if, as we may safely assume, it is nervous
energy and courage that make a horse trot superlatively fast, and if, as may reasonably be conjectured,
these qualities are derived chiefly from the maternal
side, then we shall believe that the dam and grandam
in a pedigree are of more consequence than the sire

and grandsire.[1]  And the facts seem to bear out this
conclusion.   It is extraordinary how many short
trotting pedigrees end with "a mare of unknown
breeding, but a great roadster." Such, for example,
was the dam of Mambrino Chief. Sometimes, indeed, the maternal ancestor has possessed too much
energy even for roadster purposes.  Green Mountain
Maid, the dam of Electioneer, was so high-strung that
her owner abandoned the attempt to break her to
harness.   It is said of Lady Duval, a Glencoe mare.
and the mother of two or three trotters, that "so
extreme was her nervous ambition, unless she was
permitted to rush ahead as soon as she reached the
level stretches of the roadway, she would gallop
sometimes for ten miles without cessation, and
then, when she finally concluded to behave herself,
she would settle down into a long, low, level stride
that reminded one of the daisy-cutting movement of
Lady Thorne." Many other similar examples might
be cited.

"Notice in a field of brood mares." remarks a keen
observer,[2] "the one that herds, drives, and dominates
all the others, and (if the remaining qualities of action, blood, and soundness are equal) you can always
select her ladyship as the most successful brood mare
in the paddock."

The truth seems to be that great trotters, like great
men, inherit from their mothers what has aptly been
termed the subtle ambition to succeed.

[1] Such is the opinion of the oldest horse breeders in the world, —
the Arabs.   With them a horse is always considered as belonging
to the family of his dam. not to that of his sire.

[2] Mr. S. T. Harris.

## III.

### TROTTING HORSES.

THE trotting horse plays an important part in the daily life of the whole community, being concerned, as Dr. Holmes has pointed out, even in the early conveyance of milk-cans and in the prompt delivery of fresh rolls. These humble offices have actually been performed by horses who afterward acquired fame upon the track. Several years ago an old Dutchman, living in Western New York and engaged in the milk business, was astonished and not a little frightened by the pace which his beast set up one frosty morning. The cart was bounced over the pavements of the city where his route lay, the cans hopped and rattled in their seats, and the driver lost his breath. But he had no sooner recovered it than

he began to boast of the wonderful speed at which
the horse had carried him, and thereafter the animal
was taken out, harnessed to a buggy, on Saturday
afternoons and like occasions, for a brush on the
road with the fast trotters of the neighborhood, all
of whom he outstripped. Within a few weeks the
Dutchman's son, who had been brought up in this
country, procured an old sulky, and put the milk-
wagon steed in some sort of training. In two
months' time they appeared at a track, engaged in a
race with veteran drivers and horses of established
reputation, and beat them all in three straight heats,
— a wonderful achievement for a green trotter and
jockey, and an immense surprise to the professional
persons who had jeered at the uncouth appearance
of the newcomers.

This case bears out Dr. Holmes's illustration of
the milk-cart; nor is the other example that he suggests without foundation in fact. Some years ago, a
baker's mare in Boston, after delivering her rolls and
brown bread in the city one day as usual, was driven
to Saugus, a distance of about eight miles, and started
in a match race at the track there. In the exuberance of her spirits she ran away in the first heat,
and went around the course once or twice before she
could be stopped. But being allowed to start again,
notwithstanding this irregularity, she won the race,
and finished her day's work by bringing the baker
back to Boston, and beating all the horses that engaged with her on the road home.

It must not be supposed, however, that these animals were entirely of plebeian origin. The milkman's horse had a dash of thoroughbred in his

composition, and the baker's mare belonged to the
incomparable Morgan strain. Indeed, it never happens that a horse who is not connected more or less
closely with the equine aristocracy becomes distinguished as a trotter. There is a popular superstition
that Flora Temple, Dexter, and other celebrated
animals, were of obscure birth, and began life in
humble situations; but this, as I shall presently
show, is not the case. Dutchman,[1] to be sure, an
old-time trotter of great courage and bottom, was
first used in a string team at Philadelphia to haul
brick; but he was a horse of good breeding. He
was a bay gelding, fifteen hands three inches high,
very powerfully made, bony and strong, with a plain
but resolute face, and a fine neck and head. Dutchman's time for three miles, namely, 7.41, remained
the best on record from the year when it was made,
1839, till 1872, when Huntress,[2] a beautiful bay mare,
reduced it to 7.21¼.

There is another reason why every American ought
to take an interest in the trotter. Trotting, like
base-ball, is, as its votaries often remark, a national
sport, — national in the sense not only that it is
popular among us, but that it was created by us; and
consequently anybody in the United States who fails
to take an interest in it is so far forth out of touch
with his countrymen. There is something lacking in
him, — some obscure though doubtless valuable trait,
which, if he possessed it, would certainly make him
interesting in other directions, but which is most
conspicuously revealed in a fondness for the track.

[1] Dutchman was by a grandson of Messenger; and his dam is
said to have been by a son of Messenger.

[2] By Volunteer. Her dam was a Star mare. See page 69.

Running horses furnish a spirited and beautiful sport, but the runner can never be domesticated; whereas any man who owns a single horse may find himself in the possession of a trotter, or at least of an animal which he considers to be such, — and this comes to nearly the same thing. The very beast who drags a family carryall may, like the milkman's or the baker's nag, prove worthy of a better fate. It must be remembered that few horses trot fast naturally. They require skilful driving and training; often, also, the judicious application of weights, boots, rollers, and the like, in order to lengthen their stride or to correct other imperfections in their gait. It is possible, therefore, for a horse to have "the making of a trotter in him" during an indefinite period; and so long as the owner refrains from putting his inchoate racer to the test, his opportunity for boasting about the animal's latent speed is almost unlimited. Scoffers may throw cold water upon his pretensions, but no man can assert absolutely that he is wrong.

What, then, does a trotter look like? That is a question very hard to answer. Trotting horses range in size and shape from Great Eastern, — a big, long-legged horse, standing seventeen hands, who holds the best saddle record, namely, 2.15¾, — to Little Dot, a pony of Morgan extraction, weighing six hundred and seventy-five pounds, who was raised in New Brunswick about twenty-five years ago, grew up with a flock of sheep, was knocked about by a drunken sailor, and finally, coming into the hands of a horseman, made a record of 2.26¼. Nevertheless, there are two or three trotting types. Frank Forester remarked that American trotting horses reminded him

strongly of Irish hunters; and this is not strange,
for, as a rule, the best American trotters, like
Irish hunters, are partly thoroughbred. The Duke
of Marlborough has made recently a similar statement. "The type," he says, "is something of the
class of the English hunter with a shorter head, and
not quite such good shoulders." Palo Alto, Stamboul,
and Nelson [1] are examples of this type, except that
their heads are not short. Allerton and Axtell are
more stockily built, and show less quality; Arion,
again, is much smaller and somewhat finer than
they. These are the fastest six stallions now on
the track. They all, with the exception of Arion,
stand higher at the withers than at the rump.

A more common type, perhaps, is that exemplified
in the three mares holding the fastest records, namely,
Sunol, Maud S., and Nancy Hanks.[2] These are on
the racing machine order; they are somewhat narrow-
chested; their necks are straight; they stand higher
at the rump than at the withers. Sunol is a large
mare, sixteen hands high. Maud S. and Nancy Hanks
are smaller. The trotter of the present day is represented best perhaps by these last two mares; but it
is probable that the trotter of the future will more
nearly resemble Palo Alto and Stamboul.

When it comes to details of form, the difficulty
of fixing general rules is even greater. If there be
one invariable feature in a trotting horse it is probably this: great length from hip to hock. Such was
Messenger's conformation, derived, it is said, from

---

[1] Nelson is a beautiful horse, of Hambletonian, Morgan, and
thoroughbred descent.

[2] Nancy Hanks, it may be mentioned, was the maiden name of
Abraham Lincoln's mother, near whose birthplace the mare was
raised.

Sampson. Great length from hip to hock implies a
short cannon bone in the hind leg, and a short cannon
bone in front is also the badge of a trotter. Smuggler and Stamboul are the only notable exceptions
to this rule that I recall. Wide hips are apt to be
found in a trotting horse : this is especially true of
the Clay family. Rysdyck's Hambletonian had a
round rump, but a sloping rump is more common in
the trotter ; an excessively sloping rump, however, is
the peculiar mark of a pacer. Very oblique shoulders,
running far back, such as belong to the saddle horse
and hunter, seldom occur in a fast trotter ; and I believe that this remark would be almost equally true
of running horses. Many trotters, as we have seen,
are disfigured by tails set on low ; and this again
is a common feature in running horses. In fact,
shoulders inclined to be straight, and drooping tails,
are thought by some writers to have a close connection with excessive speed at any gait. A long body
combined with a rather short back furnishes another
indication of trotting capacity ; and this was the
shape of Flora Temple, the first horse to attain
national reputation as a trotter.

Flora Temple reduced the record for a mile from
2.25½ to 2.19¾. She was well born, her sire being
Kentucky Hunter, but in her early youth she was
considered almost worthless on account of her wild,
and, as everybody supposed, ungovernable temper.
Flora, as they called her at first, was a rough-coated
little bay mare, not over fourteen hands two inches
high, but possessed of a blood-like head, shapely neck,
straight back, and fine legs with powerful muscles.
Her birthplace was in the neighborhood of Utica,

New York, where she was sold at the age of four
years for the small sum of $13. A few months later,
for $80, she passed into the hands of a drover, who
took her with him on his way to the city of New
York. One bright morning in June, 1850, this drover
was passing through the beautiful village of Washington Hollow. He was mounted on a fine gray stallion, and kept his cattle in line, while the small bay
horse was tied to the tail-board of an open wagon
drawn by two stout mules and driven by a sleepy
negro. This interesting procession attracted the notice of one Mr. Jonathan A. Vielee, a shrewd horseman, who happened to be basking in the sun at his
stable door on the morning in question, and who, re-
marking the strong and gamy appearance of the
future Queen of the Turf, hailed the drover, and
presently "had the little mare by the nose, and was
studying every mark upon her teeth. He then "—
I quote from Mr. George Wilkes's history of Flora
Temple — " took hold of her feet : and the little mare
lifted them successively in his hand, with a quiet,
downward glance that seemed to say. 'You'll find
everything right there, Mr. Vielee, and as fair and
as firm as if you wished me to trot for a man's life!'
And so Mr. Vielee did ; and as he dropped the last
foot, he liked the promise of the little mare amaz
ingly, and it struck him that if he could get her for
any sum short of $250 she would be a mighty good
bargain.

"'She is about five years old?' said Mr. Vielee,
inquiringly.

"'You have seen for yourself,' replied the drover.

"'I should judge she was all right?' again sug-

5

gested Mr. Vielee, partly walking round the mare,
and again looking at her up and down.

" 'Sound as a dollar, and kind as a kitten,' responded the drover, as firmly as if prepared to give
a written guaranty.

" 'Not always so *kind*, neither,' said Mr. Vielee,
looking again steadily at the mare's face, ' or I don't
understand that deviltry in her eye. But that's neither here nor there. You say the mare is for sale.
Now let's know what you will take for her.' The
result was that Mr. Vielee bought her for $175.

" 'And a pretty good price at that,' said the drover
to himself on pocketing the cash, ' for an animal that
only cost me eighty, and who is so foolish and flighty
that she will never be able to make a square trot in
her life.' "

A few weeks later Mr. Vielee took his new purchase to New York, and sold her to Mr. G. E. Perrin
for $350. "In the hands of Mr. Perrin," relates the
graphic writer from whom I have quoted already,
"the little bay mare, who had proved so intractable,
so flighty, so harum-scarum, and, to come down to the
true term, so *worthless* to her original owners, was
favored with more advantages than ever she had enjoyed before. She was not only introduced to the
very best society of fast-goers on the Bloomingdale
and Long Island roads, but she was taught, when
'flinging herself out' with exuberant and superabun-
dant spirit all over the road, as it were, to play her
limbs in a true line, and give her extraordinary qualities a chance to show their actual worth. If ever she
made a skip, a quick admonition and a steady check
brought her to her senses; and when in her frenzy

of excitement at being challenged by some tip-top
goer, she would, to use a sportman's phrase, 'travel
over herself' and go 'up' into the air, she was steadied and settled down by a firm rein into solid trotting
and good behavior in an instant. The crazy, flighty,
half-racking, and half-trotting little bay mare became
a true stepper, and very luckily passed out of her
confused 'rip-i-ty clip-i-ty' sort of going into a clean,
even, long, low, locomotive-trotting stroke. Many a
man who came up to a road tavern, after having been
unexpectedly beaten by her, would say to her owner,
as they took a drink at the bar, 'That's a mighty
nice little mare of yours, and if she was only big
enough to stand hard work, you might expect a good
deal from her.'"

But Flora Temple was big enough, as her subsequent career proved. Little horses, in fact, usually
make the best weight-pullers and stand the most
work. Hopeful, whose time to a skeleton wagon for
a mile, 2.16¼, made in 1878, remained the best on
record till 1891,[1] was a small gray horse, and, like
almost all weight-pullers, a very short and quick
stepper. "If little horses of this sort be particularly examined," says a high authority, "it will commonly be found that, though they are low, they are
long in all the moving parts; and their quarters are
generally as big and sometimes a deal bigger than
those of many much larger horses." This remark
would apply to Arab coursers, who, although their
muscles are great, rarely stand above 14¾ hands; and

---

[1] In the autumn of 1891, Allerton (a grandson of George Wilkes
and of Mambrino Patchen) trotted a mile to wagon on a kite-
shaped track in 2.15.

many thoroughbreds, conspicuous for their staying powers, have had the same general conformation.

Flora Temple soon came into the hands of Hiram Woodruff, and under his tuition she became a famous race horse. She reduced the mile record, as we have seen. from 2.25½ to 2.19¾, being equally good at two and three mile heats. There were several contemporary trotters. between whom and Flora Temple very little difference in speed existed when they first encountered her; but she outlasted the others. Some of these horses actually beat her once or twice; but the longer they kept at it, the wider became the distance between them and the little bay mare, of whom it had been said that she might prove valuable if she were only big enough to stand hard work. Highland Maid, a well-bred, long-stepping bay mare; Tacony, the first horse to make a record of 2.25½; Lancet; Ethan Allen; Rose of Washington; Princess, a very handsome, high-bred mare, who came on from California expressly to beat Flora Temple; John Morgan, a big, fine-looking golden-chestnut horse of good breeding, brought from the West for the same purpose; George M. Patchen, a famous brown stallion of Morgan and Clay blood. — all these horses and many others engaged with Flora Temple, sometimes "turn and turn about," but all were badly beaten in the end. "Flora Temple," said Hiram Woodruff, "would train on and get better, when thoroughly hardened, towards the middle and close of the season. This is one of the most valuable qualities that a trotting horse can have. The greatest excellence in trotting is only to be reached through much labor and cultivation. Now, if strong work at a few sharp races overdoes a horse and knocks him off, it is a great, almost an insurmountable obstacle to his attaining the greatest excellence, even in speed for a mile."

After Flora Temple came Dexter, a brown horse with a white face and four white feet, by Rysdyck's Hambletonian. He also had remarkable courage and endurance, his dam being of the American Star family.

" Some of the Stars," Hiram Woodruff said, " have given out in the legs; but their pluck is so good that they stand up to the last, when little better than mere cripples. It is no wonder that they have great game and courage; for Star's grandsire was the thoroughbred four-miler Henry, who ran for the South on the Island here against the Northern horse Eclipse, in 1823. I went to see the race, being then six years old, and got a licking for it when I came home." The Stars were descended from Diomed.

Dexter was first sold at the age of four, bringing four hundred dollars. He lowered the record to 2.17$\frac{1}{4}$, and doubtless would have reduced it still further had he not become the property of Mr. Robert Bonner, who withdrew him from the turf. The excellence of this horse probably gave the finishing blow to an old superstition which is embodied in the following stanza : —

> "One white foot, inspect him,
> Two white feet, reject him;
> Three white feet, sell him to your foes;
> Four white feet, feed him to the crows."

The first great performance of Dexter was made in October, 1865, when he trotted under saddle against

time, being matched to beat 2.19. He was trained by
Woodruff, but ridden in the race by John Murphy, a
very skilful horseman, and one of the few jockeys
whose reputation for honesty was always absolutely
unblemished. In this match, Dexter trotted the first
half-mile in 1.06½; but after passing that point he
broke. " When he broke," Hiram Woodruff relates,
" the people cried, ' He can't do it this time!' But he
settled well, and when he came on to the home stretch
he had a fine burst in. I was up towards there, and
sung out to Johnny, as he came by me, ' Cut him
loose; you 'll do it yet!' Then Johnny clucked to
him, and he went away like an arrow from the bow.
true and straight, and with immense resolution and
power of stroke. I knew he must do it if he did not
break before he got to the score, and up I tossed my
hat into the air. I never felt happier in all my life.
The time given by the judges was 2 m. 18½ s.; the
outsiders made it somewhat less."

Of the great trotters, Dexter seems to have been
the best "all-round " horse, for none of his contemporaries was able to beat him either in one, two, or three
mile heats; and he showed his superiority to a wagon
or under saddle as well as in harness. Hiram Woodruff anticipated. but did not live to see his greatest
triumphs. " It is a long time now," he wrote shortly
before his own death, "since I took Mr. Foster to his
box, and, pointing out his very remarkable shape, —
the wicked head. the game-cock throttle, the immense
depth over the heart, the flat, oblique shoulder. laid
back clean under the saddle, the strong back. the
mighty haunches, square and as big as those of a
cart-horse. and the good. wiry legs, — predicted to

him that here stood the future Lord of the Trotting World."

Goldsmith Maid, who reduced the mark from 2.17¼ to 2.14, had almost the appearance of a thoroughbred. She was small, being 15¼ hands high; her legs were lean, flat, and wiry; her head and neck were finely cut, and indicative of good breeding; she was deep through the lungs, but so slight in the waist as to suggest a lack of constitution, although she was in reality extremely tough and lasting; her feet were small and good. It was said of this famous mare that "in her highest trotting form, drawn to an edge, she is almost deer-like in appearance; and when scoring for a start, and alive to the emergencies of the race, with her great flashing eye and dilated nostrils, she is a perfect picture of animation and living beauty. Her gait is long, bold, and sweeping, and she is, in the hands of a driver acquainted with her peculiarities, a perfect piece of machinery."

Not a few horses like Goldsmith Maid have had this peculiar thin-waisted appearance, and yet were possessed of much nervous strength and of great courage. A noted trotter described by Hiram Woodruff was of this character. "Rattler," he says, "was a bay gelding, fifteen hands high, a fast and stout horse, though light-waisted and delicate in appetite and constitution. He was a very long strider, and when going his best it sometimes seemed as though he would part in the middle." He was afterward taken to England, where the climate suited him so well that he gained in appetite, and consequently in health and strength.

Goldsmith Maid, when six years of age, was sold by her breeder for $260, having never been put to work on account of her nervous disposition. She had, however, taken a very creditable part in certain amateur running races, which were held in a grassy lane about one quarter of a mile long. These dashes always took place by moonlight, being unauthorized by the elders of the family, but secretly enjoyed by the boys on the farm. Soon after she left her birthplace the Maid was sold again for $600 to Mr. Alden Goldsmith, a famous horseman, by whom she was named. He kept her for five years, and sold her for $20,000. Her dam was a well-bred animal, probably a daughter of Abdallah, who sired Rysdyck's Hambletonian. Goldsmith Maid's sire was Alexander's Abdallah, whose origin and fate are described in the preceding chapter.

All the great trotters have had grooms, or "rubbers," as they are technically called, between whom and the horses a strong affection existed. The name of Peter Conover is linked in this way with that of Dexter. Conover not only "rubbed" Dexter, but made most of his "boots." and gave him his exercise. Dexter was an intelligent horse, and whenever Budd Doble, who drove him in his races. mounted the sulky, he would become excited and pull, thinking that a contest impended; but with his groom holding the reins he would go along quietly enough. The same thing is true of Nancy Hanks. Rarus had his "Dave" and "Barney." A colored man named Grant was transferred to Mr. Bonner with Maud S., as being necessarily appurtenant to her. "Lucy Jimmy" was, as his name denotes. the attendant of Lucy, a celebrated mare contemporary with Goldsmith Maid, and very little inferior to her in speed. "Old Charlie" faith-

fully served the Maid herself for many years, during
five of which he was never absent from her stall except for two nights. Goldsmith Maid, like Rarus and
like Johnston. the wonderful pacer, had a little dog as
a companion. "They were a great family," says Mr.
Doble, "that old mare, Old Charlie, and the dog, —
apparently interested in nothing else in the world but
themselves, and getting along together as well as you
could wish. When it was bed-time Charlie would lie
down on his cot in one corner of the stall, his pillow
being a bag containing the mare's morning feed of
oats; the Maid would ensconce herself in another
corner; and somewhere else in the stall the dog would
stretch himself out. About five o'clock in the morning the Maid would get a little restless and hungry.
She knew well enough where the oats were, and would
come over to where Charlie lay sleeping and stick her
nose under his head, and in this manner wake him,
and give notice that she wanted to be fed."

Goldsmith Maid, after her retirement from the
track, exhibited a very bad temper, and became notorious for kicking and biting. She was kept at a stock
farm in Trenton, New Jersey, and one day, after an
absence of some years. "Old Charlie" came to see her.
He was warned not to go near the mare, but nevertheless he entered her paddock. The Maid recognized
him immediately. neighed with pleasure, and, coming
up, rubbed her nose against him with every mark of
affection. At this farm, Goldsmith Maid met her old
rival. Lucy. and the two venerable mares struck up a
great intimacy; they became constant companions,
and repelled with teeth and heels all other equine
society.

I shall speak hereafter of Goldsmith Maid's remarkable intelligence in "scoring." But perhaps the most interesting fact in her career is that she made her fastest time, 2.14, at the age of nineteen; and on her twenty-first birthday Budd Doble drove her a mile in 2.16. Goldsmith Maid continued on the track for nearly fifteen years, conquered all the fastest horses of her time, and trotted in all 332 heats under 2.30. She lasted so long partly because of her good breeding, and partly, it may be, because she was never trained or worked until she had become a mature horse. The fashion now is to make the trotter's career begin while he is a colt, but although the practice has not been tested thoroughly, it must be fraught with danger. If it ever should become general, it is certain that many young horses would be overworked and ruined every year, comparatively few drivers having the discretion and patience that are required for the safe "preparation" of a colt. There have been other horses who, like Goldsmith Maid, being well bred and beginning at a mature age, lasted a long time on the track. Dutchman, who trotted his first race at six years of age, was a sound and fast horse at eighteen. Topgallant. a grandson of the thoroughbred imported horse Messenger, and the first to make a record of 2.40, is a still more extraordinary example. When twenty-four years old he trotted a very hard race of four three-mile heats against all the best horses of his day. winning one heat; and the week after he engaged in another race of three-mile heats, which he won. Old Topgallant was a great favorite of Hiram Woodruff. who as a boy took care of him. and as a young man trained, rode, and drove him. Woodruff describes Topgallant as "a dark bay horse, 15 hands 3 inches high, plain and rawboned, but with rather a fine head and neck, and an eye expressive of much courage. He was spavined in both hind legs, and his tail was slim at the root. His spirit was very high, and yet he was so reliable that he would hardly ever break, and his bottom was of the finest and toughest quality. He was more than fourteen years of age before he was known at all as a trotter, except that he could go a distance, the whole length of the New York Road, as well as any horse that had ever been extended on it."

At the close of the Civil War there was living on a small farm at Greenport, Long Island, one Mr. R. B. Conklin, a retired stage carpenter, who by industry and thrift had saved a little money. Mr. Conklin had a passion for horses, especially for trotters, and he conceived the idea that a certain colt born on his farm, and the only one that he ever raised, was destined to become the champion trotter of the world. The colt's sire was Conklin's Abdallah, whose breeding is unknown. Its mother was a gray nag called Nancy Awful, half-thoroughbred, and very high-spirited. She also belonged to Mr. Conklin, and his belief in her and in her colt became a sort of religion. Many men, no doubt, under similar circumstances, have been equally enthusiastic, but the peculiarity in this case was that Mr. Conklin had always enjoyed the reputation of being "hard-headed." His neighbors therefore came to the charitable conclusion that on this particular subject the old carpenter had gone mad. The foal was certainly very promising, long, muscular, and full of life and spirit. "From the day of its

birth," says the historian, "it was treated differently
from any other animal on the place.  As soon as it
had been weaned, a suitable stall was built in a big
barn for its accommodation, and from that day forth
nothing was left undone to secure its comfort; and
it was not long before Conklin and his colt were the
talk of that end of Long Island.  When the colt was
three years old it was broken to harness, and during
the following summer took part in a little race on
the Island, winning the contest in about three minutes.  Then the old man was more certain than ever
that he had the wonder of the world, and redoubled
his efforts in the way of care, etc., had a special stable built for the colt, with an office adjoining, where
in winter, all seated around a big fire, he would
entertain his neighbors, telling them what a great
horse that colt was going to be. . . . For the next
two years Mr. Conklin gave almost his entire time
to the care and education of this colt.  He bought
himself a light wagon, got a set of double harness,
secured an old runner. and as he was a very heavy
man, and did not want to compel the colt to draw his
weight, he hooked him by the side of the runner,
and in this manner he received his first lessons in
trotting." [1]         •

The extraordinary part of this story is that the colt,
who was called Rarus. perfectly fulfilled the extravagant expectations of his breeder and owner, becoming
the champion trotter of the world. and reducing the
record in 1878 to 2.13¼.  Mr. Conklin brought him
up well. for Splan, in whose hands Rarus passed the

<hr />

[1] This quotation is from John Splan's " Life with the Trotters,"
a very entertaining work.

famous part of his career, declared that he never drove a better broken horse.

Rarus was a rangy bay, of high courage, with a plain though blood-like and intelligent head, a good neck, but rather poor feet. Excepting the tendency to inflammation in his feet, he was a remarkably healthy horse, never losing his appetite despite the long journeys that he made and the hard races that he trotted. At one time Rarus served as a foil for Goldsmith Maid, just as in earlier days George M. Patchen, John Morgan, and other horses did for Flora Temple, and as the same Patchen and Princess did later for Dexter. But in this case there was a difference. Rarus was much younger than Goldsmith Maid, and he was controlled by a driver who had no notion of using him up in hopeless contests.

Both horses spent the winter of 1876–77 in California, where they gave some "exhibition" races, no pools being sold, and it being understood that Rarus would not attempt to win. In the spring, a purse was offered in a "free-for-all" race, near San Francisco, and both Goldsmith Maid and Rarus were entered. The betting men in general supposed that the Maid would have an easy victory, but Rarus defeated her, Splan and his friends thus winning a great sum. This race marked the end of Goldsmith Maid's public career. Rarus took her place as a "star" performer, and two years later he was sold to Mr. Robert Bonner for $36,000.

No sketch of Rarus would be complete without some mention of his remarkable friendship for a dog. When the horse was in California, a fireman gave to Splan a wiry-haired Scotch terrier pup, who was then

two months old, and weighed when full grown only
fifteen pounds. Splan in turn gave the pup to Dave,
the groom of Rarus, with a caution not to let the horse
hurt him, for on several occasions Rarus had bitten
dogs that ventured into his stall. But to this terrier,
who is described as possessing "almost human intelligence," the trotter took a great fancy, which the dog
fully returned. They became fast and inseparable
friends. "Not only," says Mr. Splan, "were they extremely fond of each other, but they showed their
affection plainly as did ever a man for a woman. We
never took any pains to teach the dog anything about
the horse. Everything he knew came to him by his
own patience. From the time I took him to the stable, a pup, until I sold Rarus, they were never separated an hour. We once left the dog in the stall while
we took the horse to the blacksmith shop, and when
we came back we found he had made havoc with everything there was in there, trying to get out, while the
horse during the entire journey was uneasy, restless,
and in general acted as badly as the dog did. Dave
remarked that he thought that we had better keep the
horse and dog together after that. When Rarus went
to the track for exercise, or to trot a race, the dog
would follow Dave around and sit by the gate at his
side, watching Rarus with as much interest as Dave
did. When the horse returned to the stable after a
heat, and was unchecked, the dog would walk up and
climb up on his forward legs and kiss him, the horse
always bending his head down to receive the caress.
In the stable, after work was over, Jim and the horse
would often frolic like two boys. If the horse lay
down, Jim would climb on his back, and in that way

soon learned to ride him; and whenever I led Rarus
out to show him to the public, Jim invariably knew
what it meant, and enhanced the value of the performance by the manner in which he would get on the
horse's back. On these occasions the horse was shown
to halter, and Jimmy, who learned to distinguish such
events from those in which the sulky was used, would
follow Dave and Rarus out on the quarter stretch;
and then when the halt was made in front of the grand
stand, Dave would stoop down, and in a flash Jimmy
would jump on his back, run up his shoulder, from
there leap on the horse's back, and there he would
stand, his head high in the air and his tail out stiff
behind, barking furiously at the people. He seemed
to know that he was as much a part of the show as
the horse, and apparently took great delight in attract-
ing attention to himself."

When Rarus was sold to Mr. Bonner, Splan sent
Jimmy with the horse, rightly judging that it would
be cruel to separate them. But in Mr. Bonner's stable
there was already a bull-terrier in charge, and one day
when, for some real or fancied affront, the small dog
attacked the larger one, the latter took Jimmy by the
neck and was fast killing him; but Rarus heard his
outcries, and perceiving that his little friend was in
danger and distress, pulled back on the halter till it
broke, rushed out of his stall, and would have made
short work with the bull-terrier had he not been restrained by the grooms.

The examples which I have cited prove that horses
are far more capable of attaching themselves to other
animals, man included, than is commonly supposed;
for neither Dexter nor Goldsmith Maid nor Rarus

was particularly affectionate in disposition. There is recorded one extraordinary case of friendship between an old horse and a young one. A trotting-bred colt, called Bay, had conceived a great fondness for a gray gelding who was pastured in the same lot with him, his affection being warmly returned. When the young horse arrived at the proper age he was sent to a trainer, but in his new quarters he became unmanageable; he refused to eat, kicked and plunged in his stall, and kept the whole place in an uproar. Finally he was returned to the farm, and put back in the field with his gray friend, where he seemed perfectly contented. His owner then concluded that he would have to send the old horse also to the trainer, as a sort of companion or nurse to the young one. This he did, and thereafter the two animals were never separated. When Bay's education was so far advanced that he was thought worthy to go on the "grand circuit," the gray gelding was taken with him from city to city. In the "palace horse car" which conveyed Bay and the other costly racers, a stall was invariably reserved for his humble friend; and whenever Bay engaged in a race the old horse accompanied the "rubbers" to the track, being always stationed in some place where the young trotter could conveniently see and speak to him between the heats. In another case, a great affection sprang up between a trotter and a goat; and certain friendships between horses and other animals have become historical. Thus the Godolphin Arabian had his cat, Eclipse his sheep, and Chillaby or the "Mad Arabian" was excessively fond of a lamb that kept the flies from him.

The 2.13¼ of Rarus was reduced the very next year

by St. Julien to 2.11¼. This is a big, slashing bay
horse, with a large but good head, wide hips, and powerful hind legs. His sire was Volunteer, who was by
the famous Rysdyck's Hambletonian, Volunteer's dam
being a well-bred mare, from whom he derived a handsome head and neck and a high spirit, these being
characteristics seldom found in the Hambletonian
strain. The dam of St. Julien was of the Clay family, which he closely resembled. St. Julien, like many
other trotters, was not educated to the turf without
the expenditure of exceeding pains on the part of his
trainer and driver, Mr. Orrin Hickock. He is a very
nervous horse, and it required months of practice before he became accustomed to "scoring," so that he
was fit to start in a race.

A year later, Maud S. reduced the record to 2.10¾,
and again in 1885, to 2.08¾, which is still the best
time for a regulation or oval-shaped track, though
on the kite-shaped track Palo Alto equalled it, and
Sunol surpassed it by half a second in the autumn of
1891. Jay-Eye-See, with his record of 2.10, held the
supremacy for a single day in 1884. He is an honest
but ugly little black horse, having hind legs of tremendous power, which propel him with the accuracy
and force of locomotive driving-wheels. Jay-Eye-See
was by Dictator, a son of Rysdyck's Hambletonian,
and brother to Dexter. Jay-Eye-See's dam was a
daughter of Pilot Jr., and his grandam was by Lexington, a famous race horse inbred to Diomed. Maud
S., as we have seen, was bred in much the same way.
Her sire was Harold, by Rysdyck's Hambletonian ;
her dam was Miss Russell, by Pilot Jr., and her
grandam was by Boston, the four-mile racer, and sire

of Lexington. Maud S. shows her thoroughbred
quality in every line. She is a medium-sized golden
chestnut, with a good neck, a large, but bony, clean-
cut, and noble head, ears that are well shaped, though
a little too big, and a large eye, full of intelligence
and courage. She has a straight back and strong
quarters. Her present owner, Mr. Robert Bonner,
says of her: "Maud S. is the most intelligent and
the most affectionate animal that I have ever owned.
She has, however, 'a will of her own,' and would re-
sent harsh treatment of any kind; but if you use
her gently and kindly you can do anything with her.
Soloman's dictum concerning children would not answer in her case. If you did not 'spare the rod,' you
would be sure to 'spoil' her. I would as soon think
of striking a woman as to give Maud S. a sharp cut
with a whip." There was a time in the career of
Maud S. when she was wild, ungovernable, and, as a
racing mare, nearly if not quite worthless. But a
long course of patient training brought her back to
her original state, and she is now perhaps the best
driving horse as well as the fastest trotter in the
world.

I have mentioned the California horses Palo Alto
and Sunol. The former, whose breeding has already
been stated, is a noble animal, of immense courage, of
bull-dog tenacity, and of sound bottom. He is a big
brown horse, with fine shoulders, a well-shaped neck,
and a handsome though not superfine head. Palo
Alto has large, intelligent eyes, widely separated,
and altogether he presents an appearance of substance, of character, and of dignity. During the
greater part of his career upon the turf he has suf-

fered from a "game" leg, and yet he has never flinched or faltered. Considering his half-thorough-bred origin, he is a little phlegmatic; it takes severe work to "warm him up," and he is apt to lose the first heat or two in a race. "Palo Alto," writes Mr. Marvin, "requires constant and vigorous driving, but there is a point beyond which it is dangerous to go." Sunol, his half-sister, has not yet been tested in a long race, but she has shown an extraordinary capacity of sustaining speed for a mile. Of all the famous trotters Sunol appears to have the least pleasant disposition; she is too intelligent to be positively vicious, but she is irritable, and perhaps a little spiteful. It is said that she has an especial dislike for her trainer and driver, Mr. Marvin, and that she shows this feeling unmistakably whenever he comes near her. Nevertheless, the two seem to understand each other perfectly. "Sunol's redeeming feature," says a California writer, "is her affection for her groom." [1]

Another half-brother of Sunol, the young Arion, [2] is commonly regarded as the greatest trotter yet produced. Arion is a small bay horse, not particularly beautiful or striking in appearance, except in one respect. His hind legs, and especially the hocks, are enormously large and muscular. To this peculiarity, no doubt, he owes his extreme speed. His disposition is superlatively good, and he is said to be full of

[1] Sunol is by Electioneer. Her dam was by General Benton. Sunol's grandam was Waxy, a thoroughbred daughter of Lexington, just mentioned.

[2] By Electioneer. His dam is Manette, by Nutwood. Arion's two-year-old record, as already stated, is 2.10¾.

life and energy. "When he went back to the stall after his wonderful mile at Stockton," relates a writer in the San Francisco Examiner, "Arion was as full of play as any frisky young thing just out of the paddock. He had just trotted a mile that would kill many great horses, but he caught hold of the groom's coat with his teeth, shook it as a terrier does a rat, and nosed around the pockets for sugar, of which he is inordinately fond. Assuring himself that the groom was out of the way, he let fly with one hind foot, and struck the wall behind him with a bang like the report of a pistol; then he looked around to see how big a hole he had made in the wood." Arion, it is said, enjoys admiration, and likes to be looked at, talked to, and photographed. "He loves everybody. There is not a streak of meanness in his composition. He would not harm a mangy dog that came into his stall to sleep." He has "large, soft eyes."

In the course of this brief survey it must have occurred to the reader that there is one respect in which all the most distinguished trotters have resembled one another, and that is in their nervous energy, their high spirit and courage. That latent flame which the Washington Hollow horseman detected in the eye of Flora Temple came out afterward in the resolute bursts of speed with which she finished her fastest miles. Dexter was represented as being "chock full of fire and deviltry," and capable of jumping like a cat. Hiram Woodruff, as we have seen, spoke of his "wicked head." Goldsmith Maid had a strong will of her own, and the excitement which she betrayed on the eve of a race showed how fine was her organization. "She would stand quietly enough," says her

driver, "while being hitched to the sulky," — although she had previously been kicking and plunging in her stall, — "but she would shake and tremble until I have heard her feet make the same noise against the hard ground that a person's teeth will when the body is suddenly chilled; that is, her feet actually chattered on the ground. The instant I would get into the sulky all this would pass away, and she would start in a walk for the track as sober as any old horse you ever saw." Rarus was so nervous that he never could have been driven with safety on the road, and his courage was of the finest temper. St. Julien was exceedingly high strung, and in hands less patient and discreet than those of his trainer might never have been subdued to the purposes of racing. Jay-Eye-See, though I know less of his personal history, is notorious for the pluck that he showed on the last quarters of his hard miles; and Maud S. is the most spirited, the most determined, and at the same time the gentlest of animals.

Sunol is described by Governor Stanford, who bred her, as "a bundle of nerves." Palo Alto[1] is a horse of immense resolution. and Arion overflows with energy. The groom who has been his constant companion night and day for the past year or more says that he never saw Arion stand quietly for a full minute. "He is never at rest, and is always at play, except when the harness goes on, and he feels Marvin's hand on the lines: then he becomes at once an old campaigner, not a frisky colt."

In all these horses we find strength of will, fineness of nerve, and a "do or die" quality that goes

[1] Palto Alto died of pneumonia after this chapter was in type.

far to redeem the trotting track from those degrading
associations with which, one must admit, it is almost
always connected.  Man may take a lesson from the
horse, as well as from the dog, in courage, in resolution, and in discipline.  It is a noble spirit that ani-
mates the exhausted trotter, who, obedient to the rein
and voice of the jockey, expends his last reserve of
force on the home stretch, and staggers under the
wire a winner by a head.

# IV.

## TROTTING RACES.

SINCE 1824, when trotting may be said to have begun as a sport. the record has been reduced from 2 minutes 40 seconds to 2 minutes 8¾ seconds.[1] Whence comes this great advance? It is due to improvements in trotting courses, in sulkies. in horseshoes, in boots and toe-weights. in harness (par-

---

[1] Since this chapter was printed, the record has been reduced by Nancy Hanks to 2.04. On this occasion, however, she drew the newly invented "bicycle" sulky with pneumatic rubber tires, the use of which is thought to make a saving of at least two seconds in a mile. Nancy Hanks is by Happy Medium, son of Rysdyck's Hambletonian : her dam was Nancy Lee, by Dictator, another son of Hambletonian and brother to Dexter. Nancy Lee's dam was by Edwin Forrest, of the half-bred Kentucky Hunter family to which Flora Temple belonged. Edwin Forrest also sired the dam of Mambrino King.

ticularly in the device of the overdraw check), in
training and driving. and finally in the speed and
endurance of the trotters themselves.   The gain in
actual speed for a short distance has been much
slighter than is commonly supposed.   So long ago as
1866. Hiram Woodruff drove Mr. Bonner's gray
mare Peerless (who was bred like Dexter, being in
part Messenger and in part Star) a quarter of a mile
at the rate of a mile in two minutes,—and this not
to a sulky, but to a skeleton wagon, a four-wheeled
vehicle, which is much heavier.   It is doubtful if
this rate of going will ever greatly be surpassed,
though it is, I think. commonly believed by horsemen that some time or other a mile will be trotted
in two minutes.   The gain will probably be not so
much in speed for a short distance as in the ability
to maintain speed for a full circuit of the track.
Even Maud S. flagged a little on the last quarter of
her fastest mile.

For the past fifty years, and especially for the
latter half of that time, much ingenuity and in-
ventive skill have been employed to afford the trotter all the mechanical assistance that is possible.
Tracks are made of an elliptical instead of a round
shape, because the two comparatively long stretches
or straight pieces thus obtained give the horse,
particularly a big-striding one, the opportunity that
he requires to get up his speed.   Courses laid out in
this way are found to be much faster than the old
tracks. which were more nearly round.   During the
past two years many tracks have been constructed
in what is called the kite shape. which resembles
a long loop, or an oval, the sides of which have

been compressed until they nearly meet. On these tracks the horses start from one end of the loop, go up one side, come back on the other, and finish at the starting point. The kite track is considered to be about two seconds faster than the ordinary or regulation track, because it consists almost entirely of two long stretches; but it is of course very unsatisfactory to the spectator, who is able to see, in any real sense, only the beginning and the finish of the race. It seems unlikely that these tracks will long be tolerated.[1]

Then, too, the footing has greatly been improved. The best tracks now have an underlayer of turf or of bog grass, which makes them springy, and the surface is soft without being deep or heavy. The sulky drawn by Dutchman, the old-time trotter, of whom I have spoken in a former chapter, weighed eighty-two pounds. Hiram Woodruff, writing in 1867, mentioned this fact, adding, "I now have two that weigh less than sixty pounds." The present weight is about forty pounds.[2] This reduction of forty pounds, or one half of the total weight. since Dutchman's day, makes a great difference in time for a mile, being probably equivalent on the average to about one and a half seconds.

[1] In Delaware, perhaps in other States also, a kite track which is down grade all the way has been constructed. This crowning absurdity was accomplished by making the return side of the loop end at a lower level than that from which the outgoing side of the loop starts.

[2] I have seen lately in a Boston warehouse a skeleton wagon that weighs but fifty pounds, and a top buggy that weighs only one hundred and twenty-eight pounds. Nancy Hanks's sulky weighs but thirty-eight pounds. Such vehicles might almost be described as works of art.

Equal mechanical skill has been exerted in another direction. Many horses cannot be driven at anything like their highest speed without danger of cutting themselves, by striking one foot or leg against another, especially when they "break"; and to protect them from injury in this manner a great variety of "boots" have been invented. Counting different sizes of these articles separately, the number of them now on sale is over two hundred. Very few trotters are able to dispense with boots entirely, and many of them could not be used as race horses at all except for these appliances. The shoeing of trotting horses, again, is an art in itself,[1] and so is the use of toe-weights, which are small pieces of brass screwed or otherwise attached to the hoofs of the fore feet. Heavy shoes and toe-weights are employed to make horses trot who otherwise would pace, to keep them level in their gait, and sometimes to cause a lengthening of their stride. The difficulty and importance of these matters may be gathered from the fact that a change of no more than two ounces in a trotter's fore shoes or toe-weights would. in many cases, make a difference of several seconds in his speed for a mile, and consequently of thousands of dollars in his value as a race horse. The necessity for toe-weights or heavy shoes lies in some defect of conformation or of gait, and when a trotter is obliged to carry a heavy load in this manner his feet and legs suffer.

---

[1] A fast horse now on the track is shod as follows: a sixteen-ounce shoe on the off fore foot, and a fourteen and a half ounce shoe on the near one; a shoe of eight ounces on the off hind foot, and one of six ounces on the near hind foot. Jack, to take another instance, wore only light tips on his fore feet when he made his record of 2.12¼.

The famous Smuggler, a noble brown stallion with a white blaze in his face, a heavy and powerful animal, was originally a pacer, and in his races he wore shoes on his fore feet weighing two pounds each; in fact, he is said to have carried at one time three pounds on each fore foot. His great strength and courage enabled him to bear this burden, but eventually it disabled him. Smuggler was once sold for $40,000, the highest price at that time ever paid in this country for a horse; and though he was capable of very high speed, he is regarded as on the whole a failure. If he made a single break in a race, he lost so much ground that he was nearly sure to be distanced. This peculiarity is explained by Mr. H. T. Helm, who says that Smuggler's stride with his fore legs is not long enough to correspond with the tremendous stroke of his hind legs, and consequently that he is apt to lose his balance. If he does so, one of two things must occur: he will either fall headlong and prostrate on the ground,—which of course does not happen,—or he will throw out both fore feet together ; in other words, gallop instead of trot. But Smuggler gallops very high in front, and therefore it is not easy for him to change quickly back again from the gallop to the trot: his speed has to be very much reduced before he can pass from one gait to the other, and in this way he loses so much ground that the other horses in the race are very likely to distance him. That a horse so severely handicapped by heavy shoes could trot such races as Smuggler did is a good illustration of equine strength and pluck.

The last factor in the development of the trotting

horse is the driver; and here we touch upon the great difference between running and trotting races. A running race may be described, with some exaggeration, as a brief but spirited flight of colts ridden by boys, whereas a trotting race is a long-drawn contest between seasoned horses and mature men, who are commonly the trainers as well as the drivers of their steeds.   Not all running horses, to be sure, are colts, nor all their riders boys, but the limit of age in the horse and of weight in the man is quickly reached.   In trotting races the jockeys are always men; the standard weight is 150 pounds, and if the driver falls below that he must carry lead enough on his sulky to make up the deficiency.   In running races, steeple-chases excepted, the weight (including that of the rider) varies, roughly speaking, from 75 to 130 pounds, and a Fred Archer who tips the scales at anything over 120 must retire to private life. Then, again, running races, nowadays at least, almost invariably consist of a single dash, whereas trotting races are in heats, the best three in five: and this affords an opportunity for stratagem and patience on the part of the driver; for courage, endurance, and even for recuperation on the part of the horse.   There is, therefore, in the trotting race, an element of subtlety which gives it a peculiar fascination.   The typical driver who has been evolved from these conditions is a spare but sinewy man, with a quiet manner and a firm mouth, — as distinctly American a person as any that can be found.   His chief qualities, so far as the horse is concerned, are sympathy and resolution.   "Confidence between the trotting horse and his driver," said the great master of the art, "is of the utmost importance: it is all in all. Some men inspire it readily, so that a horse will take hold and do all he knows the first time the man drives him. For another man the same horse will not trot a yard. The truth is that the horse is a very knowing, sagacious creature, much more so than he gets credit for. If a driver has no settled system of his own, or if he is rash or severe without cause, it is not likely that confidence will be inspired in the horse, even in a long time."

It is a fact often remarked, that some drivers succeed much better with certain equine families than with others, the reason doubtless being that they are better adapted to them in disposition. A trainer, for example, who did very well with a well known high-spirited and wilful breed failed conspicuously with another strain, of a milder and more gentle nature.

There are, indeed, some boisterous drivers, but they are not the most successful; in fact, the quality of a horseman can almost be discovered by observing the manner in which he goes up to the animal's head or enters his stall. The loud, rough fellow may be a judge of soundness, and fairly well qualified for the box seat of a hack; but he is not the man for a close finish with a tired horse, when victory depends upon calling out the last reserve of strength; nor will he make the successful trainer of a high-strung colt. The trotter, moreover, cannot be convinced by mere noise and violence: he is much too clever an animal for that, and will hardly be cheated into thinking that the jockey possesses any quality which he really lacks. But when a driver

has the required combination of sympathy and force,
the trotter is quick to recognize his master and ready
to obey him.

"One half of a horse's speed," wrote Mr. George
Wilkes, "is in the mind of his rider or driver.
When it is known to the world that a horse has
made a mile a second or half-second faster than it
was ever made before, some rider of some other
horse, nerving himself with the knowledge of the
fact, and infusing that knowledge into his horse by
dint of his own enthusiasm, sends *him* a second or
two faster still; and the result of the mental emu-
lation is a permanent improvement which never is
retraced.   Hiram Woodruff was the first to take this
mental grip of the powers of the trotting horse; and
the result in his case was, that, by dint of his own
mind, he carried him triumphantly over the gap
which lies between 2.40 and 2.18."

"Dan Mace," said Woodruff himself, speaking of
another famous reinsman, now dead, "is very resolute, and the horses that he handles know it."

To drive a trotter with art is, first, to get from
him the highest speed of which he is capable;
secondly, to keep him from making a break; and,
thirdly, to bring him back to the trot with as little
loss as possible after a break has actually occurred.
To do this well requires a light and "sensational"
hand, a sympathetic intelligence, and a vast deal of
practice.   The break is prevented, sometimes by
restraining the animal with voice and rein, when it
is simply a case of too much eagerness, but more
often by moving the bit in his mouth.   If the break
happens, the horse "leaving his feet," as the phrase

is, and going to a gallop or a run, he must be
"caught" by pulling his head to one side, so that he
will have to come back to a trot in order to keep his
balance; and in extreme cases it will be necessary to
pull him first this way, and then that. The break
does not come without premonitory signals; there
is a sort of general unsteadiness of the horse's gait,
when the change is in contemplation, and at the last
moment he moves his ears backward. "The sign of
a coming break," says Hiram Woodruff, that excellent writer from whom I have quoted so much already, "will be discovered by watching the head and
ears of the horse. The attention of the driver ought
always to be fixed upon the head of his horse. Many
a heat is lost by neglect of this matter. A driver is
seen coming up the home stretch a length or a length
and a half ahead. Both the horses are tired, but
the leading one could win. The driver, however,
when he gets where the carriages are, turns his head
to look at the ladies. or to see whether they are
looking at him. Just then the horse gives a twitch
with his ears; the driver does n't see it; up flies the
trotter, and the ugly man behind holds his horse
square, and wins by a neck."

Of all muscular pleasures, there is none, perhaps.
more fine and delicate than this of the skilful reinsman. Whirled along at the rate of a mile in two
minutes and a half. he keeps his trotter steady by a
slight turn of the wrist, thus moving the bit in the
animal's responsive mouth, and so distracting his
attention and jogging his memory. If there is any
parallel to this exercise. it will probably be found
in those clever manipulations of rod and line by

means of which an angler transfers the shy but gamy
trout from water to land. Nor is it necessary to
mount a sulky in order to experience these delights.
Mr. Vanderbilt drove Maud S. and Aldine, harnessed
to his road wagon, a mile in 2.15½; at Cleveland,
some years ago, a four-in-hand accomplished the
same distance in 2.40; and a moderately fast horse,
a moderately light wagon, and a smooth road supply
all the necessary conditions for artistic driving.

There is another function of the bit scarcely less
important, and that is to encourage and restore a
tired horse. When, at the end of a stoutly contested
heat, two trotters are struggling for supremacy, they
can be urged by the voice, reinforced either by the
whip or by the bit. A coarsely bred, sluggish animal
may, at this critical moment, require the lash, but its
application to a beast of any spirit is almost sure to
disgust and dishearten him. In some subtle way,
however, when the driver moves the bit to and fro
in the horse's mouth. the effect is to enliven and stim-
ulate him. as if something of the jockey's spirit were
thus conveyed to his mind. If this motion be performed with an exaggerated movement of the arm. it
is called "reefing," and it sometimes appears. when
it is "neck or nothing." at the end of a heat, as if
the driver were actually "sawing" the horse's mouth.
whereas in reality. he is only giving the bit a loose
but vigorous motion therein.

At this point. it might not be amiss to state the
conditions of a trotting race. for it is highly probable
that to some of my readers the following explanation
will not be superfluous.

The race is over a mile track. almost elliptical in

shape, and the judges are perched in a two-story
balcony close to the track, and near one extrem·
ity of the ellipse, so that at the end of a heat the
horses have a long, straight stretch before reaching the goal. Across the track from the judges'
stand, and high enough to clear the trotters' heads,
is stretched a wire, by the aid of which, in a very
close finish, the judges can determine which horse
has won. The race is usually "best three in five";
that is, in order to win, a horse must come in first
three times, not necessarily in succession. Thus it
will be seen, if there are many contestants in the
race, it may be prolonged to seven, eight, and even
ten heats, before any one trotter has secured three.
But if a horse has taken part in five[1] heats without
winning a single one, he is ruled out, or "sent to the
barn," as the expression is, and cannot start again.
So, also, he may be ruled out if at the close of a heat
he is very far behind the winning horse. At a point
in the home stretch one hundred feet from the judges'
stand, (one hundred and fifty, if eight or more horses
are engaged in the race,) a man is stationed with a
flag in his hand, which he drops when the winner
reaches the wire; and if any lagging horse has not
passed him when his flag falls, that horse is "distanced," and cannot start again. It is possible for a
driver to "lay up" a heat, as it is called; that is, if
his horse be tired, or for any other cause, he may
content himself for that heat with just "saving his
distance," making no effort to win. The start is a
flying one. When the judges ring their bell, the
drivers turn about at or near the distance point, and

---

[1] A recent rule makes this limit three heats instead of five.

come down past the judges' stand almost or quite at
full speed. If, when they pass under the wire, they
are upon fairly even terms, the starter (one of the
judges) cries out, "Go!" and on they rush. If,
however, the start would not be a fair one, the bell
is rung as a signal that the drivers must come back
and try again: Sometimes the scoring, as these
attempts are called, is prolonged for a long while;
but the judges are authorized to fine any driver who
comes down ahead of or behind the "pole" horse;
that is, the horse who has the inside position, or
that nearest the poles which mark the quarter, the
half, and the three-quarter mile points. All the
positions are assigned by lot. The attempt is occasionally made by a combination of drivers to tire out
or excite some particular horse by unnecessary scoring, and in former years this nefarious plan was
often practised successfully, but of late the rules are
enforced with more strictness. Even with the best
intentions on the part of all the drivers concerned,
it is sometimes difficult to get a fair start, especially
if the horses are young or badly behaved, and the
scoring is frequently spoken of as a great drawback
to the pleasures of a trotting race. These false
starts, however, afford a most interesting exhibition
of horses and men; the spectator has such an opportunity as he could not otherwise enjoy to study the
gaits of the various trotters, to note how well or ill
they "catch," and to observe the skill. temper, and
courage of the jockeys. There is a great difference
in the behavior of the different horses. Some pull
and tug on the bit, despite the signal to return, carrying their drivers down to the first turn in the

track before they can be stopped; whereas others, old campaigners as a rule, will slacken speed at once when they hear the bell, stop, and turn around of their own accord.

Goldsmith Maid, a mare whose natural cleverness enabled her to profit by a long and varied experience, showed wonderful intelligence in scoring. When turned about to come down for the start, she would measure with her eye the distance between herself and the other horses; and if it seemed to her that they were likely to get first to the judges' stand, she would refuse to put forth her best speed, despite the efforts of her driver. The result in such cases was, of course, as she foresaw, that the judges, perceiving that the start would be an unfair one, rang the recall bell. "On the contrary," says Mr. Doble, "if she had a good chance to beat the other horses in scoring, she would go along gradually with them until pretty close to the wire, and then of her own accord come with a terrible rush of speed, so that when the word was given she would almost invariably be going at the best rate of any horse in the party. . . . If she had the pole, she would make it a point to see that no horse beat her around the first turn, seeming to be perfectly well aware that the animal that trotted on the outside had a good deal the worst of it."

Close to the fence, but inside of it on the track, opposite the judges' stand or thereabout, there is always a motley group of "rubbers" or grooms, and helpers, with pails of water and sponges in their hands, and blankets, thick or thin according to the weather, thrown over their shoulders, or deposited conveniently on the fence. Here, very often, the

driver pulls up for a moment, on his way back to
the starting point after the bell has rung for a recall, while the groom hastily sponges out the horse's
mouth and nostrils, adjusts the check-rein, takes up
a hole in the breeching, or makes some other slight
change in the harness.

These are tense moments in an important race,
especially if the contestants are known to be evenly
matched, and if each driver is anxious that the others shall take no advantage of him. At such times
a reputation for courage is of some service; it is
always a temptation for one jockey to "cut out"
another, or unfairly drive in to the "pole" ahead of
him, just as one boat in a rowing race may take
another boat's water. Under these circumstances, it
is the right of the driver, whose territory is invaded
to keep on, even though a collision may result ; and
a resolute man will do so, undeterred by the fact
that spokes are flying from the wheel of his own or
of his adversary's sulky, as the two gossamer vehicles
come together. "The quarter stretch looked more
like a toothpick factory than a race-course," was face-
tiously remarked of one occasion, when the driving
had been reckless.

With this explanation, I shall venture to give a
short account of a notable race which occurred at
Cleveland, in July, 1876, between the famous horses
Smuggler and Goldsmith Maid. The latter was at
this time nineteen years old, but she was thought to
be invincible, and in this very year she repeated her
best record, 2.14, first made by her in 1874. The
Maid was, as we have seen, the fastest trotter from
the time of Dexter, who achieved 2.17¼ in 1867,

to that of Rarus, who in 1878 covered a mile in
2.13¼. A slight sketch of Goldsmith Maid was
given in a former chapter, and I have stated already
in the present chapter the chief characteristics of
Smuggler.

There were three other fast horses in the race,
Lucille Golddust, Bodine, and Judge Fullerton; but
none of them, excepting perhaps Lucille Golddust,
played a part of any importance. Goldsmith Maid
was driven by Budd Doble, a young man whom
Hiram Woodruff picked out to succeed himself in the
charge of Dexter, and who has since amply justified
the selection by intelligent training and skilful driving of many celebrated horses. He is, moreover, one
of the few jockeys whose reputations are without
flaw. Charles Marvin, who also ranks high in the
craft, sat in the sulky of Smuggler. But the judges
are ringing their bell, the horses have been "warmed
up," the rubbers are gathered at the wire, a hush has
fallen upon the vast throng of spectators, anticipation is on tiptoe, and it is time for the

*First Heat.* At the third trial, the horses received a fair start, and Goldsmith Maid, pursuing
her usual tactics, made a rush for the lead. and
secured it. The first half-mile was trotted very fast,
and for the first quarter Bodine was second and
Smuggler third. Smuggler, however, went by Bodine in the second quarter. and soon after the half-
mile pole was passed he came very close to the Maid,
but at this point he faltered a little. The cause was
not known at first to the spectators, but after the
heat a mounted patrol judge galloped in with a shoe
which Smuggler had cast from his near fore foot.

Despite this accident,— and its importance may be estimated from the fact that his fore shoes weighed two pounds each,— Smuggler came down the home stretch with tremendous speed, pushing the Maid hard; and when she swept under the wire in 2.15½, his nose was on a level with her tail. This was a great heat, and Smuggler would probably have won it had he not cast a shoe.

*Second Heat.* There was some trouble in scoring, for Smuggler broke badly, but on the fourth attempt they were sent off, Goldsmith Maid being a little ahead of the others. In going around the first turn Smuggler made one of his characteristic breaks, and had to be pulled almost to a standstill before he regained a trot. His driver therefore contented himself with just saving his distance. But the Maid was given no rest, for Lucille Golddust was close upon her heels, forcing the Queen of the Turf to trot the mile in 2.17¼. These two fast heats distressed Goldsmith Maid, but those who had backed her were still confident, relying upon the great speed and steadiness of the old mare to pull her through.

*Third Heat.* The Maid, having won the preceding heat, had the inside position, and kept it, although she broke at the first turn; but her breaks were not like those of Smuggler. To the half-mile pole she led, with Fullerton second, Lucille Golddust third, and Smuggler fourth. But after this point had been reached, Marvin called upon Smuggler for an effort. The horse answered gamely; he passed Lucille Golddust, then Fullerton, and when Goldsmith Maid turned into the home stretch Smuggler was close behind her. The race was extremely close from this point; but Smuggler gained on the Maid inch by inch, and finally dashed under the wire, three quarters of a length in advance, amid tumultous applause. Time, 2.16¼. "The scene which followed," says a contemporary and graphic report in the Turf, Field, and Farm, "is indescribable An electrical wave swept over the vast assembly, and men swung their hats and shouted themselves hoarse, while the ladies snapped fans and parasols and burst their kid gloves in an endeavor to get rid of the storm of emotion. The police vainly tried to keep the quarter stretch clear. The multitude poured through the gates, and Smuggler returned to the stand through a narrow lane of humanity, which closed as he advanced. Doble was ashy pale, and the grand mare who had scored so many victories stood with trembling flanks and head down. Her attitude seemed to say, 'I have done my best, but am forced to resign the crown.'"

"During the intermission." according to the same account. "the stallion was the object of the greatest scrutiny. So great was the press that it was difficult to obtain breathing-room for him. He appeared fresh, and ate eagerly of the small bunch of hay which was presented to him by his trainer after he had cooled off. It was manifest that the fast work had not destroyed his appetite. The betting now changed, for it was seen that the Maid was tired."

The race. however, was not over yet. Smuggler had two heats to win before victory would be his, whereas Goldsmith Maid needed only one more. She was leg-weary. to be sure, but then she could be counted on to make a humanly sagacious use of her

opportunities, and a single bad break would cause
Smuggler's defeat. Excitement subdued the spectators to perfect stillness, and not a sound was heard
except the rhythmical tramp of the five horses, as
they thundered down the stretch to the wire for
the

*Fourth Heat.* At the second attempt the judges
gave the word "Go" as Smuggler was trotting steadily, although somewhat behind the others. The
Maid, as usual, rushed off with the lead, and Lucille
Golddust took the second place, being pulled out a
little, so as to bring her near the centre of the track.
This left Marvin in a very bad position, technically
known as a "pocket." He could not slip in between the other two horses, for Doble kept the Maid
back just far enough to prevent such a move; and
if he should check his own horse sufficiently to get
past Lucille Golddust, much distance would be lost.
What he did was to remain in this helpless situation
until the home stretch was reached, thinking that
the driver of Golddust would finally get out of his
way; but this did not happen, and when Smuggler
was only three hundred yards from the wire, when
Goldsmith Maid had a long lead, when "a smile of
triumph lighted Doble's face, and the crowd settled
sullenly down to the belief that the race was over,"
then at last the driver of Smuggler pulled him back
and turned to the right, so as to get out of the
pocket, and made desperate play for the heat. Contrary to what every one expected, the horse did not
break, despite this interference with his stride, but,
keeping level and steady, came down the course,
when he saw the way clear before him, with a

burst of speed which will always be famous in the
chronicles of the American turf. His ears were laid
flat on his head, his neck was stretched out low and
long, so as to bring his head scarcely above the level
of his withers, and fire flashed in his eye.

"He trotted," writes Mr. Helm, who was among
the spectators, "with a grim desperation, that cannot readily be forgotten by the thousands who were
present. His fleet-footed and never faltering oppo-
nent, the victor in a hundred trials, the Queen of
2.14, was already thirty-five feet ahead of him.
With a gathering of resources never perhaps held
by any other, and a rate of speed never equalled on
the trotting turf, he made for the front. There can
be no doubt, I think, that he moved for six or eight
hundred feet at the rate of a two-minute gait. He
trotted then as if he knew he could and would win
the heat; and in his very eye there was the look of
win it, or perish in the attempt. Woe to the animal
or vehicle that should come between him and the
end of that race! His speed was terrific, his momentum was fearful, and his stroke as steady and
true as any ever beheld. His very appearance was
a sort of magnetism that electrified the thousands
that were present."

"It was more like flying than trotting," says the
report from which I first quoted. "Doble hurries
his mare into a break, but he cannot stop the dark
shadow which flits by him. His smile of triumph
is turned into an expression of despair. Smuggler
goes over the score a winner of the heat by a neck,
and the roar which comes from the grand stand and
the quarter stretch is deafening. The time was

2.19¾. Smuggler again cooled off well, nibbling eagerly at his bunch of hay. The Maid was more tired than ever, while Lucille Golddust showed no signs of distress."

Even yet, however, the race was in doubt.

*Fifth Heat.* It was evident that the other horses, or rather their drivers, had formed a combination against Smuggler. They worried him so much in scoring that twice again he pulled off the shoe from his near fore foot, and nearly an hour elapsed before a start was obtained. "The shell of the foot," relates the excellent writer in the Turf, Field, and Farm, "was pretty badly splintered by the triple accident, but the stallion was not rendered lame. Misfortunes, however, seemed to be gathering thickly about him, and the partisans of the Maid wore the old jaunty air of confidence." The other horses had an unbroken rest while Smuggler was shoeing, so that they all appeared fresh when the word was finally given. "Fullerton," says the Turf, Field, and Farm, "went to the front like a flash of light, trotting without a skip to the quarter pole in thirty-three seconds," but Smuggler passed him near the half-mile pole, kept the lead from that point, and won the race, although Goldsmith Maid came along with great speed on the home stretch, forcing Smuggler to trot the heat in 2.17¼, and finishing a good second.

Thus ended what was perhaps, all things considered, the best race ever trotted. Here were five heats in 2.15½, 2.17¼, 2.16¼, 2.19¾, 2.17¼, each one being gallantly contested, and the result remaining in the utmost doubt till the very close of the fifth heat. "The evening shadows had now thickened, and, as the great crowd had shouted itself weak and hoarse, it passed slowly through the gates, and drove in a subdued manner home."

There is one other race of which I cannot forbear giving a brief account, because the winner displayed the same admirable qualities as Smuggler, and triumphed where his defeat was supposed to be inevitable. There were eight contestants, but the real competitors were three, namely, Nobby, Felix, and Florence.

Nobby was a very peculiar horse: a dark bay gelding, with a long neck and body, a fine head, and altogether a thoroughbred and even greyhound appearance. His gait was long, low, and smooth. He was however a wild breaker, and extremely nervous. "The twitter of a canary bird on a limb," said John Splan, his driver, "would have more effect on Nobby than a full brass band on an ordinary horse." Both his mouth and feet were in bad condition, but Splan. who took the horse for the first time on the day of the race, poulticed his feet, and relieved his mouth by driving him with an easy bit and nose-band attachment. He also stuffed the horse's ears with cotton, so that he should not be scared or worried to a break by the shouting and whipping of the other drivers. "Nobby," said the contemporary report in the Spirit of the Times, "impresses you with the idea that he is constantly trying to lose the race by making a mistake. Splan drove him as carefully as if he were handling eggs." Felix was a bay gelding. and a horse of speed.— much speedier. in fact, than Nobby; but, as a reporter of the race remarked. "he has a soft spot in him somewhere when pinched." Florence was a beautiful mare, also fast, and a good breaker. All three, it should be mentioned, were driven by masters of the art.

The *first heat* was won by Florence after a sharp contest with Felix, Nobby making no effort. In the *second heat* Nobby outstripped the others on the home stretch, but made a wild break, passing under the wire on a run, and Florence was awarded first place. In the *third heat* Nobby again broke badly, and Felix won after another hard contest with Florence. In the *fourth heat* Nobby showed his quality. At the three-quarter pole Felix led him by four lengths, but from this point Nobby began to gain inch by inch, Splan driving him with great patience and skill. His long neck showed nearer and nearer to the sulky of Felix, as the two horses approached the judge's stand, until at last they were side by side. Then Felix seemed to fall back, and Nobby won amid wild hurrahs. "I have seen his sire do the same thing in California," said a noted horseman who was among the spectators. In the *fifth heat*, however, Nobby made another disastrous break, and Felix won easily. Five heats had now been trotted, and the coming heat would decide the race if it fell either to Felix or to Florence. Nobby, so far, had only one to his credit. This brings us to the

*Sixth Heat.* It had begun to rain a little: the track was sticky, and all the horses were tired. "Their courage," says the report, "was cheered by sherry." It is more likely, however, that Nobby was treated to champagne and seltzer water, that being the agreeable dose usually administered by Splan under similar circumstances. Only the winners of heats, Felix, Florence, and Nobby were allowed to start; the others, who had not secured a single one out of the five heats that had been trotted, being "sent to the barn," in accordance with a rule already stated. The pools sold fast and furious on Felix against the field, twenty-five dollars to six, for what slight chance Nobby ever had was thought to be gone.

Now came one of the most stubbornly contested heats ever seen on a trotting course. At the start Felix showed much more speed than the others, and was a length ahead at the quarter pole, with Florence second, and Nobby trotting steadily in the rear. At the half-mile pole Felix had gained three lengths more, and looked, as the sporting phrase is, a sure winner. Soon after this point was passed Florence gave place to Nobby, and "now," said the Spirit of the Times, "Splan began to show his tactics, 'wait and win.' His gain to the three-quarter pole was almost imperceptible, and Felix still kept a long lead; but from this point Splan began to use every particle of speed that was in his horse. When they turned into the home stretch Felix was swung out to the middle of the track, where the footing was better but Nobby was driven close to the pole. 'I can't spare a foot of distance,' was my thought.' Splan afterward remarked."

"Nobby gamely entered into the spirit of the task: a stern chase, it is true, but gradually he lessened the gap. At the drawgates, where the path was hard, he wavered, as if about to break, but Splan steadied him with a slight pull, and on recovering his stride

he now measured the distance to be overcome.
Slowly but surely came he nearer to Felix; within
a few lengths of the wire they were almost even.
Just at the last moment Splan roused Nobby for a
final effort, and landed him first under the wire by
a neck. Time, 2.25."

*Seventh Heat.* Twilight was coming on as the
tired horses scored for the word. At the third trial
they received a fair start. Felix broke almost immediately, and lost three lengths, but Florence gave
Nobby no rest so long as her wind and courage
lasted. She hung close to the wheel of his sulky
until they had got midway of the second quarter,
when Nobby began to draw away from her. At this
point Felix came along, and the driver of Florence,
seeing that she had "shot her bolt," kindly pulled
her out from the pole to the centre of the track, thus
allowing Felix to slip into her place. Florence then
dropped behind, but Felix continued to gain, and
at the half-mile pole he was trotting neck and neck
with Nobby. From this point, as before, Felix out-
trotted Nobby, and when they turned into the home
stretch for the last time he had a good lead of three
full lengths. Again the driver of Felix brought
him out to the centre of the track, and again Splan
hugged the pole. The brush down the home stretch
was an exciting one. Felix trotted fast, but behind
him still pegged away the unconquerable Nobby, and
the distance between them was reduced inch by inch,
until at last Splan brought his horse up on even terms
with the other. They were now but a few yards
from the goal. Both horses were exhausted, and
Nobby could not be aroused by the voice, for his ears

were stuffed with cotton. Splan took "the last, dying chance," as he called it. Running the risk of a break, which would have been fatal, he leaned forward and touched Nobby lightly on the shoulder with his whip. The move was successful. Nobby kept steadily to a trot, but, gamely responding to the appeal, made one final effort, and fairly staggered under the wire, a winner by a head.[1] Time, 2.28¾.

Thus ended a memorable contest. It was won by the horse who proved himself the slowest trotter and the worst breaker of the three competitors, — won through his own courage and endurance, and through the skill and patience of his driver. "But who cares to see a race which falls to the slowest horse? The race should be to the swift," is a comment that might perhaps be made. Such a criticism would be founded upon a false notion of sport. All sports practised for the amusement of a spectator are noble according as victory in them depends upon the exercise of moral and mental qualities. The attentive reader of Boxiana will conclude that, taking the history of the ring as a whole, the fight was usually won by the man who had determined that he would not be beaten; and from this circumstance alone a very fair argument might be made — how nearly adequate need not here be considered — in support of pugilism.

In trotting races, for the reasons already stated, and as is apparent from the illustrations that have been given, there is a peculiar opportunity for the exercise

---

[1] Since the writing of this chapter, Nobby has been sold at auction. He brought $2,000, and his purchaser, as the sentimental reader will be glad to learn, was John Splan.

of admirable qualities on the part of both horse and man. It is true, that, so far as the drivers are concerned, their skill is often prostituted to the exigencies of the pool-box, but no accusation of this sort was ever brought against a trotter. The breath of suspicion may at times have rested upon Splan, but the name of Nobby is untarnished. In the two contests just described, all parties to the fight honestly exerted the qualifications that nature and experience had given them; and although victory perched first here and then there, the prize finally fell, as should be the case, to superior courage, endurance, patience, and skill.

## V.

### ROAD HORSES.

AMONG the irregular acquaintances of my boy-
hood, I remember a certain Ed Hulbert, who
was wont to express his notion of felicity in the following concise and oft-repeated phrase: "A smooth
road and a sharp trot!" There may be nobler ideals;
pursuits might perhaps be thought of which combine
pleasure with intellectual improvement to a greater
degree; and certainly it must be admitted that a
young or even a middle-aged man should always be
provided with an excuse for driving instead of riding,
such as that he is lame, or has already taken an equivalent amount of exercise in some other form, or desires
to be accompanied by his wife. But these difficulties
surmounted, (or shall we say disregarded?) the combination of "a smooth road and a sharp trot" will

8

supply no small amusement. Only the horse lover, indeed, can enjoy it to the full, — subtly communicating through rein and bit with his steed, appreciating the significant play of his ears, and rightly interpreting that lively, measured ring of his feet upon the road which indicates a sound and active stepper. But there are some incidental delights, such as the quick conveyance through fresh air and a passing glimpse of the scenery, which everybody enjoys. My old acquaintance would have thought but meanly of the man who gave a wish to view the country as his reason for driving; but then the Ed Hulbert standard cannot always be maintained, and something must be pardoned to the weakness of human nature.

In a sense, every horse driven by the owner for pleasure is a road horse. The fast trotter who speeds up and down the Brighton or the Harlem road, drawing a single man in a gossamer wagon; the round, short-legged cob; the big, respectable, phlegmatic Goddard-buggy animal, who may be seen in Boston any fine afternoon hauling a master very much like himself out over Beacon Street; the pretty, high-stepping pair in front of a mail phaeton; — all these are road horses, but none of them, excepting sometimes the trotter, is a roadster in the strict sense. The road horse *par excellence* is a beast of medium size, who can draw a light carriage at the rate of seven miles an hour all day without tiring himself or his driver. He should be able to travel at least ten miles in an hour, twenty miles in two hours, sixty miles in a day; and by this is meant that he should do it comfortably and "handily," as the term is, and feel none the worse for the exertion. Such roadsters are rare, — much more so now, in proportion to the total number of our horses, than they were twenty-five years ago, or before the war; the reason being that the craze for fast trotters has thrown the roadster into the shade. Of course, almost any sound horse can be urged and whipped over the ground, "driven off his feed," perhaps, and so travel these distances in the time mentioned. Nothing is more common than for some broken-down animal to be pointed out by his cruel and mendacious master as one for whom ten or twelve miles an hour is only a sort of exercising gait; the poor beast having very likely been ruined in the effort to accomplish some such feat which was beyond his capacity. The mere fact that a horse has gone a long way in a short time tells little about his powers; the more important inquiry is, What was his condition afterward? A liveryman in Vermont declared not long ago, that at one time and another he had lost twelve hundred dollars' worth of horseflesh through the ignorant and murderous driving of customers who had endeavored to keep up with a certain gray mare, of extraordinary endurance, that was owned in his vicinity for several years.

A horse that will step off cheerfully and readily eight miles an hour, a pace so moderate that one never sees it mentioned in an advertisement, is much better than the average; one that will do ten miles in that time and in the same way is an exceptionally good roadster; and the horse that goes twelve miles an hour with ease is extremely rare. A stable-keeper in Boston, of long experience, tells me that he has known but two horses that would travel at this last-mentioned rate with comfort to themselves and the driver, though he has seen many others, pulling, crazy creatures, that would keep up a pace as fast, or even faster, till they dropped. Of these two pleasant roadsters, capable of covering twelve miles in sixty minutes, one trotted all the way, up and down hill, whereas the other walked up the steep ascents, and went so much the faster where the grade was favorable. The latter method is easier and better for most horses.

The capabilities of a roadster having now been indicated in a general way, the first and most obvious inquiry is, What will be the conformation and appearance of a horse likely to possess them? Upon this subject it is dangerous to dogmatize. For example, a flat-sided, thin-waisted animal is apt to be wanting in endurance, and yet there have been some notable exceptions to this rule. A leading quality of the road horse is shortness; that is, his back should be short, and, it may be added, straight. The same is true of his legs, especially as regards the cannon-bone. A short cannon-bone is perhaps the most nearly indispensable characteristic of a roadster. The knees should be large, the hocks well let down, and the hind quarters closely coupled to the back. The belly should be of good size, and round. George Borrow, a thorough horseman, makes the old hostler in "Lavengro" say: "Never buy a horse at any price that has not plenty of belly. No horse that has not plenty of belly is ever a good feeder, and a horse that an't a good feeder cannot be a good horse." He should have great depth of lung and a moderately broad chest. Good, sound feet of medium size, and pastern joints neither straight nor oblique, are essential. It is no harm if his neck be thick, but it is absolutely necessary that he should have a fine head and clear, intelligent eyes, with a good space between and above them. An English authority declares, "There was never yet a first-class race horse that had a mean head," and I believe this is equally true of roadsters. The ears also are an important point; they should be set neither close together nor wide apart, and it is of the utmost consequence how they are carried. A lively, sensible horse, one who has the true roadster disposition, will continually move his ears, pointing them forward and backward, and even sideways, thus showing that he is attentive and curious as to what takes place about him, and interested to observe what may be coming. A beast with a coarse head, narrow forehead, dull, timorous eyes, and ears that tend to incline away from each other when held upright, and which are apt to be pointed backward, — such a horse is one to avoid as certainly deficient in mind, and probably in courage and in good temper as well. Many lazy, sluggish animals of this sort are considered eminently safe for women to drive; and so they are until the harness breaks or something else frightens them, when they become panic-stricken and tear everything to pieces. On the other hand, a high-strung but intelligent horse will quickly recover from a sudden alarm, when he finds that after all he has not been hurt. The manner rather than the fact of shying is the thing to be considered.

When we come to inquire how good roadsters are bred, the answer can be given with more confidence, for the source of their endurance and courage is always found either in Arabian or in thoroughbred blood.

These two terms were at one time more nearly synony-
mous than they are now. A thoroughbred (as we have
seen, and as the instructed reader will scorn to be
told) is one whose pedigree is registered in the English
Stud Book, the first volume of which was published in
1808. A preliminary volume, called "An Introduction
to a General Stud Book," issued in 1791, contained
the names of the chief mares and stallions of racing
stock then living. These are the "foundation" horses
from which the present thoroughbreds, English and
American, have sprung. They were almost entirely
of Oriental descent. Arabs were imported to England at a very early period, but not in such numbers
as to effect any decided improvement in the native
breed until the reign of James I. This monarch established a racing stable, and installed therein some
fine Arabian stallions. Charles I. continued the same
policy, and the royal stud which he left at Tutbury
consisted chiefly of Arab-bred horses. Soon after his
execution, it was seized by order of Parliament; but,
happily, the change in dynasty did not interfere with
the conduct of the stud. Cromwell, as is well known,
had a sharp eye for a horse, and the best of the King's
lot were soon "chosen" for the Lord Protector.

Charles II., again, had no less a passion for horses,
and almost the first order that he issued, after landing in England, was one to the effect that the Tutbury
nags should be returned to the royal stables. This
monarch imported some Arabian stallions, and a col-
lection of mares called Royal Mares, purchased on
the Continent. Their breeding is not entirely known,
but many of them were Arabs or Barbs. The Royal
Mares figure in the first volume of the Stud Book.

Many private breeders also added to the Arabian stock in England; but it was not until the first half of the eighteenth century that the three horses were imported who have exercised the greatest influence upon the race of English thoroughbreds. These were the Byerly Turk, the Darley Arabian, and especially the Godolphin Arabian, or Barb, — probably the latter. The last named was a dark bay horse about fifteen hands high (Arab horses seldom exceed 14¾ hands), with a white off heel behind. He is said to have been stolen from his owner in Paris, where he was employed in the menial task of drawing a water-cart, and his pedigree was never ascertained. It is the fashion of English writers to decry the Arabian blood; and it is true that the present thoroughbred, owing to many years of good food and severe training, is a bigger, stronger, swifter animal than the Arab;[1] but the latest and perhaps the highest authority on this subject, William Day, makes the significant admission, that all the best thoroughbreds now on the English turf trace back to one or more of the three Arab horses whose names have just been mentioned.

The chief reason why a good roadster must have

[1] Some years ago, Haleem Pacha, of Egypt, who had inherited from his father, Abbass Pacha, a stud of Arabs estimated to have cost about $5,000,000, made a match with certain merchants at Cairo to run an eight-mile race for £400 a side. The Cairo merchants sent to England and bought Fair Nell, an Irish mare, thoroughbred, or nearly so, that had been used by one of the Tattersalls as a park and covert hack. She was a beautiful bright bay mare, with black legs, standing about 15 hands 1½ inches. The match took place within two weeks after Fair Nell landed in Egypt, and she won with ridiculous ease, beating the Pacha's best Arab by a full mile. She did the eight miles in 18½ minutes, and pulled up fresh.

thoroughbred or Arab blood in his veins is, that from
no other source can he derive the necessary nervous
energy. This is even more important than the superior bony structure of the thoroughbred or Arabian.
Exactly what nervous energy is, nobody, I presume,
can tell; but it is something that, in horses at least,
develops the physical system early, makes it capable
of great exertion, and enables it to recover quickly
from fatigue. The same, or, more correctly, a similar
capacity, is remarked in mankind. Readers of Arctic
travels, for example, must often have been struck by
the fact that it is almost invariably the men, and not
the officers, who succumb to the labor and exposure
of a sledge journey. Loosely speaking, it may be that
in the educated man, especially in the man whose
ancestors also have been educated, the mind has acquired a degree of control over the body which cannot otherwise be attained. So also with horses. A
thoroughbred is one whose progenitors for many generations have been called upon to exert themselves to
the utmost; they have run hard and long, and strug-
gled to beat their competitors. Moreover, they have
had an abundance of the food best adapted to develop
bone and muscle. Then, again, the care, the grooming, the warm housing and blanketing, which they
have received, tend to make the skin delicate, the
hair fine, the mane silky, the whole organization more
sensitive to impressions, and consequently the nervous
system more active and controlling.

This same nervous energy usually prevents the roadster from being what is known as a family horse, for
he lacks the repose, the placidity and phlegm, of that
useful but commonplace animal; he is apt to jump

like a cat, and to dance or run a little now and then in exuberance of spirits and superfluity of strength. Occasionally, to be sure, a horse is found who has great courage and endurance, and at the same time a perfectly temperate disposition. Such was Justin Morgan, head of the great roadster family, whose origin I have described in a previous chapter.

If the partisans of this family are not quite so fanatical as those of the Arab, it is because they are more numerous than the latter, and consequently the less driven to back themselves up by extravagant assertion. But they are not wanting in enthusiasm.[1]

As to Justin Morgan, the immortal soul, his history is a matter of profound indifference. Nobody cares whether his mother was a Jones from Connecticut, or a Smith from Massachusetts. But Justin Morgan, the little bay colt which the schoolmaster took in payment for a bad debt, has kept the name bright for more than a century. This is sad indeed, and yet greater men than Justin Morgan have suffered a similar fate. How many horsemen are aware that Ethan Allen was preceded by a biped of the same name, a brave officer of the Revolution, who commanded our forces at the taking of Ticonderoga?

The case of General Knox is even worse. He was one who cut a wide swath in his day, — a leader in the Revolution, a brave soldier, a counsellor much relied upon by Washington, a man of wealth, of birth and

---

[1] "The Perfect Horse," a work by the Rev. W. H. H. Murray, is devoted to the praise of this family. A good illustrated history of Justin Morgan and his descendants, by Linsley, is now, I believe, out of print, and a more elaborate account of the family is in preparation by Mr. Joseph Battell, of Middlebury, Vermont.

breeding, — altogether, a personage of great importance. And yet not long ago, when a certain rustic
youth reared in Vermont paid his first visit to St.
Albans in that State, in company with his mother,
he stood aghast before a bronze statue there which
represented a two-legged animal, clad in human clothes,
and having apparently the attributes of a man. Underneath in large letters were inscribed the words,
"General Knox." "By gosh, mother," exclaimed the
astounded youth, "I always thought General Knox
was a horse!" And so he was, and a very good one
too, as we shall presently see.

The gait of the Morgan horse is highly characteristic.
Though sure-footed, he is apt to carry his fore feet
close to the ground, taking short elastic steps, which,
even when quickened to a rapid trot, seem to cost him
the least possible effort. There is no swaying of the
hips, no shaking of the whole frame, no pounding
with the fore feet or high lifting of the hocks, but a
smooth, easy, gliding motion. The Morgan both trots
and gallops with his limbs well under him.

A longer, wider gait is commonly associated with
the trotting horse. In fact, until within the past few
years it was thought that the ideal trotter carried his
hind feet so wide as to plant them outside of the track
left by his fore feet. Many, perhaps most, fast horses
do travel in this way; but, as a rule, the very fastest
step no wider behind than in front. A long stride is
however nearly, if not quite, essential to extreme
speed; and many Morgan horses, when moving at
their best pace, lengthen their gait very much, and go
perceptibly nearer to the ground. The Morgan action
in front is, as a rule, not big enough for superlatively

fast trotting, which is best performed by a peculiar and very graceful round motion of the fore legs. Some fast trotters have positively high action in front, — so high as to seem like a waste of power. This is especially true of Allerton, a Wilkes-Mambrino Patchen stallion whose record is 2.09¼. This excessive action is also found in some Morgan strains, especially among Sherman Morgan's descendants.

Country doctors are great adherents of the Morgan horse. "The Morgan," writes one of this class, "will trot all day, except when ascending a hill. As he approaches it, he will raise his head higher and higher. First, one pointed ear, then the other, will snap backward, then forward, as if he were asking permission to gallop; and then, if the driver does not object, he will lay both ears flat to his head and skim the rise like a bird, always striking into the same tireless trot when he reaches the summit."

It was from a country doctor — and I trust a veracious one, for he was my grandfather — that I heard, long years ago, the following story. He was driving late one very dark night in autumn over a strange road. A violent rain had fallen during the preceding twenty-four hours, so that the highway was badly washed. Presently his horse, a Vermont Morgan, made a leap, and crashed through what seemed to be the upper branches of a tree, taking the gig after him very neatly. This was a little unusual, but still no harm had been done. Half a mile or so farther on. the horse made another jump: then came a crash and a shiver as before, and the gig reeled over another tree, as it appeared, poised for a moment on one wheel, and righted itself as the horse resumed his trot.

By this time the Doctor knew that he must be near
a considerable river, with high banks, which flowed
through those parts, and very soon he heard the
waters roaring on the rocks below. But now his
horse came to a dead stop, refusing to cross the
bridge. The Doctor urged him forward, and he took
a few steps, but then moved back in his tracks. This
was repeated twice. Finally, vexed at such unusual
obstinacy in an animal long accustomed to rough and
nocturnal travelling, the Doctor struck him with the
whip. The horse squealed with disgust at this treatment, shook his head, advanced as before, and then
backed again, and cast an inquiring glance behind him
at his master. Now at last, the Doctor, dismount-
ing, went forward to reconnoitre. And this is what
he saw. The flooring of the bridge had been swept
away completely by a flood; nothing was left but the
sleepers running from bank to bank, and it was on one
of these sleepers that the horse had walked out so far
as he could with safety to the gig and its occupant.
The obstructions half a mile and a mile back, which
the roadster had jumped, were brush fences put up
to stop travel on the highway until the bridge could
be repaired.

Now that we are in the vein, I trust that the reader will pardon me if I relate another anecdote of a
Morgan roadster. This was a chestnut mare belonging to an old and highly respected "Vet." [1] One very
dark night the Doctor was driving toward home at a
fast trot on a level road, and in his proper place on
the right hand side of it. Presently he heard, though
he could not see. a wagon approaching at a rapid rate

[1] Dr. Flagg, of New Bedford, Massachusetts.

in the opposite direction; but as his lights were burning brightly, and the highway was a broad one, he thought nothing of it. Suddenly, however, before he could stop her, his steed made a violent jump to the left, crossing the road, and barely had she done so, when the approaching wagon, driven, as it appeared, by a drunken man, dashed by in the track which the Doctor's buggy had just left. The intelligent mare had waited till the last moment, thinking that the vehicle which she heard, would keep to the right, as it should have done; and then, foreseeing that a collision was otherwise inevitable, she had sprung out of the path of danger.

I have sketched in a preceding chapter the most speedy and highly finished branch of the Morgan stock, which is that of the Lamberts, descended, through Ethan Allen, from Vermont Blackhawk. Vermont Blackhawk had also a son called Vermont Hero, and Vermont Hero was the sire of General Knox [1] (whose name I have mentioned), a famous trotting stallion, and the founder of a subsidiary roadster family. This animal had every excellence except that of beauty. He was a stout, short-legged black horse, about fifteen hands high, with a good plain head. The Knox horses bear a wonderful family resemblance, and they are noted for their courage, endurance, docility, and intelligence. No branch of the Morgan family is more serviceable or more amiable than this one, and, with the possible exception of the Lamberts, none is more speedy.

[1] His dam was by Searcher, a half-bred horse descended from Diomed, and his second dam was also of Diomed blood. Searcher's dam was a Morgan. General Knox was therefore a combination of Morgan and thoroughbred.

The Lamberts and the Knoxes are, as I have said, decendants of Sherman, the handsome little chestnut son of Justin Morgan.

There are also two families of fine roadsters and trotters descended from Bulrush, another son of Justin Morgan. These are the Fearnaughts and the Winthrop Morrills. Both of these families are inbred to Justin Morgan, and they show a great deal of quality and of spirit, notwithstanding the fact that Bulrush was a coarse horse, with a very heavy mane and tail, suggestive of Canadian blood on his dam's side. This fact goes far to prove that Justin Morgan was well bred on both sides. For if his dam had been — as some writers assert — a coarse-bred Canadian mare, like the dam of Bulrush, then inbreeding among the descendants of Justin Morgan, especially in the Bulrush line, could hardly have produced horses so fine and bloodlike as are many of the Fearnaughts and of the Morrills. The Fearnaughts are usually chestnut horses; much resembling the Lamberts, but somewhat larger, and perhaps a little more fiery.

Another excellent family of roadsters is that of the Drews. The original Drew, a Maine horse, was foaled in 1842, his sire, it is said, being a pure thoroughbred, a bay horse sixteen hands high. Drew was a dark bay or brown. standing fifteen and a quarter hands, and weighing about a thousand pounds. He had good shoulders and a fine neck " light at the head, deep at the body," and well arched. His body was small: his hips were long and beautifully turned. He had stout legs, long pasterns a thin mane. and a nice short coat. His dam also was very well bred, being by Sir Henry. a son of American Eclipse, out of a mare by Winthrop Messenger. Her name was Boston Girl. The Drews, as might be presumed from this origin, are fine, spirited, hardy horses, with much style and dash, and very intelligent. One of them, a handsome bay stallion called Dirigo (whose dam was nearly thoroughbred), used to be driven without bit or rein through the town where his owner lived. Guided by the voice and whip of his driver, the horse would speed down the main street at a 2.40 gait, stop, turn around, and do whatever was required of him.

One of the best roadsters ever known in New England is Bay Fearnaught, whose sire was a Fearnaught and whose dam was a Drew, so that in him these two hardy and courageous strains are united. His owner, Mr. David Nevins, once drove Bay Fearnaught from South Framingham to the Somerset Club in Beacon street, Boston, a distance of twenty-two miles or more, in one hour and twenty-eight minutes. The horse was driven to a sleigh containing two men, and the going was very good. Reckoning the distance at twenty-two miles exactly, he maintained a speed of just fifteen miles an hour. Bay Fearnaught has trotted a mile to road wagon in 2.35, and two miles to a road wagon (wagon and driver weighing three hundred pounds) in 5.16. This horse is now twenty-three years old, and his owner reports him as being "sound as a bullet, and still able and willing to go fast."

Given a roadster such as I have described, and a light, open wagon fitted with a stout spring, with lamps, and possibly with a small break; given also a sympathetic companion and a mackintosh, — and, if you like, we will throw in a dog: thus provided, and

with all New England stretching out before you, what
more delightful than to take the road at any time between April and November!   It is pleasant to start in
the freshness of a summer morning, with the prospect
of seeing a new country, and with the comfortable
assurance that it is a matter of no consequence if
you become lost in traversing unknown paths.   Your
horse, I assume, has rested well, there is a cheerful
air of anticipation about his ears, and the wheels turn
smoothly and lightly on the newly oiled axles.   It is
pleasant to stop at noon in a patch of woods, beside
some mountain stream or at the edge of a lake, where
better quarters can be had than any tavern or summer
hotel affords.   The roadster is taken out, the dog lies
down at the foot of a tree, stretching himself with a
sigh of content, and a sort of gypsy camp springs up
on the instant.   After a half-hour's rest comes luncheon for man and beast; the steed taking his oats
out of a pail or nose-bag, the dog sharing lamb-sand-
wiches with the two other carnivorous members of the
party.   This meal concluded, — and there is no law
against lighting a small fire in order to have a cup of
hot tea or cocoa, — time remains for a nap, or for read-
ing a novel, or, better yet, for reclining at ease and
absorbing impressions from nature.   A fresh start is
made about two o'clock, or later if the weather be
very hot, the Houyhnhnm having first been made to
look spick and span, and able for his task.   It is pleasant then to drive past green fields and groves of pine
in the pensive light of late afternoon, and to watch the
shadows lengthening on the mountains; it is pleasant
as the cows are coming home. as the sun is setting,
and as the frogs begin their nightly chorus. to ap-

proach your destination, looking forward to supper and a bed, and leaving behind a day long to be remembered. Even the mishaps that befall the adventurous traveller, such as losing the road on a dark night when a thunder-storm is raging, and finding himself on a disused path through the woods instead of the highway, — even experiences of this kind are delightful in the retrospect.

The evening may be less enjoyable. New England taverns have a bad name, and they deserve it. Still, there is occasionally a good one, and there are others that possess some collateral attraction. The best, perhaps, are usually found in county towns where tradition lingers. I remember one such, well situated on a New Hampshire hill. The village was very small, containing three or four shops, a court-house, a miniature jail, and the tavern, a rambling structure with low ceilings. The rooms were but tolerable, the cooking was scarcely that, and yet the place had an air, a flavor, an attraction, which at first I was unable to resolve. At last I discovered that it consisted chiefly in this : the proprietor, a full-bearded, high-colored man of the old school, invariably and constantly wore a tall silk hat; the only one, in all probability, for ten miles around. Unthinking persons may perceive no significance in this; but, rightly considered, the high hat indicated a certain sense of self-respect, as well as a certain feeling for form and ceremony. If the hat had been assumed only when the wearer went outside, then it would have been simply a protection from the elements, or at best a matter of display for the villagers; but being worn constantly indoors, without regard to times or sea-

sons, it ceased to be a hat and became a badge. There
was another good feature of this hotel; the office, a
long, low room, had a big open fireplace, where logs
of wood burned cheerfully on a frosty night in autumn. The hostler, moreover, was an excellent one.
True, he fairly reeked of chloroform (New Hampshire
is a prohibition State), and his memory was not of the
best, being unable to carry "four quarts of oats"
more than fifteen minutes, or to distinguish it at the
distance of half an hour from a bran mash; but he
was gentle with his horses, and groomed them well.

If the roadster is to be kept in good condition, and
to come out fresh every morning, his master must be
liberal with fees and vigilant in his oversight. Hostlers, — I say it with reluctance, — especially in large
stables, are, generally speaking, worthless, drunken
creatures; and here and there a tavern-keeper is found
base enough to cheat a horse out of his oats. "But,"
some self-indulgent reader may exclaim, "one might
as well stay at home as to go off on a journey and be
bothered with a horse." This would be distinctly the
argument of a Yahoo, and if any one is in danger of
being deceived by it I would refer him to what the
famous Captain Dugald Dalgetty said upon the subject: "'It is my custom, my friends, to see Gustavus
(for so I have called him, after my invincible master)
accommodated myself; we are old friends and fellow
travellers, and as I often need the use of his legs, I
always lend him in my turn the service of my tongue
to call for whatever he has occasion for;' and accordingly he strode into the stable after his steed without
further apology."

Horses often fall ill or break down on a journey, and

this usually happens not from overdriving, but from allowing them to get cold, from watering them when they are hot, from feeding them when they are tired, and from general neglect. A tired roadster seldom gets a bed as deep and soft as he ought to have. The famous Mr. Splan remarks upon this point as follows: "What horses want is plenty of fresh air, to be comfortably clothed, and to have a good bed at all times. No matter how well you feed or care for a man, if you put him in a bad bed at night he will be very apt to find fault in the morning, and I think it is the same with a horse." The feet of a road horse also need attention, and his shoes are all-important. Most country blacksmiths do their work like butchers, paring and burning the foot to fit the shoe, instead of adapting the iron to the hoof. Still, within a radius of five or ten miles it is usually possible to discover a single good workman in this regard, and the traveller can get upon his track by inquiring of horsy men in the vicinity. Every village in New England contains at least one enthusiastic person who is raising colts with the confident expectation of turning out a $20,000 trotter. This man will know who is the good blacksmith of the neighborhood.

A word or two may be permitted here concerning the harness of a road or driving horse. With a light carriage, and where the country is level, breeching can be dispensed with, and a well made horse commonly looks better without it. Blinders, again, or winkers, are usually superfluous. An intelligent horse once accustomed to an open bridle is apt to shy less thus harnessed, for he can look about more freely. Besides, in the case of a skittish horse, it is an advantage for the driver to be able to watch his eye, as well as his ear. Some pulling horses go better with blinders, and some nervous horses may be safer with them. It is a matter for experiment in the particular case.

The question of check reins is not disposed of so easily, although many good people have convinced themselves that check reins under all circumstances are cruel and unnecessary. I know of one person whose great object in life, apart from the earning of his daily bread, is to do away with this part of the harness. The check rein, as all horsemen know, is often essential to the safety of human life and limb. People who write tracts or letters to the newspapers condemning it *in toto* have no knowledge of horseflesh beyond what they derive from an acquaintance with some sedate family nag of mature years. If they had a stableful of young horses to exercise in harness in winter weather, they would change their minds on this point. Many gay horses can be driven in perfect safety provided they wear check reins, especially if they wear the over-draw check; whereas the same horses without checks would be likely at any moment to put their heads down and run away, or, if they had a touch of deviltry. to kick up behind. It should not be forgotten that the use of the check rein makes it possible to use an easy bit, where without the check a severe bit would have to be employed; and any horse in his senses would prefer a check to a severe bit.

But apart from these cases, which, after all, are few in number compared with the great mass of horses in the service of man, the check has another function, which is to steady the horse, and to make it easier

for him to perform his work; but if the check be too
tight, it becomes a hindrance and a vexation, instead
of a help.

Charles Marvin relates an experience with a yearling which shows the very great importance of not
checking a horse too high : —

"There was a certain colt at Palo Alto that showed
remarkably well in the paddock, but after we got him
in harness we found that he could not exhibit a trace
of respectable speed. I drove him one day, and found
that he could not trot a three-minute gait. . . . After
vain and discouraging work I gave him up for that
day, thinking that perhaps he was out of humor, and
sulky, and a little bit tired. The next day I tried him
again, but with no better results. . . . So I unhitched
him and turned him loose on the miniature track, and
away he went as well as ever. A little study showed
how he carried his head and how he balanced himself.
I changed the check, harnessed him again, let his
head free so that he could carry himself in his own
way, and that same day he showed me a quarter in
better than forty seconds."[1]

It is natural for some horses to carry their heads
low, for others to carry them at a medium height, and
for a few to hold them high. But the check rein as
commonly used disregards these natural differences,
and pulls up the head of the unfortunate animal to a
point which suits the whim or vanity of his owner.
Even horsemen of great experience frequently err in
this matter. The owner of Lady De Jarnette, a beautiful Kentucky mare, a noted prize-winner, always
drove her with a particularly short, over-draw check,

---

[1] Training the Trotting Horse, page 218.

which he thought necessary. Her record was 2.29¼.
One day, at his request, John Splan drove the mare,
and by the simple device of letting out the check rein
a few holes, Mr. Splan reduced her record to 2.24½.

"Any one," he says, "could have driven the mare
the same mile, as she was very steady, and it required
no particular skill to manage her. She simply wanted
to be properly harnessed. It is just as easy to choke
a horse by checking him too high, and forcing the
tongue back into the entrance of the throat, as it
would be in any other way. I have seen one or two
horses die in harness that I am sure were choked to
death." [1]

The horse should never be checked on the driving
bit, for this practice tends to spoil his mouth. Even
when a side check is used, it should be attached to a
small rubber or leather-covered flexible bit, not connected in any way with the driving bit. This arrangement is an uncommon one, but I have tested
it thoroughly, and am convinced of its superiority.

Of course, when a horse has the weight of a carriage
to draw, the discomfort of a check rein too short is
greatly increased. Splan says: "I think that, as a
rule, road horses are checked entirely too high. To
place a horse's head in that position, and then ask him
to pull five hundred pounds of weight at a high rate
of speed, is wrong. The horse is not only uncomfort-

---

[1] I quote from the instructive work "Life with the Trotters," to
which I have referred in a previous chapter. Mr. Splan is a horseman of great acuteness, and as a driver cool, resolute, and full of
resource. A man of much experience on the track once remarked,
"If a horse were going to trot for my life I should like to have him
conditioned by Budd Doble and driven by John Splan."

able, but at a great disadvantage. I notice that in drawing weight most horses hold their heads in a medium position."

As to the over-draw check, useful as it is in some cases, I am free to say that I wish it had never been invented, so grossly is it abused. How often do we see some wretched victim of man's cruelty straining up hill with his neck in an abnormal position, or standing still and denied the poor privilege of hanging his despondent and weary head. Nevertheless it is extremely probable that the same horse, if equipped with a moderate side check, would perform a journey more comfortably than if he wore no check. If his head were free, he would be apt to carry it somewhere between his fore legs, going more carelessly as he became tired, stumbling, and perhaps falling before he reached his destination; whereas a moderate check would hold him together, and sustain his *morale*. The driver who gets out at the foot of every steep hill and unchecks his horse is, generally speaking, more humane than the man who dispenses with it altogether; and upon a journey, or upon a long afternoon's drive in the family carriage, this amount of trouble ought not to be begrudged. Besides, the exertion of hopping in and out (in addition, of course. to walking up all the steep pitches) will tend to ward off that stiffness which is likely to attack the legs of a lazy passenger.

In a word, then, the check rein is sometimes necessary to the proper control of the horse, and more often it is an advantage to the horse himself; but when drawn too tight, especially if it be an over-draw check, it is a hindrance and a vexation. and frequently an

instrument of torture. I like to drive a horse without check, martingale, blinders, or whip.

One great point in all-day driving is to make the
noonday stop before the roadster begins to tire. Every
horse has his distance, which is easily ascertained by
experience, though allowance must of course be made
for the state of the weather and of the roads. To this
extent he will go along cheerfully, with ears and tail
in their normal position; but drive a little farther,
and he begins to lag, his curiosity is gone, his ears
lose their vivacity, his tail droops, and he wants to
stop. It is well to make the noonday halt before this
point is reached, even though half the journey be not
completed.

When it comes to undertaking a really great distance, such as sixty or seventy miles in a day, or fifty
miles for two or three days consecutively, then intelligent driving and the best of care are indispensable.
Every foot of the road must be watched, advantage
taken of all the good going and slight declivities, the
bad spots avoided as much as possible, and the movement and condition of the roadster kept under vigilant observation from morning till night. Unless the
driver can sympathize with the horse, so as to know
exactly what his frame of mind and bodily condition
are all the way along, he is incompetent to handle
him to anything like the best advantage. When a
day's work of extraordinary length is attempted. the
best plan is to stop for half an hour or so in the middle of the morning. and also in the middle of the afternoon. in order to give the roadster a short rest and
a luncheon of oats, making a longer halt, of course,
at noontime. The recent Badminton work on driv-

ing states the old English custom in this regard as
follows : —

"Before the advent of railways, fifty miles in a
day was not considered too much for a pair of horses
to do, and that in a lumbering travelling carriage.
The rules laid down for such a journey were, to go
ten miles and bait for fifteen minutes, giving each
horse an opportunity to wash out his mouth, and a
wisp of hay; then to travel another six miles and stop
half an hour, taking off the harness, rubbing the horses
well down, and giving to each half a peck of corn.
After travelling a further ten miles, hay and water
were given as at first, when another six miles might
be traversed; and then a bait of at least two hours
was considered necessary, and the horses were given
hay and a feed of corn. After journeying another ten
miles, hay and water, as before, were administered, and
the rest of the journey might be accomplished without
a further stop, when the horses were provided with a
mash for their night meal, and if the weather were
cold and wet some beans were thrown in. This calcu-
lates a pace averaging six or seven miles an hour."

I am acquainted with a Morgan filly, five years old,
that, without any special preparation, travelled last
fall from the White Mountains to Boston, one hundred
and forty-seven miles, in exactly three days, with perfect ease. The first day she went but thirty-five
miles, the second fifty-four, the third fifty-eight. Her
owner furnishes me with the following account of the
last day : —

"I started from Portsmouth at eight A. M., drove
fifteen miles, and stopped for three quarters of an
hour, taking the mare out, rubbing her legs well, and

giving her two quarts of oats. I then drove twelve
miles, and stopped again in a patch of woods for two
hours. The mare had some hay, procured of a neighboring farmer, with three quarts of oats, and was well
groomed. Starting again at about four o'clock, I drove
to Salem, arriving there soon after six, the distance
being about fifteen or sixteen miles. The horse
seemed perfectly fresh, but as my three days would
not be up till eleven P. M. (inasmuch as I started at
eleven A. M. on the first day), I concluded to stop for
dinner. The mare was put into a stable and rubbed
down. Her legs were bandaged, and she was provided with some hay and two or three quarts of oats,
which she ate greedily. At seven thirty she was harnessed again, and came up to Boston as readily as if
she were out for the first time that day. Her eye was
perfectly bright when I arrived, she exhibited no
sign of fatigue, and would doubtless have been good
for twenty miles more."

This was a creditable performance to have been
done so easily, especially as the road from Portsmouth
is flat and sandy. A moderately hilly road is much
less fatiguing. The same filly, it may be added, when
but three years old, made seventy miles in a day of
twelve hours, drawing a skeleton wagon. Such a
journey would have ruined most young horses, but
the next morning, when turned out to pasture, she
threw up her heels, as sound and lively as any colt
in the lot.

Another Morgan mare,[1] of similar appearance, being
black, and "a compactly built, nervy, wiry animal of
the steel and whalebone sort," is credited with going

---

[1] The property of Mr. Farnum, of Waltham, Massachusetts.

eight miles in thirty-seven minutes, returning over the
same ground in thirty-six minutes. On another occasion she accomplished forty-three miles in three hours
and twenty-five minutes. This is great roading.

Vermont Champion, a son of Sherman Morgan and
grandson of Justin Morgan, was once driven by his
owner, Mr. Knights, from Concord, Vermont, to Portland, Maine, with a load of pork. The trip down,
presumably in a sleigh, took three or four days, the
distance being very nearly, if not quite, one hundred
and ten miles. On arriving at Portland, Mr. Knights
found a letter that had been sent by stage, informing
him of illness in his family; and the next morning he
started for home, which he reached about eight o'clock
in the evening of the same day. "Old men are now
alive," says my informant, "who saw Champion the
next day, and who state that he looked fit to repeat
the exploit."

But perhaps the most remarkable horse of which I
have been able to obtain a trustworthy account is Joe
Renock, a blood bay inbred Morgan stallion of great
style and beauty, kept for many years at Sherbrooke
in the Province of Quebec. He stood about 15.1
and weighed about eleven hundred pounds. A former owner thus describes him: "He had the handsomest head I ever saw on a horse. His neck was
perfect; so was his body. He had the most beautiful
long mane and tail that ever graced a horse. In
passing your finger through them, the hair felt as soft
as silk. He had as perfect a set of legs and feet as
ever was seen. His legs were of the flinty kind, as
clean and smooth as those of a deer." Like Justin
Morgan, Joe Renock was excellent under saddle.

especially as a charger. Colonel Lovelace, an English
officer, a veteran of the Crimea, who rode Joe Renock
on one occasion, declared him to be the most perfect
saddle horse that he had ever seen. But it is for his
roadster qualities chiefly that I cite him here. Mr.
John Harkness, an old horseman, and, as I am informed on good authority, a truthful man gives the
following account. [1]

"On one occasion I drove this stallion ninety miles
in one day, under adverse circumstances, which I will
relate. I started with him on a journey of a hundred
and fifty miles. It was on the first day of August,
1869. Joe Renock carried about one hundred pounds
of surplus flesh, and was hitched to a phaeton top
buggy, holding my wife and myself. I calculated to
make the journey in three days. I left home at six
o'clock in the morning and drove to Drummondville,
a distance of about fifty miles. I landed in Drummondville at noon of the same day. I am wrong in
saying that I drove him. I should say he pulled me
every inch of the way. He would not pull to fight
his driver, but he would go right up on the bit, and
keep his driver busy all the time.

"I put him up, intending to stop for the night at
Drummondville. After he cooled off, I took him out
and groomed him. After I got through with my job,
I led him out by the halter, and he played around me
like a squirrel. My wife stood on the veranda and
remarked, 'He feels well after his drive.' I told her
to get ready, and we would drive to a place called Moscow, about twenty-five miles farther, as I did not like
to stay at Drummondville.

---

[1] In the American Horse Breeder of April 22, 1892.

"The day was hot, and it was a sandy country, which made it hard wheeling. I left Drummondville at two o'clock, and he pulled me by the bit all the way to Moscow. When I got there the sun was quite high. I then reined him for Sorrell, fifteen miles beyond, and the last three miles were through a sandy pine wood. Here he commenced to rave so much that I was obliged to get out of the buggy at two different times, and hold him by the bit until I rested my arms. So much for Joe Renock, after driving him ninety miles.

"I rubbed him dry, and he was in the stable before sunset. I hitched him up the next morning, and he went up to the bit every rod of the sixty miles, the balance of my journey, and did his last with as much ease as any mile in the trip." [1]

Like most other great horses, Joe Renock derived his energy and strength largely from his dam, who is thus described by the Vermont farmer who owned her: "She was a blocky fifteen-hand dark brown or black mare with white strip and one white hind foot, full of pluck and nerve. No better mare ever trod the green hills of Vermont. I have driven her for hundreds of miles, and followed her for days on the farm. I have known her to be taken up from the pasture and driven seventy miles in a day, and it did not take her all day to do it." Joe Renock, foaled at Poultney, Vermont, about the year 1857, was this mare's last colt, she being then twenty years of age.

The shortest time for one hundred miles is that made by Conqueror, harnessed to a sulky, at Centreville, Long Island, in 1853, which was eight hours.

[1] See also page 200 for an instance of good roading.

fifty-five minutes, and fifty-three seconds. Several
other horses have done this distance in less than ten
hours. Fifty miles were trotted at Providence, Rhode
Island, in 1835, by a horse called Black Joker, in
three hours and fifty-seven minutes. Several horses
have trotted twenty miles within an hour, the first to
do it being Trustee, a half-bred horse. One of the
few defeats that Flora Temple ever suffered was in a
match to trot twenty miles within an hour, harnessed
to a skeleton wagon; "that kind of going on in a
treadmill sort of way," as Hiram Woodruff remarks,
" not being her strong point."

An American trotting horse, called Tom Thumb,
said to resemble a Canadian pony, and owned by Mr.
Osbaldestone, in England, covered one hundred miles
in ten hours and seven minutes, the vehicle weighing
nearly or quite one hundred pounds. An English-
bred mare was afterward matched to accomplish the
same task.   "She was," according to Youatt, "one of
those animals rare to be met with, that could do almost anything as a hack, a hunter, or in harness.   On
one occasion, after having, in following the hounds
and travelling to and from cover, gone through at
least sixty miles of country, she fairly ran away with
her rider over several ploughed fields. She accomplished the match in ten hours and fourteen minutes.
. . . She was a little tired, and, being turned into a
loose box, lost no time in taking her rest. On the
following day she was as full of life and spirit as
ever.  This is a match," Mr. Youatt continues, "which
it is pleasant to record; for the owner had given
positive orders to the driver to stop at once on her
showing decided symptoms of distress, as he valued

her more than anything he could gain by her enduring actual suffering."

No sensible person will care to drive fifteen miles in an hour or seventy in a day, except as a feat; but if you wish to travel forty or fifty miles, it is a great thing to have a roadster who is capable of going seventy or eighty. To ride behind a tired horse is fatiguing and depressing in the extreme, whereas there is a sense of exhilaration in covering a long distance which is yet well within the known powers of your steed. In fact, a good roadster is something like a satisfactory bank account, — your pleasure in his capacity is great almost in proportion as the drafts which you make upon it are small.

# VI.

## SADDLE HORSES.

WHAT are the marks of a good saddle horse? Perhaps the most important one is the possession of "riding shoulders," — i. e. long, sloping shoulders, terminating in rather high, thin withers. Such shoulders are indispensable for a good jumper, as a horse always lands on his fore feet. and they make the animal easy to sit. It was said of Fair Nell. the Irish mare who beat Haleem Pacha's best Arab in an eight-mile race,[1] that "she had such beautiful shoulders. with so much before you, and with such an elastic stride. that it was easy, even delightful, to sit on her, although her temper was hot, and at times she plunged violently."

[1] See page 119.

A saddle horse should have a rather short back, the least bit curved, which is the true Arab formation. Mr. S. W. Parlin has indicated this shape in the following description of Flying Eaton, a noted Maine horse: "While he had a strong, broad loin and excellent coupling, there was a graceful downward curvature of the spine in front of the coupling which gave him in some degree the appearance of being slightly sway-backed, — a conformation often found among the descendants of Sherman Morgan." [1] "Just the curve," writes Mr. Palgrave, describing the Arab horses in the Emir's stables at Haïl, "which indicates springiness without any weakness."

But it must be admitted that the rule as to short backs is fairly riddled with exceptions. Very speedy horses, as distinguished from weight-carriers and "stayers," commonly have backs of medium or even greater length; and Whyte-Melville states that the best three weight-carriers he ever knew all had the fault of being overlong in the back.

Other marks of a good saddle horse are short cannon bones, strong quarters and hocks, — it is an old stable aphorism, "No 'ocks, no 'unter," — a neck rather long, so that his wind may be good, feet rather small, so that he may step lightly, and pasterns somewhat oblique and yielding. A short, straight pastern makes a hard gait, and is apt to break down, and a pastern too long or too oblique is an even greater indication of weakness. The pastern of a saddle horse is next in importance to the shoulder. Upon it depends his elasticity, and to a considerable extent his jumping power, and

[1] See page 197.

10

it is at this point that race horses most frequently give out.

A good saddle horse, like a good horse for any other purpose, should be well "ribbed up." A considerable space between the last rib and the hip bone almost invariably indicates a want of toughness. Animals thus built usually require more grain, and are capable of less work, than "close-ribbed" horses. A thin waist also commonly shows a want of strength; but, as I have remarked with reference to harness horses, this is by no means an unfailing sign. The famous steeple-chaser, Emblem, a beautiful bay mare with wonderful shoulders, had no "middle piece," and yet she was a noted stayer. Hempstead, an American gelding remarkable as a jumper, was another instance of a wasp-waisted but strong horse. It may be doubted, however, if in these and in other like cases the want of strength is not supplied by extraordinary courage and resolution. A coarse-bred horse that was also thin-waisted would probably show, as well as feel, a lack of endurance.

A horse with low withers is, generally speaking, unfit for the saddle, especially if he stands higher behind than in front, — a conformation apt to be found both in fast runners and in fast trotters. When such horses have good legs and feet, they can carry a light man without danger of becoming knee-sprung, but weight-carrying is not their forte, and I am inclined to think that they will never trot so fast under saddle as they will in harness; whereas, as a rule, a trotter is estimated to be about three seconds (per mile) faster under saddle than in harness. During one whole winter I rode a horse of this shape, never allowing him to gallop, but often urging him to a fast trot; and yet in all that time only once did he strike the long, rapid gait of which he was capable, and which he would invariably show when harnessed to a light vehicle. This motion, the extended trot of a really fast horse, is very peculiar, and usually not very comfortable to the rider, the hind legs being well brought up under the animal at every stride, and also, in many cases, going wider than the fore feet, so that the man in the saddle feels as if he might be thrown over his horse's head. And yet some trotters step so smoothly that they can be sat close at a 2.30 gait.

If your object in riding is mainly that of exercise, almost any sound, active horse that does not stumble will answer the purpose. If his trot be hard, the more exercise you will get, and the better practice you will have. The worst horses to ride are those cold-blooded, nerveless animals, which, tiring after a few miles, let themselves go, and actually tumble down, unless kept up to the mark, rather than take the trouble to remain on their legs. Many coarse-bred cobs are of this character. They wear a deceptive appearance of strength, have stout limbs and broad chests, but lack nervous energy and courage.

I remember taking a faint-hearted cob, the property of another, from the town in which I lived to the city where he was to be sold at auction on the following day, a distance of fifteen or twenty miles. Before we had accomplished one quarter of the journey, while cantering down a very slight decline. the cob fell. It is no joke to break the knees of a friend's horse, and the sympathetic reader will easily imagine — as I shall

never forget — the feeling of horrid anticipation with
which I glanced at his legs. But fortunately, the
ground being soft, the hair had not been taken off, so
that the cob's selling value remained as it had been.
I remounted, and "carrying his head in my hand,"
rode the rest of the way, divided between the fear of
being late for an important engagement and of spoil-
ing the horse, to say nothing of my own neck. But
when your mount arrives at this condition, when he
feels like a block of wood beneath you, all his elasticity being gone, and especially if he begins to stumble, the better plan is to get off and walk. The most
skilful riding cannot with any certainty keep him on
his legs. However, if your journey be a matter of
life and death, or if you prefer to take the gambler's
chance of finishing it without an accident, your only
course is to maintain a firm hold of the bit,— not a
dead pull, but a "sensational," enlivening pull, and at
the same time to touch up the faltering nag with whip
or spur. If he is allowed when tired to drop into
his natural lethargic condition, he will quickly be
down in the dust.

Stumbling horses will sometimes fall even when
going at a walk; they do so most frequently at a jog
trot, and the likeliest spot for such an accident is near
the bottom of a hill, where the ground still declines,
but, the steepness of the descent being past, the horse
relaxes his attention. "It is not at a desperate 'hiv-
erman' pace, and over very bad roads, that a horse
tumbles and smashes his knees, but on your particularly nice road, when the horse is going gently
and lazily, and is half asleep, like the gemman on
his back."

It is usually thought that high-stepping horses are less likely to fall than low steppers or "daisy-cutters," but this I believe to be an error. Some horses occasionally fall, but otherwise never stumble, whereas a low-stepping horse may stumble frequently, but never come down, always saving himself with the other leg. It is a matter chiefly of legs and feet, and of courage; but a nag who puts his toe down first is almost sure to be a stumbler.

I need not say that the saddle horse, above all others, being necessarily an intimate companion of his master, should possess intelligence and good temper; he should have fine, well-bred ears, a large, expressive eye, a tapering nose, and nicely cut, expansive nostrils. To bestride a lop-eared, coarse-headed beast would give little satisfaction to a person of proper equine susceptibilities. But it is astonishing what small importance professional horsemen commonly attach to this vital matter of intelligence, the reason perhaps being that they take the purely mechanical view of the horse, considering him merely as a creature who is able, or unable, as the case may be, to get over the ground and to carry a weight. I have known many instances where jockeys or dealers, being employed to buy a horse for a customer, have picked out an animal which had all the requisites except the saving one of good sense.

I remember one case in particular where a keen judge of horseflesh was sent to Kentucky for a saddle horse. The man paid a large price and came back with an admirable beast, young, sound, thoroughly taught, good in harness as well as under saddle, fast, and, except for the shape of his head, very handsome.

But the head was ill-shaped, and the eye had the uneasy, glassy, indescribable, but easily recognized look of a stupid and dangerous animal. Such he proved to be; and after being half starved to "keep him down," and then "fed up" to make him look fat again, he brought matters to a crisis by running away. Whereupon he was sold at auction for about one twentieth of the sum that he had cost.

Only the other day, a trainer of many years' experience assured me that there was nothing in the expression of a horse's eye, — nothing at all; the only significance was in the shape of the head. Now the shape of the head is significant, but not more so than the eye.

The horse that I have described as suitable for the saddle is, as the reader will doubtless have perceived, most apt to be found among half-bred animals,—meaning those that have some fraction. it may be a very large or a very small one, of thorough-bred blood.— and the nearer thoroughbred, the better.

Good carriage horses are often described as hunters of a large pattern; the Cleveland Bays were part-bred horses; the Yorkshire Coach Horse Society counts a thoroughbred out cross ("two in and one out") as not disqualifying the animal thus bred for recording in its book; and in general it may be said that good horses for riding and driving are half-breds.

But, as no horseman needs to be told. the half-bred is often a very poor animal, combining the defects of both strains and this is especially the case when all the hot blood is on one side, and all the cold blood on the other. The produce of a thorougbred horse and a cart mare is sometimes a grand beast, with the spirit of its sire and the strength of its dam; but more often animals thus bred are leggy, slab-sided, and nerveless.

The same result is likely to follow when two horses of about equal breeding, but of very antagonistic qualities, are mated. General Knox and Lady Thorne were nearly, if not quite, the best trotting horse and mare of their day. Lady Thorne was out of a thoroughbred mare by a horse bred in the same way. The dam of General Knox was also by a thoroughbred. But General Knox was a coarse, stout-limbed, rather heavy-headed horse, whereas Lady Thorne had the quality of a thoroughbred, and, as might have been expected, their foal, General Washington, proved to be a rangy, weedy beast, far inferior to his sire and dam. However, some of General Washington's colts are very fine animals, the inherited excellence which was latent in him having appeared, as often happens in similar cases, in the second generation.

When it comes to racing. or steeple-chasing, and even to fox-hunting in the fast counties of England, something different is required. Of late years the best steeple-chasers have commonly been thoroughbred; and it is said that no horse with the slightest taint of cold blood in his pedigree can now live in "the first flight" of the Quorn hunt.

It is a fact of some interest, that during the past forty years or so both fox-hunting and prize-fighting have undergone a similar change, in each case a long, slow process having been replaced by a short, quick one. The newly invented "hurricane rushes" correspond to the tremendous bursts of speed with which the Leicestershire riders now chase the fox; and the loser's fate in a modern prize-fight is commonly de-

cided in about the same time that it takes to kill the
speedy Reynard of the present day.

The time may come when the universal horse for
harness or for saddle will be a thoroughbred. "Thoroughbreds," says one writer in the Badminton volume
on Racing, "are the best for all kinds of work, except
of course that of heavy draught horses," and thoroughbred mares have been used for ploughing on at least
one farm in England. The thoroughbred horse is not
necessarily a long-legged greyhound kind of beast.
Even at this day, though not so commonly as when
the process of developing a racing machine from
Eastern stock began, thoroughbreds are found with
comparatively short legs, well rounded bodies, necks
inclined to arch, and in general not devoid of those
graceful curves which, in the modern racer, have
mainly been supplanted by straight lines. Such a
thoroughbred is Mr. Burdett-Coutts's hunter sire, True-
fit; such also is the well known American horse, Duke
of Magenta; and such was Glencoe, one of the most
beautiful horses ever imported to this country.[1]

In this neighborhood most men who ride own but
one saddle horse, and commonly their stud begins and
ends with him. He should be, therefore, an all-round
horse. fit to carry his master from a suburban home to
the city, and to do this day after day on hard roads.
He should also be ready at all times for a spin across
country, — a fast trotter, a fairly good jumper, and.

---

[1] Glencoe was foaled in 1831, and imported in 1837. He was
by Sultan: dam, Trampoline by Tramp; second dam, Web by
Waxey. Many trotters, including Jay-Eye-See with a record of
2.10, trace to Glencoe through their dams. His thoroughbred son,
Rifleman, is the sire of Colonel Lewis, whose record is 2.18¾.

above all, an intelligent, docile, sound, tough horse. But we see very few such. Some men ride pretty, fat cobs, that have little " go " and no endurance ; others are mounted on tall, bony, blood-like animals, good for hunting, but not suited to a daily journey over macadamized roads and pavements. Others again ride long-legged, coarse-jointed, coarse-haired chargers that have no indication of good breeding except the quite unnecessary amount of daylight which is visible beneath them.

What is wanted is a compact, elastic, rather small horse, with legs and feet of iron. Such pre-eminently is the Arab, and it cannot be doubted that, if Arabs of pure lineage could be bred in this country, they would furnish a useful and popular breed of saddle horses. Their inferiority to thoroughbreds as racers is incontestable, but beside the point.

In India, imported English and Australian horses give the Arabs, three stone, country-breds two stone, and Capes fourteen pounds. "These country-bred horses," says an English officer, "having a strong dash of thoroughbred English blood, are generally faster than Arabs, for say six furlongs, but do not stay as well." The same authority, after speaking of the comparative slowness of Arabs, continues : "Yet, for all that, there is a great deal to be said in their favor as high-mettled racers. They are, as a rule, game, honest, and grand stayers ; so sound that an inexperienced owner may take all sorts of liberties with them in their training without breaking them down ; docile and easy to ride." Another peculiarity of Arab horses, which shows the homogeneousness and fixed character of the breed, is the fact that they can all run about equally fast.

The endurance of the Arab is probably greater than
that of any other living horse. A match against time
was won in 1840 by an Arab horse at Bungalore, in
the presidency of Madras, who travelled four hundred
miles in four consecutive days. Mr. Frazer, in his
" Tartar Journeys," relates that an Arab carried him
five hundred and twenty-two miles in six days, rested
three, went back in five, rested nine, and returned in
seven. What thoroughbred could do as much? But
I am bound to add, some authorities think that the
thoroughbred horse can outstrip and outlast the Arab
over any distance. Mr. S. Sidney, for example, a
very high authority, believes this to have been true
of Fair Nell, the Irish mare already mentioned.

The following description of Leopard, one of the
two Arabian horses presented to General Grant by the
Sultan in 1876, indicates so clearly certain points of a
good horse, and especially of a good saddle horse, that
I cannot forbear quoting it in full.[1]

"In front of the stables (at Ash Hill, near Washington), upon a beautiful table-land overlooking acres of
meadow pasturage with scattered barns and hay-ricks,
was a level spot of close fine turf, splendid to show
horses upon. Upon this the colored groom Addison
led out the Arab, Leopard. He was a beautiful
dapple-gray, fourteen and three quarters hands high;
his symmetry and perfectness making him appear
much taller. As he stood looking loftily over the
meadows below, I thought him the most beautiful
horse I had ever seen. With nostrils distended and
eyes full of fire, I could imagine he longed for a run

---

[1] It is taken from Mr. Randolph Huntington's interesting book,
"General Grant's Arabian Horses."

in his desert home. Addison gave him play at the halter, and he showed movements no horse in the world can equal but the pure-bred Arabian. He needed no quarter-boots, shin-boots, ankle-boots, scalping-boots, or protections of any kind; and yet the same movements this Arabian went through would have blemished every leg and joint upon an American trotting horse, even though he had been able to attempt the impossible activity.

"He was now brought to a stand-still that I might examine him; not cocked on one leg, pointed in another, or straddled, as our horses would be after such violent exercise, but bold and erect on all fours, as when first led out.

"I began at his head. The ear was very small and fine, much as it was in old Henry Clay. The muzzle was small and fine, the mouth handsome and lips very thin, as were the nostrils. Between the eyes he was full and broad, while the eyes themselves were large, brilliant, and of the speaking kind. I lifted the lids, and they too were thin and delicate, not coarse and heavy, as in our big-mouthed, thick-lipped, long, heavy-eared American horse. The jowls were very deep, but wide between (the peculiarity so much condemned in Henry Clay). The windpipe was large and free, running low into the breast. The neck was beautifully arched, giving the impression of a thin crest, which I expected to find from numerous writers' reports. Imagine my surprise when, upon running my hand from between the ears down, I found a big, thick, hard crest,[1] as if a three or even four inch new cable rope were inside. This was exactly such a

[1] This is a characteristic of the Barb, but not of the Arab.

crest as was in old Henry Clay, — it lopped over like
a bag of meal with old age; and I remembered having
an old Messenger stallion, years before, with exactly
such a crest, which, falling over in the same way with
age, was a great torment to my pride.

"The fetlocks could not be found; there were none.
The warts at point of ankle were wanting, and the
osselets were very small.   Large coarse osselets show
cold, mongrel blood. . . . The mane was very fine and
silky, falling over so as to cause one to believe the
crest was a knife-blade, with blade up, for thinness.
. . . Now for his gaits.   I had Addison lead him on
the walk to and from me, say a distance of two or
three hundred feet, that I might see the position of
his feet in walking.   There was no twisting behind,
nor paddle in front, but straight, clean, elastic stepping.   I now had him pass me at the side, that I
might see his knee, and his hock and stifle action.
From the walk I had him moved upon the trot, and at
either walk or trot every movement was perfect.   The
knee action was beautiful; not too much. as in our
toe-weighted horses, nor stiff and staky, as in the
English race horse, but graceful and elastic, beautifully balanced by movement in the hock and stifle."

It cannot be doubted, I think, that the Arab horse
has no superior for what might be called miscella-
neous saddle use, and in particular for polo.   Many
of the best polo ponies in England are pure Arabs,
and others are partly of Arab blood.   The English
polo players state, moreover, that the Arab bred
ponies are instructed in the game more easily and
quickly than any others.

In this country the first breed of saddle horses was

that of the Narragansett pacers. These horses appear
to have resembled very closely the palfrey of the Middle Ages, and they were developed for the same purpose, namely, as a means of easy locomotion at a time
when roads were bad and vehicles uncomfortable.
The Narragansett pacers were in their heyday about
the middle of the eighteenth century, and they originated, as the name implies, in Rhode Island, not far
from Newport. "They carried," said a writer in
the North American Review many years ago, "fair
equestrians from one to another of the many hospi-
table dwellings scattered over the fields of ancient
Aquidneck in Bishop Berkeley's time."

How these horses were bred cannot now be discovered. There is a tradition, which Frank Forester
seems to accept, that they were of Spanish origin;
and there is reason to think that the place of their
breeding was that long neck of land on Narragansett
Bay known as Point Judith, — the scene of many a
shipwreck. In the latter part of the seventeenth century there flourished one John Hull, a rich and pious
merchant of Boston, at one time Treasurer of the Colony. In a letter written in 1677 to one who owned
the tract just mentioned jointly with himself, Mr. Hull
proposed to shut it off from the mainland by a stone
wall, "that no mongrel breed might get thereon," and
in the enclosure thus made to rear "a very choice
breed for coach horses, some for the saddle, some
for draught."

Mr. Hull, it thus appears, contemplated the rearing
of harness as well as saddle horses, and it is a fact,
gathered from the custom-house records, that carriage
horses as well as pacers were afterward numerously

exported from Rhode Island. The only evidence,
however, that I can find, tending to show that Mr.
Hull's project was carried out is the following in-
dignant and righteous letter written by him some
years later to one William Heffernan : "I am informed that you are so shameless that you offered
to sell some of my horses. I would have you know
that they are by God's good providence mine. Do
you bring me in some good security for my money
that is justly owing, and I shall be willing to give
you some horses, that you shall not need to offer to
steal any."

At all events, the Narragansett pacers had a wide
reputation, and were sold in great numbers. In an
account of the American Colonies, published at Dub-
lin in 1753, and written by a clergyman of the English
Church, we find the following : "The produce of
this Colony [Rhode Island] is principally butter and
cheese, fat cattle, wool, and fine horses, that are exported to all parts of the English Americas. They
are remarkable for fleetness and swift pacing; and
I have seen some of them pace a mile in little more
than two minutes, a good deal less than three."
This last statement is doubtless exaggerated, but not
more so than is to be expected even from a clergyman
writing about horses.

Since the Narragansett pacers became extinct, we
have had no family of horses in New England bred
especially for riding, although the Morgans, of whom
I have spoken so often in the course of this book, are
excellent for that purpose. The trot of the best and
lightest Morgan families is peculiarly fit for the
saddle, being short, smooth, and, above all, extremely
elastic.

This quality of springiness or elasticity is almost, if not quite, the most important one that a saddle horse can possess. Certainly as regards road riding, an elastic trot, whether long or short, is the best gait for pleasure or for exercise, or for accomplishing a distance. No attention whatever has been paid during the past fifty years to the production of a Morgan saddle horse, but the breed still contains the material for a quick-stepping, tough, and showy animal very well adapted for city and suburban use, — what is called in England a "hack." Riding in the rural districts of New England — and this is true in almost equal degree of the Middle, and perhaps also of the Northwestern States — is nearly a lost art. There are whole townships where it would be hard to find a saddle, unless it were some antiquated, moth-eaten contrivance, covered with cobwebs and stowed away in a hay-loft.

The equine interests of New England, Boston excepted, all centre in the trotter. But this was not so formerly. Wherever ten men of Anglo-Saxon blood are gathered together, there will be found two at least who love horses, and to whom trials of speed between horses soon become a necessity. The passion for trotters set in early in the present century, but before that horse racing was common in the Eastern States, as elsewhere; and well-bred horses from Canada were often imported for riding and racing purposes. To this fact, indeed, is due much of the best roadster blood in New England. The Drew family thus arose, and some of the swiftest, handsomest branches of the Morgan family derive, on the maternal side, from well bred mares of English stock brought from Canada and the Provinces.

The sport was to be sure severely condemned by all serious people, and no church-member could attend a horse race with impunity.  Nevertheless horse racing sometimes claimed its victims among the very elect. There is a true story on this head recorded of one Deacon R., of Bennington, Vermont.  The Deacon liked a good horse, and always had in his barn two or three animals that answered this description.  In particular, about the year 1818, he owned one that was known to be a very fast runner; and so, when some wicked sporting men from New York came up to Bennington with a race horse which they offered to match against anything that could be produced in the town, the wicked Bennington boys bethought themselves of the Deacon's horse.  A match was made, to be run off secretly, in the dead of night, and one Martin Scott (who afterward became a gallant officer in the United States Army) was selected to borrow and ride Deacon R.'s runner.  Accordingly, Martin Scott burglariously entered the stable at midnight, muffled the animal's feet, and quietly brought him out and rode him to the track.

The race was over a mile course, and all went well till the home stretch was reached; then the Bennington horse fell back, and it looked as if the strangers would win.  But at that moment the Deacon himself, or his ghost, rose up behind the fence, and screamed aloud, " Put the whip to him, Martin ; put the whip to him, I tell you."  Martin, though seized with a great fear, retained sufficient presence of mind to follow these providential directions.  He put the whip to his mount vigorously, and won the race by a head.  Thereupon Deacon R. appeared on the track.

waving his hat and shouting with triumph ; but presently, recollecting himself and his deaconship, he
went up to the successful jockey and exclaimed, with
every indication of anger, " Martin Scott, you young
reprobate, you have stolen my horse, and if you do
not immediately return him to the stable, and give
him a good rubbing down I shall report you to your
father." And thus the Deacon won a horse race, and
still preserved his standing in the Church. Nevertheless, although riding steadily declined from this
time on, New England furnished some excellent cavalry in the Civil War, mounted chiefly on Morgan
horses which out-travelled and outlasted the larger
but less enduring animals ridden by the cavalry regiments of the West.

The Narragansett pacer being extinct, and the Morgan trotter undeveloped as a saddler, the only riding
horse born and bred in the United States is now to
be found in Kentucky. Kentucky, from the very
beginning of her history, has been noted for well-bred
horses, especially in the " Blue Grass " district. A
scientific person of reputation who made a study of
that region tells us that there are certain products of
the land which indicate infallibly the geological formation. Whenever, he relates, he met a tall, handsome
girl, with a good color in her cheeks, he knew that
he had struck the Blue Grass belt, with its lime-
impregnated soil, and there was no need to pound
the rocks with his hammer, or curiously to inspect
the earth. The girl was sufficient evidence of latitude and longitude ; and with her went rolling fields
of rich pasture, substantial barns, and paddocks full
of high-born colts and brood mares. The State was

settled in 1775, and so early as the year 1802 a Frenchman named Michaux, travelling in this country on a behest from his government, reported of Kentucky that "almost all the inhabitants employ themselves in training and meliorating the breed of horses." And he describes these horses as being "elegantly formed, having slim legs and well-proportioned heads."

Another old traveller, writing in the year 1818, declares: "The horse, 'noble and generous,' is the favorite animal of the Kentuckian, by whom he is pampered with unceasing attention. Every person of wealth has from ten to thirty of good size and condition, upon which he lavishes his corn with a wasteful profusion."

Within the past few months a society has been organized and a stud-book established in the interest of the Kentucky saddle horse, a dozen stallions being named as foundation horses.[1] About half of these stallions were thoroughbred, the other half being pacers of mixed breeding; and this fact indicates the origin of the Kentucky saddler, namely, that he is a cross between the pacer and the thoroughbred. Most of these Kentucky pacers were of Canadian stock, and they are described as "a hardy, substantial race." It was from this same stock that old pacing Pilot, whose son Pilot Jr. has attained reputation as a progenitor of trotters, was descended. There is a close

---

[1] Their names are here put down: — Denmark, by imported Hedgeford; Brinker's Drennan, by Davy Crockett; Sam Booker, by Boyd McNary; John Dillard, by Indian Chief; Tom Hal; Coleman's Eureka; John Waxey, by Vanmeter's Waxey, Cabell's Lexington, by Blood's Black Hawk; Copperbottom; Stump the Dealer; Texas, by Comanche; and Prince Albert, by Frank Wolford

relationship in some cases between Kentucky trotters and saddlers. Thus the thoroughbred John Dillard has sired the dams of many trotters; and not a few trace to Denmark. Denmark, also a thoroughbred, was a black horse of great style and substance, and his descendants, as a rule, take after him in a marked degree. Denmark founded the chief saddle strain in Kentucky. Tom Hal, the saddle stallion, is of the same family as Tom Hal, Brown Hal, and Hal Pointer,[1] pacers of celebrity on the track.

The old-time Kentucky pacer afforded the chief means of locomotion in that State, the highways being scarcely fit for wheeled vehicles. Only a few years ago, it was proposed to build a good turnpike from a certain "back" county to the nearest railroad; and a provident farmer of the old school was called upon to assist the project with a contribution. But he refused. The intention was to build a "twelve-foot" pike; and the farmer rebelled at such extravagance. A three-foot track was wide enough, he declared, for his horse, and anything more was superfluous. "The old saddler," writes a modern Kentuckian, "shuffled along the path where it was level, and went a half trot over the hills. He suited the country folk well in that day, but would be out of place now." The word "shuffling" aptly describes the pace, which is an awkward, inelegant gait. It was the same in the old Kentucky pacers that it is in the modern pacer of the race course, but when the Kentucky half-bred saddler came into being this ugly gait was supplemented by one smoother and more graceful.

---

[1] Since this chapter was put in type, Hal Pointer has paced a mile in 2.05¼.

The modern Kentucky saddle horses are taught the following gaits : — (1.) The flat-footed walk, or ordinary walk. (2.) The running walk. (3.) The amble. (4.) The rack or single foot. (5.) The trot. (6.) The canter. (7.) The gallop.

The running walk is simply the ordinary walk accelerated. An ambitious colt ridden toward home, kept back from a faster gait, but urged to walk more speedily, will gradually fall into it. The action is more springy and pronounced than that of the ordinary walk, but mechanically it is the same. The sensation it transmits to the saddle is a very slight up and down motion. A Kentucky horse will running-walk at the rate of five or five and a half miles an hour, and keep it up all day without fatigue to himself or to the rider.

The amble is a slow pace, both near feet leaving the ground and returning to it simultaneously, followed by both off feet also moving together. The amble is a gait of about four and a half miles per hour, and it communicates to the saddle a slight rocking motion.

In the rack or single foot the feet follow each other at equal intervals (or half-intervals), there being twice as many hoof-beats as there would be at a trot or pace of the same speed. In other words, the two near feet do not strike the ground together, as in a pace, but at regular intervals. The sound of the footfalls is one, two, three, four, instead of one, two, as it would be in the same period of time at a pace. This is the smoothest of all gaits. "You are sitting in an arm-chair." remarks Colonel T. A. Dodge, to whom I am indebted for these particulars, " at a speed of from seven to fif-

teen miles an hour." And he adds : " I once owned a
racker who could do a full mile in three minutes under the saddle, and you could carry a tumbler full of
water in your hand without spilling a drop of it."

The trot requires no description. In this gait the
off fore foot and the near hind foot strike and leave
the ground exactly together, followed by the near
fore and off hind foot.

The canter is not considered perfect in a Kentucky
horse until he can perform it at a rate no faster than
a fast walk. To " canter all day in the shade of an
apple tree," is a well known saying. On this head
an old trainer informs me, " I have taught horses
to canter around a pole which I held in my hand
with one end planted in the ground." A well-broken
Kentucky horse will of course change lead in the
canter, and start with either foot leading, at the will
of the rider.

The gallop is an inartificial gait, and belongs rather
to hunters and to polo ponies than to the saddle horse
proper. " It may be used occasionally," states a high
school enthusiast, " but no one goes galloping along
the road except a Sunday rider."

Of course it is no advantage to have a horse with
all these gaits unless the rider is skilful enough to
keep them separate. If the man is less instructed
than the horse, a sad confusion of paces is apt to
obtain. On the whole, a well-bitted, well-suppled
horse, with a good trot and a good canter, would be
more useful to the ordinary rider than would one of
these highly accomplished saddlers.[1]

[1] The readiness with which Kentuckians accommodate themselves to the New York market may be gathered from the follow-

The Kentucky horses are handsome and docile, and they jump well. Some of them are up to a great weight. I have seen one in particular that weighed about twelve hundred pounds, a smoothly turned, round built horse, of proud and lofty carriage, fit to carry a commander-in-chief; instructed in the movements of the *haute école*, and so thoroughly disciplined that his owner as he sat in the saddle was able to crack an enormous whip over the horse's head without causing him to budge an inch. I have another in my stable at this moment, a coal-black fellow, standing about 16.1, and weighing at least twelve hundred pounds, with a powerful, sloping shoulder, high withers, and a short back, capable of sustaining the heaviest rider. This horse has a long, curved neck, finely cut ears, powerful hind quarters, and a gentleness and intelligence that I have never seen surpassed.

Another type of the Kentucky saddle horse is exhibited in a beautiful little bay mare, called Pea Vine, bred by Colonel T. A. Dodge. She is a tough,

ing humorous remarks, which I quote from a newspaper published in the heart of the Blue Grass region : —

" A new kind of saddler has come into fashion of late, known as the Parker, or New York saddler. A class of business men in the East want something to jolt up their livers and give them a deal of exercise on a short road or in the parks. The gait can scarcely be described, and should be seen to be appreciated. It requires a high degree of intelligence in the horse to enable him to acquire it. He must cross his feet, take short, high steps, and come down hard ; he must go backward as well as forward, sidewise, and obliquely. He must cut up all sorts of didos. The combination of a business man who does n't know anything about riding, a plug hat, and a trained 'Parker' would draw in any Kentucky town almost like a circus. But then we have them. Our horsemen can put up anything in their line that the trade demands."

wiry, nervous creature, always dancing about on her
small feet, and arching her thin neck, but perfectly
tractable. Pea Vine, like the other two horses just
mentioned, goes well in harness.

We have one more breed, if not of saddle horses, at
least of saddle ponies, namely, the broncos. The
bronco, a rat of a horse, with ewe neck, a hammer
head, a short hip, and an easy, loping gait, is supposed to have descended chiefly from Spanish horses
brought to this continent in the seventeenth century.
Privation and cold have reduced him in size, stripped
him of all purely ornamental parts and qualities,
and developed his capacity for endurance.

"The toughness and strength of the bronco," writes
Colonel T. A. Dodge in an interesting paper,[1] "can
scarcely be exaggerated. He will live through a winter that will kill the hardiest cattle. He worries
through the long months when the snow has covered
up the bunch grass, on a diet of cottonwood boughs,
which the Indian cuts down for him; and in the
spring it takes but a few weeks for him to scour out
into splendid condition."

Another writer, Colonel R. I. Dodge, relates that a
pony carried the mail three hundred miles in three
consecutive nights, and back over the same road the
next week, and kept this up for six months without
loss of condition.

"The absence of crest in the pony," Colonel T. A.
Dodge continues, "suggests the curious query what
has become of the proud, arching neck of his ancestor,
the Barb. There are two ways of accounting for this.
The Indian's gag-bit, invariably applied with a jerk,

---

[1] Harper's Magazine for May, 1891.

throws up the pony's head, instead of bringing it down. as the slow and light application of the school curb will do, and this tends to develop the ewe neck. Or a more sufficient reason may be found in the fact that the starvation which the pony annually undergoes in the winter months tends to deplete him of every superfluous ounce of flesh. The crest in the horse is mostly meat, and its annual depletion has finally brought down the pony's neck nearer to the outline of the skeleton." The latter is doubtless the true explanation.

It is astonishing what effect cold and privation have in stunting the growth of horses, and, conversely, how quickly warm housing and abundant food will increase the size of a small breed. Some interesting experiments of this nature have recently been tried with broncos. It was found that colts by a thoroughbred sire and out of a bronco dam grew no bigger than the ordinary bronco when they were subjected to a like degree of exposure and of comparative starvation; whereas colts bred in the same way, but housed and fed in the winter season, grew very much larger. It is a question, however, whether these more delicately nurtured horses will prove as strong and tough as the others.

It is difficult to say what is the relative speed of the bronco. Like any pony, he gets into his stride so quickly that he might for a short distance, as a quarter of a mile, beat a larger horse, even a thoroughbred. But for a mile or more the thoroughbred would be the faster, and when it comes to longer distances, the result would probably be the same. Still, there is some evidence to show that it would take more than an average thoroughbred to beat a good bronco for ten or twenty miles. Many years ago, an army officer on the plains offered to match his charger, a Kentucky thoroughbred, with the swiftest pony owned by a certain Comanche tribe. The Comanches, it should be added, are the best horsemen of their race, being the only Indians who show any fondness, or even mercy, for their steeds, or any skill in breeding them. Their favorite color is the piebald. The chief accepted the offer on one condition, namely, that the race should be for a distance of not less than fourteen miles. This match never came off, but the terms made by the chief are significant of his opinion as to wherein lay the superiority of the bronco.

In another case the trial was actually made. Some Kickapoo Indians, who, like almost all red men, are desperate gamblers, bought a race horse of a white man in Missouri, and took him out on the plains, a journey of many hundred miles, for the purpose of matching him against a certain Comanche pony. They used great care with the horse, carrying with them the grain and hay to which he was accustomed, and they were perfectly confident of success. In fact, they proposed to bet everything that they owned on the result. Each man wore his entire wardrobe on his back, — an Indian, like Lever's Irishman, puts on all his finery at once, — and they converted the rest of their property into a drove of ordinary horses, which they took along to wager with the Comanches. But the Comanche pony won, and the Kickapoo Indians returned on foot, and nearly naked.

In many parts of the West, broncos are driven as well as ridden, and a pair of them harnessed to a light carriage make an excellent team for long journeys. In the early days of California, the fast stage-coaches, famous for tearing down mountain roads and skirting the edges of a precipice, were horsed chiefly, if not entirely, by broncos. But the endurance of this animal as a roadster has been exaggerated. The truth is that broncos are ridden and driven great distances in a day, not so much because they can accomplish the task with impunity, as because they are cheap, and their owners are cruel. If a bronco is ruined by a long drive, it is easy to replace him.

Broncos are commonly intelligent, but they are also apt to be vicious. In fact, the breaking which they undergo, and which has been practised upon many generations of their ancestors, could hardly fail to leave them otherwise than vicious. "Buffalo Bill" has made the buck-jumping of a bronco familiar to the people of two continents. Nor is it easy to make them go safely in harness. A neighbor of mine once hitched to a light road-cart a pony that had been ridden for some years. He took many precautions in the way of straps and ropes, so that kicking was rendered impossible. Finally, when all was ready, he mounted the cart and drove quietly out of the yard. I watched him as far down the road as I could see, and no old horse could have gone more steadily or better than this bronco. But, as it soon appeared, he was only biding his opportunity. When he came to a bridge over a river, which he had often crossed before, the pony without the least warning, jumped the rail, taking man and cart along with him, and dropped the whole establishment in the flood. It was in the spring, and ice was running, but with some difficulty the horse, as well as the man, was rescued; and this was his last as well as his first appearance in harness.

The best polo ponies bred in America are broncos crossed with thoroughbred stallions, and they are raised chiefly in Texas. I am aware that some horsemen believe the pure bronco, in his best form, to be equal in capacity, and even in "quality," to these half-bred ponies, — a fact which they explain by his descent from Spanish horses or Barbs. So far as speed is concerned, this may be true. Pale-Face, an unmitigated bronco from Wyoming, won a race at Boston in 1891; but I doubt the existence of broncos having the quality and docility of the bronco-thoroughbred.

Some of the most charming pieces of horseflesh that I have ever known were half-bred polo ponies. Schoolmaster,[1] winner of all the prizes for which he was eligible at the Boston Horse Show of 1890, is an example. Schoolmaster, a medium-sized brown pony with a plain but good head and an intelligent eye, has the strength of a little cart horse and the speed of a deer. He weighs seven hundred and fifty pounds. His legs and feet are perfect; cannon bones short; hind quarters well let down; and, above all, he satisfies the supreme test that used to be applied by a famous judge of race horses in England, for "*he stands pretty.*" Schoolmaster is "up" to a weight of two hundred pounds, and has carried it for several seasons without sustaining puff or splint. There are few ponies, however, of which so much can be said. Their short, strong backs, and great courage enable

[1] The property of S. D. Warren, Esquire.

them to carry heavy men, but the work injures them. Splints and strained cords, especially, of course, in the fore-legs, tell the tale at the end of a season.

A good part of Schoolmaster's power — and in a less degree this is true of polo ponies generally — lies in the muscles of his back. These are so powerful, that when he shies, or even meditates doing so, the rider feels as if there were a group of radiating steel springs beneath the saddle, which, if their full power were expended, might shoot him off into space. Schoolmaster, however, is a very tractable animal; he has been known to run away out of high spirits, but by a good rider he is easily controlled with a snaffle, or even with a straight bit. In fact, the tempers and dispositions of these half-bred polo ponies are almost invariably good. They are high-strung, nervous, and extremely sensitive. requiring very gentle treatment. I have known one that would tremble if a horse sneezed in the box next to her. Indeed, so far as mental qualities go, the thoroughbred element seems completely to predominate in their composition. But they are not so tough as might be expected, being poor eaters of hay, and rather sensitive to cold. I have sometimes thought that their manner of life at the East does not suit them. In their colthood, at the West, they live outdoors the year round, wear no blankets, and get little if any grain. It may be that the change, often a sudden one, to the housing, blanketing, and high feeding which they receive here, tends to impair their stoutness.

Broken to harness, these American polo ponies go well and steadily, and their short, easy trot, closely resembling that of the Morgan horse, carries them

over the ground at a rate which few larger horses
can equal for a long distance. As a rule, they are
not, of course, fast trotters. but I know of one, a
half-bred roan pony, with a beautiful blood-like head
and sloping rump, that has the big, wide gait of a
true trotter. This pony, I have no doubt, could trot a
mile in three minutes or better, and he is also a fast
runner and a good jumper. Occasionally, one finds
among these half-bred ponies one with a longer back,
lower-carried head, and longer neck than are common,
looking exactly like a diminutive race horse. I have
ridden one such, a chestnut mare, extremely nervous,
thin-waisted, long and low, a sort of toy thoroughbred, highly intelligent and capable of being tamed
and taught like a pet dog. But this pony is nearly
clean bred.

A writer in the recent Badminton volume on Riding states that in selecting a polo pony the object
should be to get one resembling as closely as possible
a race horse *in petto*. It is dangerous to differ in
any degree from so high an authority, but I should
have thought that the ideal polo pony, though in
other respects resembling a thoroughbred race horse.
is shorter in the back. Certainly the work is so different that some difference in construction might be
presumed to exist. The polo pony must be a weight-
carrier. It is notable, also, that the portraits of superior polo ponies given in the Badminton volume
represent, most commonly, short-backed animals ; and,
finally, such is the shape of the Arab and of the Barb,
— both of which breeds furnish excellent polo ponies.

The training of saddle horses is a matter with
which I shall not attempt to deal. inasmuch as it has

recently been treated by more than one good writer and thorough horseman.[1] American horses are as a rule so intelligent and well disposed that they are easily taught to carry a man, though to educate any horse in the niceties of the art requires a master hand. The chief difficulty, especially if the animal be at all nervous, is to teach him to stand still while being mounted; and this should be a long, cautious process. Mount him first in the stable, with the groom holding him by the head. After a time, let him stand free while you mount; and, later on, let the man hold him outside, near the stable and facing it, while you get on. And so by degrees accustom him to be mounted in the open.

It is a great mistake to try experiments in this or in any other matter with a green horse. I remember that many years ago, riding a young untrained horse alone at night, it occurred to me that, if I got off, it might be difficult to get on again. From this obvious reflection, it was but a step, in my own mind, to a well-grounded suspicion that I was afraid to try. And this being settled, — in that awful forum which we all carry about within us, — it appeared absolutely necessary that I should dismount then and there; and so off I jumped. Getting back was, as I anticipated, no easy task, but after much backing, shifting, and circling about the road on the part of the horse, I put foot in stirrup and was in the act of throwing my right leg over the saddle. Just then.

[1] The reader is referred to the Badminton volume on Riding and Polo; to "Patroclus and Penelope," by Colonel T. A. Dodge; to "Modern Horsemanship," by E. L. Anderson; and to "Horsemanship for Women," by T. H. Mead.

however, most inconveniently, the beast started on a dead run, and I found myself clinging to his neck. This was bad, but worse followed, for the animal kicked up behind, and shot me off so that I turned a somersault, and fell on my back in the highway. However, I pulled myself together, walked homeward a mile, the horse having preceded me, found him grazing, and, leading him up to a convenient hen house, got on, to my surprise, very easily. That same night I mounted the same horse again, first in the stable, then in the yard, and finally, with some difficulty, in the street; but for months, if not for years afterward, he was apt to resist my ascent to the saddle.

This misadventure taught me two lessons, both of which I commend to the youthful reader. The first is, that, in mounting a horse disposed to be fractious or restive, the main thing is to have a good hold on the reins, and to be prepared to keep him in check if he shows any disposition to bolt. I do not mean by this that you should hang on to the bit and drag yourself into the saddle by means of the reins. Nothing could irritate the horse more than that, or tend more to spoil his mouth. But you should have a short, firm hold of the reins, and be ready, mentally, to pull him up if he should start. In mounting such horses, it is important to move quickly and quietly; any delay or clumsiness, or irresolution, might easily convince the horse that you were his inferior at the game.

The second and more general lesson, already indicated, that I learned from my nocturnal experience is the folly of forcing matters with young horses,

or of attempting feats out of mere bravado, though
one's self be the only spectator. The true rule is
neither to go out of your way to meet danger, nor
to decline the opportunity when it comes. Anybody
who is much in the saddle will sooner or later find
an occasion to test his mettle; and if one have the
happiness to play polo, or, more especially, to ride
to hounds, such occasions will be frequent. Of all
the manly arts, horsemanship is the one where mere
strength and size count the least, and skill and courage the most.

A small, weak man with "hands" can manage a
beast which a big, strong man without them cannot
keep from running away. On the other hand, muscle
and endurance have full scope in the saddle. Assheton Smith used to tumble his hunters over fences too
high to be jumped; for nearly fifty years he averaged
about fifty falls a season, and yet he never received
more than one serious injury. Assheton Smith was
a born fox-hunter; but other men, handicapped by
nature, have shown their prowess in the saddle. To
think of Anthony Trollope, riding "straight," though
old and half blind, and sounding, as he humorously
said, the depths of every ditch in Essex, — to remember such achievements is to raise one's standard
of human courage and pertinacity.

The late R. H. Dana used to say that every man
ought at least once in his life to face death. For the
modern man, sport must commonly supply, if not
a proximity to death, at least a certain hardness of
experience which in former ages war, or travel, or
tournaments, or duels afforded. There is a keen joy
which civilization seems to whet, rather than to

deaden, in physical exertion, even in physical fatigue, still more in the agony of a contest. It is good and pleasant to put on the gloves and face an antagonist some ten pounds heavier than yourself, who would not hesitate to send in a stinging straight counter on the nose, if you gave him the opportunity; the sensation of being thrown absolutely on your own resources under these circumstances is exhilarating and wholesome; it is good, also, to handle a shell in rough water, with the consciousness that the least mistake or flurry on your part would serve to capsize or swamp your frail craft; and good is it — nay, best of all — to bestride a young and fiery horse, whose safety as a vehicle depends upon your power to grip him with leg and knee, and to guide and restrain him with a firm, light hand.

# VII.

## CARRIAGE HORSES AND COBS.

A SCIENTIFIC person once declared — and Mr. Ruskin scornfully rebuked him for the assertion — that the amount of coal consumed in any given country will measure the degree of civilization to which it has attained. The same remark has been made in regard to sulphuric acid, and doubtless it could be applied to many other commodities with that mixture of truth which is sufficient for an epigram. Of carriage horses, for example, it might be said that their quality (if not their quantity) is an index of civilization; for the carriage horse changes his character from century to century, almost from year to year, as wealth and skill augment, as highways improve, as vehicles become lighter, as railroads are brought into play, as people use their steeds for pleasure and for show rather than for long and necessary journeys. When Horace Walpole paid an electioneering visit to the country in 1761, after an absence of fifteen years or so, he found that a great improvement had taken place, and he explained it as follows: —

"To do the folks justice, they are sensible and reasonable and civilized; their very language is polished since I lived among them. I attribute this to their more frequent intercourse with the world and the capital by the help of good roads and post chaises, which, if they have abridged the King's dominions, have at least tamed his subjects."

The primitive carriage horse was a pony, unacquainted with grooming, ignorant even of the taste of oats; and the vehicle that he drew required no roads, a path through the forest sufficing for its progress. And yet, oddly enough, this ancient vehicle is still employed in this country. Within a few months of the present writing, I have seen it conveying a squaw and a papoose around the circus ring; and the red men have constructed it in that identical form for centuries, and still use it in some of the Western reservations. This woodland carriage is made, as doubtless the reader knows, by taking a couple of long poles, and affixing them to the horse's neck in such a manner that they drag on the ground behind his heels, the load being fastened on the end of the poles.

Next to these tepee poles, as the Indians call them, or *trainaux* in the French Canadian tongue, came, in this country, the sledge of the Appalachians. There are old men still living in the mountains of Kentucky and of Tennessee who have never even seen a wheeled vehicle. They use, all the year round, a sledge made of bent saplings fastened with wooden pins and rawhide thongs.

The invention of the solid disk-wheel was a stroke of genius which should have immortalized the name of its author, and yet history records neither that nor his nationality. It is certain, however, that he lived thousands of years before the Christian era. The disk-wheel being in use, ingenious men gradually punched holes in it to reduce the weight, until at last they arrived at the modern spoked wheel. Centuries more elapsed before anything that can be dignified with the name of carriage was built. It was about the beginning of the thirteenth century that carriages were first used by the nobility in England; and the roads were so bad and the vehicles so heavy that they were of little service until toward the end of the sixteenth century. A contemporary account of the city of London, written in 1550, speaks of the streets as being even then "very foul, full of pits and sloughs, very perilous and noxious." Fifty years later, coaches had become so numerous that a bill was introduced in Parliament to restrain their use, one argument in its favor being that the watermen were losing custom because people travelled by the road instead of by river. This bill was rejected, but in 1660 Parliament reduced the number of coaches in London from two thousand to four hundred. About the same time, the present custom of driving for pleasure and for show in Hyde Park was established.

But until the end of the seventeenth century coaches and chariots must have afforded very rough riding; for springs were not invented till about 1665, and in their first form they appear to have mitigated but slightly the jolting of the vehicle to which they were applied. Pepys speaks of riding in a carriage thus equipped belonging to Colonel Edward Blount, which Pepys found "pretty well, but not so easy as he pretends."

How far from easy the seventeenth century carriages must have been is shown by the numerous crude inventions that were made from time to time with the view of improving them. Evelyn, for example, in the year 1665, records the following in his Diary : —

"Sir Richard Bulkeley described to us a model of a chariot which he had contrived, which it was not possible to overthrow in whatever uneven way it was drawn, giving us a wonderful relation of what it had performed in that kind, for ease, expedition, and safety ; there were some inconveniences yet to be remedied : it would not contain more than one person, was ready to take fire every ten miles, and, being placed and playing on no fewer than ten rollers, it made a most prodigious noise, almost intolerable. A remedy was to be sought for these inconveniences."

If this astonishing vehicle was really considered wonderful for "ease and expedition," — and Mr. Evelyn was not given to irony, — it may be imagined what were the qualities of the ordinary chariot, upon which it was supposed to be an improvement.

But whatever the ancient carriage lacked in comfort, it made up in splendor. It was richly decorated, painted in gay colors, emblazoned with pictures, and fitted with hangings and cushions of silk and velvet.

On May-day, in particular, it was the custom for everybody who owned a coach to go abroad in it with such display as his means and taste would permit. The first time when Pepys took part in this fashionable amusement was in the year 1669. Shortly before, he had purchased a fine coach, and had it painted in yellow and silver, and he had also paid a visit to the horse-market at Smithfield of which he wrote, — and there is nothing archaic in the remark, — "Here do I see instances of a piece of craft and cunning that I never dreamed of concerning the buying and choosing of horses."

Pepys had defended himself against the wiles of the jockeys by taking along one Mr. Ned Pickering, a gentleman whose counterpart might easily be found at the present day. Mr. Pickering, younger son of Sir Gilbert Pickering, was bred to the law, but seems never to have followed that or any other profession, having picked up a living in devious ways. Roger North speaks of him as "a subtle fellow," — the very description of a successful Jock. And this subtlety appears to have grown upon Mr. Pickering with years, — perhaps by reason of too frequent visits to Smithfield, — for toward the close of his life he tampered with a will made by Sir John Cutts, and, being detected, narrowly escaped imprisonment for the offence.

By advice of this connoisseur, Pepys bought a pair of fine black horses at a cost of £50, and the bargain seems to have been a good one, for the Diary thereafter records nothing but satisfaction with the steeds, and in due course Pepys made Mr. Pickering a slight present in recognition of his services.

The new coach-owner thus describes his first May-day parade: "And so anon we went along through the town, with our new liveries of serge, and the horses' manes and tails tied with red ribbons, and the standards gilt with varnish, and all clean, and green reines, that people did mightily look upon us; and the truth is I did not see any coach more pretty, though more gay than ours, all the day." But this was not his first appearance in Hyde Park in his own coach. That occurred a few weeks before, and Pepys has described it thus: "Thence to Hyde Park, the first time we were there this year, or ever in our own coach, where, with mighty pride, rode up and down, and many coaches there; and I thought our horses and coach as pretty as any there, and observed so to be by others."

Later still, toward the middle of the eighteenth century, began that very great and rapid improvement — noted, as we have seen, by Horace Walpole — in highways, vehicles, and horses, which increased the rate of travel from four or five to twelve miles an hour, and culminated with the introduction of railways.

The carriage horse, it need scarcely be said, became lighter and more active according as the weight that he had to draw, and more especially the friction of the roadways, diminished. Originally he was simply a beast of burden. the first English carriage horse being of the old black cart or shire horse strain, a huge, ungainly animal, with a big head and shaggy fetlocks. Contemporary with the cart horse coachers were the "running footmen," with their wands of office. The chariots which they attended progressed

so slowly that these functionaries could easily go
ahead, when necessary, and engage apartments and
refreshments at the next inn where a stop was to be
made.  They were also extremely useful in putting
their shoulders to the wheel, when, as often happened. the vehicle stuck in a rut or in some "perilous slough."  Later, in the seventeeth century, many
Flemish mares were imported to England for carriage
horses.  They had more style and quality, but lacked
endurance, as Gervase Markham pointed out in his
well known work.  The cream-colored coach horses,
which are still bred in the Queen's stables, though
they have seldom been used since the death of Prince
Albert, are descended from the same strain.    In
France, the Norman breed furnished the carriage
horses of the sixteenth and seventeenth centuries,
and one writer speaks of the "richly mottled grays"
that drew the coach of Richelieu.

It is an apt illustration of the conservatism which
prevails in, or perhaps more correctly is an essential
part of, forms and ceremonies, that the state carriage
horse of England has always been a century or so
behind the times.  Shire horses were used to draw
Queen Anne's coach, though they had been given up
by private persons for many years before she came to
the throne; and in the same way, during the present
reign, the Hanoverian horse has held a place in the
royal stables to which he is entitled only on the
score of antiquity.  Another similar example was to
be found, until lately, in the steeds that horsed the
chariots of the Roman cardinals.  These too were of
Flemish origin. "of great size, as fat as prize oxen,
proud and prancing at starting, — all action and
no go."

As the Flemish mare succeeded the shire horse, so the Cleveland bay succeeded and vastly improved upon the Flemish importation. Cleveland bays are still bred, constituting with their cousins, the Yorkshire coach horses, and with the stout fast-stepping hackneys, the three strains of harness horse now to be found in England. I shall have a word to say about them all.

The Cleveland bays originated, as the name imports, in Cleveland, a district of the East Riding of Yorkshire, and they date from about the middle of the eighteenth century. Remotely, they sprang from a cross between the native black cart horse, already mentioned, and the thoroughbred; but the type became a fixed one, and is thus described by Frank Forester : —

"The Cleveland bay, in its natural and unmixed form, is a tall, powerfully built, bony animal, averaging, I should say, 15 hands 3 inches in height, rarely falling short of 15$\frac{1}{2}$, or exceeding 16$\frac{1}{2}$ hands. The crest and withers are almost invariably good; the head bony, lean, and well set on. Ewe necks are probably rarer in this family than in any other, unless it be the dray horse, in which it is never seen. The faults of shape to which the Cleveland bay is most liable are narrowness of chest, undue length of body, and thinness of the cannon and shank bones. Their color is invariably bay, rather on the yellow bay than on the blood bay color, with black manes, tails, and legs. They are sound, active, powerful horses, with excellent capabilities for draught, and good endurance so long as they are not pushed beyond their speed, which may be estimated at from six to eight miles an

hour on a trot, or from ten to twelve — the latter
quite the maximum — on a gallop, under almost any
weight."

But the Cleveland bay did not long continue in his
original form; there were more and greater infusions
of thoroughbred blood, so that he became "finer,"
more speedy, a little longer of limb, and in all respects a superior animal for the coach and the saddle.
The country gentlemen were great breeders and users
of Cleveland bays. "A squire," it is said, "of two or
three thousand a year, in the midland or northern
counties, did not consider his stable furnished without five or six full-sized, well-bred coach horses";
and if he went a journey of fifty or seventy-five
miles, he would be conveyed not only in his own
carriage, but by his own steeds. Noblemen counted
their carriage horses by the score; for in those
days they travelled in some state. Six-in-hand for
gala or ceremonious occasions, and four for every-day
purposes, were the usual number. But times have
changed. "The old duke always journeyed to London with six post chaises and four, attended by out-
riders. The present man comes up in a first-class
carriage with half a dozen bagmen, and sneaks away
from the station in a brougham. smoking a cigar."
The reader will remember that even Sir Pitt Crawley,
most penurious of men, was met by a coach and four
at his park gates, where he and his companion Becky
Sharp had been set down by the stage.

County running races also contributed very largely.
though indirectly, to the improvement of carriage
horses. Local magnates liked to be represented at
these races by horses of their own breeding, and con-

sequently there was a wide diffusion of thoroughbred
sires. Under these influences, the improved or half-
bred Cleveland bays lost their distinctive color in a
large degree, chestnuts, iron-grays, roans, and dark
browns becoming frequent among them. Still, there
are in existence even at the present time many Cleveland bays of the correct color, with legs black from
the knee down, and with that "list," or strip of black,
running from the withers to the root of the tail, which
is considered to establish beyond a doubt the purity
of their blood. A dark brown coat with a cinnamon
muzzle was supposed to indicate a tough and hardy
beast, and animals thus marked are seen occasionally
nowadays. Blacks were the least common, this color
being avoided, as suggestive of a cart horse origin, unless it could be traced directly to a thoroughbred sire.
Particular colors came to be associated with particular
districts. Thus, in one neighborhood it would be the
ambition of every carriage owner to have a gray Sir
William or a brown Sir Peter, as the case might be ;
whereas in another district a black this or a chestnut
that would be considered an indispensable inmate of
a gentleman's stable.

The most potent influence in developing the carriage horse was, however, that mania for fast travelling in coaches and post chaises which could be
satisfied with nothing less than ten and even twelve
miles an hour. Anybody who has actually driven ten
or twenty miles at this rate in a light carriage — not
simply heard or talked about it, which is a more common occurrence — can imagine what a task it was for
four horses to travel at such speed, while hauling a
load of four tons or more. Nothing but a strong dash

of thoroughbred blood, and hardly that, could supply
the requisite wind and limb.

One of the best of those colored plates that illus-
trate the road in coaching days shows both what kind
of horse was used, and what was the effect upon him
of the work. It is a picture of " The Night Team "
putting to in the frosty moonlight at a roadside inn,
while a few passengers, muffled to the eyes, shiver
on top of the stage. Three of the four horses, the
wheelers and the off leader, are bays, — broken down,
but still powerful. The ribs clearly show through
their short, nicely groomed coats; their fine, well-bred
heads, topped by small, aristocratic ears, hang mourn-
fully down; their knees are fearfully sprung; their
hind legs are twisted and swollen. Altogether, they
give the impression of having accomplished some
tremendous feats, and of being still able to perform
the like when well warmed to their work. The
fourth horse, the nigh leader, is a gray, young and
sound, but vicious. He wears a broad bandage over
his eyes, to prevent shying at "objects," and two or
three hostlers are struggling to get him within the
traces, while he plunges about with head and tail
high in the air. The fast mail coaches broke down
many good horses before their time; and if anybody
had upon his hands an unmanageable brute, such as
the English system of breaking was eminently fitted
to produce, he doubtless put him into one of those
horse-taming and horse-killing machines.

During the past fifty years many of the best Cleveland bays have been exported, — so many that the
deficiency in the London market has been supplied in
part by carriage horses brought over from Germany.

Not long ago, an an English agricultural journal inquired, with much feeling and with less attention to grammar, "When royalty or nobility wants a pair of upstanding London carriage horses, where goes the thousand guineas that hardly fetches them?" "Not," answering its own question, "to the struggling English occupier, but to the broad expanses of the Continent." Even the great job-masters of London (two of whom supply no less than five hundred pairs of carriage horses each to their customers, not counting single brougham and victoria horses) had recourse at one time to the Flemish horses. They were cheap and good-looking, but so washy and soft, so deficient in bone and endurance, so defective in those very points which Gervase Markham condemned in them two hundred years before, that, after a few years' trial, they were commonly given up by the job-masters.

Closely allied to the Cleveland bays are the Yorkshire coach horses. Separate stud-books are maintained in England for these families, although in many instances the same animal is recorded in both books, whereas in this country one compilation of pedigrees does service for both strains. The differences between them are thus stated by Mr. Burdett-Coutts:—

"The Cleveland bays, in what I may call their aboriginal form, are agricultural horses, with plenty of grand points in their frame, but with no elegance of 'turning,' and without any action, and therefore totally unfitted to produce from themselves alone the big carriage horse. The Yorkshire coach horses have both the qualities above referred to, but they, again,

if kept to themselves, will in a very short time become high on the leg and light of bone, and consequently equally unfitted to draw the weight of a
big barouche or a state coach." What is wanted, he
goes on to say, is "the big harness horse, standing
from 16 hands to 16.2 in height, with the bone and
shortness of leg, the depth and grandeur of frame,
which are in the Cleveland, and are not in the Yorkshire coach horse; with the quality, elegance, and
action which are in the Yorkshire coach horse, and
not in the Cleveland; and with the 'long, elegant
top line,' which is only produced by a combination of
both."

Both the Cleveland bays and the Yorkshire coach
horses are moderately high steppers, and usually
incapable of a really fast trot.

A third family of carriage horses is that of the
hackneys, whose stud-book, like the others just mentioned, is a very modern one, dating from 1882. Their
origin is remotely the same as that of the Cleveland
bays and the Yorkshire coach horses, — a mixture
of thoroughbred and cart horse; but in the hackney
family there is an intermediate strain, namely, that
of the old Norfolk trotter, a fast-trotting, plain, serviceable, moderate-sized beast, that had a great reputation in his day, and from which, in part, many of
our own trotters are descended. The best hackneys
now extant trace back almost invariably to one particular horse, called Marshland Shales, who was foaled
in 1802. He stood 14.3, was of a dun color, and is
said to have descended from the great race horse
Eclipse. George Borrow, in a passage of "Lavengro,"
which I venture to quote here, although it is a familiar

one, tells how he saw Marshland Shales at a fair in
Norwich, when he was a boy, and the horse was old: —

"Nothing very remarkable about that creature, unless in being smaller than the rest, and gentle, which
they are not.   He is almost dun, and over one eye a
thick film has gathered.   But stay, there is something
remarkable about that horse; there is something in
his action in which he differs from all the rest.   As
he advances, the clamor is hushed, all eyes are turned
upon him.   What looks of interest, — of respect!
And what is this?   People are taking off their hats;
surely not to that steed!   Yes, verily, men, especially
old men, are taking off their hats to that one-eyed
steed, and I hear more than one deep-drawn Ah!
'What horse is that?' I said to one very old fellow, dressed in a white frock.   'The best in Mother
England,' said the very old man, taking a knobbed
stick from his mouth, and looking me in the face,
at first carelessly, but presently with something like
interest.   'He is old, like myself, but can still trot
his twenty miles an hour.   You won't live long, my
swain, — tall and overgrown ones like thee never
does; yet if you should chance to reach my years,
you may boast to thy great-grandboys that thou hast
seen MARSHLAND SHALES.'"

The hackney is almost too plain to be called a carriage horse, and yet he has some style, a great deal of
strength, and much more speed than the larger and
more elegant sort.   Many hackneys, indeed, have
showy and beautiful action.   Moreover, having been
bred in something very like its present form for a
hundred and fifty years, the type is more likely to be
reproduced than is that of the Cleveland bay or York-

shire coach horse. An American horseman of national reputation, the importer and owner of some excellent hackneys, writes to me as follows: "The Norfolk and Yorkshire hackneys are a distinct breed of horses; with some thoroughbred and other crosses, of course, but still a distinct breed. They stamp their characteristics on their progeny in a very marked and decided manner, — more marked than any other breed of horses that I know of." And he goes on to describe them: "The Norfolk and Yorkshire hackneys are from 14 hands to 15.3, or even 16 hands high. The average is perhaps 15.1½. A good hackney is a horse of considerable substance, with plenty of bone, fine quality, good length, on short legs, and with riding shoulders. He is a fast and good walker, and his trot is bold, straight, and true, and fast enough for him to go ten to fourteen miles an hour. Many Norfolk and Yorkshire hackneys have trotted better than a mile in three minutes. The fine weight-carrying hacks one sees in Rotten Row, and the splendid teams that are paraded at the meets of the coaching and four-in-hand clubs in Hyde Park, are nearly all hackneys."

Of late years there have been imported to this country many representatives of all these families, the Cleveland bay, the Yorkshire coach horse, and the hackney, — some of them fine specimens, and some of them hardly worth their passage money. In fact, many of the animals exhibited at our horse shows, and sometimes actually winning prizes, as English carriage horses and coaching stallions, have been coarse, clumsy brutes, but a slight distance removed from the cart horse, and frequently not even sound.

The next type of carriage horse to be considered is the French coach horse. A great antiquity is commonly set up for this family by its admirers, but I have never been able to find any evidence in support of their assertions. Moreover, it is difficult to discover exactly what was the origin of the French coach horse. It is commonly said to have been a cross between the English thoroughbred and the Arab. It is certain that the English thoroughbred figures largely in the pedigree, and there may have been infusions of Arab blood; but the French coach horse has a bulkiness of form and a mildness of temper that indicate some other element, and it is probaly that of the ancient and admirable Percheron family. The French coachers are large, handsome horses, usually chestnut, sometimes bay, and occasionally black in color. They have very fine, intelligent heads, rather short necks, broad chests, good sloping shoulders, and the best of legs and feet.

In one respect, that of speed, they are far superior to any strain of English coach horses. In order to satisfy the government test in France, a coaching stallion must trot two miles and two fifths at the rate of a mile in three minutes, and this on a turf track. They are also, as a rule, more gentle and docile than the English carriage horses, but a little inferior to the latter in point of "quality," and not possessed of so proud a carriage. Very few French coach horses have been imported to the Eastern States, but there are many in the West.

The action of a carriage horse should be bold and free; but excessively high action, being incompatible with speed or endurance, is a fault in the true coacher.

13

High-steppers, or park or sensation horses, as they are sometimes called, stand by themselves, — in a small and very expensive class. Their gait is not merely, or even chiefly, a means of locomotion, — it is an end in itself; and very pretty is the effect of their peculiar up-and-down step, especially when they are driven at a slow trot, with all the accessories of a fine equipage. They travel as if they had springs in their hoofs, their knees at the upward stroke seeming almost to touch the musical, well burnished pole chains with which they are often and most suitably harnessed. The high-stepper expresses, so far as a horse can do it, the insolence of wealth. In his prime he would furnish a good text for a sermon, and in his decay he might point the moral of a pathetic tale.

These horses are distinctly for show, not for use. "You may drive your steppers," one authority remarks, "very slowly for the most part, and fast a short distance, if they shine in a fast trot, for two hours or so every day; but if you want to go ten miles out of town and back, you must fall back on a useful pair, or hire post horses."

The best of our sensation horses come from Maine, perhaps because its stony pastures tend to make the horses that run in them step high. The deep snows which prevail during the long winter in that latitude probably have a similar effect. A man wading through snow steps uncommonly high, and it is the same with a horse. Ten years ago a really high-stepping carriage horse was almost unknown in this country, but we raise many of them now; the demand partly causing the supply to exist, and partly calling it forth from its hiding place where it existed before. A "Down

East " farmer raises a colt or two from good stock, which, being turned out for several years on a rocky hillside, and having also, it may be, a tendency in that direction, acquire the habit of lifting their feet particularly high when they trot. The owner looks upon this action as a defect rather than a merit, but fashionable people in New York and Boston think otherwise: it soon becomes known that the dealers who go from farm to farm will pay a good price for horses with excessively high action, and accordingly such horses are bred.

But is there no family of American coachers? Good horses having been raised in this country for at least one hundred and fifty years, is it possible that in all that time we have not produced a typical carriage horse of our own? Alas! no, although we have ample material for the purpose. One of the most brilliant performers that appeared on the trotting course during the season of 1890 was Pamlico, a five-year-old stallion, owned in North Carolina, but bred in Vermont. Pamlico won many races, obtained a record of 2.16¾ in a fourth heat, and proved himself to be a very enduring and speedy trotter. But, besides being a trotter, Pamlico, except for some want of height, is almost an ideal coach horse. He is of a rich bay color, with black points: his back is short, his shape round and smooth, with neither the angularities nor the high rump that are associated with the trotting model; his neck inclines to arch; he has a handsome head, with fine ears, large eyes, widely separated; and, race horse though he is, Pamlico possesses the bold, proud action of a coaching stallion.

Now Pamlico, though an unusual, is not an excep-

tional type, and the same element from which he
derives his coaching appearance is found in a large
proportion of our trotting stock. Pamlico's grandsire
and our most famous trotting stallion was Rysdyck's
Hambletonian, who died about fourteen years ago.
As I have mentioned in an earlier chapter, he was descended in the paternal line from Mambrino, one of
the best and stoutest thoroughbreds that ever ran in
England; but his dam was by Bellfounder, and Bellfounder was a Norfolk trotter of the purest stamp.
Here, then, we have the same element upon which the
English hackney is based.

The Hambletonian family possesses a wonderful
aptitude for retaining its own and assimilating other
good qualities; and when united with strains possessing the nervous energy and the "quality" in which
it is deficient, it rises to a high degree of excellence,
as in the Volunteers, the Almonts, and many others.
The Hambletonian carriage horse is an easy poten-
tiality.[1] Other trotting families, notably the Mambrino Patchens and some of the Clays, contain similar
material.

Carriage horses thus bred would have unusual speed.
They would be a race of trotting coachers, and those
that lacked the fineness of a carriage horse would
nevertheless be strong, serviceable animals, easily sold
at a fair price; whereas the strictly trotting-bred
horse, like the strictly running-bred horse, is apt to
prove good for nothing if not good for racing.

In speaking of Pamlico, I mentioned his bold, high
action. This he does not inherit from his Hamble-

[1] It has been realized to a considerable extent at the Payne
Stock Farm in Hinsdale, Massachusetts.

tonian sire. The Hambletonian gait is a long, wide, distinctly trotting gait. But Pamlico's dam was a Morgan, of the Lambert family, and he derives his showy action from her. Some of the best carriage horses and cobs in the world have been bred in much the same way that Pamlico is bred.

I will state some examples. Fifty years ago there was a big horse in Franklin County, Maine, called the Eaton horse.[1] He was a sorrel, and he weighed 1,450 pounds. Like Rysdick's Hambletonian, he was a long-striding, lumbering beast, and most of his descendants resembled him in these respects: they were fast, but sluggish, and poor roadsters. However, crossed with small, high-stepping Morgan mares, the Eaton horse produced no less than three fine families of carriage horses, cobs, and roadsters, one of which attained distinction on two continents and in three countries.

The first of these families was that of Flying Eaton, a handsome bay horse standing about 15¼ hands, and weighing about 975 pounds. Flying Eaton inherited the high action of his dam. He had a beautiful arched neck, a heavy but fine mane, a tail well carried, a short back, with that slight graceful downward curvature of the spine which is a feature of the Arab formation. Despite his excessive knee action, his motions were easy and elastic; and he was a courageous, tireless roadster. Flying Eaton had great intelligence and one intellectual quality which is frequent in the dog, but less common in the horse, namely, a sense of humor.

---

[1] He was sired by the Avery horse, and he by Bucephalus, a big chestnut horse supposed to be a grandson of Messenger. The dam of the Eaton horse was also said to be a Messenger.

"If a stranger entered his stall," relates a former owner, "he would act as if he was going to kill him, and yet he was perfectly kind. It was only his fun. Whenever a woman entered the stall, he would be extremely gentle. I used to let him loose in the stable, and he would come rushing, stamping up, showing his teeth and acting as if he meant to slaughter me on the spot. But when he reached me he would poke his nose in my face as pleasant as could be, and invite me to stroke him."

Altogether, Flying Eaton was a perfect cob, with speed and endurance such as very few cobs indeed possess.

Within a few miles of the small town where Flying Eaton was foaled, a stout little Morgan mare very much like the dam of Flying Eaton used to be driven by a farmer's boy. She also was a high stepper, and so courageous and ambitious that she never could be persuaded or compelled to walk while in harness. The hills are very steep and long in that neighborhood, but she invariably surmounted them at a lively trot; and on the one or two occasions when a serious attempt was made to moderate her impetuosity, she resisted so strongly as to upset the vehicle in a ditch. This little mare became the mother of a very handsome, high-stepping chestnut colt (his sire being the Eaton horse) which, though weighted with the name of Shepherd F. Knapp, made a reputation in this country, in France, and in England. Mr. Burdett-Coutts speaks of him as being "unsurpassed for pace and action," and he conjectures that this horse derived his gait and style from the Norfolk trotter blood of Bellfounder. But this is a mistake; Knapp, as we have seen, had not a drop of that blood.

Shepherd F. Knapp was larger than his half-brother, Flying Eaton, but much like him in action and in character. He was exported to England in 1864. Afterward he was sent to France, where he trotted a race of two and a half miles and defeated another American-bred horse. The time was 6.14, or a little better than at the rate of a mile in 2.30. Shepherd F. Knapp sired Capucine, the fastest, gamiest trotter ever bred on the Continent, and it is said that his blood has also improved the breed of French coach horses. It is certain that in England, whither Shepherd F. Knapp was soon returned, his descendants and those of his son Washington are among the best hackneys ever raised there, being noted for their beauty and quality, as well as for their speed. It is not unlikely that among the very hackneys recently imported to this country are some that have descended from the little gray mare that used to trot so gallantly over the steep hills of Franklin County, Maine.

The last of the three families which I have mentioned as descending from the old Eaton horse, crossed with Morgan mares, is that of Troublesome.[1] This horse never attained more than a local reputation, and his colts had the common defect, inherited from him, of hitting their fore legs; but his roading qualities were such as to entitle him to mention along with Flying Eaton and Shepherd F. Knapp. Troublesome was a handsome, round-bodied bay horse, of great style and spirit. He weighed about eleven hundred pounds, and was very speedy. His knee action, like

---

[1] Troublesome was sired by the Norton horse, and he by the Eaton horse, out of a Morgan mare. The Norton horse was one of the handsomest horses ever raised in Maine.

that of Flying Eaton and of Shepherd F. Knapp, was extremely high.

Troublesome belonged for many years to "Squire" Abner Toothaker, a prominent man in the little village of Rangeley, at the head of Rangeley Lake, in the backwoods. In those days Rangeley was at least fifty miles from the railroad, and, as the Squire's business often took him far from home, it was necessary that he should have good roadsters. More than once he drove from Bangor to Phillips (a village twenty-one miles "out" from the lake) in one day, although the distance is ninety miles; and there was a standing offer on his part to drive Troublesome one hundred miles between sunrise and sundown, for a bet of one thousand dollars.

Squire Toothaker was a hard-visaged old gentleman, who always sat a little sideways in his carriage, and clucked viciously to his horse out of the corner of his mouth. Once he drove Troublesome to a sleigh seventy-six miles in one short day, besides racing him three or four additional miles against horses which he encountered at a village *en route*. On another occasion he drove from Greenvale to Phillips, a distance of eighteen miles, in one hour. I have traversed this road several times: it is rough and hilly, and, though it descends for perhaps two thirds of the way, there are several long, steep hills to ascend. I know that it takes a good horse to cover this road without distress in two hours. But Troublesome did it in one hour.

Troublesome had a son called Wild Tiger, who also was out of a Morgan dam. The name is an ambitious one, but the horse seems to have deserved it. He too was a bay horse, with four white feet, and a dash of white in his face. His knee action was excessively high; he carried his head high, and, altogether, he showed so much dash and power and spirit, and seemed to go so fast, — he could in fact trot a 2.40 gait, — that he presented a very formidable appearance. It is said that nobody ever looked behind and saw Wild Tiger approaching, without turning aside and giving him the road. Nevertheless, at a gait of six or seven miles an hour, Wild Tiger was temperate enough to be driven by a woman; but when his blood was up, it took a strong man to control him. One winter day, Squire Toothaker drove this horse from Phillips to Augusta, fifty-two miles, in five and one half hours. The snow-drifts near Phillips were so deep that it took him one hour to go the first five miles, so that he drove the remaining forty-seven miles in four hours and a half. Wild Tiger pulled all the way, and came out fresh the next morning.

Now these successes in breeding were not accidental, for, as we have seen, in three separate cases, a family of extraordinary merit sprang from the union of the Eaton horse with a quick and high-stepping Morgan mare. So, also, as I have stated, a similar cross between the Hambletonian stock and Morgan mares has resulted equally well. Why, then, do we not continue to raise such incomparable hackneys as Shepherd F. Knapp, and such tough, speedy, and beautiful cobs as the Flying Eatons? The answer must be that our farmers are absorbed in the pursuit of that *ignis fatuus*, as it commonly proves, the remunerative trotter.

I have spoken of the Flying Eatons as cobs, but perhaps incorrectly. What is a cob? The term is so ambiguous that many stanch horsemen exclude it from their categories. Generally speaking, any small-ish, chunky horse, especially if his tail be cut short, is a cob. The modern hackney usually stands a little too high to be called a cob. The old Morgan horse —of the small type—was a perfect cob, powerful, speedy, docile, enduring, and possessed of great style. He was a saddle as well as a harness cob. The Morgan race has lately been revived, largely with the object of using it as a trotting cross. This purpose is a laudable one, and yet the Morgan cob should also be preserved.

Not long since, in a small New England village, I came by chance upon a perfect specimen of this variety. It was a little bay mare, with a rather long body and round barrel. She stood on short legs. and must have been less than fifteen hands high, but she had the strength, in all the moving parts, of a sixteen-hand horse. Her neck was thick but not coarse. her head small and Arabian in shape, with fine, aristo-cratic, intelligent ears, and an eye flashing with spirit and courage. She was nineteen years old when I saw her, and hollow-backed, but still so spirited as to re-quire a man's hand upon the reins. A cob of this kind is capable of an immense amount of work, and will perform it upon half the food required by a big horse.

The ordinary cob is fat and faint-hearted. well fitted to draw a village cart gently about a village. but likely to go to pieces if put to any severe task. He has the bulkiness of a small cart horse, but lacks the nervous energy needed to make him a good roadster or a good saddle horse. He shines at horse shows, his broad back being admirably adapted for the display of trap-pings and caparisons; and he is a source of wealth to fashionable dealers. A small "blocky" horse with a rather pretty head, weak legs perhaps, and no speed, will go a-begging in the country for $125 or $150; but in the hands of the city dealer, clipped, docked, and hogged, he easily brings $250 or $300. He is no longer a "little horse," but a "cob."

The modern fashion of using cobs and small horses generally for carriage purposes is an improvement in several ways, and chiefly because it is more humane; the wear and tear of their feet upon the pavements being considerably less than it is in the case of a large horse. Formerly the London job-masters had no horses in their stables under sixteen hands high; now they have many, chiefly for single brougham use, from fifteen hands upward, and the same tendency prevails in this country. In fact, the use of small carriage horses followed the introduction of those less bulky and lighter vehicles that are due chiefly to the skill and originality of American builders; but it is doubtful if heavy carriages, even, are not drawn more easily, as a rule, by horses that weigh from nine hundred to ten hundred than by those that weigh from ten hundred to twelve hundred pounds. Such, I have found, is the common opinion of American horsemen, and such seems to be the experience of English coach drivers.

"In these days," writes the Duke of Beaufort, "when the road coaches only carry passengers, and no luggage to speak of, even if there is any at all, we should prefer, for all sorts of roads, short-stepping and small, though thick horses. They are infinitely pleasanter to drive. Anybody who has had the ex-

perience of taking off a big, lolloping team of rather
under-bred horses, who are very tired, and have been
hanging on the coachman's hands for the last two
or three miles of the stage, will understand what a
pleasure and relief it is to feel the quick, sharp trot
of a little team of fresh horses."

When, however, it is a question of hauling a heavy
load, such as an omnibus, at a jog trot on level ground,
then the big horse is required.  There must be a good
weight to throw into the collar.  Moreover, when
horses are well bred and well shaped, neither beefy
nor leggy, but bony and muscular, they can hardly be
too big.  "A pair of fifteen-hand horses," an English
authority writes, "will always have to be pulling at
an ordinary phaeton; whereas the same carriage seems
to roll after a pair of 15.2½'s of its own motion, leaving them light in hand, well collected, and with full
play for their action."

This statement, however, is not, as might be thought,
inconsistent with the opinion just expressed concerning the superiority of small horses as fast weight-
pullers.  They are better for this purpose, not because
they are small, but because they usually have the relative shortness of limb and of stride which are mechanically adapted for pulling a moderate load at a
brisk pace.  When these characteristics are found in
larger horses, as, for example, they often are in the
Percheron family, you have animals that are capable
of great tasks.  A span of Percherons are said to have
drawn an omnibus around a mile track in four minutes; and the gray Norman-Percheron stallions that
drew the diligence from Calais to Paris in pre-railway
days trotted and galloped at the rate of eleven miles

an hour, equalling the speed of their better bred English contemporaries, but not, it is true, keeping it up so long; their stages being but five miles in length, whereas the English stages were ten miles.

But whatever the size of the carriage horse, and whatever the use for which he is intended, — whether he is to be a big, prancing coacher, or a fast-stepping barouche horse, or a useful, medium-sized animal, or a stout one for a brougham, or a showy one for a phaeton, or an all-day nag for a comparatively light carriage and long drives, — whether he is to be a horse. a cob, or a pony, — let him have the inward energy and the outward grace that only a dash of thoroughbred or Arab blood can supply. Half-bred horses are not only the most useful, but the most beautiful, the world over.

# VIII.

## CART HORSES.

EVERYBODY who cares for the beautiful or the picturesque, whether or not he be touched by the true hippic passion, must take an interest in cart horses. They are attractive and pleasant to look upon merely as animals, quite apart from the fact that you can put bits in their mouths, and cause them to expend their strength at the will and in the service of man. The generic difference in this respect between cart horses and racers is well indicated by Mr. Hamerton.

"The race horse," he says, "has the charms of a tail coat, of a trained pear tree, of all such superfine results of human ingenuity, but he has lost the glory of nature. Look at his straight neck, at the way he holds his head, at his eager, anxious eye, often irritable and vicious! Breeders for the turf have succeeded in substituting the straight line for the curve, as the dominant expressional line, a sure and scientific manner of eradicating the elements of beauty. No real artist would ever paint race horses from choice. Good artists have occasionally painted them for money. The meagre limbs, straight lines, and shiny coat have slight charm for an artist, who generally chooses either what is beautiful or what is picturesque, and the race horse is neither picturesque nor beautiful."

Certainly there is some exaggeration here. Many thoroughbred horses are good-tempered and affectionate, and not unduly nervous. In the recent Badminton volume on Driving, there is an account of a young thoroughbred mare, that, having never been in harness before, was attached one day to a dog-cart, and driven thirty miles up and down hill, without showing the least fear or resistance. A thoroughbred of this character commonly has large, luminous eyes, more beautiful than those possessed by any other dumb animal. The delicately cut ear, the round, thin, quivering nostril, and even the smooth and shining coat, — these, again, are surely forms of the beautiful, though not of the picturesque. It must be remembered, also, that among thoroughbred horses there is a great variety of structure and disposition. Many of them are comparatively short in leg, with round body and curved neck. Such was the old type of thoroughbred when the Arab blood from which the present race has chiefly been derived was "closer up," as horsemen say.

In the main, however, Mr. Hamerton's remarks on

this point are just, and the typical thoroughbred especially the typical English thoroughbred, is the nervous, irritable, inartistic animal that he describes.

The cart horse, on the other hand, is a common and appropriate figure in painting.

Among the minor pictures by Turner in the National Gallery at London, not the least interesting is one which represents a stout gray farm or cart horse, taking his ease in the stable, and eating hay from a well filled rack above his head. He stands in a wide stall, heaped with yellow straw and flooded with sunshine, so that the scene is one of equine pleasure and repose, delightful to the human eye on that account, as well as for its harmonious and beautiful coloring.

There is another homespun sight which English artists never tire of representing. It is that of a string of farm horses, whose day's work is finished, at nightfall. With the harness still upon their backs, they have been ridden or led to drink at a cool, elm-shaded stream, where they stand, fetlock deep, some slowly and luxuriously slaking their thirst, while others gaze idly about, their heads half raised above the surface of the water. This is one of those familiar though foreign sights, as to which an agreeable confusion is apt to arise in the mind of an American; for he does not always clearly remember whether he has seen them in reality or in a picture, or read about them in a novel, the truth often being that his knowledge has been derived in each of these ways. Of all equine pictures, none, I suppose, is better known than Rosa Bonheur's Horse Fair. Her noble Percherons, drawn with fond fidelity, are perhaps the most ideal representation of cart horses in the world, and yet no exaggeration of the reality.

Almost all the accessories of the cart horse, his trappings, the uses to which he is put, the place in which he is kept, the loads that he pulls, are picturesque. Most often one thinks of him as an agricultural character, a true son of the soil, who slowly draws home a huge pile of hay, or is found at the plough, turning up long, glistening lines of rich earth. There is nothing spick and span about his stable, but, on the contrary, it is marked by picturesque disorder, — plenty of straw about, the stalls, mangers, and roof tinted a rich brown by the long lapse of time, cobwebs hanging luxuriantly overhead, deep mows of hay, and capacious grain-chests within easy reach to hold his provender.

Nor does the cart horse fail to harmonize with his surroundings in the city, where he receives more grain and more grooming than are obtainable on the farm. His shape, though still round, is here more elegant, his neck takes a prouder curve, and his coat becomes smooth and glossy: fit servant of commerce; solid and substantial as the Bank of England; conscious of his strength, like a merchant of indisputable credit; able to transport the wealth of the Indies from wharves to warehouses, or to draw towering piles of wool from the railroad to the factory. Smaller animals may clatter over the massive pavements of the city, but the cart horse, with his slow, majestic step and proudly bent head, is its proper denizen of the equine race.

Long established and wealthy firms do not hesitate to borrow splendor from the excellence of their cart

horses. Those of the London brewers especially —
the twelve Beer Kings, as they used to be called —
have a world-wide reputation. Formerly, each brewer
had an equine color of his own ; and they were "as
particular," says a recent writer, "about the colors
and matchings of their dray horses as of their own
four-in-hands, or the court chariot pairs of their titled
wives. One was celebrated for a black, the original
dray horse color; another, for a brown, a roan, a gray,
or chestnut team. But at present, such is the demand for horses of this class that they are compelled
to be content with any color, and to moderate the
old standard of height." The brewers' horses, it
may be remarked parenthetically, are fond of beer,
but they are allowed to have it only when recovering
from illness ; at such times it is of service as a tonic.
Horses take naturally to intoxicating liquors , beer,
spirits, and more frequently wine, are often administered to trotters in a long-drawn contest, and with
excellent results. Champagne and soda-water, as I
have stated in a previous chapter, is the pleasant
draught which one famous driver employs on these
occasions.

The "city horses" of Boston, used to carry off
ashes and garbage, have long enjoyed a high reputation for strength and beauty, and the excellent condition which they almost invariably show testifies to
the horsemanship of the official, whoever he may be,
having them in charge. There is in the same city a
noted patent-medicine house, whose stalwart four-in-
hands may be supposed to symbolize the strength of
their drugs. Twenty years ago there used to be a
cigar and candy pedler traversing the mountainous

region in the northwestern part of Massachusetts,
who had a large, gayly painted wagon, drawn by four
stout, handsome gray horses, in which he took a
proper pride; but one night the whole establishment
perished in the flames, the stable where the pedler
put up having taken fire, and the team was never
reproduced.

Between the cart horse and his driver there usually exists, in one respect at least, the ideal relation,
that is, the driver serves also as groom. Man and
horse labor together, and when the day's work is
done it is the driver who gives the hungry and tired
beast his supper, his bed, and perchance his rubbing
down. Thus the horse associates with the man the
pleasures as well as the toils of equine life. I confess that often, vexed by legal problems, I have looked
out of my office window and envied the teamsters in
the street. To be in charge of a good, sleek, fat pair
of cart horses, to live in the open air, to digest anything that you may see fit to impose upon your stomach, to have a face beautifully colored by the elements
and by whiskey, thoroughly assimilated, — is not this
to be happy? There is a certain negro teamster,
who, as it appears to me, stands at the acme of un-
intellectual existence. He drives a very fine pair
of jet-black horses, belonging to a coal merchant.
These horses have taken many premiums at horse
shows, and they bear the appropriate names of King
Cole and Chloe. Evidently the negro is wrapped up
in them. Once or twice, at least, every year, he exhibits the animals at a show or fair, and on these
occasions he has nothing to do except to talk; and I
know of no machine that runs more easily and pleas-

antly than the tongue of a horseman under such circumstances. I discovered accidentally one day that the very color of the horses is a source of pleasure to him. It was in winter, and the streets were heavy with snow and slush. The team pulled a big load of coal so neatly out of the slough, that a bystander was moved to express his admiration at their prowess. "Huh!" exclaimed the colored man, grinning from ear to ear, "you see, Mistah, them horses is *black!*"

The arched neck of the cart horse is a thing not only of beauty, but also of utility. Unless he arches his neck, he cannot be "collected," so as to pull with an economy of strength. Anybody who has ridden much on the front platform of a horse car must have noticed a great difference in the action of different teams — according to the ability of the driver — when a heavily loaded car is to be started. Some horses throw up their heads, and strike out wildly with their fore feet, making a violent effort, and slipping on the pavement. Others, better trained, start more slowly, stepping shortly on their toes, their legs well under them, their necks arched, — and this is the true way.

Here, also, as in the case of road horses, I think that a proper check rein may be beneficial. The check rein of a cart horse, as commonly used, is attached neither to the headstall nor to the saddle, but is simply a bridle rein, buckling on the bit, and passing around the top of the hames. It does not pull the horse's head up, but rather pulls it in, thus tending to arch the neck and to steady the animal. In going up hill even this form of check would be out of place, but on level ground it must, I think, be of assistance.[1]

There is an affinity between the lighter kinds of cart horse — many of whom, such as the Percheron, are very active — and the war horse. The famous Justin Morgan, of whom I have spoken in previous chapters, founder of the great road horse family, was not only the best weight-puller of his time, besides being a fast runner, but, though a small animal, was also much in request for musters and other military occasions, on account of his superb carriage and commanding appearance. A horse of this kind, but weighing two or three hundred pounds more, would have made an ideal charger for a knight of the Middle Ages. The knight himself, his armor, and the armor worn by the horse, were estimated at nearly or quite four hundred pounds. In fact, so heavy and cumbersome were the horseman's accoutrements that two squires were often needed to exalt him to the saddle, and, once overthrown, it was difficult for him to rise without assistance. The suffocation of some hapless contestant who had the ill luck to fall upon his stomach was a not uncommon incident of a passage at arms. To carry a knight in full armor required a beast of great size and strength, and doubtless, like the modern fire-engine horse, he was most usefully employed at one of two gaits, a walk or a hand-gallop. The knight did not ride him, as a rule, except when some martial business was on hand. At other times, his squire bestrode the war horse, the knight himself

[1] Such, I find, is the opinion of an English Vet. R. S. Reynolds, M. R. C. V. S. of Liverpool, who has published a little book called "An Essay on the Breeding and Management of Draught Horses."

travelling more quickly and. comfortably upon his jennet.

By most of the authorities the war horse of the Middle Ages is identified with the old black cart horse, or shire horse, of England. A recent work by Mr. Walter Gilbey is entitled "The Old English War Horse or Shire Horse," thus assuming that they were one and the same; and the late Mr. Walsh was also of this opinion, for he wrote as follows: "From time immemorial this country has possessed a heavy and comparatively misshapen animal, the more active of which [sic] were formerly used as chargers or pack-horses, while the others were devoted to the plough." And he gives the following unflattering account of him: "In color almost invariably black, with a great fiddle-case in place of a head, and feet concealed in long masses of hair depending from misshapen legs, he united flat sides, upright shoulders, mean and narrow hips, and very drooping quarters." Such was the shire horse, — so called because he was raised almost exclusively in the Shires or Midland counties.

Shire horses are still bred, but they have been improved by crossing with Flemish stallions. The London dray horses are mainly shire horses, and since the shire horse is the only purely English cart horse, — that is, the only one of English origin and raised on English soil, — it is fashionable in England to speak of "shire horses," and never of "cart horses." Nevertheless, when a society was formed in that country, some years ago, to improve the breed of agricultural horses "not being Clydesdales or Suffolks," the name "English Cart Horse Society" was taken. The fact is, that hunters, coachers, and race

horses are now raised more numerously than cart
horses in the shires, and hence the term "shire
horse" is inaccurate, as well as somewhat vague.
The old black cart horse, or shire horse, is now most
nearly represented by the black horse of Lincolnshire.

One hesitates to conclude that the beautiful, high-
mettled charger of the Middle Ages, as he has been
described by poets and romancers, was really a dull,
ugly beast, with "misshapen legs," and "a great
fiddle-case in place of a head." Was it such a steed
that carried the Disinherited Knight in his encounter
with Brian de Bois Guilbert? Sir Walter Scott relates, that "the trumpets had no sooner given the
signal than the champions vanished from their posts
with the speed of lightning, and closed in the centre
of the lists with the shock of a thunderbolt"; and
the charger of the Disinherited Knight is described
as "wheeling with the agility of a hawk upon the
wing." It is possible that the English shire horse,
or war horse, was improved by crosses of Arab blood,
for Arab horses might have been brought into England at the time of the Crusades. Isaac of York, it
will be remembered, supplied Ivanhoe with the horse
and armor which he used when he overthrew Brian
de Bois Guilbert, and awarded the crown of beauty to
Rowena; and the thrifty Jew exclaimed to Rebecca,
as they gazed upon the conflict, "Ah, the good horse
that was brought all the long way from Barbary, he
takes no more care of him than if he were a wild
ass's colt!" In this, however, Isaac of York must
have been misreported by Sir Walter. No Barbary
horse or Eastern horse of any description was ever
big or strong enough to carry a knight in armor,

although, as I have suggested, it is possible that the native horse of England obtained some beauty, grace, and agility by an infusion of Eastern blood.

Mr. Gilbey, so far as I know, is the only writer who has endeavored to prove, though others have asserted, the identity of the war horse of the Middle Ages with the old black cart horse of England; and he relies almost entirely upon the evidence of coins and other graven representations. But in such figures much must be allowed for the taste or caprice of the artist, and I suspect that Mr. Gilbey's series might be impugned by others. For the period beginning about the year 1500 he shows the famous white horse of Albert Dürer, that has indeed the characteristics of a cart horse. But in the College of Arms there is preserved an illustrated roll, known as Tournament Roll, commemorating a grand tournament which took place at Westminster on February 12, 1510, in honor of Queen Katherine; and the war horse represented by this roll is a much finer beast than Albert Dürer's. He has a beautifully curved neck, a small, well shaped head, and he is disfigured by no long hairs at the fetlock joints. This picture may of course be idealized, but it is as good historical evidence as the coins produced by Mr. Gilbey. The whole matter is one of not very profitable conjecture, but it is worth remembering that the Middle Ages, during which the war horse was in daily use, constituted a long period, and it is hardly credible that in this time a true war horse should not have been developed, more active, spirited. and beautiful than the shire horse. One writer, indeed, of a date as early as the sixteenth century, speaks of his high action, —

which would be natural in such an animal as I have imagined, but which was never seen in the shire horses.

But, however this may be, the shire horse is a beast of great antiquity, though much improved during the past two centuries. In fact, there are some living members of the breed whose pedigrees can be traced back for at least one hundred and fifty years, and this is more than can be said of any other existing cart horse family. One reason for the improvement is a mechanical discovery as to the muscular action of the cart horse. It used to be thought that he did his work by perpetually tumbling against his collar, as it were, thus bringing his weight to bear, and consequently that his fore quarters ought to be as heavy as possible; it was no harm if his shoulder bone were straight, and as for his hind quarters it did not matter much what they were. But this notion has been exploded, and it is now perceived that a cart horse pulls by muscle rather than by weight, and more by the muscles of his hind quarters and legs than by those of his fore quarters. The structure of a cart horse should therefore bear a general resemblance to that of a racer or trotter, except that his legs should be shorter, his shoulder less oblique, and his rump not higher than the withers.

The Saturday Review once made some excellent observations on this subject, as follows: " There are many points, indeed, which good horses of nearly all breeds share in common. For instance, the following descriptions, taken at random from different newspapers: he is ' thick, level, and strong '; he ' stands on short, well formed limbs, and, like several good horses, he sports curls of hair on his fetlocks'; 'he is of good substance, deep-bodied, and set off by those powerful yet sloping shoulders,' etc. ; 'he has also a deep body, with great muscular development in his rump, quarters, thighs, and gaskins,' — although they might equally apply to certain cart horses, were one and all written of race horses. . . . An excellent judge, again, once wrote that horses 'with strong backs and loins, wide hips, and great muscular quarters, with sound and well shaped hocks, generally win,' — not prizes at agricultural shows, as cart stallions, but races at Ascot."

Another English breed of cart horses, or, in this case, more properly farm horses, was the Suffolk Punch, which once became almost extinct, but has lately been revived in a somewhat different form. These were sorrel horses, smaller and more active than the shire horse, and noted for their docility. They stood low in front, and were disfigured by very upright shoulders; but they were round and stout, and had good heads. Readers of "Sandford and Merton" will recall the delight of Harry when his father, Farmer Sandford, received the present of a span of Suffolk Punches from Mr. Merton, father of the wicked but repentant Tommy. Harry rushes into the house to announce the arrival of two strange and beautiful horses, whereupon, says the tale, the elder Sandford, who in all other respects is represented as a sedate and even phlegmatic person, "started up, overset the liquor and the table, and, making a hasty apology to Mr. Merton, ran out to see these wonderful animals. Presently he returned in equal admiration with his son. 'Master Merton,' said he, 'I did not

think you had been so good a judge of a horse.
I suppose they are a new purchase which you want
to have my opinion upon, and I can assure you they
are the true Suffolk sorrels, the first breed of working
horses in the kingdom ; and these are some of the
best of their kind.'" Being undeceived, he at first
refused the gift, but was finally persuaded to accept
it, to the great content of both Harry and Tommy.

The stanchness of the Suffolk Punches was prover-
bial, and they would have been called in the language
of the modern sale stable, "dead-down, true pullers."
This quality was often displayed at pulling matches,
where the competing teams would fall upon their
knees at a given signal (the ground being strewed
with straw or sand), and in that position move a
great weight. The only account I have ever seen of
the origin of this breed states that it was formed
by crossing Norman stallions with the Suffolk cart
mare.

Perhaps the most popular breed of cart horses
now used in England is the Clydesdale. This, as
the name implies, is a Scotch family, but its origin
is obscure, though tradition ascribes it to a cross
made by an unascertained Duke of Hamilton between the draught mares of the country and some
Dutch stallions. Clydesdales, with the exception of
the Percherons, have more "quality" — that is, finer
characteristics and a better bred appearance — than
any other cart horses. Their coat is more silky, their
ears are smaller, their heads and necks more beautiful, and the whole body is more finely turned. Their
faults are a tendency to be too long in the leg, somewhat light-waisted, and, occasionally, a little hot in

temper. Their color is bay, brown, or black. Some
of these horses are very beautiful, and very large also.
In Cassell's Book of the Horse, there is an excellent
colored illustration of Prince Albert, a magnificent
Clydesdale stallion, seventeen hands high.

The only peer of the Clydesdale is the Percheron.
This horse, as everybody knows, is usually gray in
color, though sometimes black, and less frequently
chestnut or bay. The Percheron stands on somewhat shorter legs than the Clydesdale, and is more
compactly built, his head and ears being as fine as
those of his rival, and commonly even smaller. He
carries a long, thick mane, but wears less hair
than the latter on his fetlock joints. In England
hairy fetlocks are considered a mark of beauty;
but they retain both dirt and moisture, and consequently, unless carefully cleaned and dried, produce
"scratches."

Nothing is certainly known as to the origin of the
Percheron, though some writers assert that he is descended in part, at least, from Arab stock. There is
no positive proof of this, and the assumption rests
chiefly upon an undoubted resemblance between the
Arab and the Percheron, notwithstanding the great
difference between them in size and weight. The Percheron has the same intelligent and gentle disposition as the Arab, and, like him, a compact body, an
arched neck. large eyes, and a tail well set on. There
seems also to be a tendency in the breed to revert to
a smaller type; some very fine Percheron stallions
stand no more than 15 hands. and the best of them
rarely exceed 16½ hands. This tendency would indicate a derivation from smaller ancestors; and it

renders the Percheron a more desirable cross than the Clydesdale, when the object is to obtain a road horse or a light cart horse. The Percheron's trot also is faster than that of the Clydesdale, which constitutes another reason for his superiority in this direction. The Clydesdale, on the other hand, being a more rapid walker than the Percheron, and being unlikely to breed smaller animals than himself, makes the better cross when the object is to produce a heavy cart horse.

Many stories are told of feats performed by Percherons, some of which I have mentioned in the preceding chapter.

M. du Hays, equerry to Napoleon III., relates the following : " In 1845, a gray mare accomplished this match. Harnessed to a travelling tilbury, she started from Bernay at the same time as the mail carrier from Rouen to Bordeaux, and arrived before him at Alençon; having made fifty-five and three fifths miles, over a hilly and difficult road, in four hours and twenty-four minutes."

Another case vouched for by M. du Hays is thus reported : " A gray mare, seven years old, in 1864, harnessed to a tilbury, travelled fifty-eight miles and back on two consecutive days, going at a trot and without being touched by the whip. The following time was made : the first day, the distance was trotted in four hours, one minute, and thirty-five seconds ; the second day, in four hours, one minute, and thirty seconds. The last thirteen and three quarters miles were made in one hour, although at about the forty-first mile the mare was obliged to pass her stable to finish the distance."

The finest Percheron that I ever saw was a coal-black stallion, not of great size, high-headed, compactly built, with flowing mane and tail. This fellow had short, quick, smooth action, exactly like that of the Morgan roadster family, and he was said — doubtless truly — to be capable of trotting ten miles an hour with ease. The resemblance between the Morgan and the Arabian horse has often been remarked upon, and it was honestly come by, for the English thoroughbred horse that sired the original Justin Morgan was of Arab descent. In shape, also, as well as in action, there is again a resemblance between the Morgans and the Percherons ; and so, on the whole, it seems not unreasonable to infer that the New England roadster and the French cart horse have a common origin, both being descended, not wholly, but largely, from the "primitive horse," as the Arab is sometimes called.

No other breed, except possibly English half-bred animals, equals the Percheron in ability to draw a heavy load at a fast pace. The post and diligence horses formerly used in France, as we have seen, were Percherons. From Boulogne to Paris the pace was ten miles an hour, although the road was paved. The harness and reins were of rope. and the hostlers in charge of the big gray horses that did the work were women. The coachers, before being put to, or after they had been taken out, would often engage in a fight in the inn-yard, biting and kicking one another viciously ; and on these occasions the woman hostler. who was quite equal to the emergency. would quickly appear upon the scene, and, with a few well directed kicks from her wooden sabots, put an end to the combat. The gray stallions that have for many years drawn the omnibuses of Paris were always of Percheron, or of the kindred Norman stock.

It has frequently occurred to me that a family of superior road, and perhaps coach, horses might be developed by crossing the Percheron with the original Arab breed. Horses thus bred could not fail to be sound, tough, gentle, and, I should think, handsome. Certainly, if the Percheron is really derived from the Arab, such a cross would give size to the latter without introducing any element so foreign as to result in a hybrid, heterogeneous sort of animal. The cross between the thoroughbred and the cart horse does not usually turn out well; occasionally, to be sure, the produce preserves the strength and size of one family with the action and courage of the other, some noted hunters having been bred in this way. More often, however, the half-bred horse of this description is a slab-sided, nerveless beast, of little good for any purpose. But between the Percheron and the Arab there is an affinity sufficient to prevent such a result from their union. In one instance, at least, this has been tried, Mr. Parker, of West Chester, Pennsylvania, having bred a colt by the Jennifer Arabian, out of Rosa Bonheur, an imported Percheron mare. The horse thus bred is described as "a wiry, handsome colt, who was sold to go to Oregon, where he proved a valuable sire." A cross between the Morgan and the Percheron ought to be equally good.

Large numbers of Clydesdales, and Percherons in still greater abundance, have been imported to this country, but, unfortunately, the demand, especially at the West, has been for very big horses. The consequence is that the Percheron family has been corrupted on its native soil, Flemish and other inferior blood being introduced, in order to get the immense size wanted for the foreign, and particularly for the American market. Many of the Percherons winning prizes at our horse shows are of this type, — huge, overgrown, lethargic creatures, ungainly, slow, and wanting in endurance. The smaller horses of both the Clydesdale and Percheron breeds, the latter especially, are almost invariably the better. M. du Hays gives the height of the true Percheron stallion as ranging from 14¾ to 16 hands, but the height of Percheron or so-called Percheron stallions imported to this country varies from 15½ to 17 hands. In weight they vary from 1,400 to 2,200 pounds; the average being about 1,700. The mares average about 1,550 pounds in weight, and range from 15 to 16¾ hands in height. The size and weight of the Clydesdale importations are about the same, whereas, if the best and purest of both breeds were imported, the Percherons would be the smaller.

Fashion and caprice, instead of knowledge and judgment, are apt to determine the characteristics even of a cart horse. In the West, as I have indicated, elephantine animals are preferred; and in New York the favorite cart horse is a big, rangy, high-standing beast. In Boston, on the other hand, shorter-legged, broad-chested, round-bodied, short-backed, quick-moving horses are sought for; and this type is undoubtedly more efficient and lasting, besides being, as I think, a great deal more picturesque.

Most of the cart horses used in this country are raised at the West, though many also come from

Pennsylvania. It is doubtful if they could be bred with profit in New England, but seemingly it would be profitable for farmers at the East to buy Percheron, or half-bred Percheron, or Clydesdale colts at the age of two or three, work them moderately, and sell them again at the age of five or six. Under this system, the horses would come to the market in much harder, better condition than the corn-fed animals of the West, and consequently they would bring a better price. Upon the farm, the colt would be able to perform enough labor to pay his way; and the difference between his value at three and his value at six years of age would be clear profit. It is in this manner that Percherons are brought up in France; the farmers who buy them from the breeders, farmers also, working them moderately until they are of an age to be sold.

The enormous shire horses that are used in London as dray horses receive their education in the same way. "The traveller," says an English writer, "has probably wondered to see four of these enormous animals in a line before a plough, on no very heavy soil, and where two lighter horses would have been quite sufficient. The farmer is training them for their future destiny; and he does right in not requiring the exertion of all their strength, for their bones are not yet perfectly formed nor their joints knit, and were he to urge them too severely he would probably injure and deform them. By the gentle and constant exercise of the plough he is preparing them for that *continued and equable* pull at the collar which is afterwards so necessary."

In England it is customary to use heavy shire horses

15

on the farm, and they are of an almost incredible slowness; so slow are they, in fact, that William Day [1] seems almost to be jusified in his assertion that agriculture in England might be revolutionized simply by increasing the efficiency of the farm horse. In that country, a team of horses and a man are considered to have done a fair day's work if they have ploughed three quarters of an acre, and more than this is seldom, if ever, accomplished. In the United States, on the other hand, the ordinary stint is about an acre and a half: just double what it is in England. Day estimates that in drawing a load of a ton the English farm horse walks at the rate of one mile and a half an hour, whereas a coach horse, in a fast coach, drawing exactly the same weight, (but not covering more than nine miles in a day,) travels at the rate of eleven miles an hour. A more exact comparison can be made with van or furniture-wagon horses. Four of these will travel twenty-three miles in a day, hauling six tons, at the rate of three miles per hour: just double the speed of the farm horse, that draws one ton instead of a ton and a half, (which would be the share of a van horse in a team,) and goes fourteen miles instead of twenty-three.

In ploughing, the cart or shire horse walks even slower, doing but one and one fourth miles in the hour, and this although the draught is estimated at only three and three fourths hundredweight. "Is it any wonder, then," exclaims the writer whom I have just mentioned, "that we should so often see the poor creatures with staring coats and shivering with cold when dawdling along against this mighty draught,

[1] The Horse: how to Breed and Rear Him.

or that the ploughman, wrapped up in a top-coat that might resist the rigors of a Siberian winter, creeps after them, as frigid and benumbed an object as the animals themselves! "

He also tells the following incident, vouching for its truth : "A farmer who lived at Longstock, near Stockbridge, many years ago, was one day walking about his farm with a facetious friend. They noticed a plough, with horses and man, in the middle of a field, and the friend suggested that it was standing still. The farmer declared it was moving, and a dispute arose and ran high between them as to which was the case. To settle the question, they hit upon the expedient of getting a fold-shore, and setting it up in a line with the horses' heads and some conspicuous object beyond. But the ploughman now observed them, and, suspecting what they were about, became troubled in conscience, and whipped up his horses, which then quickened their pace, so that the fact that they were really moving became obvious; and," says the writer, "we may see examples of the same sluggishness every day of our lives."

In the United States, in the eastern part at least, the farm horse can hardly be called a cart horse, for he is comparatively light in build. It is in the city that we find the cart horse in his noblest form and highest condition, and there he will doubtless continue, until the warehouses crumble to dust and grass grows in the highway. The car horse is fast disappearing; and every lover of dumb animals will rejoice that this should be so, for the electric current that invisibly takes his place has no capacity for suffering.

The heaving flanks, the tortured mouth, the nervous
eye, of the car horse, — the excruciating sound of his
iron-shod hoofs slipping and clashing over the pavement in a vain attempt to start a heavy load, — these
will soon be things of the past; and the animal that
was but one of a thousand, that never received a
kind word or a caress, that sweated and strained and
wore himself out in the service of a heartless and
impersonal master, will have been released by Science.
He will soon become but a memory in those very
streets where the cart horse, more fortunate and more
lovable animal, seems destined to walk for centuries
yet in proud security.

## IX.

### FIRE HORSES.

EVERYBODY knows that a fire-engine horse is a large, strongly built, handsome animal, with a broad forehead and an intelligent eye. He wears neither check nor blinders, and is never blanketed, except when he stands out in the street; but his coat is nicely groomed, his hoofs are well oiled; he is usually in the pink of condition; his social affections and faculties are highly cultivated; interested looks follow him when he takes his daily exercise; and, seen in full progress to a fire, he is an object of respect and admiration, almost of terror.

His work is different from that of any other horse in the world, and it requires a peculiar combination of qualities. The fire steed must be able to draw an extremely heavy load at a smart gallop; in short, his

function is that of a running draft horse. Engines,
with the men who ride on them, usually weigh about
8,000 pounds, or four tons; some are a thousand
pounds lighter; others as much, or nearly as much
heavier. The chemical engines are less ponderous,
varying from 2,500 (this kind employs but one horse)
to 7,500 pounds. The hose carriages attached to the
fire engines, and drawn by one horse, are, as a rule,
about half the weight of the engines, but sometimes
much more. Two-wheel carts were formerly used
for this purpose, but they have been superseded, in
Boston and in most other cities, by four-wheel wagons, which, though not so picturesque, are much easier
for the horse, inasmuch as none of the weight comes
upon his back.

Hook and ladder trucks, with their men, vary in
weight from 4,350 to 10,600 pounds, the trucks which
reach the last mentioned figures being hauled by three
horses, harnessed abreast. This form of "hitch"
is also coming in use for the heavier class of engines, or "steamers," as they are called. The engines
usually fit the street car tracks, which is a great advantage; whereas the hook and ladder trucks are too
broad for this, and they are so extremely long that a
large part of the weight is far from the horses, which
of course makes it more difficult to haul; but, again,
the load is more "springy," not so dead as that of
the engine, and the two kinds of apparatus are, on the
whole, about equally difficult to pull. Some of the
longest ladder trucks, as most of my readers know,
are provided with a steering contrivance for the
hind wheels, so that the helmsman, who sits immediately above the axle, is able to turn them sharply

in going around a corner. By this device the necessity of a wide turn is avoided, and the driver is
able to "cut" the corners as closely as if he had an
ordinary length of vehicle behind him.

Sometimes a tough spiral spring, made of steel, is
inserted in the trace of a fire horse's harness, near the
whiffletree, the object being to lessen the strain at
starting. This ingenious device enables the horses
to exert their strength against a yielding connection
instead of a dead weight, — a certain momentum being acquired before the whole load moves. On the
same principle, the couplings which unite a train of
loaded cars must be somewhat loose, in order that the
locomotive may start the train. Motion is then com-
municated from the first car to the second, and so on,
as the spectator readily perceives; whereas, if all the
couplings were tense, the whole train would have to
start at once. The spring just described might be
used with all draft horses.

In the city proper, where most of the runs are
short, the whole distance is usually covered at a gallop, unless some hill or obstruction intervenes; and
this performance tries the animal of whom it is required through and through, so that if there be a
weak spot in him it is soon discovered. In the first
place, he must be big and heavy. Boston fire horses
vary from 1,200 to 1.600 pounds, — very few indeed
quite reaching the maximum, and most of them
weighing about 1,400 pounds, — rather less than more.
But the fire horse must also be active, as well as big
and strong; he must have good feet, good wind, and,
finally, to execute his ordinary task, he must be in
hard condition. When the horses are first bought,

they are almost invariably fat and soft; but they are immediately assigned to a station, without any training or preparation. Consequently, they must be humored, and, if need be, restrained somewhat, during their first months of service. Should they be driven fast at this time, they might easily become "touched in the wind," or otherwise disabled; and this sometimes happens through careless or unskilful driving. The best and strongest horse in the world, if out of condition, cannot safely be called upon for an extraordinary effort. (There is a hint here, by the way, for fat or elderly people who persist in running for trains.)

Elsewhere, the weight of fire horses is commonly about the same as it is in Boston. In Cambridge, in Lynn (which has an excellent department), and in Providence, they have none over 1,400 pounds; in Chicago the limit is given as 1,450; but in Brooklyn comparatively light horses are used, their weight varying from 1,150 to 1,350 pounds; and the veterinary surgeon attached to this department states that he prefers those approaching the minimum.

As a rule, short-legged and short-backed horses are the best for drawing engines. It is indeed a general equine principle that "weight-pullers" should be formed in this way: they are more nimble, take shorter steps, and recover themselves more easily, than longer-legged and longer-striding animals. The trotters who make fast records to skeleton wagons (much heavier than sulkies) are almost invariably of such a construction. I have been told of a pair of tough roans built thus, and weighing not much more than 1.200 pounds, who could pull a heavy engine at wonderful speed; but, unfortunately, the near horse had a habit of balking on the threshold of the engine-house, when harnessed for a fire, which so delayed the apparatus that his subsequent speed did not make up for the time lost, and he was retired to private life.

One of the best, oldest, and lightest engine horses in Boston is also built on this model. He is a rather plain brown fellow, weighing only about 1,175 pounds, with a strong, short back, splendid shoulder, and stout limbs, with big knees and short cannon-bones. His expression is extremely gentle and intelligent. At present he serves as the off horse on a chemical engine, his mate being a handsome dapple gray, with white flowing tail. The brown horse is reckoned by the enginemen to be twenty-two years old, having been in the service for many years. I suspect that there is some exaggeration in this statement, but he is certainly an old horse. His mate is ten, and considerably larger, but the two step well together, and make a fast team. Their driver assured me that he had once given the protective company a fair beating in a race to a fire.

Of the gray horse, a good, and I believe, on investigation, a true story is told. In the same building with the chemical engine is an ordinary steam-engine, the two " houses " being connected by hallways. At one time the gray horse was transferred to the other engine, and put in one of the stalls behind it. In the middle of the first night after this change had been made, an alarm of fire was sounded. The steam-enginemen tumbled out of bed, rushed down to the engine floor, and found one horse standing in his place by the pole, ready to have the collar fastened about his neck; but the gray was missing. They looked in his stall, but it was vacant; "neither hide nor hair of him" could be found, and it seemed clear that the animal had been stolen by some bold thief. Presently, however, a horse was heard moving about in the adjoining house, and it proved to be one belonging to the chemical engine, which had already gone to the fire. He was of course immediately put in the place of the missing beast, and the engine finally got under way. The fact was, that when the alarm sounded, and the doors of the stable flew open, the gray had gone to his old place on the chemical engine, and pushed aside the horse already standing there, who, finding that he was not wanted, returned to his stall. The men, in the hurry of the moment, harnessed such animals as offered themselves, and were off without discovering the mistake.

There is a reason why ladder truck horses should be taller than engine horses: the apparatus which they draw is at a much higher level from the ground than is the bulk of an engine, and consequently a low-standing animal would waste part of his efforts in pulling downward instead of pulling forward. Some ladder truck horses are shaped in one important respect like Maud S., Sunol, and other fast trotters and runners, namely, higher at the rump than at the withers, and with long hind legs. This is not considered a good conformation for a cart horse; but it seems to answer well where, as in the case of a ladder truck, horses are required which have height and speed as well as strength.

Such being the kind of horse needed for fire en-

gines, let us now visit a new recruit in his quarters.
The weather being warm, the doors of the house are
open, a rope being stretched across the entrance. Directly in front of us stands the engine, a polished
mass of copper and nickel, with scarlet wheels. The
driver's seat is a small box, just big enough to hold
him, and behind it, rolled up separately, are strapped
the blankets. The harness is suspended from the
ceiling in such a manner that it can be let down when
the horses stand under it. Back of the engine, and
some yards distant as a rule, a partition, composed
chiefly of doors, runs across the house. Behind this
partition are the stalls ; the horses facing the engine,
and the front of each stall being a door, with a window in it. Bridles are worn night and day, the bits
being slipped out when the animals eat their oats, but
kept in while they chew their hay. Some horses,
whose mouths are tender, are bridled, in the stable,
with the bit hanging loose.

Now, then, we will suppose that an alarm of fire
strikes, the hour being midnight. The horses are
lying down, out of sight and fast asleep ; the men
are upstairs in bed, — all save one, who dozes in a
chair beside those mysterious telegraphic instruments
grouped in a corner near the front door. The gas
burns brightly, but there is not a sign of animation
about the place. It is all so miraculously clean, so
neat, well ordered, burnished, and polished, so nearly
deserted, so absolutely quiescent, and yet so bril-
liantly lighted, that it appears rather like an illusion
than a reality. The engine might be the huge and
magnificent toy of a giant. It looks much too fine
for real use.

But, as we were just saying, an alarm sounds, and the scene changes. In a corner of the ceiling, near the front door, is a circular opening, through which, rising from the floor, passes a shining brass pole. When the men are called out, they throw themselves on this pole, and come down like a flash of lightning; the feet of the second man almost touching the head of the first, and so on. The horses scramble on their legs, the doors in front of them fly open, and out they rush, their heavy iron-shod hoofs thundering over the floor. Each horse goes to his proper place; the driver, from his seat, lets down the harness; two or three men standing at the pole snap the collars together, fasten the reins to the bits, and off they go. There is nothing more to be done: the girths are not used in running to a fire; the traces are already attached to the whiffletrees and the pole-straps to the collars, so that the fastening of two collars and four reins constitutes the harnessing. Often, perhaps commonly, the horses are harnessed and everything is ready for a start before the gong has finished telling the number of the box. Half a minute is about the maximum time for companies in a first class department to make ready and leave the house; and the ordinary time is, I believe, fifteen or twenty seconds. The fire marshal of the Chicago department informs me that, "on the test of a certain engine, with men in bed and horses in stalls, the hind wheels of the apparatus crossed the threshold in eleven seconds." For the Brooklyn department the time is given as "from four to eight seconds, according to distance of horses from the engine."

To teach a green nag to come out of his stall at the

signal, and range himself alongside the pole, is not so difficult as might be imagined. We will suppose that a span of new horses are assigned to a certain engine, the old pair, as is the custom, being taken away at the same time. The surroundings are strange and more or less terrible to them, but they are handled very gently and carefully, and gradually lose their fears. The schooling begins at once, the driver being assisted by the other men. The ordinary signal is given, as if for a fire; the stall doors open; the horses are led out, put in position, harnessed, and in a few minutes led back; and then the process is repeated perhaps half a dozen times. Great pains are taken that the animals shall not strike against anything, or by any means become frightened. The unusual spectacle of a harness suspended in the air is apt to disturb them at first, but they are led slowly up to it, induced to smell of it, to inspect it on all sides, and thus to learn that it is perfectly harmless. In the same way they are made familiar with all the other objects about them, being continually patted and encouraged.

The chief traits of the horse are the great strength of his memory, especially of his faculty of association, and his timidity. The fireman's task, therefore, is first to convince his pupil, by gentle treatment, that no harm threatens him, and then to establish a connection in his mind between the proper signal, the opening of the stall door, and a progress thence to his station by the engine pole. After being led to their positions what it is thought may prove a sufficient number of times, the horses are allowed to come out at the signal of their own accord, a man standing behind to touch them up a little if they do not start promptly

when the gong sounds and the doors open. Of course
no two horses learn with equal rapidity, and the difference between them in this respect is greater than
might be supposed. Two weeks constitute about the
average period of instruction, during which time two
or three lessons a day are given: but horses have
been known to learn in one lesson; and others,
again, have been months in arriving at the same
proficiency.

A pair of gray horses, newly purchased for an
engine in Boston, were led out three times in the
manner just described. They were then left to themselves: the gong sounded, the stall doors opened, and
the pair trotted out, each going to his place alongside
the pole. They had caught the idea at once. These
horses are remarkable not only for intelligence, but
for strength and speed. They are both, and the off
one especially, of a type different from that of any
other fire horses that I have seen, being very tall (the
off one is seventeen hands), rangy, slightly wasp-
waisted, and having fine, thin necks. and small. well-
bred heads. These nags are built after the fashion
of the once famous Conestoga horses of Pennsylvania.
They are great gallopers, and the hose-wagon steed has
hard work to keep up with them; but this too is a remarkable animal. He is one of the oldest horses in
the department, having served ten years, and being,
naturally, a little stiff in the legs; but his strength is
so great and his courage so good that even these powerful, flying grays cannot draw away from him. He
is a big brown horse, with a great shoulder, the best
of short legs, and a noble countenance. His original
cost was the unusually large sum of $450, but the bar-

gain has proved a good one for the city. Old as he
is, being sixteen or seventeen years at least, he is
thought to have made the best run of his life a few
weeks ago, galloping all the way to the fire, a distance
of a mile or more. A little blood trickled from his
nostrils when he pulled up behind the engine, but
otherwise he seemed none the worse for the immense
exertion.

Another big horse, of the greyhound type already
described, — that is, having long hind legs and standing higher at the rump than at the withers, — was
four months in learning the business. He is a gray,
with a long, rather coarse head, and small "mouse"
ears out of proportion to his size, for he weighs 1,380
pounds; but this evidently mongrel beast is not altogether devoid of intelligence, being steady enough
on the street to serve as a leader when three horses
are used, and on one occasion, when the whiffletree
fell on his legs, he refrained from running away.
This horse is used with a ladder truck, and his education was finally accomplished by fencing in his
path from the stall to the pole with ladders, a method
often employed.

Sometimes it is not want of mind, but nervousness,
which makes a fire horse slow to learn the trade, just
as some nervous children have difficulty in applying
their minds. Such was the case with Peter, a well-
bred black horse, used for many years in Boston with
a ladder truck. Peter was a noble, strong, spirited
animal, and, once taught, he became as prompt and
trustworthy as any horse in the department. On one
occasion, shortly after his purchase, Peter, exasper-
ated by the schooling, broke away from his instructors,

jumped cleanly through an open window without touching the sash, and ran down the street in search of amusement. At another time, while waiting in the blacksmith shop, his shoes having been taken off, but not yet replaced, Peter heard the twelve o'clock alarm strike. This he knew indicated the hour of his dinner, and accordingly Peter made off, without saying "By your leave" to the smith, and presently appeared at the ladder-house door, neighing for admission.

This fine animal met with a sad fate not long ago. While running to a fire, he came in collision with one of the protective wagons, and his leg was broken in two places, so that he had to be shot where he fell in the street. Something even worse happened several years ago to a fire-engine horse in Boston. He was struck by the pole of another engine, which came out of its house just as the first engine dashed by; the force of the blow, unknown to his driver, broke the animal's leg, but he kept on, travelling, of course, on three legs only, and pulling his share of the immense weight behind him, till the place of the fire was reached, nearly or quite one quarter of a mile further. Then the poor beast dropped to the ground, never to rise again. The fire horse is subject to accidents like these, but we must remember that the fireman's danger is greater yet.

It happens occasionally that a horse is bought who proves to be altogether too nervous for the business: he is in a continual state of tension, will not eat unless taken out of his stall, and is so worried with apprehension of an alarm that it is impossible to use him as a fire horse. In a few other cases, the nervousness,

though not so extreme, is sufficient to disturb the
animal's health, to impair his digestion, to prevent
his taking the needed amount of rest, so that eventually he too, after being doctored perhaps for an
imaginary disease, is transferred to some more peace-
ful occupation.

Now that we have seen how a fire-engine horse is
instructed, and where he lives, it might be interesting to know in what manner his daily life is ordered.
He takes breakfast, in Boston, at five or half past,
in some houses as late as six o'clock, — the meal consisting, as a rule, of two quarts of oats. After breakfast, he receives a thorough grooming, and about ten
o'clock he goes out to walk for an hour, with an
occasional trot, one horse of a pair being ridden and
the other led. At half past eleven or twelve he has
dinner,— two quarts of oats again,— which also is the
allowance for supper, at half past five or six. Some
old and some delicate horses have nine quarts of oats
per day. Usually a bran mash is given once a week,
and in some houses a little bran is fed every day. In
the afternoon the horse has another hour of exercise,
supposing that no fire has occurred. ' Hay is allowed
at night only, and in most of the houses it is fed from
the floor, so that the horse can eat it while lying
down. For several reasons this method is far better
than feeding from a rack, especially for the fire horse,
who takes a long while to eat his hay, inasmuch as the
bit remains in his mouth. In most cities the grain
allowance is about the same as it is in Boston, although in Chicago the horses are fed just twice as
much, twelve quarts per day, and in Brooklyn, as I
am informed, the allowance varies from twelve to

eighteen quarts, which is excessive. In Chicago, it would seem, the fire horses do more work than is required in Boston. Ten companies in the heart of that city average thirty-six runs per month; whereas in Boston the average varies, according to the situation, from eight or ten to twenty-five runs per month. In the suburbs many companies do not go out more than once a week, on the average. The hour for bedding down varies from half past five to eight P. M., at the discretion of the driver. It would be better to make this duty obligatory at the earlier hour, and better yet if the bedding were left under the horses by day as well as by night, especially in the case of those companies which do the most work. The more a horse lies down, the longer his legs and feet are likely to endure; and by the supply of a soft and perpetual couch he can often be induced to lengthen his hours of repose.

At eight P. M., it is the custom all over the city to call the horses out and harness them to the engine, and at this time visitors are apt to drop in. Both firemen and horses are always well known in the vicinity, and many civilities pass between the neighbors and the occupants, human and equine, of the engine-houses. The children especially are friends with the horses, calling them by their names, and often treating them to candy and other luxuries. In fact, whenever a fire-engine horse is introduced to a stranger, he expects to receive some dainty, and will poke his nose in the visitor's hands and pockets: nor is he easily discouraged by failure to find anything, being evidently convinced that nobody would be quite so mean as to enter his stable without bringing at least a lump of sugar or the fraction of an apple.

There is a handsome gray horse in the Central Station, in Boston, who has a great liking for ice, and, when out for exercise, he can never be persuaded to pass an ice wagon without first thrusting his head in behind and helping himself to a small piece. It is needless to say that the firemen make great pets of their four-footed companions, and are a little inclined to exaggerate their good qualities, — " the finest pair in the department " being discovered in almost every engine-house. There is, too, a favorite horse at each station, — not always the strongest or handsomest, but the most affectionate, docile, and sociable; and the visitor is always taken first to this animal's stall, whose virtues are thereupon extolled with generous enthusiasm.

From December to April every engine-house in Boston contains an equine guest, as an extra horse for making up a "spike team," in case the streets are blocked with snow. Usually this horse is not owned by the department, but is loaned by an ice company or a contractor, — his keep being reckoned as payment for his services. The new-comer does not serve as a leader: one of the regular team is put in that post, the extra horse taking the other's place at the pole. Some of the engine horses show great intelligence and discretion as leaders. On one occasion a spike team was dashing through a narrow street, where there was barely room to get between a wagon on one side and a light carryall, with women and children in it, on the other. The driver found that he had no control over his leader, and feared a bad accident; but the horse threaded his way so carefully and accurately that the engine swept past the carriage without touching it. When the engine stopped, it appeared that the leader's bit was hanging loose, and that he had served as his own driver.

This same animal, a big bay horse, is also credited with some clever work in his own interest. Immediately in the rear of his stall was a slide where the oats came down, as he had full opportunity to observe at feeding time. But how could he get them? He was confined in his stall, not of course by a halter, but by a rope stretched behind him, and fastened by an ordinary open hook. First, he discovered that, with some difficulty, he could turn in the stall far enough to get hold of the rope with his teeth, and after many attempts he succeeded in unhooking it. It was then an easy task to step across to the slide, pull it open with his teeth, and thus set running the reservoir of grain above. Two or three times he was found, after achieving this feat, standing in a deluge of oats, and industriously stowing them away in a compartment furnished by nature. But the firemen checkmated him by putting on the rope a snap hook, closed by a spring; and there it may be seen, at once proving the occurrence and preventing its repetition.

There is another sagacious leader, called John, one of a span of large, handsome, dark, mottled grays, used on a ladder truck. These are among the very finest horses in the Boston department: they are strong and symmetrical, with small, clean-cut heads, large eyes, and courageous but gentle expression. John, especially, is as kind as a dog, a favorite with the women and children of the neghborhood, a great pet of the firemen, and quiet as a mouse in the stable, but on the street full of life and animation, and playful enough

to have thrown, at one time and another, everybody
who has ridden him to exercise, except the captain.
John's sense of discipline is so strong that he draws
the line there. While used as a leader his stall is
different from the usual one; and when on one occasion, having occupied it for some weeks, the third
horse was dispensed with, and John was put back in
his old quarters, he rightly and sagaciously concluded
that his former place on the engine should also be resumed, and accordingly, at the next alarm, he ran to
the pole, instead of going in front.

The finest engine horse that I have seen is, I think,
the near one of a dark gray team used in Boston.
This is what horsemen call "a big little 'un," that is,
a stout animal on short legs. He is a comparatively
small horse, standing 15 hands 3 inches, and weighing
1.320 pounds; but he is big where bigness is required.
He has a broad chest, a tremendous shoulder, deep
lungs, a big barrel, a short back, and strong hind
quarters. His legs are flat and clean, his feet of just
the right size, and he has a broad forehead and an intelligent eye. Possibly his shoulder is a little too
upright, and there is a suspicion of hollowness in his
back, but otherwise he seemed to me an ideal engine
horse. His mate is handsomer in some respects, and
more gentle, but a trifle too long in the back and
legs.

Beside the engine, hose-wagon, and ladder truck
horses, there are others, used to haul coal and supplies, to carry men and tools for the repair of wires,
etc. These are chiefly old, partly broken down animals, no longer fit for the hard and rapid work of
running to fires. Then there are smaller nags, weigh-

ing from 950 to 1,050 pounds, employed by the engineers in their light wagons. These horses, especially such as are used by the chief engineer, get more practice in running to fires than any others, and they become very clever in picking their way through a crowded street, breaking into a gallop whenever they see an open space before them, and pulling up promptly to avoid collisions. The tough, intelligent, short-stepping Morgan is excellently adapted for this purpose, and one of that breed has been used for eight years past by the veterinary surgeon connected with the Boston department. Another, used by a district engineer, is of about the same size and pattern, and of the same gamy disposition.

The protective (insurance) wagon steeds, though not, strictly speaking, belonging to the fire department, should not be disregarded in this account. They show more "quality" than fire-engine horses, weigh less (about 1150 pounds), stand higher in proportion, and look like powerful coach horses. There are two protective wagons in Boston: one in the heart of the city, which weighs, with the men, about 7,800 pounds; and the other, which is much lighter, at the South End. One or both of these wagons respond to every alarm of fire in the city, so that the horses attached to them do a great deal of work. On a certain Fourth of July, one of these companies was called out on nineteen different occasions in the twenty-four hours; the horses not becoming cool enough throughout that time to be fed, and being supported by draughts of oat meal and water.

The arrangements in the protective houses differ, for the worse, from those of the fire department. The stalls are in the main room where the wagon is kept, and at the back of the building is an entrance, the doors of which are apt to be open. The animals are thus exposed to strong and frequent draughts, very bad for horseflesh; and they are also continually annoyed by the noise, by the glare of lights kept burning all night, and by the coming and going of visitors and officials. The object of this arrangement is, of course, to save time; but if the horses stood six feet farther back, and were protected by a partition, probably only one or two seconds more would be required to bring them to the pole. Moreover, they are so often out at night that the suggestion already made in regard to engine horses applies with more force to those engaged in this service, namely, that bedding should be left under them at all times. In the South End house the stalls are open at both ends, so that the horses stand in a thoroughfare for cold breezes; and this was formerly the case in the other station. In the latter house there were for eight years a very fine pair of grays, who were sold, not for unsoundness, but because they were worn out by want of rest. One of them also became vicious. The fact is, that, with the possible exception of man, the horse is the most nervous animal in the world, and the least able to endure continual and multiplied annoyances. These grays were last seen drawing a hack, and they have probably long since passed to some lower and more painful stage of equine degradation.

Connected with a fire department there is usually a veterinary hospital, and in Boston this is situated on Tremont Street; being part of the building in which a ladder truck is stationed. It consists of a

single box stall and several straight stalls, but the
health of the horses is looked after so carefully that
these accommodations are sufficient.  When I visited
the place it contained but two patients.  One was a
fine gray engine horse, who, while running to a fire,
came in collision with a "tow" horse, and was thrown
down.  His knees and hind legs were badly cut, but
none of these injuries proved serious, and he was
soon on the road to recovery.  The other patient, also
an engine horse, was suffering from a bad leg, caused
partly by improper shoeing, and partly by the state
of his blood.  With the exception of these two, all
the horses in the department, numbering about two
hundred, were in working order, — an excellent
showing.

Fire horses, as a rule, give out first and chiefly in
their feet.  Standing so much as they do on wooden
floors, their feet have a tendency to become dry and
hard, but this is counteracted by a permanent stuffing
of tar and oakum, held in place by a leather pad.
Almost all the fire horses of Boston wear these pads,
and usually on the hind as well as on the fore feet.
In other cities, the same result is accomplished by
periodical stuffing of the feet with some one of the
many materials which horsemen use for this purpose.

The worst trouble, however, arises from the concussion produced in the foot by the hard paving-stones
of the city.  This is bad enough for any horse, but
especially bad for the fire horse, because, owing to his
great weight, his galloping speed, and his heavy load,
he pounds his feet with tremendous force.  Often a
pair of engine horses whose feet have begun to give
out are transferred to a suburban station, where, the

roads being less hard and alarms less frequent, they go on very well for some years longer. Great pains are taken with the shoeing, which is under the direct charge of the accomplished Vet employed by the department. Horses used in the city proper wear corks on all their feet, to give them a better grip on slippery pavements, car-tracks, etc.; but in the suburbs corks are dispensed with, the shoes without them having this advantage, — that they let the foot down lower, so that it supports the weight of the horse in a more natural position. The frog of the foot is intended by nature to lessen the concussion by receiving part of the blow itself; but with an ordinary shoe, especially with one having corks, this function of the frog is very imperfectly discharged, the frog being kept off the ground by the shoe. What the city fire horses (perhaps I might say, what horses in general) need is some method of shoeing which will protect the wall of the foot, and at the same time allow the frog to come in contact with the ground.[1]

Fire horses also throw their shoes very frequently, catching them in car-tracks and other projections. In fact, a team can hardly go to a fire without losing at least one shoe among them; and the continual re-shoeing tends, of course, to wear away the hoof. It is desirable, therefore, to make it grow as fast as possible, and for this purpose it is kept well oiled. Ev-

---

[1] Possibly this result might be accomplished satisfactorily by the Charlier process, which consists in channelling the wall of the foot at its base, and inserting in the circular groove so formed a steel shoe. By this method the walls of the foot are protected as with the ordinary shoe, but, the foot not being raised from the ground, the frog comes into play, just as if no shoe at all were worn.

ery driver has his own specific, upon the peculiar and wonderful properties of which he will descant with much enthusiasm; but the best of them is probably not more efficacious than a rag tied about the coronet, and kept well moistened with cold water.

Despite the severity of their occasional labors and the hard usage to which their feet are subjected, fire horses in Boston last a considerable time. They are bought, usually, at the age of five or six years (costing about $325), and they remain in service, on the average, about seven or eight years. In other cities their duration and cost are nearly the same. In Cambridge, where few of the streets are paved, fire horses are said to last from seven to ten years; but in Brooklyn this period is put as low as six years, — about the length of time that a car horse endures.

In Boston there are at least half a dozen veterans of ten years' standing, and some who have served as fire horses even longer than that. The old hose-cart horse of whom I have spoken already has a record of at least ten years' service. There is another seasoned Houyhnhnm, — a dark chestnut, of the same heavy, low-standing shape, who has seen twelve winters in the business. About five years ago it was thought that he ought to have an easier life, and accordingly he was transferred to an outlying station, where fires seldom occur. But on the occasion of the first alarm to which he responded the old fellow bolted, and made a complete wreck of the hose-cart by dashing it against a stone wall. This was his protest at being removed from the house to which he had become accustomed, and from the society of his familiar friends, human and equine; and so he was put back in the old place, where he still remains in full employment. He is reckoned to be seventeen years old, and he has a contemporary, also a hose horse, who entered the department in the same year.

This is Grief, so named because of his melancholy aspect. He has a way of standing with his fore legs wide apart, his head hanging down between, and a doleful expression of the face. A visitor, who saw him once in this attitude, remarked that he would make a good "image of Grief," and the name seemed so appropriate that it was adopted by common consent. "Grief" is duly inscribed in large letters over his stall, and as Grief he is known through the department and to all the neighbors. Grief is a remarkable horse; in color a rich mottled brown, and in shape much resembling the other old horses already described. He has a massive, well formed shoulder, strong, straight fore legs, powerful hind quarters (too long a cannon-bone, however), a good neck, slightly arched, a rather intelligent, clean-cut head, but mulish ears. His peculiarity is a philosophical, phlegmatic disposition. He has a hearty appetite and a sound digestion, but he never shows the least impatience for his meals. Other horses paw and neigh when they hear the premonitory rattle of the oat-box, but Grief never betrays the least sign of curiosity or of interest. The children of the vicinity often come to this house to give the horses candy, and the span of bays who draw the engine always recognize their benefactors, and will follow them about the stable. But Grief, though glad enough to be fed, never takes the slightest notice of any visitor beyond swallowing what is offered to him. He sleeps a great deal, ruminates still

more, and allows nothing outside of business to disturb or excite him; and hence, no doubt, his excellent
state of preservation.

But Grief awakes when the alarm strikes. However long or steep the road, however fast may gallop
the stout young bays in front, he always keeps up
with the engine. The strength and nervous force
that he accumulates in the stable Grief expends lav-
ishly on the way to a fire. His eye is then full of
spirit; his expanded nostrils display the red glow
within; his neck curves to the task; his splendid
shoulder strains against the collar. He looks twice
the size of the horse that was dozing in his stall a few
minutes before. Arrived at the scene of action, he
draws up as close as possible to the engine. Grief
likes to get where the sparks fall in showers about
him, and there he will stand, shaking his head to dis-
lodge the burning particles, pleased with the shrieks
and roar of the engine, with the shouts of the men,
with the smoke and flame of the conflagration. At a
great fire in Boston on Thanksgiving day, 1889, the
engine which he followed was burned within twenty-
five minutes after it left the house; but Grief stood
by it, firm as a rock, till the flames came near and he
was hurried away by his driver.

The patriarch of the department is, however, not
Grief, but another horse, stationed in East Boston, and
called Old Joe. His age is variously estimated, but
I gather that it is at least twenty years, and possibly
twenty-four. Joe is not so impassive as Grief; he is
more like the rest of us, being swayed by curiosity,
touched by social affections, and dependent upon society. He has a gentle, intelligent, courageous eye,

and a good head. His great age is indicated by an
extremely hollow back, but otherwise he is still a
grand-looking horse. He, too, is a mottled bay or
brown, and not unlike Grief, except that he is even
larger. In fact, the four old fire horses whom I have
particularly described would have made a great team
in their youth, — broad-chested, deep-lunged, low-
standing, short-backed fellows, with immense shoulders, roomy stomachs, and strong hind quarters. Joe
is now an engine horse. His mate, though in comparison with him a mere colt, is in truth an oldish
beast; and the two agreed some time ago that they
would trot out no more from their stalls when the
alarm sounded (having as it seemed to them, done
that sort of thing quite long enough), but would pro-
ceed from the stable to the pole at a dignified walk.
This resolution has been kept. The firemen have
tried to hurry them, but without success. Rattan
rods (such as schoolboys used to be whipped with)
are hung behind their stalls, and descend automati-
cally when the alarm strikes; but the old horses laugh
at this gentle flagellation; they refuse to hurry their
pace, and, alone among the fire horses of Boston, they
advance with slow and measured step from the stable
to the engine house.

The only remaining question which we have to ask
is this: What becomes of them all? What fate is in
store for Old Joe, for Grief, for that veteran hose-
cart steed, who gallops with his heavy load till the
blood runs from his nostrils? When thoroughly
worn out, fire horses are sold, or, more commonly,
handed over to a dealer in part payment for new animals. In some cities, in Brooklyn, in New York also,

I believe, they are disposed of at auction; and inasmuch as a certain distinction attaches to them even in decrepitude, they always bring a little more than they are worth as beasts of burden. At most, however, they sell for a song. Broken down horses are bought by poor men; they have scanty fare, little or no clothing, hard boards to lie on, and, commonly, severe toil to endure.

The cast-off fire horse must sadly miss his good oats and hay, his clean, warm stable and comfortable bed, his elaborate grooming and gentle treatment, his companions, brute and human, the caresses and sweetmeats to which he was daily treated. Removed from all these luxuries, his life broken up by a sudden and painful revulsion, we may be sure that the equine veteran, who spent his best years in helping to save our property from destruction, must very shortly present a spectacle of misery and despair. The next bony animal that the reader sees pulling a tip-cart may be a once proud and petted fire horse, for whom the only possible boon is now the axe of the knacker.

## X.

### ARABIAN HORSES.

THERE is no other race in the world by whom good birth is valued so highly as it is by the Bedouins of Arabia. And yet in their form of government these nomadic clans are the most democratic of people. Every Arab finds himself the member of a tribe, but if he chooses to leave it, he can do so without let or hindrance. He may take refuge with strangers, or pitch his tent in solitude and isolation. Even when the majority determine upon war or upon some warlike expedition, the minority are not obliged, either by law or by public opinion, to join with their fellows. They stay at home, if they prefer, without discredit. Each tribe has a leader, a sheikh, elected by universal suffrage, but his authority is very limited, and his commands are enforceable only so far as they commend themselves to the popular judgment. The sheikh is an agent rather than a ruler. All matters of real importance are decided by vote. The sheikh leads the tribe to new camping-grounds, settles small disputes, transacts political business, entertains strangers, and keeps open house at all hours of the day and night. This last is perhaps his chief function. The humblest shepherd addresses the sheikh by his Christian name, and neither in dress nor in conduct does he affect any superiority. Moreover, the possession of wealth will not procure a man distinction or respect among the Bedouins, any more than the possession of office ; and this is remarkable, because the Bedouins love money to the point of avarice.

But to high birth the Arab, democrat though he be, renders homage most sincere. There are among the Bedouins certain families of traditional good breeding. For such families a respect almost reverential is shown ; and it is from their members that the sheikhs are usually chosen. Nor is this high value erroneously attached to noble blood. Good breeding and good birth are nearly always found together in the desert, and the sheikhs are commonly distinguished by the quiet elegance and dignity of their manners. If a sheikh be deficient in this regard, he is almost invariably a man of inferior origin, raised to command by force of his own talents and energy.

The respect which the Bedouins have for high birth in their horses is, if possible, even greater. becoming absolutely fanatical. Lady Anne Blunt [1]

___

[1] Mr. Wilfrid Blunt and his wife, Lady Anne Blunt, made two journeys to the desert, and their observations are recorded in two

speaks of the reports which reached her party in the desert as to the extraordinarily fine pedigree of a particular horse owned by a certain old man. "'Manéghi Ibn Sbéyel'[the title of the horse's family], they kept on repeating in a tone of tenderness, and as if tasting the flavor of each syllable." The travellers made a considerable detour in order to see this famous animal. When they arrived at the tent of his owner, they found that he had gone to borrow a donkey for the purpose of moving the family furniture to a new camp; for "a horse of the Manéghi's nobility could not, of course, be used for baggage purposes." Presently, however, the old man appeared, riding his high-born steed, which proved to be "a meek-looking little black pony, all mane and tail."

Mr. Blunt expresses the opinion that the Arabian horse is degenerating through in-breeding, and more especially because animals of the best families, though individually inferior, are preferred to superior individuals, but members of families belonging to an inferior rank. However this may be, it is certain that the extraordinary excellence of the Arabian horse in his present form could never have been developed or maintained had it not been for the extreme care which the Bedouins bestow upon equine descent.

They have no written pedigrees; it is all an affair of memory and of notoriety in the tribe. Certain

interesting books, written chiefly by Lady Anne. These are, " The Bedouin Tribes of the Euphrates," and "Our Pilgrimage to Nejd." They lived among the Bedouins for some time, and what they report about the Arabian horse, his qualities, his descent, and the families in which he is grouped, agrees in all substantial respects with the account, presently to be mentioned, given by Major Upton.

alleged pedigrees of Arabian horses, couched in romantic language, and represented as carried in a small bag hung by a cord around the animal's neck, have been published; but these are forgeries, gotten up probably by horse-dealers, Egyptian, Syrian, or Persian. The breeding of every horse is a matter of common knowledge, and it would be impossible for his owner to fabricate a pedigree so as to deceive the natives, even if he were so inclined. The Bedouins, it seems necessary to admit, are, in general, great liars; and they will lie (to a stranger) about the age, the qualities, or the ownership of a horse; but they will not lie about his pedigree, even when they can do so with impunity. To be truthful on this subject is almost a matter of religion, certainly a point of honor, in the desert.

How far back do these pedigrees run, and what was the origin of the Arabian horse? These questions it is impossible to answer definitely. The Bedouins themselves believe that Allah created the equine genus in their soil. "The root or spring of the horse is," they say, "in the land of the Arab"; and again, "It was Allah who created him, for the happiness of believers."

This pious belief is shared by a few generous souls in England and America, a small but devoted band, who gallantly defend the cause of the Arabian horse against his only rival, the modern English thoroughbred. Chief among these faithful was the late Major R. D. Upton, who visited the desert himself, and who has recorded his experiences and his views.[1] Major

[1] "In Newmarket and Arabia," a small book, which was first published in 1873; "Gleanings from the Desert," a later work

Upton concluded that the horse was found in Arabia "not later than about one hundred years after the deluge, . . . if indeed he did not find his way there immediately after the exodus from the ark, which is by no means improbable," and this probability the author then proceeds seriously to consider. According to Major Upton and a few kindred spirits, all other breeds are mongrels, and the only way to obtain horseflesh in its best and purest form is to go back to the fountain head, to the horse of the desert.

Naturalists, I believe, have not yet determined where the genus originated; but they gather that three allied animals, the tapir, the rhinoceros, and the horse, have all descended from a common ancestor of the eocene period. Of these three, the tapir and the rhinoceros certainly are found in many parts of the world. The immediate precursor of the horse was the small animal called Equida, which was exceedingly common both in America and in Europe. Fossil skeletons have also been found in almost every part of America, varying but slightly from the skeleton of the present horse, although externally the animals which they represent may have differed from him as widely as does the zebra. It is possible, therefore, that, contrary to the usual opinion, horses existed on this continent in a wild state before the coming of the Spaniards. These facts as to the wide distribution of both the ancestors and the first-cousins, so to say, of the primitive horse, tend to show, although of course they fail to prove, that he also was

only a part of which, however, is devoted to horseflesh; and a paper concerning Arabian Horses, published in Fraser's Magazine for September, 1876.

widely distributed, not confined even to the salubrious region of Arabia.

But there is one argument in favor of the Arabian being the primitive horse, which I have chanced upon, and which I here present to those enthusiasts who will appreciate it. There is a conjecture of Darwin's that the dark stripe running along the spine of some horses, and occasionally extending to the shoulders and legs, may indicate a "descent of all the existing races from a single dun-colored, more or less striped primitive stock, to which our horses occasionally revert." In the Cleveland Bay family this dark stripe, or "list," is valued as a mark of pure blood; it is found also in the Exmoor breed of ponies, and in some other strains.

Now Major Upton reports an observation made by him upon horses in the desert as follows: "A line somewhat darker than the general color of the animal is to be seen in *colt* foals, running in continuation of the mane along the spine, and to be traced for some way even among the long hair of the tail. I never saw it in a filly. . . . It can be traced in old horses and in those of a very dark color. . . . It appears as the first or primitive color of the animal, which tones away by almost imperceptible degrees from the back to the belly; it may be seen in lines on the males of other wild animals. At certain seasons, and as the horse ages, and dependent also in some degree on his condition, the dark color spreads over the shoulders and upper parts of the body, . . . as if shaded with black." To be sure, Major Upton states that this phenomenon is "totally different from the markings of the zebra, quagga, or any of the hybrids"; but nevertheless it seems to he essentially the same. Zebras and quaggas are of the equine family; and this peculiar marking of the Arabian horse would, on Darwin's hypothesis, indicate that, if not himself the primitive horse. he at least stands nearer to that animal than does any other existing *equus*.

However, this discussion has no practical value, nor is it essential even for the Arabo-maniacs to prove their case historically. This fact is sufficient, and cannot be controverted, namely, that the Arabian horse is the only one now extant of a fixed type. His antiquity is such that in comparison with him all other breeds are mongrels of yesterday. It is conjectured that he dates back to the time of Ishmael; and it is reasonably certain that the present breed existed in the days of Mahomet.

This is antiquity enough. The English racer, as I have stated, is a modern product, his stud-book dating from the year 1808. According to the standard of the desert, therefore, the English horse is a parvenu; and although he is bigger, stronger, and faster than the Arab, he is less sound, beautiful, intelligent, and gentle. Moreover, as must be the case with a new breed. the English thoroughbred varies greatly in size, in shape, and in many other characteristics; whereas the Arabian, though each family has its peculiarities, is much more nearly of one type, and almost of one size. Pure Arabians range from 14 to 15 hands. being commonly about 14.2. Very rarely one stands as low as 13.3, or as high as 15.1. An English officer, speaking of Arabian horses as racers, says, "They can all gallop about equally fast."

In estimating the Arabian horse. or in comparing

him with his English contemporary, it must be borne
in mind that an Arabian of absolutely pure breed is
an animal which few European eyes have ever looked
upon.  Of all the Oriental horses imported to England
in the eighteenth century, and upon which, in great
part, the English thoroughbred is founded, only one,
the famous Darley Arabian, procured by Mr. Darley
in the latter part of Queen Anne's reign, is known
to have been of pure lineage.  It is probable that
no thoroughbred Arabian horse has yet reached our
shores, except Kismet, a stallion recently brought
over, who died a few hours after landing; and perhaps the only Eastern mare of that degree ever in
the United States is Naomi, a late importation from
England, to which country she was taken by Major
Upton.

There are no wild horses in Arabia, although there
is a widespread belief to the contrary.  This animal,
as an old writer explains, "can live only of man's
hand in the droughty *Kháfa*."  The pure-bred Arabian
horses are the possession, almost exclusively, of a
single great Bedouin clan, known as the Anazeh, and
of this clan a tribe called the Gomussa have the best.
Even among the Bedouins, apart from the Gomussa,
there are not many animals of the highest stamp.
" I doubt," says Mr. Blunt, "if there are two hundred
really first-class mares in the whole of Northern Arabia.  By this I, of course, do not mean first-class in
point of blood, for animals of the purest strains are
still fairly numerous, but first-class in quality and
appearance as well as blood."

Across Central Arabia extends a vast territory
called the Nejd, composed of sandy deserts and rich

pastures. This whole region is a plateau, and the atmosphere is dry and bracing. It is under such conditions that horses thrive, and here was the original home of the Arabian horse. In Flanders, where the air is humid, and the pastures are moist and rank, horses grow large, but they have flat feet, inferior sinews, lymphatic temperaments, and soft hearts. Flemish nags have been imported largely to England for many hundred years, being cheap, big, and showy; bnt they have always been noted for their lack of endurance. Even among thoroughbreds unsoundness is frequent in the British Isles, due in great part to the moist climate. The English horse, when transplanted to India or to Australia, becomes much improved in the quality of his feet and legs, and this improvement is doubtless the effect chiefly of a drier climate.

The Anazeh spend their winters in the Nejd, migrating in spring as far as the Euphrates, and it is among the wandering tribes of this clan that the Arabian steed in his purity must be studied. The Anazeh, and the Bedouins in general, keep their mares, but sell many of their horses, and it is from the horses thus sold, crossed with inferior mares, that the animal known in Europe and in India as an Arab is bred. The Bedouins call these half-breds "the sons of horses," and they look upon them, as well as upon all other breeds but their own, with the greatest contempt, stigmatizing them as *kadishes*, or mongrels. The desert is almost surrounded by horse-growing countries, and it is touched here and there by great horse markets. On the west and northwest is Syria, where many of these bastard

Arabs, the "sons of horses," are raised. The chief horse market of Syria is Damascus, on the shore of the desert. Opposite, on the eastern shore, in almost a straight line from Damascus, is Bagdad, the capital of Turkish Arabia, another great horse market; and south of Bagdad, between the Euphrates and the Tigris, there is a wide stretch of country where many half Arabs are bred, chiefly for sale in India.

The Arabian horses, so called, that are found in Turkey, especially in Constantinople, in Egypt, in Syria, and in India, are not the true coursers of the desert, but their "sons." They are commonly gray, and hence the popular idea that gray is the normal color of the Arabian horse. As a matter of fact, the Bedouins prefer bay with black points, — not objecting to three white feet, — and this is the most frequent color among the Anazeh mares; next comes chestnut, then gray. Black is a rare and inferior color. White horses are much esteemed, but seldom occur. Roans, piebalds, duns, and yellows are never found among pure-bred Arabs. The two Arabian stallions sent to General Grant as a present from the Sultan of Turkey, in 1876, are both grays, and though they were supposed to be pure bred, the probability is, I cannot help thinking, that they are kadishes, "sons of horses," not horses themselves. Neither money nor high office can command the flower of the desert. Even Abbass Pasha had only a few really thoroughbred mares, and yet he spent five million dollars in gathering his famous stud at Cairo.

This man appears to have had a notable passion for horseflesh. On one occasion he despatched a special mission to Medina for the sole purpose of procuring a rare work on farriery. At another time he sent a bullock cart from Egypt all the way to Nejd to bring home a famous mare, old and unable to travel on foot, that he had purchased from the Anazeh. A Bedouin, who had been sent to Cairo by one of the chiefs of Nejd, was shown over the viceroy's stables, by order of that official. On being asked his opinion of the blood, he replied frankly that the stables did not contain a single thoroughbred. He added an apology on the part of his chief for the animals which he had just brought to the viceroy from Arabia, declaring that neither Sultan nor sheikh could procure colts of the best strain.

Bagdad is on the very edge of the desert, and the Pasha of that place has unlimited resources; but Mr. Blunt says · "Although his Excellency's horses were, as a lot, good of their kind, they were very different from real Arabs; and on comparing them with those of the Anazeh their inferiority was conspicuous, and their history could easily be understood. They were very nearly all gray."

In the centre of Arabia, in the district of Nejd and on the border of the desert, is the city of Haïl, where for many years has existed the famous stud of the Emir of Haïl. Emissaries of this dignitary are constantly on the lookout for mares, wherever they can find them, and not infrequently *ghâzus*, or marauding expeditions, have been sent out by the Emir against this or that tribe, for the express purpose of capturing some particular mare whose fame had spread over the desert. It was of the animals in this stud that Mr. W. G. Palgrave's oft-quoted de-

scription was written. Out of his two interesting
volumes [1] this passage alone has survived : —

"Remarkably full in the haunches, with a shoulder
of a slope so elegant as to make one, in the words of
an Arab poet, 'go raving mad about it'; a little, a
very little saddle-backed, just the curve which indicates springiness without any weakness; a head broad
above, and tapering down to a nose fine enough to
verify the phrase of 'drinking from a pint pot'; . . .
a most intelligent and yet a singularly gentle look;
full eye; sharp, thornlike little ears; legs, fore and
hind, that seemed as if made of hammered iron, so
clean and yet so well twisted with sinew; a neat,
round hoof, just the requisite for hard ground; the
tail set on, or rather thrown out, at a perfect arch;
coat smooth, shining, and light; the mane long, but
not overgrown nor heavy; and an air and step that
seemed to say, 'Look at me, am I not pretty?'—
their appearance justified all reputation, all value, all
poetry. The prevaling color was chestnut or gray.
A light bay, an iron color, white or black, were less
common. . . . But if asked what are, after all, the
specially distinctive points of the Nejdec horse, I
should reply, the slope of the shoulder, the extreme
cleanness of the shank, and the full, rounded haunch,
though every other part too has a perfection and a
harmony unwitnessed (at least by my eyes) anywhere
else."

And yet Mr. Blunt says of this same stud: "Of
all the mares in the prince's stable, I do not think
more than three or four could show with advantage
among the Gomussa." He admits, however, that

[1] "Central and Eastern Arabia."

their heads were handsomer than those of the Anazeh mares. The latter are built more nearly on a race-horse model, having greater length of body and of limb. The Nejd[1] horses are perhaps prettier, though not so bloodlike. Unlike the Anazeh mares, they stand higher at the withers than at the rump. " Every horse at Haïl," writes Mr. Blunt, " had its tail set on in the same fashion ; in repose something like the tail of a rocking-horse, and yet not, as has been described [by Mr. Palgrave], thrown out in a perfect arch.' In motion the tail was held high in the air, and looked as if it could not under any circumstances be carried low."

It has been suggested that this phenomenon is partly, at least, the effect of art; that before the foal is an hour old its tail is bent back over a stick, the twist producing a permanent result. But this is probably a slander.

There is one family of American trotters, that of the Mambrino Patchens, which alone among American-bred nags is distinguished for the beautiful carriage of the tail, and, as I have mentioned in a previous chapter, jealous persons sometimes make the same insinuation in reference to these horses that was directed against the stud of the Emir of Haïl.

All Arabian horses carry their tails well, and, next to the head and its setting on, the tail is the feature which the Arab looks to in judging a horse. " I have seen mares gallop with their tails out straight as colts, and fit, as the Arabs say, to hang your cloak on," Major Upton remarks. A family of horses renowned in the desert is descended from a mare of whom the

---

[1] Nejd, a district, is the general ; Anazeh, the particular term.

following tradition exists. Her owner was once flying from the enemy, and, being hard pressed, he cast off his cloak in order to relieve the mare of that unnecessary weight. But when, having distanced his pursuers, he halted, what was his surprise to find that his cloak had lodged on the mare's outstretched tail and still hung there! From this incident, the heroine of the story has figured ever since in the unwritten pedigrees of the desert as "the Arab of the Cloak."

Occasionally, though not often, one sees an American-bred horse, especially if it be a colt, galloping in the pasture with its tail carried so high that the hair divides and falls forward like a streamer. This is a very common sight in the desert. "I have seen a mare, an Abayan Sherakh," writes Major Upton, "galloping loose, with both head and tail high to an extent such as I could hardly have believed had I not seen it. Her tail was not only high, but seemed to be right over her back, and, besides streaming out behind like a flag, covered her loins and quarters. It was a splendid sight to one who can appreciate a horse." A single horseman mounted on a mare that carried her tail in this superb manner, and galloping in the distance, away from the spectator, has often been mistaken in the desert for three horsemen riding abreast.

What does an Arabian horse look like, — a mare of the desert, of noble birth, belonging, we will say, to the tribe Gomussa, of the clan Anazeh, and valued for her high descent from Nejd to the Euphrates, from Damascus to Bagdad? Let us imagine her coming forward at a walk. She advances with a

long, swinging stride, the hind feet considerably overstepping the print left by the fore feet, — overstepping
from twelve to eighteen inches, — sometimes, if careful observers may be trusted, even as much as two or
three feet. Above all, she swings her head from side
to side, and looks about with curiosity, as she goes.
This mark of alertness and vivacity is among the
Bedouins a *sine qua non* of good breeding. The son
of a certain sheikh being about to purchase a horse,
asked advice of his father. The old man answered
simply, "Get one whose ears are ever in motion,
turning now forward and now backward, as if he
were listening to something."

In truth, a well-bred horse, the world over, exhibits
similar indications of a lively spirit, and of an inquiring mind. There is no pleasure in the use of a
horse who fails to prick his ears, and to keep them in
motion; and it would be a short but not seriously
inadequate description of a good roadster to say that
you can drive him fifty or sixty miles in a day without taking the prick out of his ears. The head of our
Gomussa mare is the first and chief part of her to be
examined.

Whyte-Melville wrote: —

"A head like a snake, and a skin like a mouse,
　An eye like a woman's, bright, gentle, and brown,
With loins and a back that would carry a house,
　And quarters to lift him smack over a town."

This comparison of the head of a horse to that of
the snake has often been criticised, and yet I think
an Arab would perceive the force of the simile. The
head of an Arabian horse when he is excited, writes
one, "seems to be made up of forehead, eyes, and

nostrils," and this suggests the raised head of a hissing snake.

What gives the head of the Arabian steed this peculiar appearance is chiefly the prominence of the forehead, — greater in the mares than in the horses. A small head the Arabians particularly dislike, as indicating a small brain, but the size should be in the upper regions of the skull. From the top of the head to a point between the eyes will often measure as much as from the last mentioned point to the upper edge of the nostril. Morever, the forehead, between and below the eyes, should be slightly convex or bulging.[1] The space around the eyes should be free of hair, so as to show the skin underneath, which at this part is particularly black and lustrous. The name for the original breed of Arab horses, now divided into five families, is Keheilan, from *kohl*, antimony, the Arabian horse having by nature that dark circle about the eye which the women of Arabia are wont to obtain by the use of antimony. Sometimes the whole face, and even the ears, are entirely free of hair. The cheek-bone should be deep and lean, and the jaw-bone clearly marked. There is great width of jaw and depth of jowl. In fine, the head of the Arabian horse is large where the brain is, and large in the breathing apparatus, but small in all the unessential parts. The face narrows suddenly below the cheek-bone, and runs down almost to a point. "A nose that would go in a pint pot"

---

[1] This feature, which, by the way, distinguishes the Touchstone family of English thoroughbreds, is not to be confounded with that of a convex or "Roman" nose. The latter points to a low descent, and is associated with obstinacy.

is an old description of the Arabian cast of countenance.

But the profile of the Arabian horse terminates, not "with the nostril, as in the English race horse, but with the tip of the lip." "The nostrils," Mr. Blunt states, "when in repose, should lie flat with the face appearing in it little more than a slit, and pinched and puckered up, as also should the mouth, which should have the under lip longer than the upper, 'like the camel's,' the Bedouins say." [1]

> "Fine his nose, his nostrils thin,
> But blown abroad by the pride within."

The ears, especially in the mare, should be long but fine and delicately cut, like the ears of a gazelle. This agrees with our Western notion on the subject, for small "mouse-ears," as they call them, are not liked by our horsemen. As to the carriage of the ears, Major Upton well describes it as follows : "The ears, to be perfect, should be so placed that they point inwards. so that the tips may almost touch. The outline of the inner side of the ear should be much curved, and, as it were, notched about half-way down."

Next to the head and ears, the Arabs value the manner in which the head is set on the neck. This point, or rather form of juncture. they call the mitbeh. It especially refers to the shape of the windpipe, and

---

[1] "The nostril. which is peculiarly long, not round, runs upward toward the face, and is also set up outward from the nose, like the mouth of a pouch or sack which has been tied. This is a very beautiful feature, and can hardly be appreciated except by sight. When it expands. it opens both upwards and outwards, and in profile is seen to extend beyond the outline of the nose." — Major Upton.

to the manner in which the throat enters or runs in
between the jaws, where it should have a slight and
graceful curve. "This," Major Upton adds, "per-
mits of a graceful and easy carriage of the head, and
. . . gives great freedom to the air-passages. The
Keheilan is essentially a deep-breathed and a good
and long-winded horse."

The peculiar rounded prominence of the forehead
already described, the Arabs call the jibbah; and the
jibbah, the mitbeh, the ears, and the tail are the
parts as to which they are most particular. These
points indicate breeding, and breeding is all that the
Arabs care for in a horse.

For the rest, the Arabian horse, in his highest form,
exhibits great length. He stands over much ground,
as the phrase is, although his back is short. There is
a common notion that the Arabian at rest keeps his
legs well under him; that he belongs to that type of
which it is said "all four feet would go in a bushel
basket"; but this is erroneous. Often, on the other
hand, the Arabian stands with his fore legs bent
backward from the knee, which is thought to be a
good formation or habit. In the length of his body,
in the length of his hind legs, which is extreme, and
in the fact that he stands higher behind than in front,
there is a resemblance between the Arabian horse, at
least the Anazeh horse, and the typical American
trotter. Maud S., for example, has these peculiarities. Sunol has them in still greater degree. The
Anazeh mares, moreover, are very long from hip to
hock, and this again is the almost invariable formation of the trotting horse. The body of the Arabian
is elegantly shaped. His ribs are more deeply arched

than is usually the case with our horses, and consequently he swells out behind the shoulders in a graceful curve, whereas both the running horse and the trotter are very apt to be what is called slab-sided.

Another peculiarity of the Arabian is the great length of his pastern joints, to which is chiefly due the remarkable springiness and elasticity of his gait. "He is so light that he could dance upon the bosom of a woman without bruising it." And a quaint writer thus describes a mare of the desert: "All shining, beautiful, and gentle of herself, she seemed a darling life upon that savage soil, not worthy of her gracious pasterns." Nor, despite its length, does this joint ever break down with the Arabian horse, as happens so frequently with the English racer. Grogginess and knuckling over are unknown in the desert.

As to the legs of the Arabian, they are as hard as flint; spavin, curb, and ringbone are very infrequent. In speaking of a certain Anazeh mare, a bay with black points, Major Upton declares that her legs appeared to have been cut out of black marble, and then highly polished. The knees and hocks of the Arabian are large, as they are in all good horses. "A Bedawee, whose mare had a foal running by her side, being pursued, feared that his steed would not do her best, out of consideration for the foal; therefore he struck at the foal with his lance, and it fell back disabled. But when the Arab stopped his mare, the foal shortly made its appearance; and although it had been wounded in the hocks, it had made such good play that it was called the father or possessor of good hocks. It is a strain most highly esteemed."

Another family is descended from "the Mare of the Old Woman," whose story is as follows. A Bedawee had been pursued for some days through a long and devious course. On the way his mare gave birth to a foal, but her master soon mounted again and continued his flight, leaving the little creature to its fate. However, when he stopped at night to rest, the infant appeared, having followed all the way, notwithstanding its extreme youth, and thereupon he gave it to an old woman, who brought it up by hand; and this foal, "the Mare of the Old Woman," became the mother of a noted family.[1]

As to the manner in which the Arabs treat their horses, it is pleasant to be assured that neither romance nor tradition has exaggerated its kindness and familiarity. "Their great merit as horse-breakers is unwearied patience. Loss of temper with a beast is not in their nature, and I have never seen them strike or ill use their mares in any way." If Providence provided Central Arabia as a region peculiarly fit for breeding sound horses, it would seem also that the ancient Arabian race was specially designed to have the nurture and training of these high-bred animals. The Arabs have a saying which is indicative of their character. "A noble may labor with his own hands, without disgrace, in three cases, — for his horse, for his father, and for his guest."

It is clear that rough treatment would soon convert Arabian horses into demons. Mr. William Day, the well known English trainer, conjectures that the ill

---

[1] The endurance of young foals is surprising. I know of a case in which a foal only ten days old travelled by the side of its dam, a Morgan, over fifty miles in about twelve hours, without injury.

temper and ferocity which characterize some strains
of the English thoroughbred come from the Arab
blood in their ancestry. Hence he infers that Arabian horses are bad-tempered. His conjecture is very
likely correct, but his inference is a vicious one. It
is not improbable that a generation or two of the old-
fashioned English groom, with his rough "Come up,
horse!" and dig in the ribs or kick in the belly,
added to the use of whips and spurs and severe bits,
would sour the temper and awake the resentment of
so highly bred and finely organized an animal as one
of Arabian descent. But in the desert viciousness in
the horse is absolutely unknown. The Arab rides,
without saddle or stirrups, on a small pad fastened in
place by a surcingle. As for bridle and bit, he has
none. The horse is guided by a halter, the rope of
which the rider holds in his hand, and he is controlled by the voice. "I have never seen either violent plunging, rearing, or indeed any serious attempt
made to throw the rider. Whether a Bedouin would
be able to sit a bare-backed, unbroken four-year-old
colt as the Gauchos of South America do is exceedingly doubtful."

The Arabian mare has no more fear of her master
than a dog would have with us, and she is on terms
of almost canine intimacy with the whole family.
An old traveller in the desert describes an incident
on a wet evening at the sheikh's tent: "Evening
clouds gathered. . . . The mare returned of herself
through the falling weather, and came and stood at
our coffee fire, in half-human wise, to dry her soaked
skin and warm herself as one among us. She approached the sitters about the hearth, and, putting

down her soft nose, kissed each member of the group, till the sheikh was fain to rise and scold his mare away."

"Ali's tent," writes Mr. Blunt, "was partly occupied by a filly and a bay foal, the latter not a week old, and very engaging. It was tied up, as the custom is, by a rope round the neck, while its mother was away grazing, and neighed continually. It was very tame, however, and let me stroke it, and sniffed at my pockets, as if it knew that there might be some sugar there."

No wonder, then, that the Arabian foals are described as being gentle and familiar. They do not run away when they are approached at pasture; they are not to be intimidated by the flourishing of sticks or by the waving of garments. If they happen to be lying down when one comes near them, they continue in that position, instead of scrambling to their feet in alarm; and they have an engaging habit of using their masters as rubbing-posts. All this is true, in general, of our trotting-bred American foals. The fact is that any colt, whatever its origin, if treated with uniform kindness, will become by the age of six or eight months as tame and fearless as the pets of the desert.

The manner of rearing the Arabian colt is as follows. It is weaned at the tender age of one month, instead of being allowed to run with its mother for four, five, or six months, according to our custom. but it is then fed on camel's milk, which is very nutritious. So soon as it is weaned, the dam goes out to pasture, and the foal remains close by the tent, being tied by a cord around the neck, or around the hind

leg above the hock. The children play with it, and
when it is a year old they mount it occasionally, and
thus it gradually becomes accustomed to carrying
weight. Before it attains two years of age it has
been ridden by a half-grown boy, and a year later it
is put through some long and severe gallops. The
Bedouins maintain — very unreasonably, as Western
experience shows — that, unless a horse has done hard
work before he is three years old, he will never be fit
to do it afterward. It may be, indeed, that Arabian
and "thoroughbred" horses can do hard work in
their colthood with impunity; but of half-bred, still
more of cold-blooded horses, Shakspere's adage still
holds true:

> "The colt that's backed and burdened being young
> Loseth his pride, and never waxeth strong."

When the Arabian colt is about two and a half
years old, besides being taught to gallop in the figure
of an 8, and to change his leg, so as to become supple,
he is ridden by his master on a journey. The consequence of this heroic treatment is, that splints are not
uncommon in Arabian horses, and sometimes their
shank bones become bent permanently. Occasionally,
also, the colt gets a pair of broken knees by being
ridden over rough ground at too early an age. But,
strange to say, the Arabians make no account of such
a blemish. Their horses, when full grown, never fall,
despite their careless way of walking. "The Arabian
horse is too sure of his footing to be careful, except
on rough ground, and there he never makes a false
step."

I own a Morgan mare which has precisely the
same peculiarity. On ordinary roads she will not

take the pains to avoid an obstacle such as a stone,
and will frequently trip over it, knowing full well
that she can always save herself with the other leg.
But I have driven this same mare down a mountain
side, where the only road was the dry bed of a rocky
stream, and there she picked her way in perfect
safety, without taking a false step.

The smallness of the Arabian horse is due partly,
at least, to scantiness of food. "Horses, mares, and
colts, all alike, are starved during a great part of the
year, no corn being ever given, and only camel's milk
when other food fails. They are often without water
for several days together, and in the most piercing
nights of winter they stand uncovered, and with no
more shelter than can be got on the lee side of the
tents. Their coats become long and shaggy, and they
are left uncombed and unbrushed till the new coat
comes in spring. At these times they are ragged-
looking scare-crows, half starved, and as rough as
ponies. In the summer, however, their coats are as
fine as satin, and they show all the appearance of
breeding one has a right to expect of their blood."

The cow-pony of our Western and Southwestern
States is akin to the Arabian, being descended from
the Barbs (in part Arabian) that the Spaniards
brought over when they conquered South America;
and the cow-pony and the Arabian horse fare very
much the same in winter, and undergo a similar
change in spring. "The cow-pony," writes Colonel
T. A. Dodge in a private letter, "in many places, in
the winter, looks like a bear. His hide becomes fur,
and his legs are as big as barrels. But when he
scours out in the spring, he is as fine as any thorough-

bred. He comes of the same stock which produced
the English thoroughbred, and he has had the very
best of training in running away from wolves and in
hunting his fodder. In other words, with him the
species is a survival of the fittest. . . Barring his
attenuated form, which comes from his annual starv-
ing, he is one of the most astonishing creatures ever
made."

The last touch of romance is added to the Bedouin
when we learn that he is not in any sense a horse-
dealer. The town Arab is often a dealer in horses,
but the Arab of the desert treasures the glorious
animal for his own sake, and not as a merchantable
commodity. If he has a mare to sell, there she is, —
you may take her or leave her; but the owner will
make no attempt to exaggerate her virtues or to
apologize for her defects. "He knows little of
showing off a horse, or even of making him stand to
advantage; but, however anxious he may be to sell
him, brings him just as he is, dirty and ragged, tired,
and perhaps broken-kneed. He has a supreme contempt himself for everything except blood in his
beast, and he expects everybody else to have the
same." The Arabian horse is frequently blemished
by lance wounds and other injuries, and especially
from firing with the hot iron. This is the sovereign
remedy among the Arabs for man and horse, and
upon both animals it is practised to a cruel and
ridiculous degree. Mr. Palgrave mentions one case
where a deep circular wound had been burned upon
the skull of an insane man, the injury being sufficiently great to cause the madness which it was
intended to cure.

Often, indeed, it requires the eye of a skilled horseman to detect the merit and high breeding of a mare
fresh from the desert, in her winter coat and winter
condition.   An old traveller relates how such a mare,
sent by a Nedji prince to an Egyptian Pasha, was
criticised by those who saw her: "Merry were these
men of settled countries, used to stout hackneys.
'The carrion!' cried one, for indeed she was lean
and uncurried. 'The Pasha would not accept her,'
said another.   But a Syrian who stood by quietly
remarked, 'A month at Shem, and she will seem
better than now.'   And some Bedouins who were
present declared her worth to be thirty camels."

It is true, as this traveller sagely declared, that
men of "settled countries, used to stout hackneys,"
often prefer an inferior horse to the pure-bred Arabian.   The Barb, for example, has a bigger crest and
is more on the prancing order.

I have touched already upon the views of the
Arabo-maniacs.   With them the problem of horse-
breeding is a very simple one. the solution being to
discard all other breeds as mongrels, and to go back
to "the primitive horse." the horse of the desert.
On the other hand. most practical men engaged in
the business deride this notion.   "I cannot help
thinking," writes one such. "that of all insane ideas
the maddest is that which some enthusiasts have of
permanently improving English race horses by an
admixture of Arab blood. as if the difference between
the various breeds of horses were not the result of
climate, selection, stable management. work, and
training."   It is, I believe, a fact — so malleable
is horseflesh — that a thoroughbred foal, born in

India, of parents imported from England, bears un-mistakable evidence of his birthplace; and in the second or third generation the colonized thorough-bred loses all resemblance to the native English stock.

No doubt, as the writer just quoted maintains, the race horse of to-day cannot be improved by an infusion of Arab blood. He is bigger, faster, than the Arab, and could beat him over any distance short of one hundred miles; perhaps indeed over any distance whatever. It is probably the same in regard to trotting horses; and yet, as I have mentioned, the Arabian formation, especially as it is found in the Anazeh family, closely resembles that of a typical trotter. Moreover, the Arabian trotting gait seems to be much the same as that of our horses. Thus Major Upton writes : " When trotting, the hind legs of the Arabian appear to be, and often may be, too long, and there is too much reach for a pleasant trot-ting pace [not for speed]; yet with good riding some will trot grandly." This is precisely what might be said of an American trotter if used as a saddle horse. However, the Arabian horses are deficient in trotting action forward; and on the whole it is very doubtful if any gain in trotting speed could be made at this late day by an Arabian cross.

But if the object were, not to obtain a race horse, either at the running or trotting gait, but to produce a family of fine saddle or driving horses, especially the former, for general use, then indeed it might be well to breed from Arabian stock. Success would be certain. The only question would be whether you could reach your end the more quickly by this means, or by breeding from the best of our own horses; and this is a problem which nothing short of experiment can solve. It must be remembered that no serious attempt on a large scale has ever been made in this country to raise horses with a view to beauty, intelligence, courage, and soundness; and these are the respects in which the Arabians excel.

Moreover, the perfectly natural way in which they take to jumping, an exercise of which they have not the slightest experience in the desert, shows that the Arabian horses are entirely harmonious in all their parts, and therefore adaptable to any use that might be required of them. Lady Anne Blunt relates: "The mare I rode on the journey carried me over the raised watercourses by the Euphrates in the cleverest way in the world; off and on, without the least hanging or hesitation, and always with a foot ready to bring down in case of need." One of the mares brought home by Mr. Blunt was let loose in his park on the night of her arrival, and forthwith she jumped the fence, five feet and six inches high. The lower rails were then pulled down, and she was walked back under the top one, a thick, oaken bar, several inches higher than her withers.

Few Arabian horses have been imported to this country, especially of late years; but it is a striking fact that, when one hears of some extraordinary feat performed by an American horse, it is not infrequently added that his dam or grandam, or some more remote ancestor, was "said to be Arabian." I saw not long ago, for instance, in a Maine pasture, a little roan mare, not otherwise remarkable in appearance, but of a distinctly Arabian cast of countenance. She had a nose that would "go in a pint pot," a neat head, fine ears, and a large, intelligent, though wicked eye. This little mare is reputed to be a remarkable road-ster, and a former owner declares that he once drove her from Gardiner to Phillips, Maine, in five hours and a half. The distance is fifty-five miles. The dam of her grandsire was a half-bred Arab, and the foal at her side when I saw them showed even more distinctly than its mother the Arab strain in its ancestry.

The dam of the famous Flora Temple was by a "spotted Arabian horse." Leopard Rose, a spotted mare that made a sensation on the track in 1889 and 1890, winning many races, and getting a record of 2.15¼, was by Killbuck Tom, and he by a circus horse said to be of Arab descent. Numerous like instances might be cited. Of course, no pure Arabian was ever "spotted," but I am inclined to think that some at least of the animals thus described had Arabian blood in their veins. Still, the point is doubtful.

One of the best roadsters in Maine of recent years was a mare descended from "Royal Tar," a mysterious white stallion who is said to have swum ashore from a vessel wrecked near Eggemoggin Reach, and who not improbably was of Eastern birth.

The grandam of this roadster is described as an "ordinary" black mare, and her sire was Tom Knox, a black horse; but she, like her dam, inherited the white color of her grandsire, Royal Tar. She was once driven eighty-seven miles in a day of fourteen hours, hauling two people in a top buggy, doing the last thirty-six miles in four hours. and winding up with a race of some miles down the road from Bucks-

port to Bangor, which she won. This mare weighed
about nine hundred pounds; her back was very short;
her eyes were "large and expressive"; she was low-
headed, and a hard puller. I ought not, however, to
speak of her in the past tense, for my informant adds
"She is now nineteen years old, and has n't seen a
windpuff."

An old gentleman who has owned many valuable
horses told me lately that the best and most intelligent of them all was a medium-sized gelding, with a
dash of Arab blood. One very hot day he drove this
horse sixty miles in a heavy buggy, putting up toward
night at the house of a friend. After the nag had
thoroughly cooled off, the negro groom in charge
mounted and took him out for a bath in a neighboring
river. The horse enjoyed it so much that he swam
hither and thither for a considerable distance with
the darkey on his back, and, finally coming ashore,
he finished the day's work by taking the bit in his
teeth and running away on the high road for three or
four miles out of pure lightness of heel and heart.
"Massa," said the negro, when he led this extraordinary animal to the door on the following morning,
not daring to get in the vehicle and drive, "Massa,
this hoss am de debil!"

One experiment now making in this country with
regard to Arabian horses deserves mention. Mr.
Randoph Huntington is a veteran horseman, whose
devotion to the Henry Clay family of trotters (descended from the Barb, Grand Bashaw) and to the
Arabian horse may be described without exaggeration
as heroic. I have quoted in a previous chapter his
description of old Henry Clay. For many years the

Clays were the victims of prejudice, the result partly
of ignorance, partly of designed misrepresentation;
and Mr. Huntington, like the horses that he loved,
was a perpetual target for ridicule and abuse. Of
late, however, the value of this strain has asserted
itself so clearly that it cannot be denied by the most
envious person. Mr. Huntington owns the Anazeh
mare Naomi, and he has established a stock company,
with headquarters on Long Island, for the purpose of
breeding a family of Clay-Arabian horses. What
may be the capacity of these Clay-Arabians, as they
are called, I do not know, but some of them are animals of extreme beauty and finish, as symmetrical as
their Oriental ancestors, and much larger.

As an Arabo-maniac, Mr. Huntington has stood
almost alone in this country. He had one predeces-
sor, a Kentucky gentleman, a breeder of running
horses, who staked his fortune and his hopes upon
the success of his Arabian stud. Twice this man
visited the desert to buy horses, having become convinced that on his first attempt he obtained none of
the pure breed. The enterprise was a failure, and he
died bankrupt and broken-hearted.

It would be interesting to know how far the Arabo-
maniacs have been influenced, unwittingly of course,
by the halo of romance which surrounds the courser
of the desert. At all events, it is a generous enthusiasm which this far-away steed kindles in the breasts
of his few and scattered devotees among English-
speaking people. The passion for horseflesh is, I
hold, a sort of divine madness; and Arabo-mania is
one form of it. Let us deal with it gently.

## XI.

## THE CARE OF HORSES.

SO many treatises have been written concerning the horse and his stable that I should do better, some critics might think, to let the matter alone. But my excuse is this: I do not mean to write a treatise, but only a chapter; and, unless my knowledge of horse books is at fault, the modest task of putting the essentials of the subject in so brief a form has never yet been attempted. The present essay will contain no long Latin words, no medical terms, no vague prescriptions; it will merely treat of those commonplace things which more learned authors are apt to omit. Nor do I pretend to write for the typical horseman, who would scorn to obtain information from the printed page. He knows already all that man can know. I have not forgotten the anger and contempt with which a certain blacksmith, a good mechanic, moreover, once told me of a present that he had just received from a grateful customer. It was a work on the diseases of the hoof, written by a Vet of five times his experience and ten times his information. "To think," he exclaimed, in the tone of one whose pride had received a wanton insult, — "to think that any book could teach me anything about the foot of a hoss!"

Now I fear that we horsemen are all more or less like this blacksmith; and accordingly I address myself, not to the craft, but to the ordinary horse owner, who has acquired no special knowledge of the animal, and who does not enjoy the services of a stud-groom. Nevertheless, I make bold to say that among the following pages will be found a few original remarks, worthy the attention even of a horseman. It would be odd indeed had I failed to pick up an idea or two concerning matters that lie so near my heart. And here I might repeat what was said to me last summer by a middle-aged farmer, a rough, grizzle-headed "Down-easter." We stood in his barnyard on a pleasant Sunday afternoon, while a weanling filly — whose high merits had just been pointed out — contentedly chewed an enormous and horny thumb extended by her master for that purpose. Suddenly the farmer turned to me, — being careful, however, not to disengage his thumb, — and remarked, with an obvious and unusual effort at introspection, "I like a good horse awful well!" So do I, — so, I am persuaded, does the reader, — and accordingly, with his permission, we will put on our hats, and saunter out to

## The Stable.

The first thing to notice is that the occupants poke their heads out as we approach. This means that they are kept in box stalls, and are accustomed to be petted and to be fed with apples, carrots, and other equine dainties. I am a believer in box stalls. A horse loose in his box — and he should not be tied unless for some special reason — gets an appreciable amount of exercise in walking about his quarters. The difference in this respect is so great that often a horse, whose legs stock in a straight stall, will remain perfectly smooth if he be given the run of a loose box. So also, the animal in a box stall, having more freedom of movement, is much less likely to take to kicking, cribbing, or weaving, — all these vices being induced by ennui and restlessness. But the chief advantage of a box stall is that it gives the horse more opportunity to lie down, to stretch himself, and to roll. He likes to lie, as a dog does, with his head flat on the ground, and with all four legs stretched out at length, and this attitude is impossible in a straight stall unless it be extraordinarily wide. Every stable should contain at least one box stall, to be occupied by the horses in turn, or in case of illness.

The more a horse lies down, the longer will his legs and feet last. Therefore, in a straight as well as in a box stall there should always be bedding under the horse, and, if tied at all, he should be so tied that he can lie down at ease. It is a common, almost an invariable, fault of grooms to tie up their horses too short, lest they should get cast. But with nine horses out of ten — forty-nine out of fifty, I think I might say — this precaution is unnecessary. In straight stalls I tie my horses so that they can rest their heads flat on the floor, and I have never had one injured by so doing. In many stables, if an animal is seen to lie down in the daytime, it is at once concluded that he must be ill. But give a horse bedding and sufficient halter rope, and it will soon become habitual with him to lie down for a part of the day as well as of the night. I have noticed especially that horses like to recline in the morning, after they have finished eating, comfortably snoozing while they digest their breakfast. Horses that are out of the stable all day, such as cart and hack horses, should always have their hay at night on the floor of the stall, in order that they may eat and lie down at the same time. This plan, as we have seen, is usually pursued with fire horses, and its advantages are plain. The disadvantage of the method is that it would, in some cases, entail a waste of fodder, but the waste would be slight.

I do not quite share the modern prejudice against the old-fashioned hay-rack. It is dangerous, the authorities say, because hay-seeds are likely to fall from it into the animal's eyes. This may be so, but I never heard or read of any such actual case. The disadvantage of a hay-rack placed on the floor is that the horse can eat from it easily and quickly: whereas with the high hay-rack, protected by numerous bars, he has some little difficulty in pulling out his fodder, and hence will be longer in consuming it, thus facilitating digestion, and giving him something to do. The best arrangement, it seems to me, would be a rack placed at a medium height, and well defended by bars or slats.

By this time, however, I assume that the reader and myself have put our heads over the first door, and are looking inside the stalls. There are five in this row, and the solid partitions between them run up to a height of less than a foot beyond the withers of an ordinary sized horse. At that point the partition is continued by three horizontal rails, to prevent neighbors from biting each other. An iron network would be better, perhaps, but I used a discarded lightning rod which happened to be on hand. Thus, a clear space over all the stalls is obtained for light and air, and more especially for social purposes. A horse should always be able to see his neighbor; and if there is but one loose box in a stable, it should be contiguous to the straight stalls. A horse shut up in a box stall, made, as it sometimes is, with a solid door and but one small window, is forlorn and unhappy. In some stables the partitions between the loose boxes are composed entirely of iron network, — a good arrangement unless it should render the stalls draughty.

The reader will observe that my loose boxes face the south, that there is a window in each, and that the door is cut in two, having an upper and a lower part. Thus, the temperature can be regulated in a considerable degree. Good dimensions for a loose box to contain a horse of medium size are twelve feet by twelve, but a box ten feet by ten, or perhaps even smaller, would be better than a straight stall. Mr. G. Tattersall states the proper size of a hunter's box as twenty-two feet long and thirteen feet wide. In a recent work will be found a plan for making loose boxes convertible at will to straight stalls.[1]

If the latter are used, they should be as wide as possible; and they should be long, not less than twelve feet. Short stalls have three disadvantages: they allow two contiguous horses to kick each other, —a possible but infrequent evil; they fail to protect the hind legs from draughts; and, worst of all, they enable the occupant to stand with the toes of his hind feet in the gutter, which usually runs behind the stalls. This is a bad position, being certain, if long continued, to result in a straining of the cords and muscles of the pastern. It is said in all horse books that the stall should slope backward but a trifle, only just enough for purposes of drainage; but I go further, and declare that it ought not to slope at all. I believe that the natural position of a horse is with his fore legs actually lower than his hind legs, and certainly he should never be put in a stall where his fore legs must stand in the least degree higher than his hind legs.

Perfect cleanliness can be obtained by having the stall floored with slate, sloping as much as may be desired. On the top of this is laid a removable floor of wooden or metal slats, so supported that it is exactly level. On this the horse stands, and, as it is easily taken up, the slate floor can be flushed with water every morning. It may be doubted if a stable should ever have a pipe or gutter connecting with a sewer, the danger of its becoming clogged is so great.

[1] "Stable Building and Stable Fitting," by Giraud. London: B. T. Batsford, 1891.

The bedding, acting as an absorbent, should always be the main reliance for drainage.

The necessity of sunlight in a stable is now so well understood that it need not be dwelt upon. The horse, having a peculiarly fine organization, is especially sensitive to the presence or absence of sunshine. A good Vet will never perform an operation on a cloudy day if it be possible to postpone it; and where distemper, or any other disease, runs through a stable, it will, I believe, invariably be found that the lightest cases and quickest recoveries occur in the stalls that receive the most sunshine, although none of them may be actually dark. So also it is now commonly understood that stables should be cool, — a truth which English horsemen have been very slow to learn. Even "Nimrod," an advanced writer with new and sensible theories about hunters, thought that horses could hardly be kept in the pink of condition if the temperature of their quarters fell much below seventy-five degrees! To their hot, ill ventilated stables many English writers ascribe the former excessive prevalence of roaring, now fast decreasing in England, and in this country almost unknown.

A temperature of fifty-five degrees is not far from the right one in winter, and any degree of cold above freezing will be borne by horses with perfect comfort, provided they are well blanketed. The real enemy of the horse is not cold, but dampness; and against that he is to be defended at all points. If a horse begins to cough, let him be put in the sunniest, driest part of the stable, and he will recover the sooner, even though his new situation be much cooler than the old one. Dogs in damp kennels always have rheumatism, and horses have even less affinity than dogs for dampness. Dryness of climate, says a recent writer, "is the great factor in producing not only sound feet, but sound limbs, tendons, and bone." However, it is time to look a little closer at our stalls, and to see what they contain in the way of

## BEDDING.

Here is a gamy-looking black mare standing on a deep bed of dark brown stuff which might be, and indeed has been, mistaken by the unsophisticated for a muck-heap. I need hardly say that it is peat-moss. It is not nice to look at, and one would rather see his horses knee deep in golden straw; but it has this great advantage: it cannot be eaten even by the most voracious animal, and consequently it is suitable for horses that devour their bedding and get too fat. Moreover, it keeps the feet soft. No horse bedded with peat-moss ever requires to have his feet stopped; and it is invaluable in cases where the hoof is defective or deficient, and needs to be "grown out." Further, it is free from odor, and incombustible. Sometimes peat-moss renders the frog too soft, so that the horse, especially if he be used unshod, is apt to become foot-sore, but this bad effect might always be avoided by a frequent renewal of the peat-moss.

And this brings us to the question of expense. The material costs about $2.50 per bale, and each bale will supply one box stall or two straight stalls. The peat-moss should be forked over every day to mix the wet and the dry. But how long does it last? That depends almost entirely upon the habit of the particular horse in eating his hay; if he eats it up clean, the peat-moss bedding will last a long time. The black mare before us was bedded down seven weeks ago, and her bed will last a week or two yet, perhaps longer. Other horses, that scatter their hay and trample it under foot, need a fresh bale every two or three weeks, and perhaps the average time that it lasts in good condition is four weeks. Thus it appears, on the whole, that peat-moss is a cheap form of bedding.

In summer, sawdust frequently renewed makes a good bed, but it is too cold for winter, except as a substratum with straw on top. Where I live "meadow" hay cut near the river can be had for $6 or $7 per ton. It is not quite so clean as straw for bedding; but some of it will be eaten by horses, and, unless their work is fast work, it forms not only a cheap, but also a wholesome food. The best straw for bedding, as everybody knows, is rye straw, which usually costs about $20 per ton, and is more economical than oat straw, which costs about half as much. The bedding should of course be well dried in the sun; meadow hay can thus be used twice, oat straw two or three times, and rye straw half a dozen times or more.

The chief points to be observed about bedding are, first, that it should always be kept under a horse, for the reasons previously stated, and, secondly, that it should be used profusely. A horse likes a deep soft bed. — such as he does not usually have in New England. An English groom will bed down his horses in a manner to make a Yankee stare. But if the truth were known, liberal bedding is not only beneficial to the horse, it is also economical. If much straw be used, it can all be dried, and used again and again, whereas, if the supply be stinted, a large part of it will become so dirty as to be incapable of further use. Bedding is only less important than

## FEEDING.

Under fed, hard worked horses sometimes fall in the street from sheer weakness, induced by want of oats. On the other hand, many, perhaps most, gentlemen's horses are fed too high. In city stables, especially in boarding and club stables, the horses receive too much grain and too little hay. Consequently they are apt to have a shrunken appearance, and to become what is known as "grain-burnt."

For young horses and colts, hay three times a day, and plenty of it, is indispensable. The physiological reason for this was well stated by Hiram Woodruff, as follows: "In order to thrive, the horse, young or old, must not only have his stomach supplied with a sufficient quantity of nutritious food, but also with enough matter not so highly nutritious to distend it. A horse or a colt fed only on the substances which go to make up his substance would starve, though you gave them to him in the greatest abundance." And he adds, on the same subject: "While the animal is young, a good distention of the stomach is calculated to produce that roundness of rib which we see in so many of our best horses. Now this capacity of the carcass . . . is not going to be obtained by the feeding of food in the concentrated shape. Bulk is required, and the pulp and essence need not be given in large quantity until the organization is formed, and extraordinary exertion is required of the horse."

"Make your head early, my boy," was a piece of advice solemnly given to me by an old toper, when I was about twelve years of age; and if I were to admonish a colt in the same spirit, I should say to him, "Make your stomach early."

Much benefit is often obtained from a change of food. Thus, if a horse does not do well on oats and hay, he may be tried with provender in place of oats. "Provender," as the term is used hereabout, means oats and corn ground up together; and sometimes the mixture is subjected by the miller to a steaming or cooking process, with good results. This is of course a heavier food than oats, and more fattening; but it may safely be given in cold weather. In cold weather, also, a little whole corn (cracked corn is always to be avoided) can be fed to advantage. A pint of corn in two or three quarts of bran, made into a mash with boiling water, constitutes an excellent supper on a wintry night for horses that are doing very little work. But for riding and driving horses, the chief reliance in the way of grain, year in and year out, must be oats.

As to the quantity proper to be given, no rules can be laid down, because horses differ so much in this respect. Here, for example, if the reader will accompany me to the end of the row, are two contiguous stalls occupied respectively by a big bay mare and a small black one. The bay mare is a handsome creature, with an aristocratic head, large mild eyes, and hunter-like legs; but her back is too long, the coupling is loose, and her constitution is soft. The black mare, on the contrary, is a short-backed, compact, tough, wiry animal, and she will do twice the

work of the bay mare on exactly half the food. This
bay mare has another peculiarity, she bolts her oats
without stopping to chew them. To correct this, an
old bridle is always kept hanging at the door of the
stall, and when her oats are given to her the bit is
slipped in her mouth. It would be well also, in the
case of such horses, when kept in loose boxes, to
have a manger made in the shape of a long narrow
trough, running the length of the stall. If the oats
were scattered over this manger, an additional hindrance to bolting them would be provided. A "slow
feeding" manger has been patented, and is now on
the market, which accomplishes the same object by
doling out the oats through a small aperture.

Ground oats can sometimes be fed with advantage,
but a horse that bolts his grain is apt to be a "soft"
horse, and to feed him on ground oats would aggravate
this tendency. Not long since, I happened to take
up a disquisition on pigs, and my eye fell upon this
passage : "A hog ought to eat his food up clean, but
he ought not to make a mad rush for the trough;
that shows an inferior constitution." I believe that
this remark is equally true of horses.

After what I have said of the two animals just
mentioned, the reader will hardly need to be told
that the bay mare seldom if ever requires a bran
mash; whereas the black mare has one twice a week
through the winter, when grass is not obtainable.
The office of a bran mash is to loosen the bowels, cool
the blood, and purify the system. At the close of a
long, hot day's work, give a horse a good cleaning, a
bran mash, and a soft bed, and it is wonderful how
fresh he will come out in the morning. And here — at

the risk of causing some horsy person to throw down my book in disgust — I will state this elementary fact: A bran mash,[1] consisting ordinarily of six quarts, is made by pouring boiling water upon the bran, stirring it, and then covering it with a thick cloth or otherwise, and letting it steam for fifteen or twenty minutes. The cloth may then be removed and the bran given to the horse, in winter while it is still warm, in summer when it is cool.

All tough healthy horses need bran, or its equivalent. In fact, this general proposition may be laid down: strong horses kept on stable food have a tendency to tightness of the bowels, just as delicate horses have the opposite tendency. In the latter case, a simple remedy, to be used whenever necessary, is a cupful of ordinary wheat flour mixed with the grain or put in a pail of water. In some stables the horses are "salted" when they receive a bran mash; but the better plan is always to have a lump of rock salt in a little rack by itself, where it will not contaminate the oats. Thus the horse can help himself according to his needs. When salt is given only occasionally, the animal is sure to take a great deal, and to follow it up by drinking immoderately of cold water. Colic has often been caused in this manner.

Bran is a kind of artificial grass, and in summer I prefer to let my horses graze a little, or, if this be impracticable, to have grass cut for them, which they like much less. Not many years ago it would have been thought madness to give grass to a horse in full training; but this is done nowadays with great benefit.

---

[1] I use the generic term "bran," but I mean "shorts," which have more body than bran.

in the case both of runners and trotters. If possible, let the horse graze in the early morning, while the blades are still wet. The grass is sweeter and more juicy at this time, and the dew is an excellent medicine for the feet.

When horses have their shoes removed and are turned out to pasture, care should be taken not to make the change too sudden. Many a fine animal has been killed by direct transition from a warm stable and blankets to the open air and cold ground. Let the blankets be taken off while the horse is still kept under cover; and turn him out at night for the first time. If he is turned out in the morning, he will feed all day, and at night-time lie down, and, very likely, catch cold; but if he is turned out hungry at night, he will keep on his feet all or nearly all the time till morning; and the first night is of course the dangerous one. Another good plan is to take the horse in the first night just before you go to bed; and finally, it is practicable to turn a horse out blanketed. A second surcingle sewed to the blanket and passing around the flanks can be used. A horse in active service can thus be given a night out with safety.

Now, however, as I observe that the reader is becoming bored, we will move on to the grooming-room; but as we pass by the hay-mows I cannot refrain from this remark: the popular notion that horses like coarse hay best, and thrive best upon it, is a huge mistake. The second or third quality of hay as it would be deemed in respect to coarseness is the best. Nine city horsemen out of ten, I am aware, would deny this proposition: but the tenth is the man who has tried the experiment.

But here we are at the watering trough, and despite my implied promise, I shall button-hole the reader for a moment more before we leave the main stable. Horses require water that is pure and soft. Many well-bred nags will not drink from a pail in which another animal has already had his nose. The Arabs regard pure water as of the highest importance; and they do not hesitate to risk their lives, as by leaving camp at night when the enemy is near, in order to water their horses at some fresh spring of which they have knowledge. This is the form in which they describe a man of thoroughly bad and contemptible character:—

> " His horse drinks troubled water,
> And his covering is full of holes."

The oftener a horse drinks in the course of the day, the less he will drink. Therefore, the best plan is to have water always before him at his meals. It was found by experiment at the Duke of Beaufort's stables, that under this, the modern system, a horse drank only five gallons, whereas, when watered but twice during the day, he drank eight gallons.[1] Of course, if the comparison had been made with three instead of two waterings a day, the discrepancy would not have been so great. At Badminton, I believe, slate troughs are used for this purpose. A better plan, perhaps would be to have pail-holders fixed alongside the grain mangers. Then a pail of fresh water could be put in whenever the horse was fed.

---

[1] From this it seems necessary to infer that formerly at Badmington horses were watered but twice a day, although it is difficult to believe that so preposterous a system was practised.

With a permanent watering trough in the stall, there must be danger of the water becoming stale, and also of the horse's drinking from it when he comes in heated by his work.

The next best thing to having water constantly before the horse at his meals is to give it to him frequently, four times a day being the minimum. Should he be watered before or after eating? All the books say before, but in this country the almost universal practice is to give it afterward. The theory of the books is, that, when a horse is watered after his feed of grain, the water tends to wash the latter out of his stomach, where it should digest, to the gut or second stomach. But it seems to be more natural for the horse, as it is for man, to drink after eating rather than before, provided he cannot drink while eating. A horse who is both hungry and thirsty will refuse water until he has had food. There is another consideration which I have never seen mentioned, namely, that a horse is likely to eat his grain more slowly, and to chew it better, if he is thirsty, than if he has just been watered. My own way is to water him after he has eaten his grain, and before he has his hay. At Palo Alto the horses are watered two hours after eating. Whatever the system adopted, there is one time at which almost all horses like to drink, and that is about nine or ten at night, when the stable is, or should be, visited by the groom or master, the beds arranged if they need it, surcingles looked to, and the horses watered.

As to watering on the road, very good horsemen differ widely in their practice, some eschewing watering troughs almost altogether, whereas others drive up to every trough, and let the horse drink his fill. Neither example, in my opinion, should be followed. The best way is to water the roadster often in hot weather, but to give him only a little at a time; in cold weather, less often. Some horses indeed can be allowed with impunity to drink all they want; well-bred nags especially, although they like to plunge their noses deep in the trough, do not often drink to excess. However, by watching the effect of water upon his horse's bowels, the driver will soon learn how to treat him in this respect.

Even in the stable certain soft horses, whose blood is apt to be heated, should have their appetite for water restrained; they like the feeling of it going down their throats, and will drink greedily. It would be well if such animals were always bitted before being watered; thus they would be compelled to drink slowly, and a less quantity would satisfy them. As a rule, the healthiest horses drink the least. More than one good pailful should never be given at a time to any horse. But let there be no interference with nature in respect to water without good reason. Beyond doubt, some ignorant and fanciful grooms keep their charges in torment for want of it.

One general remark more, and then the reader shall be allowed to escape from the vicinity of the trough: very cold water should always be tempered before it is given to a horse, especially in summer. Now let us enter the small room in front, whence proceeds that periodic whang of the currycomb on the floor, which indicates that within goes on the important process of

## GROOMING.

The necessary tools are a currycomb and the brush that accompanies it, a mane brush, a good, soft cloth. a scraper, towels, a pick for the feet, sponges, and a pail. To these may be added with advantage a softer brush, almost like a hat brush, and a chamois skin. Combs and cards should be banished to the cow stable. To discriminate a good groom from a bad one is a matter for the experienced eye of about fifteen seconds. If a man undertakes to clean your horse, whatever the circumstances, without first removing his coat, you may be sure that he is a sluggard and an impostor. The retention of his waistcoat even gives reasonable ground for suspicion, and the real workman is almost sure to let down his suspenders and roll up his sleeves. When, as will happen sometimes at a New England tavern, a young man wearing spectacles, and with the languid air of a divinity student, looks after the stable, I take off my own coat.

There are four places in especial on the horse which a lazy or incompetent groom will neglect, and which may be examined as a criterion. These are the inside of his ears, the crevice, so to say, under his jaws, the inside of his hind quarters, and the part under his tail, which should be cleaned with a wet sponge at least once a day. for much dust and dandruff collect there. The root of the mane is also frequently a neglected spot.

Perhaps the cardinal principle in grooming is this: the currycomb should not be employed on the horse, but on the brush. Now the ordinary horse owner will declare that this statement is applicable only to the stables of rich men, where grooms are abundant; and such, I confess, was long my opinion. But when finally I tried the experiment with my own hands, I quickly discovered the mistake. The truth is, that a horse can be cleaned not only much better, but much quicker, without the currycomb, used upon him, than with it; the reason being that the currycomb applied to his skin irritates it, and therefore produces more dandruff than it removes. The true way to clean the horse is to rub him round and round with the brush; and to supplement this by smoothing down the hair with a cloth or a chamois skin, or both. Thus he can be made and kept perfectly clean. Even a mane brush is too severe for a very fine-coated animal. An Indian Sayce does his work almost entirely with the palms of his hands. A wet wisp of hay or straw is very effective in taking up dandruff; but the main reliance must be the currycomb brush.

"If a horse is clean," writes Major Fisher,[1] "no scurf or grease of any kind should ever adhere to the hand when rubbed over the skin. If your groom assures you to the contrary, and says that you must expect a *little*, he lies, and knows it too."

It is related of Mr. Jefferson that he was accustomed at Monticello, his Virginia home, whenever a horse was brought round from the stables for his morning ride, to rub the animal's coat with a cambric handkerchief, and if any grease or dirt appeared on it, the negro groom was reprimanded, and the horse sent back to the stables.

---

[1] Author of "Through Stable and Saddle-Room," perhaps the most practical work on the subject of horse-keeping ever published.

Another common mistake relates to the virtues of
"rubbing down." On a hot day, for example, a traveller arriving at his destination flings the reins to the
hostler, and tells him to give the horse "a good rubbing down." But what the animal needs is to cool
off, whereas rubbing tends to heat. A better treatment would be as follows. Take off the harness, and
immediately sponge with cold water the parts under
the collar or breastplate and under the saddle. Thus,
and thus only, are sore backs and shoulders prevented.
If there is any swelling, or as a precaution in hot
weather, it is well to use arnica and water, in the
proportion of two to one. Next sponge his nostrils
and dock; then with a damp, but by no means a wet
sponge, wipe the dust from his whole body; and,
finally, let him drink two swallows of fresh water,
and put him in a stall with plenty of bedding. When
thoroughly cool he may be watered moderately, then
fed, then groomed, watered again, and put to bed. It
is best, of course, especially in hot weather, to have
the horse walked about awhile instead of being put
in his stall at once.[1]

I remember seeing, years ago, a perfect illustration
of what might be called fanatical rubbing down. It
was in a trotting race of many heats, one of the competitors being a little bay stallion, much noted at the
time, called William H. Allen. The practice then was
to rub the horses dry with towels between heats, and

---

[1] "When a journey has been long continued and severe, the
horse should not be immediately put into a stable, but ought to
be walked gently about until the circulation of blood in the feet has
had time to accommodate itself to the altered conditions of rest.
By this means laminitis (inflammation of the feet) is averted."
Mr. George Fleming, F. R. G. S.

William H. Allen was led under a tree for that pur·
pose.   But being a nervous horse, and his skin doubtless being tender from continual rubbing, he strongly
objected to the practice, and spent the whole time of
what should have been his intervals of rest in vain
attempts to kick his tormentors, lashing out at them
with his hind legs, and pawing and striking with his
fore legs.   He lost the race, partly perhaps because
he was handicapped by these unnecessary exertions.
The practice nowadays is, after a brief scraping and
drying, with the application of liniment and sometimes the bandaging of the legs, to walk the horse
about, blanketed according to the weather.

After very long drives I rub my nags' legs with a
strong solution of arnica and water, or, perhaps better, with a mixture of arnica. New England rum, and
water in about equal parts.   Alcohol is of course the
essential ingredient.   This should be applied from a
point above the hock or knee to the foot, and on all
sides of the leg; it tends to prevent spavin, curb, and
windgalls.   There is nothing like rubbing of the legs
for a tired horse.   The animal stands in his stall
with drooping head, eyes nearly closed, and appetite
gone.[1]   Now take him in hand, clean him well but
quickly, then gently pull his ears, and rub his legs
for half an hour if necessary, not up and down, but
downward so as to induce a proper circulation of
the blood, and to soothe the muscles.   Before long
his eyes will open, his head will be raised, his ears
pricked forward, and you will soon have the satisfaction of seeing him munch his hay.

---

[1] I have seen horses in this condition, but not as the result of
my own driving.

In cold weather the advantages of rubbing down are more real: but if the horse be in a sweat, and the stable be cool, there is danger in the process, unless three or four men can be employed in it. "The horse must immediately be rubbed dry, when he comes in," say most of the books; but in the mean time, for it cannot be done in a moment, the horse catches cold. The better way is to let him stand for a minute or five minutes, according to the temperature, and "steam off," then blanket him, and rub his head and neck dry. Every stable should have at least one hood, to be used, for example, when a horse goes to the blacksmith shop in excessively cold weather, and more especially to be used in the stable. In cold weather, whenever a horse comes in thoroughly wet, either with rain or sweat, I put on a hood, removing it as soon as the hair is dry. If the whole body be wet with rain, one thick blanket should be put on, to be followed in about five minutes by another, and perhaps two more, for under these circumstances heavy blanketing is necessary. The water will go to the top blanket, leaving the one next to the horse perfectly dry, — although this result is the opposite of that which the inexperienced person would expect.

And how about the legs? Their proper treatment is summed up in the old stable aphorism: "If they are wet, dry them; if they are dry, leave them dry." Nothing could be more irrational than the practice, formerly common and not yet extinguished, of sluicing the horse's legs with water immediately on his coming into the stable. This might perhaps be done without harm, if the legs could be dried at once after the washing; but this operation would be a long one, and nine times out of ten it would be slurred. Windgalls occur far more frequently in hot weather than in cold weather, and by way of preventing or reducing them I think it well to wash the horse's legs on very hot days, provided that he is perfectly cool at the time.

But no matter how muddy the going may be, the legs ought not to be washed on that account. My method is to brush off so much of the mud as will come off, and then to have the legs bandaged, but not tightly, with flannel or woollen bandages, to be left on, usually half an hour or more, till the hair is perfectly dry. Then they are taken off, and the legs brushed and rubbed clean.[1] Care should be taken to have the bandages come down low, so as to cover the hollow place back of the fetlock joint where "scratches" appear. If this method be pursued. and if plenty of vaseline be used on the heels, and in the spot just mentioned. reinforced occasionally by glycerine, say once a week, scratches and mud fever can be avoided absolutely.

From the legs of the horse. it is a natural transition to

## THE FOOT.

Extreme dryness and extreme moisture are the chief enemies of the equine foot, and they both produce thrush, which is a kind of white decay, indicated by a peculiar and offensive odor. Commonly it attacks the frog, and sometimes the sole of the foot. If taken in hand early. it can be cured by the application of common salt saturated with petroleum ; and the most severe case will yield to a solution of blue vitriol and

---

[1] This is the plan recommended by Major Fisher.

vinegar. The blue vitriol, about two ounces, may be
put in a quart bottle of water, filled with vinegar, the
vinegar to be used when it has aquired a rich green
or blue tinge. It is best applied by means of a small
oil can with a spout. Thus the liquid can be directed
where it is needed. without touching the sound parts
of the foot. Tar and many other remedies are also
used for thrush.

When the horse is groomed in the morning, his feet
should be well picked out. and in summer washed.
In most good stables, the foot is washed also when
the horse comes in. I have noticed that horses seem
to enjoy this process ; and a thorough soaking of the
hoof when they are groomed in the morning, and
again when they come in after work, will go far to
keep their feet soft and healthy. Care should be
taken, especially in winter, that nothing but the hoof
is wetted. It is very easy for the groom to splash a
little water on the heels and under the fetlock, and
thus scratches may be induced. For this reason, the
safer plan is to omit washing the foot in winter unless
your groom happens to be absolutely trustworthy.

At grass, the foot never becomes hard, but when
the horse stands on straw or wood it is apt to become
hard and dry, and many horses require to have their
feet stopped once a week. The time-honored material
for this purpose is a mixture of cow-dung and earth ;
but if it be used, the foot should be well washed the
next morning with soap and water. In city stables,
oil-meal and bran are commonly employed. A recent
invention for this object is petrolatum, — a packing
saturated with petroleum. It comes in pails which
are sold at $1.50 apiece, and a pail will last a long

time. This kind of stuffing is clean, easy to apply, and effectual except in extreme cases. When the foot is very dry, I do not find that it answers the pur pose. Some authorities, moreover, maintain, and I believe rightly, that oil should never be applied to a hoof, because it renders the horn brittle, and impairs its quality. This is the opinion of Charles Marvin, the well known California trainer, whose intelligence and great experience with horses give weight to the assertion. Mr. George Fleming, also, whose prize essay, "Practical Horseshoeing," is the best work on its subject that I have ever seen, holds the same view.

Another method of "stopping," and a very good one, is to put a wet sponge or a handful of moss in the hoof, keeping it in place by a small stick, or, better yet, by a thin piece of steel, stretched across the foot, and inserted under the rim of the shoe. Finally, felt pads can be bought for seventy-five cents a pair, which are secured to the foot by means of an iron toe-piece and a strap and buckle. Thrown into a pail of water, these pads will in a few minutes absorb moisture enough to last all night; and they are convenient to use on a journey. After a very long drive, especially in summer, the horse's fore feet should be stopped as a matter of course.

Where shoeing has to be done frequently, as in the case of fire horses, it is important that the hoof should grow fast, in order to supply the necessary waste of horn. Some horses also, as the result of disease, of bad shoeing, or of bad formation, have a deficiency of hoof. In such cases it is common to apply oil to the hoof; but, as I have stated already, many good

authorities condemn this practice, and I am inclined
to think that cold water is better. Wet rags tied
around the coronet will serve the purpose; and a
sponge arrangement for the outside of the hoof can
be bought. Peat-moss bedding also, as I have said,
encourages a quick growth of horn; and probably the
very best means for this purpose, though one not
often practicable, is to turn the horse out in a pasture, part of which is salt marsh. I have known an
extraordinary growth of hoof to be promoted in this
manner.

For rheumatism and sprains, also, sea water is a
remedy. Its tonic and strengthening effect upon
horses is remarkable. In one case that fell under my
observation, a severe lameness in the shoulder of a
little bay mare was cured by a course of sea baths.
Her owner took her into the water with him one day
as an experiment: the mare liked the process, and
followed her master into the waves every day thereafter for a month, by which time she had completely
recovered.

In another case, a horse received a severe sprain in
one of the hind ankles. Hot and cold water were applied alternately till the inflammation disappeared,
and then a bandage was put on, and kept wet with sea
water. In four days the ankle was as good as ever.

I might add here, that, in all cases of sprains, perfect rest is absolutely necessary; and there is no
better remedy than cold water, applied by means of
a linen bandage, continually wetted. But the bandage
should be taken off at night, for it will become dry in
an hour's time or less, and in that condition it is heat-
ing and harmful. For sprain of the hock, or of other

parts inaccessible to a bandage, or for a sore back. when the skin is not broken, pure alcohol is a remedy which I have found efficacious.

And now I have a word to say about

## SHOEING.

The first principle of shoeing is, that the foot should be reduced by paring or burning only with the greatest caution, and in the least possible degree. Indeed, some of the latest authorities declare that the sole of the foot should never be pared or burned, and that the heels should never be "opened out," i. e. that the horn between the bars of the foot and the frog should never be cut away.

But I think that in some exceptional cases the sole of the foot should be pared, and that, more frequently, it is best to "open out" the heels. Of course the sole of the foot grows continually, and the theory is that the superfluous or old part comes off naturally in flakes. But sometimes, especially when the horse is shod in such a manner that the bottom of his foot is absolutely removed from contact with the ground, the sole fails to wear off as fast as nature intended, and as a result it begins to encroach upon the frog. In such a case it should be pared. And so as to the heels. If the heels of a colt be examined, a small wedge-like opening will always be found between the bars and the frog. Sometimes in old horses this becomes entirely closed, and when that happens, I think it should be opened to preserve the normal condition of the foot.

However, as a rule, neither sole, frog, nor bars should be touched, and the wall of the foot should

be pared only enough to keep it level, and to prevent
undue length at the toe. The amateur may be sure
that a blacksmith whose practice is to pare or burn
the sole of his horse's foot is a bad blacksmith; and
he may almost be sure that one who does not pare
or burn is a good blacksmith. In former days it was
the custom to pare the sole almost to the quick, for
absolutely no reason; and consequently, whenever a
shoe came off, the horse was immediately disabled.
The reader of fiction or poetry of the last century, or
of the first half of the present century, will remember
that, whenever the traveller's horse cast a shoe, the
rider was obliged to dismount forthwith, and to lead
the animal with slow and painful steps to the nearest
smithy. But if the foot be left undisturbed, protected
by its cover of horn, the loss of a shoe need not be
made good for a day or a week. On country roads a
horse with sound feet should be able to travel for a
week or so without shoes; and if he is driven or
ridden only enough to keep him exercised, he may
dispense with shoes altogether. This at least is true
where the roads are soft, but where the roads are
hard it would not be true.

On the other hand, the position that no horse ever
need be shod — which books have been written to
maintain — is an absurdity. A city dray horse wears
out every month an iron shoe at least one third of an
inch thick. Would the horn of his foot last so long?
The ordinary growth of horn is only about one quarter
of an inch per month; and although the unshod hoof
may grow somewhat faster, it does not grow fast
enough to compensate for the wear and tear of ordinary roads. Horses in the wild state, and horses

turned out in stony pastures, frequently become so
foot-sore that they can hardly step; and before shoes
were invented regiments of cavalry were sometimes
disabled from the same cause. Certainly, if shoes
were not necessary, such a clumsy device as that of
skins, like sandals, bound about the horse's foot,
which were once in use, would never have been employed. Historians tell us also that plates of metal,
fastened by strings, served the same purpose for hundreds of years. Even the mustang's feet lack the
toughness of iron. "In the mountains," relates Colonel T. A. Dodge, in a recent paper, "where the sharp,
flinty stones soon wear down the pony's unshod feet,
this Indian [the Apache] will shrink raw hide over
the hoofs, in lieu of shoes, and this resists extremely
well the attrition of the mountain paths."

I have even seen it stated in books, that a horse
unshod can travel on smooth ice better than if he
were shod with corks. This, I say, has been stated
as an absolute fact, and elaborate reasons have been
given for it; and yet I know from my own experience
that a barefooted horse is perfectly helpless on smooth
ice. On rough ice indeed, or on snow-covered roads, he
will travel fairly well without shoes, stepping shorter,
of course, than if he were shod. but on smooth ice he
cannot take a step with safety. Unshod colts are frequently lamed by slipping in icy barnyards or fields.
I remember once narrowly escaping a fall while riding
a barefooted horse. In the middle of the street, which
sloped a little to the sidewalk on each side, I had no
difficulty; but the horse shied off, struck the smooth
ice, and we found ourselves skating down toward the
gutter, with a prospect of tumbling when we reached

the bottom; but just before we brought up against the curbstone, I turned the horse's head gently to the left, and he, understanding what was wanted, jumped lightly to the sidewalk, and so kept his feet.

The second great principle in shoeing is that the foot should be allowed to come as nearly flat to the ground as possible.[1] The office of the frog is to sustain a part of the concussion which the foot and leg receive when the horse steps; and this it cannot do when the shoe is so built up on corks or otherwise that it keeps the frog clear of the ground. When the frog is thus deprived of its natural use, the blood fails to circulate in it, and it becomes atrophied or diseased. In such a case, also, there is apt to be a consequent trouble in the legs, for of course the strain upon the legs is regulated by the shape and position of the hoofs; and this brings us to the third great principle in shoeing, which is, that the horse should stand upon his feet in the manner that nature intended. It is plain that if his toe be left too long, or pared too short, or if the hoof is so treated as to be longer or higher on one side than the other, or if the shoe is put on too far forward or too far back, — in these and in many other cases that might be mentioned, the legs do not bear their natural relation to the foot. The consequence is that some muscles and tendons of the leg do less, and some do more. than their quota of work. If, for example. the slope of the hoof in front is too great, the back tendons and joints of the limbs must be strained.

Even Maud S. was suffering from swollen fore legs and strained tendons when she came into the hands of

[1] See page 249, for the Charlier system of shoeing.

Mr. Bonner. But her new owner, who has made a close
study of the farrier's art, saw at once that she did not
stand true on her feet. Accordingly, he altered the
position of her fore shoes, and the swelling forthwith
disappeared from her legs. Mr. Bonner had a similar
experience with the great Sunol. For a year after
his purchase of her she remained at Palo Alto, and a
few weeks before she made her fast record of 2.08¼
Mr. Bonner paid the mare a visit. At that time Sunol
was going slightly lame in one fore foot, when first
taken out, from some unknown cause. Mr. Bonner
carefully examined the foot, and discovered that the
wall was a trifle higher on one side than on the other.
This was rectified, and the lameness disappeared.
Now, if a horse can become lame at Palo Alto from
such a cause, and the cause remain undiscovered, how
numerous and mischievous must be the cases of bad
shoeing that occur where nothing more than ordinary
skill and experience in horseflesh obtain !

There are many horses that require the mind and
eye of a thorough craftsman to shoe them properly;
and when thus shod they never interfere or over-
reach; whereas, if wrongly shod, they can hardly
take a sound step. When an incompetent smith has
to deal with such a horse, he commonly begins by
making a murderous attack on the hoof with his
knife, and then affixes to it a shoe of extraordinary
shape. A good workman, on the other hand, never
makes a shoe the shape of which differs from the
natural shape of a horse's foot. This, I think, may
be taken as an axiom, and it supplies a test capable
of wide application. The competent smith corrects
interfering or overreaching by contriving a new ad-

justment of shoes to feet, but when his work is done it will contain no noticeable peculiarity.

Some horses require to be shod with short shoes in front. I once owned a horse that, if shod too long in front, would catch a hind shoe in a fore one, and actually throw himself to the ground. It is a common fault of smiths to make the shoe too long, — so long, in many cases, that it curves in at the heel and almost touches the frog; whereas it ought to go no farther than is necessary to protect the wall of the foot from contact with the ground. For the same reason, that is, in order to let the heels and the frog have free play, corks or calkins should not be used in the fore shoes of saddle or of light harness horses, — except, of course, when the roads are icy. — and it is a question whether they are useful on the hind shoes. The ideal shoe [1] is the lightest, simplest, smallest piece of metal that can be contrived to protect the wall of the foot.

And now we come to

## BLANKETING.

The horse requires these blankets: a linen or cotton sheet for summer, to be kept on day and night unless the weather is very hot; a woollen sheet, to be used in cool summer weather; and a thick blanket, to be used in cold weather over the linen or woollen sheet, according to circumstances. A woollen blanket of intermediate weight for fall and spring is a luxury, but not quite a necessity.

---

[1] Regarded simply as a means to locomotion. When it is a question of "balancing" a trotter by means of weight in his shoes, another problem is introduced. See page 90.

In a cold stable the horse may require in severe weather two, or even three and four heavy blankets. John Splan sensibly remarks, "If it comes to a cold night, and you think you want an extra blanket on your own bed, see that the horse has one."

Beside these individual blankets the stable should contain one or more hoods, and coolers, and a rubber blanket for cold rains. The office of the hood I have already described. The cooler is a long, thin all-wool blanket, extending over the neck and fastened by safety pins. It is used when the horse comes in from work. Horsemen frequently remark, sometimes by way of an argument in favor of clipping, that, if a horse with a long coat gets thoroughly wet with sweat, he will not become dry again for hours, — often. in fact, will remain wet through the whole night. But when this happens, unless in some exceptional case, it is because of wrong management. The custom is to put on the animal's heavy clothing at once, when he comes in hot, and this causes him to sweat profusely and to become unduly heated. The proper way is to let him stand for a very short time, three or four minutes being the maximum. with no blanket, then put on the cooler, his legs and fetlocks being protected by the straw, in which he stands knee deep, or by bandages, and let him so remain until he is dry, or until he feels cool to the hand. Then he may resume his ordinary heavy clothing. Of course, judgment must be used in this process of cooling; and the time during which the cooler is employed should vary, according to the temperature of the stable and the nature of the horse, from five minutes to an hour or more. I have never known a horse to take cold under this method.

A cheap, warm, and durable blanket can be made of canvas or sail-cloth, lined with some woollen material. A horse bred in a northern latitude will do very well without blankets in winter, — except, of course, that one must always be used when he comes in wet from rain or sweat, — but he will not look well. His coat will be long, and it will "stare," and he will require more food than he would need if blanketed.

When colts or horses are exercised by being turned out in a yard or lot, it is safer not to blanket them in the stable. If an animal is neither groomed nor "covered up," nature supplies him with a thick and oily garment. Rub your hand on the hair of a colt at pasture, and you will find that it is positively sticky. In some parts of Northern New York, and I presume in some parts of New England also, it is the custom to winter horses in open yards, without sheds, where the only shelter is that afforded by the hay-rick which supplies them with food. Horses thus exposed to extreme cold and wet receive no injury, but they must suffer much discomfort, and doubtless the cost of a warm shed would soon be made up by economy in hay. Of course warm blanketing is absolutely necessary when the animal is deprived of his natural coat by

## CLIPPING.

Clipping, like every other process applicable to horseflesh, is grossly abused. To clip a horse that is obliged, as, for example, many hack horses are, to stand out in all weathers, and for long periods, is a great cruelty; and especially is it cruel under such circumstances to clip the legs which cannot be blan-

keted.    It is also in some degree cruel, and as I think
in a high degree absurd, to clip carriage horses in the
city that are seldom required to go long distances.
Such animals being kept in warm stables, and being
warmly clothed, have short coats; and in these natural coats they are far handsomer than in the clipped
condition.    Nevertheless, the common practice is to
deprive them of their hair.    Why ?    Doubtless because the labor of the groom is thus lightened, and in
these matters the man rules the master.    On the other
hand, horses that are taken out once a day, driven
hard and fast, and then brought in again, are usually much better for being clipped, since they escape
the profuse sweating which they would otherwise
undergo.

Moreover, especially in early spring, clipping often
seems to have a valuable tonic effect.    Horses that
were thin and run down have been known to pick up
with extraordinary rapidity after being clipped.    The
reason doubtless is, that in the clipped condition they
keep a certain amount of flesh which they would
otherwise have lost by sweating.    Even when a horse
stands in the stable — to say nothing of his work — he
perspires ; and if the weather is warmish he perspires
a great deal, for his heavy blanket is retained till late
spring or summer.    By clipping, this loss of flesh is
avoided ; and perhaps also the fact that the animal's
skin is comfortably cool, instead of uncomfortably
hot, has a direct effect upon his general health.

But again, under certain conditions. I have no doubt
that the sweating which a long-coated horse gets is
beneficial.    A moderate amount of sweating is good for
a horse, as it is for a man, and in the case of an animal

that has very little work, being ridden or driven only
a few miles every other day, perhaps, — in such a case
there can be no doubt that a heavy coat, and the consequent sweating, are advantageous. This is a plain
consideration, but I have never seen it adverted to
in any horse book.

Another point of some importance in deciding
whether or not to clip your horse is this: Will the
operation have a permanent effect upon his coat, making it come out earlier, or heavier, or coarser the next
autumn? Skilled opinions differ on this point; but,
as a general principle, the cutting of hair certainly
tends to affect its future growth; and there is no
reason why this should not be true of horses as of
other animals. Still, clipping the coat once a year
probably has only a slight effect, — at least, until it
has been repeated for some years.

In fine, whether or not your horse should be clipped
depends upon his coat, upon the work which he has to
do, upon the exposure to which he is subjected, and
in some degree upon the stable where he is kept. If
you wish to avoid a necessity for clipping him, be
sure that he has a thick blanket on the first cool
nights of autumn, even in September: this will tend
to keep his coat short.

The operation of clipping should not be performed
on a damp day, nor on a warm day when the pores of
the skin are open and there is a consequent liability
to take cold; and it need not be said that a clipped
horse requires at least one more heavy blanket than
an unclipped one.

And now, having brought these essays to a close, I will address to the gentle reader the same remark that was made long ago by one of my predecessors in the subtle art of horsemanship. He said, — and I trust that I have been equally fortunate, — "Lord! If I had always such a nice, attentive person to listen to me as you are, I could go on talking about 'orses to the end of time."

# INDEX.

# INDEX.